THE SEEKERS, THE DREAMERS, THE CONQUERERS— PASSIONATE MEN AND WOMEN WITH A DREAM TO LIVE FOR, A LAND TO FIGHT FOR

John Cooper Baines—The fearless Texan now in the full power of his manhood, the time has come for him to reclaim a secret fortune, a decision that may cost him his land and his life.

Andrews Baines—The brave young son of John Cooper and his noble wife Catarina, ready to fight at his father's side with the fierceness of his mother's Spanish blood and his father's Indian upbringing.

Carlos de Escobar—Proud brother of Catarina, fate took away the beloved of his youth, now destiny threatens to keep him from his one chance of happiness.

Teresa—The high-spirited beauty whose wealth frees her from the need for a husband, but whose belief in a rogue's deceitful lies may trap her in a life of grief.

Colonel Francisco Lopez—Darkly handsome, irresistibly charming, and cruelly treacherous. His flattery will lead to a deadly seduction, his evil to disaster for John Cooper Baines.

Noracia—With flashing Spanish eyes that hide a ruthless heart, she is a woman who takes the power she craves and the men she desires.

A Saga of the Southwest
Book IV

FLIGHT OF THE HAWK

Leigh Franklin James

 Created by the producers of
Wagons West, White Indian,
Children of the Lion, and
The Kent Family Chronicles Series.

Executive Producer: Lyle Kenyon Engel

BANTAM BOOKS
Toronto • New York • London • Sydney

FLIGHT OF THE HAWK

*A Bantam Book / published by arrangement with
Book Creations, Inc.*

Bantam edition / November 1982

Produced by Book Creations, Inc.
Executive Producer: Lyle Kenyon Engel.

All rights reserved.
Copyright © 1982 by Book Creations, Inc.
Cover art copyright © 1982 by Lou Glanzman.
*This book may not be reproduced in whole or in part, by
mimeograph or any other means, without permission.*
For information address: Bantam Books, Inc.

ISBN 0-553-22578-2

Published simultaneously in the United States and Canada

*Dedicated to the men and women who made America
what it is today, by believing in the timeless,
enduring virtues of honesty, humility, and hard work.*

Acknowledgments

The author gratefully acknowledges the inspired collaboration of the Book Creations, Inc. team of Lyle Kenyon Engel and Marla Engel, Philip D. Rich, editor in chief, and Bruce Rosenzweig, senior editor.

In addition, the author wishes to express his indebtedness to the University of New Mexico Press for published documentation which helped authenticate many incidents of this novel. And thanks once again to Dave Richmond, formerly manager of the gun department of Abercrombie & Fitch, for his invaluable data on the weapons of the period. Sincere thanks are also due to Joseph Milton Nance, head of the history department of Texas A & M University, and state historian of Texas, who contributed much exhaustive research to help flesh out this novel.

And finally, a deeply appreciative tribute to Fay Jeanne Bergstrom, for four years of expert, devoted transcription of the author's manuscripts.

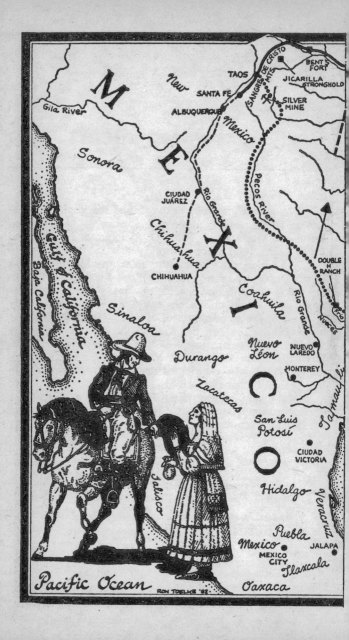

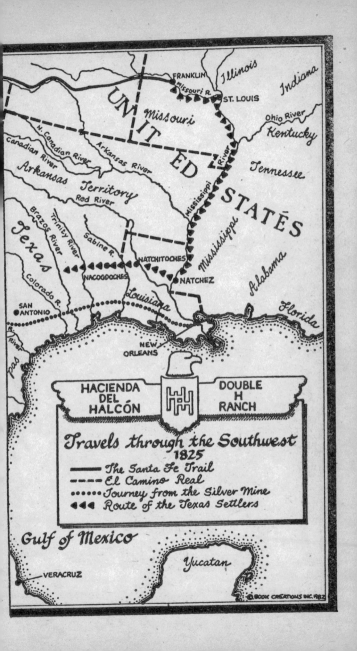

FRANKLIN
Illinois
Indiana
Missouri R.
ST. LOUIS
Missouri
Ohio River
Kentucky
UNIT
Arkansas River
ED
Mississippi River
Tennessee
N. Canadian River
Canadian River
STATES
Arkansas
Territory
Red River
Mississippi
Texas
Brazos River
Trinity River
Sabine R.
NATCHITOCHES
Alabama
Colorado R.
NACOGDOCHES
Florida
SAN
ANTONIO
Louisiana
NATCHEZ
River
NEW
ORLEANS

HACIENDA
DEL
HALCÓN

DOUBLE
H
RANCH

Travels through the Southwest
1825
——— The Santa Fe Trail
– – – El Camino Real
•••••• Journey from the Silver Mine
◄◄◄ Route of the Texas Settlers

Gulf of Mexico

Yucatan

VERACRUZ

© BOOK CREATIONS INC. 1982

Prologue

It was mid-April of 1825. Exactly two years ago, there had been a great fiesta at the Double H Ranch in Texas to celebrate the return of Carlos de Escobar to his father, Don Diego, and his stepmother, Doña Inez. Don Diego's only son had taken leave of his family sometime before this, stricken with intolerable grief over the death of his beautiful young Apache wife, Weesayo, whose death had been caused by the dissolute hidalgo Don Pedro de Menguez. Believing that he might assuage his grief by fighting for the cause of liberation, Carlos had ridden into Mexico to join the army of Santa Anna, only to become disillusioned with this corrupt and scheming officer—who grandly called himself El Libertador.

Carlos had taken a furlough, and the wily Santa Anna sent his henchmen to follow the young lieutenant in the hope that he would lead them to a mysterious cache of silver ingots. Santa Anna was craftily waiting in the wings until it was time to seize total power over the land the Spaniards had called Nueva España, and that hoard would ease his way to power. These ingots were located in the abandoned mine that Carlos's brother-in-law, John Cooper Baines, had discovered. Santa Anna's men shot Carlos and left him for dead on his journey to the Apache stronghold high in the mountains of New Mexico, where Weesayo's people lived. He stayed at the stronghold until he regained his strength, then went back into Taos to stay with his father's old friend, Don Sancho de Pladero. At last Carlos made peace with his conscience, thanks to the compassionate understanding of Padre Salvador Madura, and finally returned to his home in Texas.

1

The great ranch had prospered with the arrival of many settlers, who were becoming part of what both John Cooper and Don Diego hoped would be a strong community, well able to defend itself against attack from either renegade Indian bands or hostile Mexican soldiers. The trabajadores had built a schoolhouse not far from the spacious hacienda, which housed John Cooper and his Catarina, Don Diego and his Doña Inez, as well as Carlos. Catarina and Bess Sandarbal, along with Doña Inez, served as teachers to the children of the settlement. They also taught their own children that they were in no way privileged, and must share recreation as well as study with the children of the workers. As Don Diego himself beamingly remarked, "This is a community made of love and friendship, and it is stronger than any fort with stone walls because love is the greatest weapon of all against evil enemies."

This very month, the trabajadores had begun work on the large church that would replace the little chapel they had first built when they had followed Don Diego and John Cooper from Taos to this fertile land near the Frio River. The church would be the spiritual bulwark of the Double H Ranch, also known as the Hacienda del Halcón, after John Cooper's Indian name El Halcón—the Hawk.

Don Diego de Escobar, now aged sixty-five, enjoyed the serenity of his latter years, basking in the love that Doña Inez, now fifty-five, accorded him. His two mortal enemies in Taos, Don Esteban de Rivarola and Luis Saltareno, had paid with their lives for their crimes against the poor and the oppressed Pueblo Indians; and he foresaw no threatening shadows to darken the blissful horizon of his twilight years, seeing his daughter, Catarina, happy with John Cooper, and praying that his son, Carlos, would one day find a woman who would replace his beloved Weesayo.

Only one shadow remained, the shadow of a vulture—Santa Anna, who with his evil plots, might yet prove the most dangerous of all threats to the prosperity of the Double H Ranch.

North of the border, in the United States, Jedediah Strong Smith, of the Rocky Mountain Fur Company, discovered the South Pass, gateway to the Rocky Mountains. Russia and the United States concluded a treaty whereby Russia *recognized the parallel of 54° 40' as the southern limit of expansion, thereby defining the extent of the Oregon country. On February 9 of this year of 1825, John Quincy Adams became the sixth President of this growing, prospering young country.*

In the Southwest, trading along the great Santa Fe Trail was at last given official sanction by the new government in Mexico, and ambitious Americans were able to bring their wares by mule train, from as far away as Franklin, Missouri. In addition, settlers were arriving in ever-increasing numbers on the fertile plains of Texas, building their homes and raising crops and cattle in the new land of opportunity . . .

One

Catarina Baines, now thirty-one and in the full flower of her beauty, had come out to the corral to watch Miguel Sandarbal, foreman of the Double H Ranch, saddle a roan gelding for her son Andrew. She looked on with maternal pride as the black-haired, blue-eyed, wiry boy, not quite twelve, easily swung himself into the saddle, took the reins, and while Miguel smilingly opened the gate, rode out at a gallop, flourishing his *sombrero* in his left hand and calling to her, "See, *mi madre*? I can ride as well as Pa!"

"That's all very well," Catarina said as she turned to her tall, towheaded husband dressed in his buckskins, "but surely, Coop, you don't intend to take him along with you to San Antonio! Why, he won't be twelve until December—that's no age for a boy to go on a cattle drive!"

"Now, Catarina honey," John Cooper grinned, warily looking around to make sure Miguel did not overhear their domestic discussion, "what you're forgetting is that I'll be along with him, and so will Miguel and some of our best *vaqueros*. Besides, in this country, one grows up young and stays young—look at me, now."

"I am looking, *mi corazón*, but you certainly can't compare yourself to Andrew."

"Just remember, *querida*," John Cooper said softly, "that before my fifteenth birthday, I came back with my dog Lije from a hunt to find my father and mother murdered by Indians, along with my two sisters. I made it all the way across the wilderness, from Shawneetown, Illinois, to Taos, and to you." With this, waving at his son, who had just galloped by

5

with another flourish of his *sombrero*, he put his arm around Catarina and kissed her on the mouth.

"Oh, you!" She made a face at him and blushed. "You think a kiss solves everything, don't you?"

"Most times," he sheepishly admitted, and tried to kiss her again.

"No you don't, Coop!" Then she couldn't help giggling, and gave him a kiss herself. "I suppose you'll have your way, in spite of all a poor, helpless mother has to say about the matter. Very well, but you'd just better bring Andrew back safely."

"Now that's a promise I can make and keep for certain, *querida*." Again he kissed her, and this time, Catarina's arms locked around his neck, and the kiss was a very long and satisfactory one. "You see," he soberly went on, "it's only about seventy miles, and we're taking three hundred head of our good longhorns to a small mission where there are friendly *indios* and missionary workers. It'll do the boy good to be out on the trail with us. And for further protection, besides the musket which he knows how to shoot very well, we'll have Yankee. He'll bring us good luck, just as Lije and Lobo always brought me."

Hearing his name mentioned, Yankee, who had been trotting back and forth along the corral enclosure, sniffing out unfamiliar scents, came running up to his master and barked, as if to confirm what John Cooper had just said. Yankee was defender of the ranch and friend to all in the community, and like his predecessor, Lobo, was part Irish wolfhound and part wolf.

Catarina uttered a sigh of resignation, but there was a smile on her face. "I suppose it'll be all right, then, if Andrew goes. He really is a wonder for his age, Coop darling."

"That's what I've been trying to tell you, *mi corazón*. Besides, one day he will share in the inheritance of Double H Ranch, and the more he knows about horses and cattle and reading signs along the trail and taking care of himself when he's thrown on his own resources, the more reliable a man he'll be. I had to learn the hard way, and I didn't have my father to guide me. Don't worry, Catarina; if he makes mistakes, I'll call them to his attention. In a rugged country like this, so new and so young, nature doesn't allow you too many mistakes. That's why I want Andrew to learn quickly and to be ready for whatever comes along."

"I suppose you're right." Again Catarina sighed. "I remember how I was sheltered back in Madrid before my family came to the New World, and what a spoiled brat I was—yes, you knew that when you first met me."

"You're not that any longer; you're my sweetheart, my beloved, the best wife any man could have, and the mother of fine children. And the way you've organized the school, and are helping to bring up Carlos's children—it's just wonderful!"

Catarina eyed him, then sorrowfully shook her head. "Poor Carlos. I've been praying all this time that Teresa de Rojado back in Taos would say yes to him. I think she'd make him a perfect wife. And that's what he needs."

"Yes, I think he's at last over his grief for Weesayo, and I know he loves Teresa. Still and all, it remains to be seen if she's going to consent to marry him, *querida*."

"I'm going to pray for that in the chapel tonight, my dear one. Well, then, you'll be leaving tomorrow morning for San Antonio?"

"Yes. We'll take ten *vaqueros* and Miguel; we'll all be well armed, and we should be back in two weeks. And when I get to San Antonio, I'm going to get you an especially nice present. And one for little Ruth, and for our youngest, Carmen."

"I think, Coop, it would be a good idea to bring Charles something nice, too. I think he's a little jealous of Andrew— he said to me this morning at breakfast that he'd give anything if you'd take him along on the drive. You really shouldn't have let Andrew boast about going—not until I agreed to it. The first thing you know, our children will be turning to you if their mother says no."

John Cooper tilted back his head and heartily laughed. "Now Catarina, it's not going to come to that, not ever. In the *hacienda*, you have the first say-so with the children. And they'd best mind their manners, all of them, yes, even Andrew. But when Andrew's on the trail with me, of course he's going to be responsible just to me."

"I can never completely win an argument with you, my dear one," Catarina smiled, and went into his arms again.

"Anyway, Charles needn't be too jealous," John Cooper

confided to his beautiful black-haired wife. "I've a feeling there'll be something to take his mind off it. One of Carlos's horses is due to foal anytime now, and I'm certain he'll take all the children to watch."

"Isn't Carmen too young?" Catarina asked. "She's only three!"

"*Querida*, it isn't as if we were city folk," John Cooper explained, with the ghost of a smile hovering around his lips. "This is a little world all its own, still primitive and still isolated. And I think the best way for children to learn about birth and death is to see it before their eyes so they can ask the grown-ups all the questions they want. That's the way I was brought up, even if you did think I was a savage the first time you saw me at the dinner table."

"You'll never let me forget that, will you?" Catarina laughed and kissed him again.

John Cooper was up well before dawn the next morning to supervise the final preparations for the drive to San Antonio. He had had to ease himself very carefully out of Catarina's embrace, for she had clung to him last night and confided that she would soon bear him another child. He understood with a wave of tenderness that even though she had long since reconciled herself to his frequent absences on hunting forays or journeys to the Apache stronghold—even to Taos and sometimes New Orleans—she would have preferred if he gave up all such excursions and assumed the role of a staid husband and father.

Sleeping peacefully, she turned toward him, a beatific smile on her red lips. He bent to kiss her eyelids, not wanting to wake her.

As he eased out of the room and silently closed the door, holding his breath lest the least stir of noise waken his beloved Catarina, he found Andrew already waiting in the corridor, his eyes sparkling with anticipation. The boy eagerly looked forward to the drive, and over the past year, John Cooper had spent several hours each day instructing his son on how to survive in the wilderness. "I'm ready, Pa," Andrew boisterously announced.

"Shh, do you want to waken your mother? Sure as you're born, she'll start trying to talk me out of taking you.

Now come along—we'll have a quick bit of breakfast in the kitchen, and then we'll be off."

"I'm so excited, Pa. Thanks so much for taking me along. One day, I want to be as good as you are with 'Long Girl.'"

"Oh, do you now?" John Cooper chuckled as he put his arm around his son's shoulders and strode along to the kitchen. "Well, 'Long Girl' is a pretty fine Lancaster rifle, and to give you the straight of it, my pa told me he wasn't going to let me have 'Long Girl' until I was a better shot with my musket. And I recall—well, never mind." He had stopped because suddenly the rush of memories had come back to him: that beautiful September day in 1807, when he and the greathearted Irish wolfhound, Lije, had gone off hunting, and all he had had to show for the hunt were two mallard ducks. And he had known very well that his father was going to give him a licking for wasting ammunition and coming back with so little meat for the table. Then—there in the cornfield, out of ammunition, unable to lift so much as a finger to help his family, holding his hand over Lije's muzzle to prevent the dog from growling, he and the wolfhound had to watch as his family was massacred by Indian renegades.

There was no need to sadden young Andrew's bright spirits on this day of days with such a recollection. And of late he had not thought of it, but thought only of his happiness here on the sprawling, prosperous Texas ranch, away from the stultifying regulations of the Spanish government. For Andrew, he thought to himself, it was a wonderful time to be a boy, at the dawn of a new era. This young country was growing by leaps and bounds, and one day there wouldn't be any Spanish or even Mexican political influence left, except for traditions, like Tía Margarita's wonderful cooking. Someday there would be a huge United States of America, and, he was certain, Texas would be an integral part of it.

"Well, Andrew boy," he jocularly exclaimed as they seated themselves in the kitchen and Tía Margarita and her two helpers bustled about to serve them a quick breakfast of fruit, hot biscuits with honey, a few slices of cold chicken from supper last night, and strong coffee, "I suspect that one day you'll earn yourself a rifle like 'Long Girl,' but you'll have to prove you're worthy of it. Maybe this trip we're tak-

ing together will show me just how well you can handle a
musket. Now remember, don't get panicky. Be sure you
prime it properly; don't overload it with gunpowder; and
most of all, take your time when you're aiming."

"What if I have to shoot it in order to protect somebody,
Pa?"

"I hope to God, Andrew, we won't run into that sort of
trouble this time—or ever. One thing—a musket can't possibly have the range of 'Long Girl.' And it'll take you a good
minute to reload, so you have to make your first shot count.
Just remember that."

"I will, Pa, sure I will." Andrew tackled his breakfast
with gusto, while John Cooper smilingly watched and clapped
him on the back and nodded. "You're quick and smart for
your age. You're a good boy, and I'm proud of you. Only
one thing, Andrew, you're too young yet to know about
women, but I'll give you a little advice—especially around
your mother. She's sweet and tender, and she can't quite accept the fact that you're growing up so fast. So even if you're
a good shot and can ride your gelding as well as I can ride
Pingo, don't let on to her that you'd rather do things like that
than have her teach you book learning and such. Be gentle
with her, Andrew. One day—and I'll still be around to watch
it, I hope—you'll find a girl of your own, just as sweet and
beautiful as your mother. And she'll love you more because
you're gentle and considerate with her. You just remember
that, son."

"I know, Pa. Like the way I am with Ruth."

"Yes, I've noticed that. You take your sister's part, and
you don't let Charles bully her any. That's good, son. Always
stand up for a woman, because by nature she's physically
weaker, and she can't answer back to a man the way you and
I can. You understand that?"

"Sure I do, Pa." The boy flushed hotly, aware of his father's pride in him. He abruptly rose from the table and,
turning to Tía Margarita, exclaimed, "Thanks a lot for the
desayuno, Tía Margarita!"

"Why, you're quite welcome, young master!" the jovial
cook giggled as she made him a curtsy.

John Cooper rose, stretching himself and yawning. Then
he said to the cook, "You look after Catarina and the chil-

dren while I'm gone. There's a special reason—Catarina's going to—you know."

"Oh, *seguramente*, Señor John Cooper!" Tía Margarita exclaimed with a knowing wink. "You can count on me. I wish both of you good luck, and hurry back safely to us, Señor John Cooper."

"Thanks, Tía Margarita. Come on, Andrew. Let's go find Yankee. Do you know, he's even bigger than Lobo was at his age—nearly two now, and full of fight and spirit."

"He is at that, Pa."

As the two of them came out near the bunkhouse, John Cooper opened the door of the shed in which he usually kept Yankee when they were not out on hunting excursions or training sessions. The wolf-dog barked joyously and ran out to his tall master, then lowered his head and rubbed his muzzle against John Cooper's calf, while the latter stooped to rub his knuckles over Yankee's head, exactly as he had done with Lije and then Lobo.

"Gosh, he seems real tame, Pa!" young Andrew exclaimed, leaning forward to pet the sturdy young wolf-dog. Yankee was now almost the size of Lije, weighing a little over a hundred ten pounds, with yellow eyes, the strong fangs and pointed muzzle of a wolf, yet with the massive body and somewhat elongated tail of the Irish wolfhound. His fur was a light gray, and at first glance he seemed even sturdier and heavier than Lobo.

Though Lobo had returned to the wilds with the wolf bitch two years ago, John Cooper had still heard him bark and whine at least once a month with the coming of the full moon, as he and his timber-wolf mate loped past the Double H Ranch. But for the past four months, there had been no sign of the aging wolf-dog. And John Cooper concluded that Lije's get had at last reverted completely to self-sufficient lupine savagery; no more contact was necessary with the two-legged species with whom he had lived so long. Thus, with Lobo gone, he had spent several hours almost every day training Yankee to adapt himself to the *trabajadores* and their families. He used the same methods he had used with Lobo, rapping the wolf-dog on the nose whenever the latter showed the least enmity toward one of the ranch workers or their children.

Now astride Pingo, the palomino stallion sired by Fuego,

John Cooper looked proudly at his son and nodded: "I see you've packed your saddlebags already, and you've sheathed your musket—is it primed and ready in case you need it, Andrew?"

"It sure is, Pa!"

"That's good. And you've practiced reloading many a time with me, I know that; so I expect you to be able to bring in your share of meat during our journey to San Antonio and back. The *vaqueros* who go with us will be watching you, Andrew. They are ready to accept you because you're my son, but you have to earn their respect. I know you will."

"I'm going to try real hard, Pa; you can depend on it."

"That's the way I like to hear a son talk. All right, now, there's Miguel, and the others who will accompany us to San Antonio." Raising his voice, John Cooper lifted his right hand and called out, "I'll lead the way, riding the point. Are the cattle all ready?"

"They are, *patrón*," Miguel Sandarbal smilingly chuckled. At sixty, he was lean and wiry, his skin bronzed like that of an Indian; his closely cropped silver-gray hair, as well as his vigor and bearing, belied his age. He had accompanied Don Diego when the latter had left his native Spain so many years ago, exiled as he was to the New World on trumped-up charges of treason. And life with his *patrón* had been good to Miguel. Only last night his yellow-haired wife, Bess, now thirty-six, had whispered to him, "My husband, no one would take you for your age, so I don't want you to think about it again. There's no one on this entire ranch I'd rather have as my husband. Now you make young Andrew feel just as strong and able as you can, and I'll love you the more for it. Both of us owe that much to John Cooper Baines and Don Diego."

And Miguel, humbly grateful for the joys that the good God had granted to him in the twilight of his life, had murmured, "My dearest Bess, *mi corazón,* you don't have to tell me how to treat Andrew. I've a debt that won't ever be paid, if only because Don Diego set you free when you were enslaved by *los indios,* and gave me the chance to be your *hombre,* your *esposo.* And indeed you've made me forget my age, *querida.* You've given me two fine young sons and a daughter. Never fear; I'll watch over the boy, and it won't be long before he's just as strong and capable as his father."

Miguel was to ride with John Cooper's son at the very end of the small herd. Traditionally, the newest *vaquero* was relegated to bring up the rear, so that he might "eat dust" and become aware of his insignificance in comparison with the *ganado* he was driving.

John Cooper was interested in seeing just how Andrew would react to sudden hazards, such as the whirring of a hawk nearby, or the sinister rattle of a snake, sunning itself on a rock just off the trail. Also, since for the past three months he had taken Andrew along with him each time he went out with Yankee for a run and a trial hunt, he was eager to see whether the boy would make use of the young wolf-dog's ability to flush out game. There would probably be plenty of wild ducks this time of year, possibly a small deer, and certainly the large jackrabbits that infested this part of Texas territory. Any one of these would make a tasty supper, which the boy would appreciate the more if Yankee flushed out the game for him and he was able to kill it with his very first musket.

Riding at the front, John Cooper glanced back from time to time to see his young son and Miguel. It was a good partnership. He thought grimly to himself that if he had had a companion like Miguel to comfort him immediately after his family's death, and teach him how to face the dire necessities of survival, things would certainly have been easier for him. On the other hand, he had no wish to pamper Andrew, or Charles either, for he planned to take his younger son out on the trail the following year.

The first day was leisurely. The *vaqueros* rode alongside the small herd to maintain order and to round up the occasional stray. Their direction, east by slightly northeast, would bring them to San Antonio easily within the week, and there would be ample time for John Cooper to delight the boy with anecdotes of his life with the Indians. Andrew loved to hear how his father—when he was his age—had crossed the North American continent, living for a time with the Ayuhwa Sioux, where he had shared in the hunt and had learned the language of the Indians. Moving ever westward, he had also lived with the Skidi Pawnee and the Dakota Sioux, finally arriving in the great Southwest, living high in the mountains in an Apache village, and becoming blood brother to the chief. It was shortly after this that the nineteen-year-old John Cooper had met and fallen in love with Andrew's mother, Catarina de Escobar, who, along with Carlos, Doña Inez, and Miguel Sandarbal, had accompanied the exiled Don Diego from Spain to the New World.

The sturdy wolf-dog loped along, occasionally diverted by the sounds of birds that darted up from a thicket of flowering mesquite or from a small grove of live-oak trees. John Cooper could not blame Yankee for being distracted: it was the wolf-dog's first dangerous excursion. John Cooper was convinced that Yankee's lapses, as well as his son's, could readily be corrected with a little patient training. But already the wolf-dog—spawn of the wolf cub Mischief and an Irish wolfhound—had proved abounding in energy and enthusiasm for the monotonous, long journey to San Antonio.

During their brief stop for lunch, John Cooper rode back to the end of the herd, where he found Miguel sitting on a log, chatting with Andrew, who was reclining on the ground, eagerly listening. John Cooper dismounted from Pingo and let the beautiful brown palomino graze with the other horses on the waist-high buffalo grass that flourished on either side of the winding trail. The streams, wildflowers, thick hedges of brambles, and shallow *arroyos* filled with verdant foliage made this landscape memorable and as beautiful as that of his own Double H Ranch. "It's strange we see no settlers yet, Miguel," John Cooper speculated.

"Not even the *hacienda* of that damnable *rico* who took Weesayo prisoner, *mi patrón*," Miguel said between gritted teeth, remembering Carlos's shattering tragedy.

"I know. A courier who visited us over a year ago told me that after the death of Don Pedro de Menguez, his *peones* robbed the house, took what horses and cattle they wished, and deserted it. And before they did, they burned the *hacienda* to the ground. A fitting end, indeed."

"Amen to that, *mi patrón*." Miguel soberly nodded. Then, with a broad grin, he added, "Your *hijo* will do you credit. He's already asked me at least a hundred questions, as God's my judge. And I've been hard put to it to answer them to his satisfaction. He's a quick learner, and he's strong and wiry. Even if he weren't your son, he'd make a *gran vaquero!*"

"I'm glad you agree with me, Miguel," John Cooper quipped as he reached forward to rumple Andrew's thick shock of black hair. "Of course, at first I might have been prejudiced when I felt that he was almost ready to lead this herd to market." Then, as Andrew flushed and sheepishly looked down, the former mountain man reminded him, "I want to hear your musket sound before sunset. Keep an eye on Yankee, because he's bound to flush out some quail or ducks or maybe even a young deer. And if you're a good enough shot, I'm thinking of buying you a rifle of your own, but that all depends on how well you do with this musket, ¿comprendes?"

"¡Sí, mi padre!" Andrew confidently exclaimed as he looked up.

"Miguel, I want you to encourage him to talk in Spanish whenever the mood strikes you. So long as we're here in Texas and there are Mexicans around us, we'll have to keep up our knowledge of their tongue so that we can work together. That's why the Indian tribes of the area have learned to speak Spanish. In this land, the more Spanish a man knows, the sharper a trader he can be."

"Exactly right, John Cooper. Wait, what's Yankee doing there?" Miguel called out.

The wolf-dog had suddenly uttered a soft growl and crouched with his head lowered, as if sniffing a new and unfamiliar scent. Andrew at once sprang to his feet, ran up to his tethered horse, and seized his musket from the saddle sheath. He inspected it to make sure that it was primed and loaded, and John Cooper and Miguel exchanged satisfied nods. The protégé had made a good start on this, his first day as an apprentice vaquero!

Yankee now moved swiftly forward through the thick, bright green grass toward a clump of pecan trees. Suddenly there was a whir of wings as five wild ducks soared from the top of the tallest tree. Instantly, Andrew squinted along the sight of his musket, following the trajectory of the ducks, and holding his breath, pulled the trigger. The recoil nearly sent him sprawling, but one of the ducks plummeted to the ground.

"Good for you, muchacho!" Miguel cried out delightedly, running up to Andrew and clapping him on the back.

"A fine shot, and did you see how he never took his eye off the flight?"

"He didn't allow for the recoil, though," John Cooper said, coming up to them. "And if it had been a bear and he hadn't killed it with the first shot, he'd be in real trouble trying to get to his feet and scampering up a tree, where he could reload it." Although John Cooper was finding fault with his son, inwardly he was proud as a peacock, and the twinkle in his eyes reassured Miguel that his long-respected *gringo* friend was only pretending to be so strict. Indeed, as John Cooper well remembered, he had been living in the Ayuhwa village when he had gone after the killer bear to free the lovely squaw, Degala, from her shameful servitude. After he had wounded the animal, it had climbed up a tree after him until, reloading with desperate speed, he had managed at last to fire the lethal shot before it could reach him with its terrible claws.

By now, Andrew had righted himself, and was calling out, "Fetch, Yankee; fetch, boy!"

John Cooper put a hand on Miguel's shoulder and intently watched as the strong young wolf-dog made his way through the brush and grass, seized the dead duck by a wing, and turned and raced back to his young master. He held the duck, his yellow eyes glowing with pride and excitement, until Andrew put out his hand and knuckled his head just above the eyes, calling out, "Good Yankee, that's fine; good boy!" Relinquishing the prey, the wolf-dog moved back and sat up, his pink tongue lolling, as he watched young Andrew stoop to pick up the duck.

"Well done, Andrew boy!" his father approved. "And since you've shot it by yourself, you shall have it for supper—mind you, give Yankee a good share for retrieving it so well. I'd say he's even better than Lobo was at the same age."

"That may be true, John Cooper," Miguel agreed. "But do you think Yankee will be savage enough to defend us in case of attack?"

"I'm pretty sure he will. But then, let's hope he isn't tested on this trip." With this, he turned to call sharply to his son, "Andrew, you haven't forgotten something, have you?"

"I did, Pa," the boy apologetically agreed. Going to his

horse, he opened his saddlebag and took out powder horn and a ball, and then proceeded to prime and load his musket.

"Good boy. Never forget that, the minute you shoot. That extra few seconds you've gained by quick reloading might be the difference between your coming back alive or lying out on the trail there for the buzzards to pick you over," John Cooper grimly declared.

They started on their way again, and rode several more miles that day. They camped just as the sun set in the west, leaving the magnificent, cloudless sky a breathtaking purplish-rose, with the long shadows tracing grotesque patterns on the majestic expanse of grass and trees along this uninhabited landscape.

"There must be plenty of buffalo even this far south," Miguel murmured to John Cooper as he began to make a fire, while two of the *vaqueros* started preparations for the evening meal. There would be jerky, beans, and biscuits made out of flour, water, baking soda, and salt, and cooked in a skillet in a little grease, then washed down with strong coffee. The cattle had been bedded down for the night, and their soft lowing could be heard as the *vaqueros* ate in turns, four of them watching the cattle until their colleagues had finished their supper.

John Cooper watched Andrew pick off the duck's feathers, cut it expertly, and then cook it over a small fire, while Yankee stood by, wagging his tail and uttering a soft growl from time to time just to remind the boy that he had more than earned a taste.

And when at last Andrew offered both his father and Miguel some of the duck, John Cooper shook his head and replied, "No, boy, it's yours; you've every right to it—you shot it. And when you don't shoot anything and the game's low, you'll go without. It's a lesson you'd best learn right off, before you grow much older."

"I know, Pa. I'm beholden to you for telling me all these things. It's lots of fun."

"So far, yes," his father said quietly. "But just to remind you that it's not always all fun, you'll stand watch till midnight while the rest of us get a little sleep."

Miguel frowned as he eyed his companion, but John Cooper shook his head and muttered so that only Miguel could hear. "I don't want him to get a swelled head. That could have been just a lucky shot, and I don't want him to think that just because he shot a duck his first time out, he's a great hunter. Let's see what sort of watch he keeps and whether he can listen for sounds in the night and decide what they mean. I've taught him plenty this last year; now it's time to find out how much he's remembered of his lessons. When I was his age, I had to remember my lessons, or I wasn't allowed to go hunting."

Then he fell silent again, filling his coffee cup as he stared into the fire, recalling the scenes of his earlier life.

John Cooper had taken Miguel aside and instructed him to let young Andrew nap until about two hours before midnight, and then to let him stand guard duty till midnight. Miguel himself, of course, would be the principal guard. "It will give my son a sense of responsibility and duty, almost as if he were a soldier," the tall, former mountain man told the elderly *capataz*.

"Never fear," Miguel stoutly declared, "I'll wake him in time to stand guard, and I won't let on that I'll be there watching after him. That'll make him feel all the more important."

It was a quiet night, with scarcely any wind. From a distance came the plaintive sound of a coyote's howl, and Yankee, lying alertly beside young Andrew, suddenly lifted his head and uttered a soft growl. The boy put out his hand to pet the wolf-dog, murmuring, "It's all right, Yankee; it's just an old coyote." Miguel had wakened him scarcely half an hour ago, and Andrew had at once inspected his musket to make certain that it was loaded and ready in the event of trouble. He had taken up his position as guard about a hundred yards from where the cattle were bedded down. There was a quarter-moon, with only faint silvery light to dapple the tops of the trees and the thickets of mesquite. There were also the chirping sounds of cicadas and the occasional call of a night bird. Andrew, his eyes wide and alert, refreshed by his nap, tightly gripped the musket and stared round the area to make sure that all was well.

Now Andrew stretched, yawned, and stood up, crouching as he did so, remembering how his father had told him, "When you're on guard, never make yourself a full target. Turn sideways every now and again; crouch low like an

Indian, so if anyone's drawing a bead on you, you'll make it harder for them. And if someone ever does take a shot at you, cry out and fling yourself down on the ground and play dead. Keep your musket handy and watch, and maybe the man who's shot at you will show himself to make sure he's brought you down—then when he's in your sights, show him what a mistake he made. Little things like that, boy, could mean living to a ripe old age."

If Catarina had heard her husband give their son such advice, she might well have protested that this talk of life and death might frighten a boy so young. But John Cooper believed this advice was for the boy's own good, as well as the good of his companions who might share the danger.

From his own position near a live-oak tree, squatting down with his musket lying across his thighs, Miguel watched Andrew's alertness and smiled to himself. This indeed was a worthy progeny of *El Halcón. Seguramente,* Andrew Baines was a son a man could truly be proud of. And then he thought fondly of his beloved Bess and their own children, Timothy and Julia and, most recently, Juan, whom Bess herself had named after his father. He prayed to *El Señor Dios* that he would be spared long enough to see at least Timothy grow to a sturdy young manhood.

Three days ago, five riders had crossed the Rio Grande, having shaken off a platoon of Mexican cavalrymen who had pursued them. Three of them were Mexican, and two were white renegades with a price on their heads back in Missouri, where they had robbed and murdered two farming families. They had crossed over into Mexico and established an unholy alliance with the three Mexican outlaws, who themselves had once been *peones*.

Just before sunset today, they had seen from a distance the herd which John Cooper and Miguel were driving to San Antonio, and they had considered cutting loose a few strays, for they had not eaten in two days. They were well armed— the Mexicans had braces of pistols, and the renegades, Jack Sparling and George Purfree, had stolen two rifles and ample ammunition. All five men were also armed with knives, and the three Mexicans were murderously expert with these weapons above all others.

The five outlaws, having tethered their horses well out of

sight in a clump of pecan trees a quarter of a mile to the south, watched till the campfires were extinguished. They crept on their bellies toward the cattle, and Manuel Cardozo, the self-appointed leader of this murderous band, turned and beckoned to his two Mexican companions, indicating that they should rope two of the steers on the very fringe of the herd. Accordingly, José Féliz and Alvaro Salcado, stocky, swarthy men in their early thirties, came forward, crouching low, armed with their lariats. They promptly looped them around the steers, then led them toward the clump of pecan trees.

Yankee lifted his head and uttered a low growl, then a yapping bark. Andrew started; staring in the direction toward which Yankee was looking, he could just make out the shadows near the pecan trees. With a cry of alarm, he aimed his musket and pulled the trigger. The range was far too great for a musket, but the sound of the shot wakened the camp. Miguel called a warning, and John Cooper sprang to his feet, lifted "Long Girl" to his shoulder, squinted along the sight, and pulled the trigger. José Féliz staggered, dropped his lariat, and sprawled dead on the ground. Alvaro Salcado uttered a cry of alarm and began to drag the bellowing, protesting steers back into the trees. One of the *vaqueros* nearest him lifted his musket and fired, and Alvaro dropped dead in his tracks. Manuel Cardozo shot both his pistols at the *vaquero* but missed, and he swore angrily, then gestured to Jack Sparling and George Purfree to go back for their horses and ride away from this disastrous encounter.

But the other *vaqueros*, now wakened, had seized their guns and sent volleys into the shadowy clump of pecan trees. Cries and howls of pain attested to the accuracy of their marksmanship. Cardozo was fatally wounded, while the two white renegades received shoulder wounds. Staggering toward the horses, they mounted them and rode away, but John Cooper, with a last shot from "Long Girl," dropped Sparling from his horse. Only George Purfree, bleeding profusely from his wound, galloped westward to escape.

The former mountain man hurried to his son, lifted him in his arms, and ecstatically swung him around and around. "I'm proud of you, Andrew! If you were a soldier, you'd have a medal by now for alerting us all with your musket!"

"I wish I had a rifle like yours, Pa. I couldn't hit anyone

from this distance with that musket," Andrew said as his father set him on the ground.

"I'll get you one, and that's a promise, Andrew boy. You've earned it. Hasn't he, Miguel?"

The grizzled *capataz* grinned broadly. *"Por todos los santos,* indeed he has!"

"Now let's go see what's left of those bandits. I'm pretty certain we got all of them, but just in case one of them is wounded and lying there with a gun, we better be careful. We'll take torches with us." So, saying, John Cooper, Miguel, and a few of the *vaqueros*—who quickly improvised lighted torches—slowly approached the site of the bandit attack, ready to fire their guns if need be. Yankee was in the lead, crouching and sniffing as he stealthily went up to the bodies lying on the ground. It was clear that the three Mexicans were dead, and a hundred yards away they found the body of Jack Sparling, whom John Cooper had shot down from his horse. Even in the dim light of the torches, the former mountain man was able to make out the tracks of the horseman whom he had heard galloping away, and he also detected traces of the blood that had been dripping from the man's wound.

"I don't think that one will get too far," John Cooper said to Miguel as the *vaqueros* collected the bandits' weapons and rounded up their horses. "There's no sense in going after him. Let's just wrap their bodies in their ponchos, and in the morning we'll have two of the *vaqueros* take them and their horses into San Antonio."

"A good idea, *patrón,*" Miguel said as he and John Cooper went to help the *vaqueros*. "I am sure the governor will be glad to know these outlaws have been apprehended."

The men completed their grim task and then returned to camp. Andrew watched soberly as the horses with the dead men on their backs were tethered off to one side of the camp.

John Cooper came up to his son and put his arm around his shoulders. "I'm sorry you have to see all this, Andrew," he said gently. "I guess death is as much a part of life on the trail as anything else."

"I—I guess so," was all Andrew said, his voice quavering slightly.

Looking down at him, observing the way he held his head high and kept his emotions under control, John Cooper

was very proud of his son indeed. He pulled the boy to him
and held him tightly for a moment, then the two of them
walked away from the grisly scene, Yankee protectively trotting alongside.

Two

Thirty-four-year-old Carlos de Escobar had come to
terms with himself during these past two years after returning
to the Double H Ranch, much to the relief and joy of his aging father, Don Diego, and his stepmother, Doña Inez. Now
plunging into all the activities of the great ranch, he devoted
a good deal of time to being with his children by Weesayo,
his twelve-year-old son, Diego, and his daughters Dawn and
Inez, to whom his sister Catarina had become a kind of foster
mother. But he wasn't interested in the sheep that Miguel
Sandarbal raised upon a separate part of the vast acreage, or
the cattle that his brother-in-law had already begun to
breed with the shorthorns he purchased through his New Orleans factor. Carlos was only happy when he worked with the
horses, and had purchased, from the very same factor, a palomino stallion and two mares. He had also worked with
several of the *trabajadores* to build a small stable for these
three superb horses so that they might breed in sheltered
quarters, without being distracted by the horses of the *remuda* and John Cooper's own palominos.

His service in the Mexican army and his strenuous outdoor life had made him more vigorous than he had ever been
before, and the intensity of his features—touched by the unforgettable sadness that had never left him since Weesayo's
death—made him still more attractive to the *criadas* who

worked in the *hacienda* and gave him ardent glances and sudden, shy, stammered words whenever they had occasion to speak to him. But he knew that he was almost desperately in love with Teresa de Rojado, the beautiful young widow who had come to Taos from Havana after her husband's death to visit Don Sancho de Pladero, her father's friend.

Carlos had met Teresa at the de Pladeros two years earlier. Since that time, the young widow had used part of her large inheritance to purchase a small but luxuriously furnished villa some two miles north of Don Sancho's home. She had chosen her servants entirely from the pueblo of Taos— an elderly, fiercely devoted housekeeper, two maids, and a cook, as well as a groom and two stableboys. Like Carlos, she loved horses and had purchased several mares and a stallion. One of the mares, which she kept apart from the stallion, was her favorite mount, and she had named her Feliz because the mare always seemed so delighted when she came to her stall to have her saddled.

Also like Carlos, she was an expert with rapiers and foils, and she kept up her skill by teaching the sturdy young Indian groom to use the foil, till he was able to give her a reasonably exacting match.

Carlos had returned to Taos three times in the hopes of marrying Teresa de Rojado. Each time he had proposed to her, she had gravely shaken her head, put her hand to his, and murmured, "I cannot, *mi amigo*. I do not love you the way a woman should love the man she wants to marry. But you are good and kind, handsome and young, surely desirable to many women who could give you more pleasure than I could ever hope to do—"

And he had groaned and shaken his head and said, "Oh, no, Teresa, never say a thing like that again! It is you I want, in the most honorable of ways. You too have known what sorrow is, and I sense it and can help banish it from your life, if you will but let me."

That was where it stood, with his fear that there might be those in Taos who desired her and could offer her more than he ever could. Carlos was disappointed but not defeated, and he fervently believed that someday he would win her love.

Now on this same day that marked the beginning of John Cooper's first cattle drive in the company of his older son, Andrew, Carlos excitedly entered the *hacienda* and exclaimed to Catarina, who was coming down the corridor, "Dulce is having her foal—come watch, and bring the children!"

Catarina smilingly nodded and promptly hurried to the *hacienda*'s large nursery, which had at one time served as a classroom but, since there was now a schoolhouse, had been restored to the children's recreation room. Grave Francesca— Don Diego and Doña Inez's daughter, who had already won the sobriquet of Little Mother—was playing with her adopted sister and brother, Dolores and Juan. Meanwhile Diego and Dawn and Inez, as well as Charles and Ruth and Carmen, were busily engaged in building a miniature *hacienda*. Esteban Morales, the assistant *capataz*, whose skill at whittling had delighted the children of the Double H Ranch over the years, had painstakingly whittled out scores of squares and blocks, which he had then painted with vegetable dyes. In addition, he fabricated many miniature animals, like horses, burros, cows, steers, and sheep. He had also ingeniously carved out little figurines of men and women, and even given them costumes by gluing bits of painted bark onto them. Greatly flattered by the children's praises, he was currently making sets of Mexican soldiers, Indians, and *vaqueros*.

Esteban regarded his post as assistant *capataz* at the Double H Ranch as heaven-sent, and the former sheepherder from Chihuahua had sworn in the chapel to lead a life of exemplary devotion and loyalty to John Cooper Baines and his family. Indeed, in keeping with that vow, he had already begun work on a huge crucifix for the new church, using the very finest woods, oils, and stains.

Catarina gathered the children and herded them toward the barn, where Carlos kept his palominos. He was waiting for them at the door and smilingly ushered them in, saying, "We will have a little competition in honor of the new foal, *amigos*. Each one of you may suggest a name, and I shall choose the one most suitable. I shall bring back a very special present from Taos to the one who proposes it."

Catarina gave him a surprised look. "You're going to Taos again, *mi hermano*?"

"*Sí*, Catarina. I think you can guess why."

"It's Teresa, isn't it?" she murmured so that the children wouldn't hear as they hurried inside toward the stall where the mare lay, already beginning her labor. Luis Robardo, a *vaquero* in his early twenties, was in the stall with the mare, awaiting the arrival of the *patrón*. Luis had ridden to the *hacienda* as a courier from San Antonio and, after having seen the magnificent ranch, begged for a job. The young man had been hired by Carlos himself, once the latter had discovered that the courier was particularly skilled with horses. Now Luis excitedly called out, "It's beginning, Señor Carlos!"

"*Bueno*, Luis. Come along, *mis amigos!*" Carlos smilingly ordered. The children, without exception, adored this title from the man whom some of them called Tío Carlos, and he, in turn, was deeply touched by this mark of affection.

The door of the stall was left open so that even the smallest child could see the miracle of birth. Carlos entered and squatted down beside the beautiful palomino mare, who whinnied and lifted her head, trying to nip at him to show him that her moment had come. He stroked her head lovingly, murmuring words of solace: "*Sí, comprendo, mi* Dulce. It will all go very well; you are strong; it will be the best stallion of all of them, I promise you that. And you shall have extra sugar and carrots so you can grow strong again, once your foal is born—ah, Luis, be ready now, it comes!"

The two men, working together as a team, delivered the foal, and cleansed it quickly, so that this unsightly task would not offend the spellbound children. Little Ruth called out, "But how tiny he is! Tío Carlos, how long will it take him to be big as Dulce there?"

"Before the year is over, you'll see, *querida!* But it's not going to be a stallion; it's a mare—I was wrong this time, Dulce; forgive me. But the next one will be a colt, that I'm certain of!" Carlos stroked the mare's head again, then rose. "Well now, *amigos,* what do you propose as a name for this little mare?"

"Why don't you call her Querida, Tío Carlos?" Ruth at once called out.

Several of the other children proffered names, but Carlos's mind was already made up: "Querida it is, my sweet little niece. Now you must tell me what you wish me to bring back from Taos as your present."

Ruth drew herself up and, with a dignity that one would have expected more from grave, older Francesca, declared,

"If it isn't too much trouble, Tío Carlos, I should like a bird in a cage, just like Mama's."

Carlos burst out laughing, in which Catarina contagiously joined till there were tears in her eyes. They were both remembering Pepito, the cockatoo in the silver cage, which the governor-general of Cuba had given to Catarina, then thirteen years old, on Christmas Eve, in the year 1807, during the first stop of the de Escobar journey from Madrid to the isolated and distant village of Taos, where Don Diego was to take up his new life as *intendente*. Pepito, to Catarina's delight, continued to address her with *"Quiero, Catarina,"* a phrase she had taught the cockatoo during that period in her life when she had been a pampered, headstrong girl often in need of the admonitions from her then aunt and now stepmother, Doña Inez.

Ruth frowned and was ready to cry at hearing this grown-up laughter, but Carlos swiftly hastened to reassure her: "Oh, come, my sweet little niece, we weren't laughing at you at all. Your mother and I were remembering something that happened long before you were born. Of course you shall have your bird in a cage. And it will be very different from Pepito. That way, only you shall have it and enjoy it."

As if by magic, Ruth's face brightened, and she flung herself into her handsome uncle's arms and bestowed an energetic hug and kiss upon him.

After lunch that day, just before the early-afternoon *siesta,* Carlos de Escobar said to his father, "I wish your *permiso, mi padre,* to speak to you of something that is deep within my heart. And to you also, *mi madrastra,*" he said eloquently as he turned to look at Doña Inez, "if you will hear me."

The children had had their lunch and gone back to their rooms. Only Catarina remained with Don Diego and Doña Inez. She looked warmly at her handsome brother and surreptitiously blew him a kiss. Carlos gave her a sad smile and nodded, and then turned to his father and earnestly declared, "My duties here on the ranch are quite in order, *mi padre.* That is why I want permission from you to ride to Taos."

"Of course, my son," Don Diego said, smiling warmly. "You have more than fulfilled your duties here. Take what time you need. And, of course, you will see Don Sancho—

please urge him again to think seriously of coming to join us here. I miss my old friend."

"I understand that, *mi padre,* and I am certain he will come to Texas soon. He talked often of it when I visited him last."

"How long do you think you will be gone, my son?" Don Diego asked.

"About two months, *mi padre.* I'm sure you know—as Catarina has probably already told you—that I'm very much in love with Teresa de Rojado."

Don Diego permitted himself a knowing little smile as he turned to look first at his wife and then at his daughter. "That is true, my son. And I must say that I thoroughly approve. There is no one I'd rather welcome here than the Señora de Rojado. She will give you great joy; I am sure of it."

Carlos uttered a long-drawn sigh. "I have already visited Taos three times in the past two years and urged her to marry me, but she still says no."

"I have prayed all this time, my son, that there will be someone in this world who will share with you the long years God is sure to give you. I say this to you, before my beloved wife, Doña Inez, and my daughter Catarina; you have been a son among sons, and no father could have been more rewarded than to have you as his successor in this life."

"My father, you do me too much honor," Carlos protested, his cheeks flushing.

"I do not say these words lightly, Carlos. I can remember our journey across the Atlantic and how you, young though you were, a mere stripling, taught us all a lesson in courage and endurance. No, I pray that this time you will bring her back with you."

"I shall pray for that also, *mi padre.*" Carlos rose, went to his sister and kissed her on the forehead, and then moved around the table to kiss his stepmother on the cheek, and to shake his father's hand. Greatly moved, the white-haired *hidalgo* watched his son leave the dining room and then, anxious to hide his emotion, lifted the little silver bell and rang it peremptorily for Tía Margarita. When she entered, eyes wide with surprise at the imperious ring of the summons, he blustered, "*Mujer,* bring brandy for all of us. We wish to drink a toast to my son. Hurry, if you will!"

And when the brandy was served, he turned to Doña Inez and, taking her hand, gently said, "I pray to the good God that He will make my son happy after these years of desolation and anguish. He has righted himself from the morass of despair—but now I know that until he wins the señora's answer, he will never be truly freed from the shadows of his great sorrow."

Carlos had gone to his room to pack his saddlebags. When he had finished, he went into the chapel of the *hacienda* and knelt to pray. Bowing his head, he devoutly murmured, "Holy Mother, hear my prayer. You know well that there is no lust in my heart for the Señora Teresa de Rojado. I wish to honor her, and I will devote my life to her, if she says yes to me. You do not know how much I miss Weesayo, Holy Mother. And it is not only because of my needs as a man that I wish to marry again. The Señora de Rojado, though she was born to the aristocracy, believes as I do, that the accident of birth does not entitle us to special privilege. I love her because she is good and true and loyal. Believe me, Holy Virgin, that it is not out of selfish desire that I pray to You, Mother of our beloved Savior. I love her for she has known the anguish of bereavement as I have. I would, if it could become possible, cherish her and love her truly. Grant me this, and I shall build an altar and have Padre Pastronaz consecrate it. I call upon You with veneration and humility, and I accept Your holy will."

He crossed himself and went back to his room. As he took his saddlebags from the bed, he closed his eyes, and the lovely, tall, slim Teresa de Rojado appeared before him, riding alongside him on her mare, understanding him with such sympathy and tenderness as he had not dreamed a woman of her highborn state could grant a man—and yet, treating him like a brother, not a lover.

And for all her magnificent expertise as an equestrienne and fencer, she also had, at age twenty-nine, all the feminine graces of beauty, gentleness, and compassion. On those occasions when he had visited her, he had observed that she treated her Indian servants like equals, without any arrogant pretense of aristocratic breeding.

And so as he left for Taos that afternoon, Carlos prayed once more that on this visit he could make Teresa at last fall in love with him.

Three

By way of accolade, John Cooper let young Andrew ride ahead of the *vaqueros* and Miguel, and even a few yards ahead of himself. Andrew's eyes sparkled with pride, and he glanced back at his father with an infectious grin as, on the dusty streets, men and women called greetings to John Cooper and cheered him as a welcome visitor.

The two *vaqueros* who had gone ahead of the others had already ridden into San Antonio and turned over to the governor the bodies of the dead renegades, as well as their horses and weapons. Thus the governor himself came out on the street to welcome John Cooper, and effusively shook his hand and thanked him and his men for apprehending the bandits.

By now, the tall American was well known in San Antonio, thanks to his friendship with the cattle breeder, Joaquín Cobrara, who had recommended factors in New Orleans, Galveston, and even St. Louis, through whom John Cooper was able to import pedigreed bulls and heifers that he intended to crossbreed in order to obtain finer beef. More than this, Cobrara had been extremely helpful in recommending the bank in which the former mountain man had deposited some of the silver ingots he had found in the secret mine so many years earlier. He soon meant to deposit many more of them in this bank.

The stocky, thickly bearded cattle breeder came out of the adobe and wood-constructed one-story building where he kept his office, and effusively welcomed John Cooper, who was dismounting from his magnificent palomino. Then watching Andrew wheel his mount and ride back toward his

29

father, Cobrara chuckled and, gesturing toward the black-haired youngster, declared, "I suspect this is your oldest, Señor Baines. He handles his horse very well—a true *caballero*."

"Yes, Señor Cobrara, and he's got his wits about him. A few rustlers tried to steal some of the strays a few nights ago, but Andrew fired his musket and alerted us."

"Everyone in town knows all about how you defeated the bandits, Señor Baines. Well, my felicitations to you, Señor Andrew. You follow in the footsteps of your father, it's plain to see. And one day, Señor Baines, if *El Señor Dios* so wills, I myself or my own son, Jaime—who is only a few years older than your Andrew—may do business with your son in providing the very finest cattle for breeding."

"I'll say amen to that, Señor Cobrara. As you can see, I've brought a herd of three hundred head. They're meant for the missions."

"You come at an excellent time. Only yesterday, Padre García of the Franciscan mission was hoping there would be beef for his parishioners, who have raised enough in tithes to let him buy most of that herd of yours."

"I shall give him a very fair price. I want the goodwill of all the people of San Antonio, Señor Cobrara, and especially that of Padre García, whose charitable works are well known to me. But now I'm wondering if there's something exceptional I can take back to the Double H Ranch as a present for my family."

"As it happens, there's a fine spinet, made in France, which was shipped a year ago from New Orleans and meant for a *hacendado* who died just a week before it arrived here. I've had it in the back of my warehouse, for it appears, unfortunately, that no one in San Antonio wishes to claim it. If it had been a guitar or perhaps even a violin, I'm sure I could have sold it many times over."

"I shall buy it from you. We already have a piano at the *hacienda*, but it's old and in very bad condition, having been carted around so much. I know the family would love a new one. What price are you asking?"

"Five hundred silver *pesos*, Señor Baines. You understand that this would include the cartage from New Orleans and the money out of my own pocket that I advanced in poor old Señor Darnerio's name."

"I'll have my *vaqueros* get a *carreta* so that we can take it back safely. The terrain is not difficult, but I want to be certain that it's securely fastened, so that it's not too badly out of tune by the time I reach the *hacienda*."

"Two of my assistants will help your *vaqueros* with the *carreta*, Señor Baines. Then you'll take the herd to the mission now?"

"Yes, Señor Cobrara, and when I return, I'd like to talk to you about importing two really fine short-horned bulls and perhaps six heifers of the same species."

"I understand that M'sieu Mallard, who is my agent in New Orleans and whom you yourself know, will have a shipment from the East next spring. I shall send a rider to him tomorrow and tell him that you have asked for the bulls and heifers. And, of course, it goes without saying that I'll get you the very best price I can."

"I'm indebted to you again, Señor Cobrara. Well now, Andrew, shake hands with my good friend Señor Cobrara, and then you can ride with me to the mission."

"I'm sure my wife would be delighted if you and your *capataz*, Señor Sandarbal, and of course, your fine son Andrew, would be our guests for the afternoon meal at my villa," the stocky cattle breeder genially declared.

"With the greatest pleasure in the world," John Cooper grinned. "After the skimpy provisions we've had to content ourselves with in the past week, a dinner such as your good wife cooks will be a banquet to us. I thank you on behalf of my son and my *capataz*." Then, after making a little bow, John Cooper mounted Pingo and wheeled the palomino down the dusty street, calling to the *vaqueros*, "¡*Vámanos, muchachos!* We go to the Franciscan mission."

Joaquín Cobrara owned a magnificent home in the section of San Antonio known as Villa of San Fernando. The house was luxuriously furnished and built with *patios* and many sheltered corridors. His wife, Luisa, not quite forty and still spirited and handsome, welcomed John Cooper and Andrew and the white-haired, sun-bronzed *capataz*. Her son, Jaime, fourteen and tall and gangling, eagerly shook hands with John Cooper, and with Andrew as well. He was, as his father whimsically announced, a little awed by the tall American, whose exploits in the wilderness his father had often discussed.

There was, however, an unexpected visitor to share the festive meal, a tall, sturdy man in his late thirties, with blond sideburns and a thick beard, whom Joaquín Cobrara introduced as "the Señor Eugene Fair, from Missouri. He has come here to arrange for more *americano* settlers in this great Texas of ours."

"I'm pleased to meet you, Mr. Fair," John Cooper said, extending his hand before he seated himself at the table. "You're likely a good friend of Stephen Austin."

"I count myself fortunate to be one of his friends, Mr. Baines. He's a great man, and all of us who work with him can't say enough about what he's done toward opening up this frontier. It's our prayer that friendly settlements will prevent any possible war between our United States and Mexico. Though I confess, I'm worried about the politics south of the Rio Grande."

"They worry me, too, some," John Cooper wryly admitted. "One of these days, in my view, Santa Anna is going to try to take over, and he's the sort of man who likes battles and bloodshed—if the odds are in his favor."

"I pray God it won't come to that, Mr. Baines," Eugene Fair solemnly avowed. "But if it does, you, an American yourself, know perfectly well that we'd win hands down."

"I'm sure that's true, Mr. Fair. But what I'm thinking about are the innocent people, the old men and women, the children, and the wives and sweethearts of the soldiers who'll suffer in the event of a war between our country and Mexico. And it's all so needless. But maybe if they elect a president down there and let Santa Anna know that they'd just as soon settle things peacefully, he might not decide to lead an army against us. At least, that's what I'm hoping for."

"Forgive me, Señora Cobrara," Eugene Fair said, turning and making a courteous bow toward the cattle breeder's amiable wife. "I didn't mean to hold up your wonderful meal with a political dissertation."

"We are all friends here, Señor Fair," she beamed. "Feel free to say whatever you please. But now I shall have dinner served. And when it is over, there will be *aguardiente* and good coffee and cigars for you men to enjoy." With this, she clapped her hands, and two maids appeared from the kitchen, receiving their orders to begin serving the meal.

John Cooper smiled and nodded at his new friend. He could not, however, resist asking before they began eating, "Where do you plan to bring your settlers, Mr. Fair?"

"About thirty miles north of the Austin settlement, on the Brazos, Mr. Baines. It's good, rich land, good for farming, as well as for ranching. And, of course, it'll strengthen Mr. Austin's community."

"I can see that. Well, if you've any extra settlers, you might tell them about the Double H Ranch. My *capataz* here, Señor Miguel Sandarbal, and I are always looking for good men who would like to share their lives with us and strengthen our community. We're a good ways southwest of where you plan to be, down by the Frio River."

"That means you're not far from the Rio Grande, Mr. Baines. In the event of a war, there might be danger, don't you think?"

"In one sense, maybe. On the other hand, Mr. Fair, I hope that long before such a thing occurs, we'll have so many settlers and so many men who can take up arms to defend the land and to fight for the United States that no Mexican troops in their right minds would think of attacking. I suppose maybe that's wishful thinking, but actually, where we are, we've rarely seen any Mexican patrols at all in the past several years. They'd be more likely to come to San Antonio here, or the town of Austin."

"True enough," Eugene Fair agreed. "Well now, that looks absolutely wonderful—I'm afraid, Mr. Baines, for all I want to talk to you, my hunger is taking priority over everything else." Fair's eyes glowed as the maids carried in lavish platters of baked chicken and mutton prepared with mouthwatering spices and herbs. Vegetables and freshly baked *tortillas* accompanied these, and there were also platters of *chile con carne* and *carne asada*, for Señora Luisa Cobrara believed that the more food she served, the less danger there was that anyone would leave the table still hungry.

After the lavish meal, Luisa served some excellent French brandy and cordials, as well as strong coffee, together with a bowl of fruits and nuts. She bade her son take his leave of their guests, and then she, Jaime, and Andrew left the men to themselves. John Cooper tried one of the fine

Havana cigars, which the cattle breeder had ordered by way of New Orleans, and he puffed at it contentedly as he took a sip of brandy. Then he eyed Eugene Fair and asked, "Have you or Mr. Austin had any trouble from hostile Indians in your settlements thus far?"

"Not really, Mr. Baines. Perhaps you didn't know that about three years ago, Stephen Austin himself was captured by the Comanche, but when they found out that he was an American and not a Mexican, they released him, almost with apologies. He made a treaty with the Wichita until his colony was strong enough to dispose of the troublesome coastal Indians. I think he plans to form an alliance with immigrant Cherokee, Shawnee, and Delaware, though the Mexican government has been trying to get him to go to war with the Comanche who sometimes raid this city, as well as Goliad."

"It's my experience that the Comanche aren't really the most dangerous, even though they're perhaps the most warlike and the most expert horsemen of all the Plains Indians," John Cooper replied. "That's because they're nomadic; they move constantly wherever the buffalo go."

"That's quite right. Also, they don't send out scouts and spies to find out what their enemy is doing the way the Kiowa Apache or the Lipan do," Fair assented. "Still in all, I think I'd rather fight any other tribe except Comanche—their culture is that every man is a warrior-chief unto himself. That comes from their long years of fighting the Spaniards and opposing Indian tribes. And there's certainly no more courageous Indian anywhere in these United States. Of course, you probably also know that four years ago, when our first colonists came on the *Lively* and it was wrecked on the coast, most of the survivors were killed by the Karankawa, although others, strangely enough, were escorted by these very same Indians to their destination. Already this year Mr. Austin is pursuing a campaign against the Karankawa to drive them to the coast—I'm certain there'll be a peace treaty before much longer, since they've already appealed to the priests and civil authorities at Goliad. Also, Anastacio Bustamante, of the new Mexican government, is bringing a large troop of well-trained soldiers to assist Mr. Austin's colonists."

"Your settlers are determined not to be uprooted," John Cooper said, grinning.

"Yes, Mr. Baines. We believe that Texas should be annexed to the United States, and not become a dependent and enslaved part of Mexico, especially with the chaotic day-by-day government in Mexico right now," Eugene Fair stoutly averred.

"Well, it would be a great help to your cause if you had more settlers who'd lived with Indians the way I have," John Cooper smilingly declared. "I lived with two tribes of Sioux, as well as the Skidi Pawnee and the Jicarilla Apache. I'm still allied as a blood brother to the Jicarilla, and it's a valuable alliance. But best of all, I've a wampum belt that was given to me by the Jicarilla once—it means I'm a hunter and friend of the Indians. This has come in very handy in dealing with the Indians in the vicinity of our *hacienda;* I've even done some trading with the Apache and Comanche, and I've acquired some fine mustangs that I bred with our horses."

"I've no doubt, Mr. Baines," Fair eagerly replied, "that if you ever wanted to take on additional responsibilities, Mr. Austin would be overjoyed if you'd seek a post with him as a lieutenant in charge of defenses. There's no doubt that a man like yourself, with your knowledge of Indians, could train and also reassure many of our settlers, that they'll be able to develop their farms and ranches and live like normal citizens without any more bloodshed."

"I'll make you a counteroffer, Mr. Fair," John Cooper said, as he rose from the table and shook hands with the energetic *empresario.* "You tell Stephen Austin that there's plenty of acreage around my ranch by the Frio River. If ever his settlement gets overcrowded and he has good men and women who'd like to settle down and live normal lives, just have him send them to me. There'll always be a place for good Americans on the Double H Ranch."

Before leaving San Antonio, John Cooper asked Joaquín Cobrara to send a message to the factor, Fabien Mallard. He was planning to make a trip to New Orleans by next spring at the latest, and would appreciate it if the factor would look for attractive dress materials for Catarina and Doña Inez, as well as Bess Sandarbal. This done, he rode back to the mission to conduct business with the genial priest.

Selling the animals for a modest price, John Cooper explained, "I do not seek profit from you, *mi padre.* And the money you give me for these three hundred head will, I promise you, be spent in building a church at my ranch, where all my *trabajadores* and all our families will worship."

"You are most generous, Señor Baines. Our dear Lord will bless you for your generosity."

"Let the difference in the price which you expected to pay and which I took from you, *mi padre,* be considered my gift to your church. I am not a parishioner, but I feel great sympathy for all Franciscans, knowing how Saint Francis himself gave up his wealth and wandered among the beasts and the birds as a poor but liberated man."

"Yes, my son, ours is a gentle faith, and to my mind it is gentleness and love that will conquer the savagery of this wild land. Be assured that I shall pray for you and your dear wife and your children, including your fine son, Andrew, who, as you tell me, has already proved himself to be a man of courage." The *padre* made the sign of the cross, and John Cooper bowed his head.

While the transaction was being accomplished at the mission, Miguel Sandarbal spent an hour with one of the San Antonio merchants and filled a wagon with supplies for the Double H Ranch. Also, he purchased four dray horses from a stableman nearby to draw the wagon, as well as the *carreta* in which the spinet had been carefully packed. It was bound with sturdy leather slings and a padding of poor-quality cotton, which had been spoiled by a drenching rain.

Mounting the driver's seat, Miguel drove the horses back to the mission, where John Cooper and the other *vaqueros* waited for him. His own horse was tied to the back of the wagon and docilely followed. A *vaquero* drove the *carreta*.

They took a leisurely route homeward, avoiding some of the rougher terrain; and so, rather than riding due west and then southward to the Frio River, they took the southerly trail from San Antonio southward to the Nueces River, and from there followed its fusion with the Frio till they reached home. John Cooper not only wanted to give the spinet less jostling, but also wanted to survey the terrain to determine whether there were any Mexican troops or Indian villages in that vicinity. Eugene Fair's remarks about the conditions in Texas had given him much to think about.

He had not forgotten his plan to transfer to the vault in the New Orleans bank all the silver ingots he had found in the abandoned mine near the Jicarilla stronghold. Once the ingots were there, in a bank in the United States, it was very unlikely that Santa Anna would ever gain possession of that treasure: a treasure meant for the poor of Taos, and especially for the Pueblo Indians, who had known such long years of oppression and poverty. A portion of it—its rightful due as discoverer—was for the well-being of his family and all those who lived in peace on the Double H Ranch, and another portion John Cooper meant to give his friends, the Jicarilla Apache.

There were perhaps sixty ingots remaining in the mine, an incredible fortune. In the hands of Santa Anna, it would put a military dictator on the throne of Mexico, who would challenge even the United States and bring death and misery to thousands of innocent people. No, this treasure must be taken from the mountain before, by some ill chance, Santa Anna's spies discovered it. And although the Jicarilla Apache with their chief, Kinotatay, preserved the secret, it was also possible that a new *alcalde mayor* in Taos, or even an importunate governor of New Mexico, might wish to drive out the Indians, including the Jicarilla high on their mountain stronghold. That would mean bloodshed and misery, but it might also mean the discovery of the silver mine.

No, this transfer must be done in the very near future. It would be a long journey from the stronghold to New Orleans, and it would be wise to have strong, well-armed allies as escorts. He could expect the warriors of the Jicarilla Apache to accompany him all the way from their mountains to the ranch, and from there his own *trabajadores* and friends on the ranch would provide the escort to New Orleans. In all, it would be one of the most dangerous enterprises that John Cooper had ever undertaken, but it had to be done.

As was his wont when he rode out on cattle drives or on long hunting forays with Yankee, John Cooper had worn his buckskins. He also wore the Spanish dagger in its sheath around his neck, the dagger that he had taken as a boy from the two renegades who had tried to kill him back in the blizzard-ridden region of northern Missouri seventeen long years ago. And the wampum belt which the Jicarilla had given him was bound securely around his waist. It had not faded with the years, since he had polished and oiled it. These symbols, which almost every Indian would understand, could save his life, especially if he could not speak the tongue of a brave he encountered on the trail and who took him for the sort of *wasichu* who would draw a bead on an Indian simply because he was an Indian.

They stopped that evening to camp near a little creek, and John Cooper amused himself by sending Yankee to reconnoiter. He was quite pleased with the young, powerful animal's behavior on this journey. He hoped that when the need arose, Yankee would not back down from a fight since the advantage of having such an animal at his side in battle was in the element of surprise and terror—he could remember how Santomaro's men shrieked in terror when Lobo leaped at them as they tried to raid the *hacienda* back in Taos. Even as he thought of Yankee, the wolf-dog came trotting up to him, wagging his tail, lowering his muzzle so that John Cooper might rub his knuckles over his forehead, and uttering that characteristic purr of contentment.

The former mountain man chuckled, remembering Lobo. Then, with a kind of nostalgic sadness, he thought of Fortuna, the black raven with a lame wing that Carlos had brought back from a hunting expedition. He remembered how Fortuna's wing had healed, and how the raven had teased Lobo, flying down to peck him, whenever John Cooper had taken them on an outing.

Fortuna seemed to have left the Double H Ranch on the very night that Lobo and his timber-wolf mate circled the ranch and, raising their muzzles to the moon, howled in farewell. He had not seen Fortuna since. And remembering how valiant and faithful Lobo had been, he hoped that the God of animals and birds would reunite them for long years to come and that Fortuna would continue playfully teasing Lobo.

They wakened early in the morning and, after a quick and simple breakfast, mounted their horses and resumed the trail back to the ranch. Once again Yankee proudly trotted ahead of all of them, sniffing, glancing back with an eager look in his yellow eyes, and barking whenever there was a sudden flash of a jackrabbit racing across the plain beyond them. Several times he was tempted to take off after the rabbit, but John Cooper's stern "No, Yankee, stay!" held him obediently. Nonetheless, he glanced back with almost a humanly exasperated look, and John Cooper could not help laughing to himself. Yankee was indeed a delightful companion on the trail, and surely a diversion for his young son.

Shortly before noon, Yankee suddenly stopped dead in his tracks, lowered his muzzle, and then began rapidly racing through the thick grass toward the southwest. Intrigued, the tall American spurred Pingo and followed him, while Andrew, not to be outdone by his father, kicked his heels against his gelding and galloped after them.

Miguel Sandarbal, out of instinctive precaution, bade the *vaqueros* wait and prime their weapons, while he accompanied his master and the latter's son.

Yankee had come to a dry canyon, which had been a flourishing creek long years ago. There were thick brambles and bushes on each side of it, and beyond, a huge cluster of wild pecan trees and live oak trees, as well. John Cooper tensed in his saddle as he saw a group of four Lipan Indians on horseback, circling a wild boar. One of the Indians then dismounted and, seizing a feathered lance, ran at the boar, yelling and taunting it. It charged, swerving in its mad rush, its bloodshot eyes fixed on its enemy, and with its sharp tusks gashed his calf. The Indian uttered a groan, stumbled back, and fell. His three mounted companions hurled their lances, but all fell short, and the boar, squealing its enmity, backed up, pawing the ground as a bull might, ready to charge again.

Swiftly, John Cooper reached for "Long Girl" and drew it out of the sheath, brought it to his shoulder, squinted along the sight, and pulled the trigger, just as the boar charged the fallen Indian. Almost simultaneously, John Cooper heard his son's musket explode to the left of him, and, startled, he turned to glance at Andrew, who once again was almost dazed by the recoil and staggered in his saddle, dropping the musket.

But the boar had been halted in its charge. Sprawled onto its side, it kicked convulsively for a few moments and then lay still. John Cooper promptly dismounted and, stroking Pingo's head, murmured, "Stay, *amigo*, stay there, good Pingo!" as he hurried toward the fallen brave whose three mounted companions came closer now, their hands on their hunting knives.

Miguel Sandarbal had pulled his Belgian rifle out of its sheath and called to them in Spanish, "We are friends; he has saved your companion; do not show your weapons, or I must shoot!"

The men reined in their horses, staring at Miguel and

waiting, while their mustangs tossed their heads, whinnying and shifting from hoof to hoof.

John Cooper crouched down beside the fallen Indian, who stared at him in wonder. The Indian then put out a hand toward John Cooper's wampum belt and hazarded in Spanish, "*Amigo?*"

"*Sí, amigo,*" the former mountain man nodded.

The Indian warrior was almost as tall as John Cooper and wore breechcloth, leggings, and moccasins. His black hair was shaved off on the side of his head, while the hair on the right side was long but tied with string so that it did not fall below his shoulder. Feathers and trinkets adorned his hair, and his left ear was pierced with seven holes, the right with two. His beard and eyebrows had been plucked out, and his chest and back were smeared with several colors of paint. A red stripe circled his neck like a noose.

"The *jabalí* is yours. You have killed it; you have saved my life," the Indian said to him in a guttural tongue. John Cooper was startled: there was a likeness in this Indian's speech to the tongue of the Jicarilla. He had no way of knowing that, centuries before, the Jicarilla and the Lipan had been united as one nation. Because of the depredations of the Spaniards, the Lipan had been driven away and their power weakened. But even now, they were a warlike tribe and as valiant as the Comanche in battle.

John Cooper therefore tried a few words in the Jicarilla tongue and was pleased to find that the man whose life he had saved from the boar understood him. "I read the belt that says you are a great hunter and a friend to all of the people," the Lipan warrior hoarsely averred as he tried to sit up.

John Cooper called to Miguel: "He's bleeding, but not too badly. Let's put a tourniquet over the wound. Don't worry, his friends won't attack; I'll talk to them." Then, turning, he called to the fallen brave's three companions, again speaking in the Jicarilla tongue, "I am a friend; I am blood brother to the Jicarilla of Nuevo México."

To his surprise, they wheeled their mustangs toward the west and galloped off. John Cooper turned back to the fallen man, whose calf Miguel was now binding with cloth. "Why do you leave you thus?"

"Because I have been saved by a *wasichu,* and they

think of me as a woman now. The *jabalí* would have killed me if you had not killed it first with your firestick, which speaks with thunder. And that is your son who fired his musket also to save me?" He sat up now, pointing to Andrew, who still sat astride his gelding.

"It is my son, yes. I am John Cooper Baines, blood brother of the Jicarilla, whose chief is Kinotatay."

"My tribe has heard of the Jicarilla and the brave Kinotatay in the mountain stronghold," the Lipan said in Apache. "And we know of you also, though not by name. You are the *gringo* with yellow hair, the *wasichu* who fights with the son of a wolf beside you—and also with your own son on horseback. Already my people think of you as a demigod.

"I also know of your ranch. Three moons ago, when I rode with my brothers who now will speak my name no longer over the campfire, we came upon your land and your *hacienda*. And we knew whose it was and that you were strong, and that you were also a friend to *los indios*.

"I am Minanga, war lieutenant of the Lower Lipan—but I have lost my rank because my warriors have seen me unsaddled by a *jabalí*, which I did not kill but which wounded me. I shall be an outcast until I prove myself to them—this is our custom. We hunted buffalo here before the setting of the sun yesterday, and we found tracks and hoped to find the herd. Instead, this was my fate. The Giver of Breath has put me before you as a slave, and it is best that you kill me, so that my spirit will go to the heavens and not into the darkness."

"But I do not wish to kill you. And there are other tribes who would consider your warriors cowards that they did not come to defend their leader, their war lieutenant," John Cooper solemnly replied in the Jicarilla tongue. "Now if you wish, Minanga, I will take you back to my ranch until you are well."

"But I cannot go back to my tribe until I have counted some coup which will show them that I am not dead or a slave."

"Perhaps, then, you can be the scout of our ranch. And perhaps also, if ever we are attacked, you can aid my own war lieutenant. There are Mexicans, Texans, and Americans on my ranch, Minanga. But all of us live in peace, and we do not seek to take away the buffalo from you who were first upon this land. We seek no war with the Mexicans, either. You have heard of los Estados Unidos?"

"Yes, I have heard those words, and I have heard them from *gringos*, as well as from *mejicanos*."

"In your tongue, Minanga, these words stand for a union of states, a brotherhood of many hundreds of people—like your warriors, who will fight to make sure that no enemy takes our land. But in the land on which we have settled, a land we hope someday will be part of los Estados Unidos, we do not try to drive *los indios* away from their hunting grounds, nor from their burial grounds."

"I have heard it often said that you are a *wasichu* who would have made a good *indio*, if you had not had white parents," Minanga replied with a dour little smile, as John Cooper helped him rise. The tall Lipan winced and tested his wounded leg. "The pain is going; your man there has great magic. Is he your shaman?"

"No, he is not a doctor; he is my *capataz*, Minanga. Can you ride?"

"I will try. My horse still grazes there; he is loyal to me—more than my warriors were. Very well, I will ride back with you, Señor Baines."

"You will tell me more about your tribe after you have come to our *hacienda* and had your wound cared for. You will eat well, and you will rest."

"You have given me back my life. I am yours to command. This is the way of our people, and I am glad that it was you who saved my life, and not some other *gringo* or *mejicano*."

"Are there those in your tribe who would stand by you, even though these men have seen you fall before the *jabalí?*" John Cooper pursued.

"There are some to whom I could send word. But you see, we have no village now. We moved to this country following the buffalo. Where it goes, we go. It is our life, and without it, there is no meat for the old ones, or for the children."

"Tell me, Minanga, do you know any of *los indios* of the pueblo of Taos? Many of them are my friends."

"Yes, to be sure, I know the people of the pueblo, especially an elder there, who is named Ticumbe and is the spokesman for many of his tribe. I met him four years ago, when I went to the fair to buy maize and cotton blankets in exchange for hides and tallow and suet. And also, to buy two good horses. One of them is the one that still waits there for me. I bought him from a Mexican who had come from Chihuahua to trade at the fair."

"He is a strong, good horse, with good hocks and fetlocks. There is strong blood in him."

As John Cooper helped the brave to his black mustang, which stood peacefully grazing nearby, he asked, "You have no wife or children, Minanga?"

The Indian's face was laconic and bleak as he answered, "No, Señor Baines. My wife was raising maize in the fields many miles from here when a Waco on a raiding party rode by and, leaning down from his mustang, snatched her up and rode off with her. She was great with my first child—and I have had word that both are dead."

"Then you have no ties which would bind you to your tribe, and it may be that as scout of our ranch, you will one day be able to go back in honor."

"If the Giver of Breath has destined thus, I am not one to argue with Him who judges all," Minanga philosophically replied as, with an effort, he mounted his black mustang. "Lead me to your ranch. I trust you because you speak as with my own tongue, even though many of your words are different."

Proudly erect in his saddle, giving no sign of the pain of his bandaged calf, he held the reins of his mustang as John Cooper led the way to the waiting *vaqueros*.

Four

Just two days after Eugene Fair had met and dined with John Cooper in San Antonio, two large groups of Americans met in Franklin, Missouri, to wish one another the very best of luck. One of the groups was comprised of some eighteen Missouri traders, who would start out with their burros and horses and wagons laden with trading goods and cross the Arkansas and then the Cimarron rivers, to find a warm welcome from the enthusiastic Mexicans at Rio Gallinas (soon to be renamed Las Vegas, but never to be confused with the future Nevada metropolis of a century later). Then they would go leisurely and with high hopes into Taos at the foot of the snowcapped Sangre de Cristo range, and thence to the liberated town of Santa Fe along the newly opened Santa Fe Trail, the chief trade route to New Mexico. And over the past several years, men had come back from Santa Fe to boast of the treasures to be found for the enterprising who would pursue this trade route.

The other group was comprised of sixty-five settlers who were to travel with a guide chosen by Eugene Fair—one Simon Brown—to the new settlement some thirty miles north of Stephen Austin's newly founded city on the Brazos, whose name, San Felipe de Austin, had been selected by Governor Martínez of Texas himself.

As *empresario*, Eugene Fair negotiated with the Mexican government for a large tract of land in Texas. The settlers, in turn, promised to develop their portion of the land by building a house, growing crops, and raising cattle. Fair's group of settlers would take the paddle-wheeler to Natchez, with all

44

their worldly goods stored in the hold, disembark at that boisterous and dangerous river town, and purchase wagons and livestock and seed and tools. From Natchez, they would go on to Natchitoches not far from the Sabine River, and thence on the land route to their new home.

The settlers were from such faraway places as Ohio, Indiana, Fort Kaskaskia, and Fort Pitt. Those who had come thus far had sold their wagons to pay for their passage from Franklin to Natchez. These settlers had also heard rhapsodic descriptions of the Southwest: fertile land, where grass was as tall as a man's head, where elk and antelope and deer and even bear flourished, and where there was plenty of water as well as open space, so that a family might have freedom to grow its new roots without the presence of hostile Indians. To be sure, some of those who had earlier visited the far-off Southwest with an idea of settling there one day had barely escaped death or captivity at the hands of the nomadic tribes that still ruled this virtually unknown region bordering the United States and Mexico—but the eager settlers-to-be thought nothing of such risks.

Among the settlers, there were those who had special reasons for pulling up stakes and destroying their roots in the East or the Midwest: they wanted to start a new life and totally obliterate the shadowy past that they were all too eager to forget. There was William Maynell, for example, a dour, balding man in his thirties, who had come from a small Ohio town, where he ran a grain mill. He was a wealthy skinflint, his features bleak and peaked, with a bony nose and squinting, watery blue eyes topped by thick brows which were invariably arched in a suspicious stare. He had a wart high on his right cheek that he was continually fingering whenever he pondered what action should be taken, or what words should be spoken.

His father had been a peddler who drove a wagon through Ohio and Pennsylvania, a jovial man with the heart of a gypsy and the morals of a goat. He had seduced Maynell's mother and left her great with child, so that her stern Presbyterian parents turned her out and bade her hie herself to a brothel, once she had borne her child, for she had forfeited the right to call herself their daughter. Out of compassion, a widower in his early fifties had married her and given her the name of Maynell, and fathered another son, William's half brother, Eldon.

By the time William Maynell was fifteen, both his stepfather and mother were dead, and he and Eldon, two years younger, were taken in by his stepfather's spinster sister, a woman with a dour and suspicious nature, who undoubtedly was a great influence on both boys. Her death five years later left both brothers with a small inheritance, the house going to William, who by this time was an apprentice to a millwright in Ohio.

He was ambitious and greedy, and due to his morose boyhood, he schemed to further his own ends. The millwright died a year later as the result of a suspicious accident; he had gone down to the creek to fetch water, had stumbled and lost his footing, and had fallen into the creek, swollen by rainwater. His cries for help had brought his apprentice, who had stood by and watched him drown without blinking an eye. To Maynell, the accident was providential, and since the millwright had no family, he acquired the business. To his credit it might be said that he was ingenious with machinery; working with his hands was inordinately satisfying. Since he was hardly prepossessing of features or manners, the girls of the village did not take to him, despite his sudden affluence.

His brother, meanwhile, went to work on a nearby farm and married the farmer's eldest daughter a year later. This ensured Maynell that Eldon would never be dependent upon him: hence, all his efforts could be directed toward furthering his own material gains.

When he was twenty-six, he at last managed to find a wife, the homely, older daughter of the proprietor of the only inn in this Ohio town. She was nearly thirty, and he had been virtually her only suitor. But again Maynell was calculating. Six months after his marriage to Johanna Kurwyn, her father was found dead in his bed. The overworked and uneducated town doctor, Dr. Spurling, diagnosed the cause of death as a stroke or a flux. He did not know that the heavy woolen blanket that lay neatly folded under the bed had been used to smother the old man. A few weeks later, Maynell and his wife, Johanna, moved into the inn, and Maynell sold the mill.

At about this time, his brother, having had bad luck with the farm, approached him for a loan; the loan was granted in return for a first mortgage drawn up in such a way that the first default on the stipulated payments would result in a change of ownership. And when, some four months later, Eldon Maynell found himself unable to make a payment, his brother promptly foreclosed and turned Eldon, his wife, and two children out. The horrified townspeople took up a collection and gave Eldon and his family enough money to leave for the West in search of cheap land and a new start, and they began to ostracize his ruthless brother.

Johanna Maynell had had two miscarriages, and died, presenting her miserly husband with a puny little girl. Much to his annoyance, Maynell was obliged to hire a nursemaid to care for the infant, and engaged a sixteen-year-old orphan for the task. Her name was Annie Buckley. She was attractive but dim-witted; and that winter, in her pathetic eagerness to make certain that the baby was kept warm in her crib, she bundled her with swaddling clothes so that, quite by accident, restlessly moving about at night, the baby was smothered to death.

Once again the town doctor was called in, and adjudged the infant's death as being caused by her own puniness. William Maynell married Annie Buckley some eight months later, and made her the hostess of his inn. The inn had prospered because many families from Pennsylvania and New York had decided to move beyond to fertile, cheap lands, and many wagon trains stopped at the little Ohio town for several days, their occupants being quartered at Maynell's inn.

The dour man, inwardly brooding over all the bizarre accidents of the past, found his new wife, Annie Buckley, an encumbrance. The young woman—really no more than a girl—believed that she had carte blanche to his private fortune, and bedecked herself in fancy silks and cottons, and purchased jewelry and furs. When her husband angrily informed her that he was not made of money, she slyly taunted him with the remark, "But you are, dear husband, and you'd best please me with the things I like so much. Don't forget, I've been poor ever since I was born, and I've accommodated you in bed—though you're no real man for a healthy girl, and I can only stand you because of your money."

Annie had no way of knowing that, with this forthright speech, she had sealed her own death warrant.

It did not seem so the following month, for Maynell bought her a new buggy and some attractive new dress materials, which had just come into the town's only variety store. She appeared with him at church a Sunday later, resplendent in her green cotton dress, complete with a new hat with feathers, and the pastor smilingly approved of the devotion that the couple seemed to show as Annie held the hymnal for her husband to sing by.

Six months later, William Maynell, agitated and tearful, drove the very same buggy to the house of Dr. Spurling to inform him that he had found his young wife drowned in the little creek several hundred yards behind the inn. What was more, she was naked, and the distraught husband argued that assuredly she must have had a mental breakdown and taken her own life by this means. The doctor concurred, and Maynell was again a widower.

Although Dr. Spurling must certainly have thought it strange that the two wives and the first wife's father had all died in such a short time, he had no real reason for suspicion: there were no marks of violence on Annie's body. However, William Maynell had cunningly dosed his young wife's coffee with just enough laudanum to put her into a sound sleep, so that when he carried her, shortly before dawn, out to the creek and slid her inert, naked body into the water, she could hardly struggle for life.

Although Maynell had been cleared of all duplicity in the curious deaths of the members of his family, the townspeople shunned him. Perhaps it was because this aura of death hovered about him; perhaps it was because his unprepossessing, dour appearance singularly troubled them. At any rate, there was a slackening of business at the inn, and those travelers who did come into the little town looked elsewhere for room and board, with the Widow Amsbury, or at the Sutherland farmhouse. Month after month the antagonism gained momentum, and Maynell found himself going into the variety store to have his order filled without even so much as a "good morning," until he at last decided that he had had enough of this provincial backwater.

Therefore, about eight months after Annie's death, he sold the inn to a German immigrant family. Maynell took his cash in a worn satchel, bought a wagon and horses, and set out for an even smaller town named Courtley, Indiana, some forty miles north of what was one day to be the thriving metropolis of Indianapolis.

When he alighted from his sturdy wagon and tied the reins of two dray horses to the tethering post in front of the town's inn, he introduced himself as William Mayberry. Entering, he spoke pleasantly for a time to the clerk at the counter and engaged a room. He spent considerably more time questioning the clerk as to the town's activities and prosperity, and was apparently satisfied with the answers he received. A week later, after having deposited his cache of gold and silver coins in the bank, he purchased a small farm on the northern outskirts of town. The couple who had owned it had decided to move to Missouri to be near relatives. They left behind them a reticent but hardworking farmhand who, himself a bachelor in his late twenties, had been tempted to leave the stodgy little town and go to the West to seek his fortune. William Maynell persuaded him to take charge of the farm and doubled his paltry wages as a final inducement.

But by now—basking in the knowledge that under his new name and in a placid little settlement, no one knew his past—he felt it was time to find a wife. As it happened, the farmhand, Benjamin Carter, fell in love with a pretty, black-haired orphan girl of twenty, Naomi Blake, who had been taken on as a servant by her dead father's older sister and husband. She had worked for them for three years now, was given no wages, only a tiny room near the attic, and a grudging amount of food, just enough to keep her alive. Her aunt was a religious zealot and was forever sermonizing to her on the evils that could befall a young girl who yielded to temptation. Indeed, poor Naomi's only recreation, if it might be called that, was sitting in the parlor reading the prayerbook aloud with her uncle and aunt when there was no other work for her to do.

One of her errands carried her near the Mayberry farm, where she met Benjamin Carter. He at once fell in love with this lovely, downcast girl and, within several weeks, ventured enough courage to tell her that he wanted to marry her and leave for the West, where they could have their own little plot of ground and a house and perhaps children. Naomi was more than willing, and when her aunt and uncle had gone for the weekend to visit friends in a nearby town, she secretly met her young suitor in the barn of the Mayberry farm. There was a thunderstorm; she clung to him; and he consoled

her passionately. William Mayberry had gone out to the barn
to make certain that the horses and cows had been brought
out of the storm and safely sheltered. He heard voices, hid
behind a stall, and quickly understood what was taking place.
More than that, in their transports, the young lovers did not
see him, and he was able to lecherously look at Naomi's exquisitely lithe near-nudity.

The next day, he casually asked his farmhand whether
he had a sweetheart, and Benjamin Carter ingenuously declared that he had, and that he hoped to marry her one day.
"It's not that I'm not grateful to you, Mr. Mayberry, for dou-
blin' my wages—but I'm just as alone as Naomi is, you see,
'n anyhow, before you ask me to stay on, I've been thinkin',
as you well know, about goin' West 'n bein' a homesteader, or
such. So I may just as well, to give you a chance to find another hand, give you notice that in about a month, Naomi 'n
me'd like to take off—if you've no objection."

Mayberry gave him a guileful smirk, which passed for
an encouraging smile, and assured him that he was thoroughly in sympathy with the project. But his devious and
sadistic mind began at once to concoct a plan whereby he
could eliminate the farmhand and take possession of this delicious young creature, who would be compelled to share his
bed or else suffer the town's castigation for her great sin of
fornication.

Innocently, Naomi took what opportunities she could
from her taxing duties to steal over to the Mayberry farm
and meet Benjamin in a brief but ecstatic tryst. The natural
consequence was that the week before they both planned to
run off together to the West, she found herself pregnant. Her
aunt, who had been startled at her niece's inexplicable trans-
formation from a timid mouse into a radiant, happy, and
often forgetful girl—Naomi had neglected her housework on
several occasions—became suspicious. She confronted Naomi
and, by browbeating her, forced the tearful young woman to
confess that she was with child. In vain, Naomi pleaded that
she and Benjamin Carter intended to be married very soon.
Her aunt informed her uncle, and the two of them read a
sanctimonious sermon over her and then drove her out of the
house to lead her shameless life without any further aid from
them.

Instinctively, Naomi headed for the Mayberry farm and

went to the barn, where she was certain of finding her lover. William Mayberry, watching from the kitchen, saw them and gleefully rubbed his hands together. It was time for him to act.

Benjamin Carter urged Naomi to stay the night and sleep in the hayloft, promising to come out to her when his day's work was finished. He swore that the next morning he would get his wages from Mr. Mayberry, and the two of them would go West to find freedom and happiness. That evening, in the kitchen, Benjamin's employer was more affable than he had ever been before. He urged Benjamin to have supper with him and intimated that he might even give the lovers a wedding gift of cash, which would ease their journey. Benjamin was almost pathetically grateful, and he began to tell his employer of his plans for running his own farm and his love for Naomi, as he sipped the strong coffee that Mayberry had placed before him. It was laced with laudanum, and soon Benjamin began to yawn and then, putting his head down on the kitchen table, fell into a deep sleep.

When he was certain that the farmhand was unconscious, William Mayberry took a hammer from the chest in the corner of the kitchen and, with a single blow, killed the man. Then, dragging his lifeless body down to the cellar, he dug a deep grave and buried him.

This done, he went back to the kitchen, finished his own coffee, and wrote a note purportedly from Benjamin Carter. It went on to the effect that he had reconsidered, wished to have no encumbrances, begged her forgiveness, and wished her well. He did not know whether Naomi Blake could read or write, but he was certain that Benjamin had to this moment never written her a letter, and therefore she had no way of knowing that the handwriting was not her lover's.

Trembling with lecherous anticipation, he at last went out to the barn and found Naomi lying on a bale of hay at the back of the barn. She had fallen asleep out of exhaustion and anxiety. His eyes glinted with salacious delight as he studied her lithe body, attractive even in the drab homespun dress which her aunt herself had sewn. He touched her on the shoulder, and when she came awake with a cry of alarm, he murmured, "Please, miss, don't be frightened. I'm Benjy's employer, you know. I own this farm."

"Why—yes, sir," Naomi quavered, as she slowly sat up

and rubbed her knuckles over her forehead to try to revive herself.

"I'm afraid I've got bad news for you, miss. You see, Benjy had a long talk with me in the kitchen, and he wrote you this note. He decided he didn't want to get married after all, and he's right sorry, but he's already gone West. Here, here's what he wrote."

Naomi uttered a frightened cry and seized the sheet of paper. She could read, but the cunning murderer had reckoned correctly that, till this moment, she had never seen a sample of her lover's handwriting. She burst into hysterical sobs, and Mayberry consoled her.

"Oh, my God, this is just awful," Naomi sobbed. "You don't know how bad it is . . . I—I thought he was going to marry me, and now—and now I'm—I'm with child—and here he says he's going West without me. Oh, what shall I ever do? My aunt and uncle won't ever let me come back to the house—oh, and the child I shall have, it will surely die—"

"Why now, miss, no need to carry on like this. You know the saying, it's always darkest before the dawn. And also, every cloud has a silver lining. Suppose I were to say to you, I'm a widower, lonely, and I'm rich, too. I'd marry you in a flash, if you'd have me. Besides, this town is dead. There's nothing in it for me, or for you, for that matter, and I'm thinking of going out and settling in Texas."

Naomi stopped her weeping and stared helplessly at the homely farmer. "You mean—you mean you'd marry me and make an honest woman out of me—and not mind that I had a child by—by Benjy?"

"Of course I would! I'm lonely, you see. True enough, I'm almost old enough to be your father, but I'm rich enough to make you happy. And I'll bring up the baby like my own, and not a word ever said about it. How's that strike you?" he said with false joviality.

Though she could read and write, Naomi Blake knew very little of the world, which had narrowed down the past three years into a life of utter servitude to her stern aunt and pious uncle. She knew, on the other hand, that she had no other home, and that if she remained in this little town and bore her child, she would be driven out of it by the churchgoing residents as a scarlet woman. And so, in her despair, believing that Benjamin Carter had abandoned her, she tearfully accepted Mayberry's offer of marriage.

A week later, they were married in a little church, and as she left the church, her aunt and uncle indignantly sniffed and muttered to themselves, "Well, at least the hussy won't bring shame upon us. Good riddance, I say!"

A month later, William Mayberry sold the farm, withdrew his savings from the bank, and headed for Franklin. He had read of Stephen Austin's *empresarios,* and decided that Texas would be far enough removed from the scenes of his past life to let him start afresh with a delectable young wife. As for Naomi, she discovered that she had given up a tender lover for a cruel satyr. Her husband's carnal demands upon her sometimes nauseated her, and when he discovered this, he whipped her with a strap until she begged forgiveness. After the whipping, he callously reminded her that he had taken her in as a fallen woman and was going to give her child a name, so that the least she could do by way of gratitude was to accede to his conjugal demands.

Now, on this sunny day in Franklin, Missouri, she stood hopelessly beside him as they waited to board the paddlewheeler. He took her elbow and hissed, "Smile, you stupid little bitch; these are going to be our neighbors, Naomi girl!" And she forced a mechanical smile to her trembling lips, and inwardly she prayed that, by some miracle, her faithless lover might find her out there in the West and save her from this brutal tyrant to whom she was married.

Also waiting to board the paddleboat was another group of settlers. A coppery-haired girl of about seventeen, drably dressed in linsey-woolsey, stood behind a portly man in his late thirties, with a thick and affectatiously waxed mustache, and a tall, bony woman whose thin lips and narrowly set brown eyes and dominant chin proclaimed her a termagant. She was Cora Stilton, and the man with the mustache was David, her husband. The pretty teenage girl was Nancy Morrison, a bound girl, whose indenture the Stiltons had purchased from the town workhouse of Elyria, Ohio, where they had been born, met, married, and lived until last month, when they had decided to apply to Eugene Fair, one of Stephen Austin's *empresarios.* David Stilton was a capable blacksmith. He had been born on a farm, which his parents had lost, and it had always been his dream to work his own land. His wife, Cora, had just turned thirty and been told by the doctor at Elyria that after her three miscarriages, she could never bear a child. She came from a poor family and was the oldest of four sisters. Stilton himself had always been inept with women, and Cora had inveigled him into marriage, realizing that it was probably her last chance. She looked older than her years because his ineptitude as a lover and her own inability to bear a child had soured her. During the past year, after receiving that verdict from the doctor, she tyrannized the lovely, meek teenager by resorting to corporal punishment with a hickory switch, and at least once a week, she accused her of having been her husband's harlot and threatened to send her to a bordello.

David Stilton awkwardly tried to defend Nancy, only to be accused by his neurotic wife that his sin was the more grievous because he dared to lie with Nancy in the sanctity of their own house. It was true that Stilton covetously eyed the slim, exquisitely formed body of the bound girl, whose fresh, virginal youth excited him by now far more than Cora ever could. Yet the fact was that he had never once touched her.

As they were about to board now, Cora Stilton turned to her husband and snapped, "You've heard the captain say we're going to Natchez, and you know what sort of town that is, David Stilton! If you don't want to burn in hell's own fire when you're dead, you'll leave that hussy Nancy in one of the cribs—oh, she'll earn her keep well enough, no fear of that! She'll make a better living than I suspect you will from this farm you're so set on having. Now you take my advice, David Stilton, if you know what's good for you!"

There were other settlers who were also eager to begin life anew in a setting where there would be no political or religious obstacles to their pursuit of freedom. Couples like the Fenmores and the Atkinsons, who had never before owned land, looked forward to the primal joy of growing their own food and seeing the land flourish from their own efforts. Herschel Fenmore, a mild-mannered, bespectacled man in his mid-thirties, had been a surveyor's clerk in southern Pennsylvania, and his wife, Beth, had been a rural schoolteacher there. They had two boys, ages ten and twelve, and a daughter of six; and when Herschel's father had died two months ago and left him a thousand dollars and the old house in which Herschel himself had been born, he and Beth had daringly decided to cast their lot with Austin's *empresario*. As for Donald Atkinson, he had been the only son of a wealthy greengrocer in southern Illinois. At the age of forty, having inherited the store and grown tired of running it, as well as of the lonely life he had led as a bachelor, Atkinson had startled the town's gossips by marrying a seventeen-year-old bound girl, Cassie North. The two of them now stood at the gangplank of the paddle-wheeler, holding hands, and the brown-haired, slim Cassie, remembering the dreary life from which he had saved her, sent him a look of ineffable gratitude and devotion. He looked up at the cloudless sky and murmured a silent prayer of thanks for this bounty so late in his life. He would wait until they reached their new land, had their own little house, and then he prayed that Cassie would give him a son. As for Cassie, she, too, was praying that God would make her a good, deserving wife.

Finally, there were the couples from Missouri who owned slaves, and Eugene Fair had assured them that the Mexican government would offer no opposition to slavery, so long as they themselves were respectable and law-abiding residents on the land grant.

Among the traders who prepared to take the land route onto the Santa Fe Trail were none other than Matthew Robisard and Ernest Henson, to whom Don Diego de Escobar had given shelter and thereby risked his own career as *intendente* when Governor Manrique had summoned him to trial for having aided the two young Missourians despite all the Spanish restrictions against trade in Taos and Sante Fe. As they prepared to mount up now, Robisard said to Henson, "I can't wait to see what sort of get John Cooper got out of the wolfhound puppies I sent him, Ernest. You know, after he left Taos, he got himself a real Texas spread. From what I hear from some of the couriers, he's going to be one of the biggest ranchers out there before he's finished."

"We'll see him on the way back, and we'll bring presents for that lovely wife of his, and for Don Diego and Doña Inez, too," Ernest Henson smilingly declared.

The whistle of the paddle-wheeler announced the moment of departure for the settlers. Beyond, where the traders were ready, their guide cupped his hands to his mouth and called out, "Let's go! Santa Fe or bust!"

Five

Antonio López de Santa Anna Pérez de Librón had already begun to write his memoirs. In them, he loftily described how he had proclaimed the Republic of Mexico on December 2, 1822, then published the *Plan de Veracruz* and a manifesto,

> In which I expressed my intentions, carefully stating that these were only to be temporary, in order for the nation itself to be the true arbiter of its destiny.

After he had defeated the imperial army under the command of General José A. Echavarri, he boasted that, in these momentous times, he was "judge and jury of the destiny of my country," and that his victory "could not possibly have been more splendid!" In 1824, the newly elected Congress of a liberated Mexico convened and drew up a constitution, which was accepted by the free and independent sovereign states of what had once been Nueva España. The patriot, Guadalupe Victoria, was elected as their president. It was then that the revolution had arisen in Yucatán; the wily Santa Anna had brought peace, but wasn't rewarded with greater military rank. Instead, he was elevated to a place of prominence in the new, free nation, as he waited craftily, planning to make himself the titular head of all Mexico—perhaps not emperor, since that had been an ill-starred title which had cost Augustín Iturbide his life—but at least, *el presidente*.

Professing that the heat of Yucatán sickened him, Santa Anna sought, and received, a transfer to the province of Veracruz. There he bought his estate at Mango de Clavo, located on the road from Jalapa to Veracruz, purchasing it for twenty-five thousand *pesos*. Also, he married Inez García. Rumor had it that he desired her more attractive sister, but that his proposal to her parents was so awkward that he found himself engaged to Inez and only noted the mistake when he approached the altar. He was reported to have said with a shrug, "It's all the same to me."

On the very day when Carlos de Escobar departed on his journey to Taos, Santa Anna was being feted by his loyal officers and acolytes in the house of his good friend, Colonel Francisco López. This house was perhaps a mile away from his own estate at Mango de Clavo. And as it happened, Santa Anna's new wife was away for ten days visiting her parents.

Colonel Francisco López was thirty-five, tall, with hawk-like features, curly black hair, and a crisp, pointed beard. His eyes were a soft brown, cajoling and pleading in turns; his mouth was ripe and sensual. A bachelor, he boasted that he owned a virtual harem in his villa, and it was true that there were at least ten pretty *criadas* who served in the house as maids, cooks, housekeepers, and when these duties were performed, as docile concubines for their virile and imperiously arrogant master.

López and Santa Anna had gone to the same military school as cadets, though it had taken longer for the former to achieve his present rank. Because of his greater experience on the battlefield, Santa Anna, though also a colonel, was actually López's superior officer and, of course, far ahead of the personable but equally ambitious López in public acclaim. Like his fellow officer, López felt that the new democracy of Mexico was untenable and could easily be toppled by a strong, determined leader. Santa Anna believed that he was destined to become this leader: Francisco López, more cunning and less overt in his declarations of ambition, preferred to let his commanding officer win his victory and then wait for mistakes which would negate it, so that he himself might replace his longtime friend.

Both men were vainglorious, opportunistic, and sensual

to the extreme; to be sure, Santa Anna's recent marriage had hampered his amatory prowess, except when he was in the field and could dress up his sergeant as a priest to "marry" him to the belles of the villages that his army conquered. So it was only natural that he should envy Francisco López for the latter's bachelorhood and domestic harem.

The two men had just enjoyed a lavish banquet in the company of a dozen of Santa Anna's favorite captains and lieutenants. Four of the young *criadas* had toiled in the kitchen all morning and afternoon to prepare the bounteous repast to be offered to their master's important guests. Platters of *pollo con arroz,* suckling pig cooked with fruits and herbs, venison, bowls of thick *chile con carne* and *carne asada,* as well as platters of eggs prepared with sweet red peppers, were laid down upon the ornately set rectangular table of the great refectory in Francisco López's villa. Fruits and flans, nuts and cheeses, and rich chocolate served in silver cups inscribed with López's initials, together with *aguardiente* and wines from the Canaries and France, concluded the repast. There were boxes of rich Havana cigars and even English cheroots. If Francisco López had not emulated Santa Anna's habits of paying off his gambling debts by forging his superior officer's name to a draft on the military company's funds, he had nonetheless become almost as rich as Santa Anna by plundering defenseless little villages and threatening their *alcaldes* with physical torture if they did not contribute to the "fund for the liberation of our beloved country."

After the banquet, when the men had unbuttoned their tunics and were smoking cigars and drinking wine or brandy, López leaned forward and, with a lecherous wink at his superior officer, cleared his throat and announced, "*Amigos,* in honor of your visit, I shall now conduct a little lottery. As you have undoubtedly seen for yourselves in visiting my humble *hacienda,* I have ten *criadas* of unsurpassable docility and loveliness. There are fourteen of us here tonight, it is true, and thus four of you will go unrequited. But I am going to have my lovely majordomo, Catalina, pass an officer's hat around the table into which, shall we say, special lottery tickets have been placed. Each ticket will bear the name of the *criada* who will be your personal companion for the rest of the night. However, four of the tickets will necessarily be blank."

"But that's not democracy," Lieutenant Jorge Pisante smilingly protested. "If there are only ten of us who will have a charming bed partner, what of the other four?"

Francisco López chuckled and stroked the pointed tip of his crisp black beard. "Why, then, here is truly where democracy can be proved. The fortunate ten, realizing their deprived companions' needs, will assuredly, out of friendship and devotion to duty, offer their unlucky companions the privilege of sharing their own *novias*. And of course, if it so happens that the four who draw blank tickets from Catalina's hat should be of lower rank than their more fortunate companions, this truly will show how all of us, regardless of rank or status, work together for the greater glory of our great country."

Ribald comments greeted this satiric speech, and then López clapped his hands. There was a chorused gasp of licentious amazement and lustful anticipation: the kitchen door had swung outward, and Catalina, a tall, brown-haired girl of about eighteen, appeared with an officer's hat between both hands, which she had pressed against her loins. She was stark naked save for silken-covered slippers and a pair of emerald earrings dangling from little gold chains on her dainty ears. Santa Anna uttered a muttered oath of lustful excitement under his breath and craned his neck toward her, his dark eyes sweeping her nakedness. Then he turned back to his friend: "Decidedly, Francisco, you have imagination and taste. If I had the power, I'd promote you to the rank of general for this night."

López respectfully inclined his head. "I thank you for your flattery, *mi coronel*." With this, he made an imperious gesture to the naked young *criada*, who, seeing that all of the men's glittering eyes fixed on her, blushed violently, lowered her eyes, and moved to the very center of the table, stopping before a stocky young lieutenant, Pablo Lechaniz, who had recently been added to the staff of Francisco López. Leering, the lieutenant put his left hand to cup one of her firm breasts and, while fondling her, delved his right hand into the officer's hat and picked out one of the little square tickets. "¡Caramba! What luck I have—it's Catalina herself!" he exclaimed, shoving aside his chair and making as if to take her in his arms. But López halted him with an angry "Not so fast, *mi teniente!* You will wait until all the tickets have been drawn, and that is an order. Take your seat and count yourself fortunate that I don't declare this draw illegal. You may pass on, Catalina!"

"*Gracias, patrón,*" the Mexican girl stammered, scarlet to her earlobes. She moved quickly to a heavyset, thickly bearded captain, Ferdinand Soscelos, an officer noted for his brutality to helpless villagers. He leaned back, lifting his beaker of *aguardiente* to his lips and savoringly sipping it while his right hand hovered over the hat that she tendered in her hands. At last, he drew a ticket, examined it, and exclaimed, "I have Pepita!"

"A fortunate choice, *capitán,*" López suavely congratulated him. "She is just past fifteen, and almost a virgin. New to my service by some three weeks, I have not really had time to detail her capabilities. That is for you to do, *mi capitán.*"

"*Su servidor, mi coronel,*" Captain Soscelos said, inclining his head in a mark of respect to his superior officer. Santa Anna chuckled, amused by the little farce, while his eyes greedily contemplated the flanks and hips of the naked young servant.

At last, all ten *criadas* were chosen. As it chanced, Santa Anna, two lieutenants, and another captain had drawn blank tickets and found themselves denied partners for the night. But López, whose draw had won him Mercedes, a tall, comely *criada* who tonight was celebrating her eighteenth birthday, rose from the table, and declared, "It will be my pleasure to offer my beloved superior, who will one day govern all Mexico in his justice and wisdom, the sharing of Mercedes, if he is so inclined."

"*¡Diablo, seguramente, mi* Francisco!*" Santa Anna joyously exclaimed, as he, too, rose from the table. Francisco López consoled the other three officers: "I leave you gentlemen to solicit the goodwill of those more fortunate than you. Perhaps they will emulate my generosity. But if not, I will have bottles of brandy and wine sent to your rooms so that you may have some little solace."

As each *criada's* name had been called out in this lascivious lottery, the girl in question had emerged from the kitchen, clad exactly as was Catalina, and went over to stand beside the chair of the fortunate winner. As the men left the refectory with their consorts, the other three officers pleading their case, Santa Anna tilted back his head and burst into bawdy laughter: "Francisco, *amigo,* you're a man after my own heart. And it was good of you to offer to share Mercedes with me. She is indeed a morsel fit for the gods—"

"Or for a great emperor or *presidente,* as you choose, *mi coronel,*" López slyly interposed.

"But before we enjoy the charm of this delightful *criada,* I have something I wish to say to you, Francisco."

López stiffened and offered Santa Anna a smart salute. "I am at your disposal, Coronel Santa Anna!"

"No need to stand on ceremony. And if it is true that one day my country calls me to assume its leadership, I shall not forget my good friend and companion, who himself is a valiant soldier," Santa Anna promised.

López turned to the trembling, naked young girl beside him: "Go ahead of us, Mercedes, to the last room on the second floor of my *hacienda* and to the right. Get into bed and wait for us; do you understand?"

"*Sí, mi patrón,*" the naked servant-girl murmured, and left the dining room.

"Now that we're alone, Francisco, I want to enlist your help. It is a project I've had on my mind for some little time now, and I think that you are the very man to help me accomplish it."

"You honor me beyond my due, *mi coronel.*"

"Not in the slightest. Listen a moment, and I will tell you what I have in mind. But first, do you remember about three years ago, when the unfortunate Iturbide sent one of his officers to my camp to act as liaison between myself and him?"

"I do indeed. Was it not Coronel Ramón Santoriaga?"

"You have an excellent memory, Francisco. Yes, it was. I am not sure that you remember a lesser officer, a Teniente Carlos de Escobar."

"The name is not unfamiliar to me, but I cannot at the moment place him."

Santa Anna made an impatient gesture with his hand and shook his head: "It is not essential. But my spies tell me that Santoriaga, together with his wife and children, has gone

to live on a ranch in Texas, under the protection of an accursed *gringo,* who is the *cuñado* of this same *teniente.*"

"I understand, *mi coronel.*"

"Now, Santoriaga and the *teniente* became very close
friends. I know now that Santoriaga was not loyal to me, but
to Iturbide. Thus, in a sense, he is a traitor. But far more important than that is the secret which I sought to wrest from
this Carlos de Escobar. You see, Francisco, somewhere there
is a secret hoard of pure silver, which this *gringo* found; I
had the Teniente de Escobar followed."

"*¡Madre de Dios!*" López hoarsely ejaculated.

"Exactly. I sent two of my best *soldados* to follow this
Carlos de Escobar because I thought he would lead them to
the treasure. Instead, he went to a mountain stronghold of
the *indios.* After my men ordered him to give up his secret,
he ignored them and rode onward; they then did what good
soldiers do to traitors. They shot him."

"Then he is dead, this de Escobar?" Francisco López
speculatively asked.

Santa Anna shook his head, his face dark with glowering
anger. "No, he survived his wounds. I know this from some
of my spies who have asked the merchants in San Antonio.
And some eight months ago, one of my couriers rode past
this Texas ranch and stopped there for water and food. He
caught sight of the *teniente,* and also of the *gringo,* whose
name is John Cooper Baines."

"And so you think, *mi coronel,* that de Escobar or the
gringo can lead you to the treasure?"

"Not me, Francisco," Santa Anna suavely corrected with
a knowing wink, "but yourself. You knew Santoriaga and
were on friendly terms with him, isn't that true?"

"Oh, yes, we were good friends indeed," López smirked.
"To be sure, he didn't have the interest in women I did, but
then he was married."

"Very well. Now, *amigo,* you will go to this ranch, and
you will make yourself known to Santoriaga. You'll tell him
that you've deserted from the Mexican Army because of its
treachery in dealing with peaceful Americans. He may even
offer you a post as a soldier there, to guard that accursed
ranch. And you will keep your eyes and ears open. If ever
there is any mention of silver—learn about it, study it, and
act upon it. You see, Francisco, if you can discover that

hoard and bring it to me, you and I shall be able to rule Mexico with wealth and power. Men are bought with silver, and if you are successful in your mission, I shall have the largest and best-armed army in all Mexico."

"I swear to you, *mi coronel,* that I will carry out your mission, and that I will succeed in it."

"You are my good and loyal friend, and you shall be rewarded. Now," Santa Anna sniggered as he lifted his half-empty glass of wine and downed it with a gulp, "let us go share Mercedes."

Six

Carlos had chosen his mustang, Dolor, on his ride to Taos in his quest of winning the hand of Teresa de Rojado in marriage. First he intended to stop at the Jicarilla stronghold and spend some time with the people of his late wife. Then he would repeat Don Diego's invitation to Don Sancho to come join him on the Double H Ranch, and also he would spend some time with Padre Salvador Madura, who had replaced the murdered Padre Moraga and who gave him the strength to come to grips with the burden of his grief for Weesayo. Yes, this kindly, younger priest had shown him the meaning of false pride and misplaced guilt. Perhaps—and he brightened at this thought—if Teresa were to say yes, Padre Madura might perform the marriage in Taos, with Don Sancho and his wife and Tomás looking on.

Carlos also intended to question Padre Madura as to whether the aging, ailing Don Sancho de Pladero was still able to administer the affairs of the city, which now, because of the opening of the Santa Fe Trail, might well be more vul-

nerable to corruption and greedy ambition by the *ricos*. Yes,
there would be those who would seek to take the place of
power that the evil former mayors of Taos—Don Esteban
de Rivarola and Luis Saltareno—had held. Decidedly, now
that Mexico was ignoring all that was going on north of the
Rio Grande, and leaving Taos to its own resources, there
would be many opportunities for strong-willed, unscrupulous
*hacendado*s to achieve their ends and to tyrannize the Pueblo
Indians.

He rode on toward the distant mountain range where the
stronghold was, in a mood that alternated between eager expectation and gentle sorrow: this time, surely, he would
convince Teresa how sincere he was in his love for her; this
time also he would come again to that place where John
Cooper had brought him so many years earlier and where he
had first met Weesayo and fallen so deeply in love with her.
And when he made camp that evening, building his bed in the
thick grass near a little creek that had gone dry, he fell asleep
at once. In his dream he saw Weesayo standing outside the
wickiup of her father and lowering her eyes as his gaze rested
upon her; then she vanished, and he saw the slim equestrienne, the beautiful Teresa, a foil in her hand, lunging at him.
He smiled in his sleep, and his hand instinctively moved as if
he were parrying her lunge toward his heart.

As Carlos and his mustang neared the Jicarilla stronghold, the handsome Spaniard was overwhelmed with
nostalgia. He remembered how, after his young Apache
wife's tragic death, he had ridden not far from here to find
catharsis for his agonized spirit on the high peak of an isolated mountain. And as he neared the mountains where the
Apache lived, his mind turned once again to gentle Weesayo,
who had been the Beloved Woman, and who had fallen in
love with him, despite their differences in race, speech, and
outlook. The last time he had come there, he remembered,
had been when Santa Anna's two corporals, disguised as
peones, had followed him and shot him down. It had been
the gentle Apache girl, Colnara, whom he had first seen after
wakening from the stupor into which his wounds had plunged
him; she had reminded him of his beloved Weesayo. But wisdom had shown him that to marry her would be only to try

to bring back a ghost, and it would be as unfair to Colnara as to him. Yet he knew that he wished to see her, to wish her well, and to thank her, now that he was once again restored to his quest in life.

As he rode up the winding trail to the stronghold, he recognized the signs by which the watching scouts relayed the news of his coming. At last Dolor reached the summit and rode on level ground toward the circle of wickiups. From the largest one, Kinotatay, older, grayer, but still stalwart and erect like a young man, came out to greet him as he dismounted.

"It is good to see you again, my blood brother. Things go well with you?"

"Indeed, Kinotatay. And with you also?"

"Yes, thanks to the Giver of Breath. I now have two strong sons from my sweet Mescalero wife. And every day I watch them grow sturdier and happy in the ways of our people, though they are still not much more than babes. I pray to the Great Spirit that I shall be here when it is time for their puberty rites. I wish to see them grow into manhood."

Carlos bowed his head, knowing that Kinotatay was thinking of the tragic loss of his son Pirontikay, who had perished in the battle against the Mescalero in which John Cooper Baines had taken such an active part. Carlos also knew that the custom of the Jicarilla Apache was never to mention the name of a dead warrior, and so he murmured only, "I shall pray also that you have many long years in which to see both your sons become strong warriors, Kinotatay."

"Will you stay with us for some time, my blood brother?"

"I wish to do that with all my heart."

Kinotatay smiled and nodded emphatically. "I will give orders to have a feast in your honor."

"You are too kind, my blood brother. May I ask what has happened to Colnara, who nursed me and brought me back to life?"

Kinotatay smiled. "She has married the brave Jisente, and only two moons ago their first son was born."

"I am very glad. She was kind and sweet, and she reminded me—"

"You will not speak her name. I know to whom you refer, *mi hermano*." Kinotatay clasped Carlos's hand and squeezed it tautly till the young Spaniard winced. "I know how you were drawn to her, and I know why. But it is best that Colnara found a mate who lives in our stronghold and is free and strong. Otherwise you would always have with you the ghost of her whose name we never speak."

"And you know that I have found someone in Taos, a widow, a *gringa* born to wealth and of good blood, yet a woman who is as kind to the lowly and the poor and *indios* as I myself wish always to be."

"You have told me of this one on the journeys you have made to Taos before now, *mi hermano*. Will she accept you?"

"No," Carlos replied sadly, shaking his head. "I come this time in the hope that I may at last convince her to share her life with mine. I would be happy then. My children would have a mother, and I would have someone I care for very deeply."

"If it is the will of the Giver of Life, it will happen; do not fear, *mi hermano*. And now I will have a wickiup prepared for you, and your horse will be cared for, while you rest until the feast tonight." Kinotatay gently put his arm around the Spaniard's shoulders and walked him toward the comfortable hut that would be Carlos's residence during his stay with the Jicarilla Apache.

That night, after the joyous feast and the dancing in which Carlos himself was invited to take part and did so with enthusiasm, Kinotatay pointed out Colnara's stalwart husband and said, "He is a proud young warrior, and there are times when I must quell his spirit to make war against enemies. We have none now, but his father once fought the Mexicans, was captured and tortured by them, and escaped, though he was lame for the rest of his days. This is why Jisente sometimes forgets that not all *mejicanos* are the same, and that those who came to Mexico from across the great seas are still different. Yet he respects you, and considers you, as I do, a member of our tribe. He asks that you practice the bow and arrow against him, as well as the lance. He wishes to see if he is your equal."

"I shall be happy to test my poor skill against his, Kinotatay. It is strange how peaceful life is when one comes to these mountains. It was thus two years ago when I was in torment, and the world was black. But being here with you and your braves restored me. I owe you much, my blood brother. Perhaps in some ways even more than *El Halcón*, because it was here that I found her whose name I may not speak again. Let there always be peace and brotherhood between us. This I pledge you. And if the time should come when enemies attack you, I pledge also that I will fight by your side, even to the death." Carlos held out his hand, and the tall Jicarilla *jefe* shook it and then embraced the Spaniard.

The next morning, Carlos and Jisente, surrounded by eager spectators, began their trials. For his part, Carlos welcomed the opportunity to try his hand again at the Apache weapons, for he was thinking that when he reached Taos, he would try bouts of the foils with Teresa de Rojado. He wished to be at his physical peak, for he wanted to be his very best when he practiced with her. She would never marry him if he let her win, and it was for this additional reason that he wanted her to share his life. There would be healthful, friendly competition between them in fencing and in horseback riding, and it would add zest to their days and increase the joy of their nights together. He had thought of this often during the last six months, and now it seemed to him that he must exercise not only all of his diplomacy, but evince all of his truest feelings to win her consent.

Kinotatay himself presided at the exercises, choosing the targets and increasing the distances, as both Carlos and Jisente, quivers attached to their backs, drew their bows and took careful aim. At the first several targets, Carlos matched his Apache opponent; when the distances grew longer, Carlos just managed to hold his own by what he considered one or two lucky shots. But finally, when the target was placed at the maximum distance, it was Jisente who was more accurate, and he was acclaimed by the cheers of his companions.

The next exercise was throwing the feathered lances. Here, Carlos more than held his own. But at the conclusion of this competition, Kinotatay tied a vine at a distance of fifty feet in such a way as to make a ring, saying that the winner would throw the lance completely through the ring without touching it. This time, it was Jisente who won.

"You are truly a great warrior, Jisente," Carlos said in

the Apache tongue, which he had learned from Weesayo. "It is no disgrace to be beaten by one with your skill. I am glad that I am not your enemy, for I think that even the skill I have with my long stick, which speaks with thunder and fire, would fail before the swiftest of your arrows."

"And I, Jisente of the Jicarilla Apache, say to you before all our people that I respect you equally, and that except for *El Halcón* himself, you have come the closest to defeating me in the trial of weapons."

Carlos had brought a brace of pistols in his saddlebags, and now presented these to Jisente. "Use these to defend your chief and your people, Jisente. And when you do, think of me and know that I fight in spirit beside you."

The pleased murmur of the spectators told Carlos that he had made a friend and ally of the young warrior and had acquitted himself honorably in the eyes of these mountain *indios*. Their code of life was one of honor and truthfulness, so at variance with that of the *ricos* of Taos and Santa Fe, who secretly hated them and begrudged the 1821 Treaty of Córdoba, which had granted Indians full citizenship.

Carlos had intended to ride into Taos after a few days in the Apache stronghold, but the memories he associated with this towering mountain community kept him there as if hypnotized. He felt refreshed in spirit, enjoying the simplest of pleasures, such as playing with the children who, having witnessed his friendly rivalry with Jisente, followed him almost wherever he went. And he tried not to notice the secret warm glances that unmarried young girls sent him as he walked through the village, genially greeting an old man or a white-haired woman. He stayed eight days, and on the morning of the last day, he went to Kinotatay to thank him for his hospitality. Then, mounting Dolor, and waving his hand to the assembled villagers, Carlos went back down the winding trail, and rode toward Taos. It was the end of the first week of May in the year 1825.

Seven

The old, deaf housekeeper crossed herself as she opened the door of the rectory and saw the tall, gaunt, gray-haired man standing before her. Though he wore the costume of a Taos shopkeeper, she knew him to be Ignazio Peramonte, who, after the death of Padre Moraga, became the secret leader of *Los Penitentes*, the order of Penitent Brothers.

He gave her a faint smile and, knowing her affliction, let his lips form the words he wished to utter so that she could read them: "I wish to see Padre Madura, sister."

At once she vigorously bobbed her head, gestured for him to come in and to make himself comfortable, and then hurried into the church, where Padre Salvador Madura was hearing the confession of a fat widow whose only real sin was gluttony. After he had absolved her and gravely warned her that gluttony was one of the seven deadly sins, he added the wry advice that less indulgence at the table would undoubtedly prolong her life. Waving aside her tearfully grateful thanks, he left the confessional booth and followed the old woman into the rectory. Seeing that Ignazio Peramonte's face was drawn and cold, she hurried out, not wishing to be privy to secrets that did not concern her.

The superstitions not only of the Pueblo Indians but also of the Mexican, Spanish, and Anglo residents of Taos were deep rooted. On many a lonely hill rose a stark white cross to remind all that this was the country of *Los Penitentes*. They called themselves the Brothers of Light and still scourged themselves in secret Lenten rituals, a custom they acquired from the very first Spanish *conquistadores* led by Don Juan

69

de Ornate. For this was a harsh, unremitting land, and the discipline of *Los Penitentes* served to underline it; yet, in return, the spiritual ties that this singular sect encouraged had been instrumental in deepening the faith and the family ties of the people, as well as turning their minds to a greater intimacy with the elemental wonders of nature.

"May the blessings of our Lord be with you always, Fra Ignazio," Padre Madura said as he made the sign of the cross.

"And with you equally, *mi padre.* You'll recall that last week, you told me that someone had broken into this holy place and stolen some of the silver *pesos.* This was the money exchanged in my shop for the holy trinkets and jewelry that I made by melting down those ingots the *gringo*, John Cooper Baines, had given to you two years ago."

"I am still at a loss to understand how anyone could have known about the silver."

"I do not think that anyone actually knew, Padre Madura. But I have found the thieves. They are *peones* who work for the *hacendado* Manuel Bustamente. You will recall how he grumbled when you preached that sermon about the tithes one owes to our blessed Savior, and then had the blasphemous temerity to accuse you of thriving in luxury from the money donated to the church for good works. I wonder that you did not excommunicate him on the spot!"

Padre Salvador Madura shrugged. "What would you do, Fra Ignazio? There will always be those who complain because they are selfish and narrow-minded and see only what they want to see. It is true that I purchased a new chasuble and for my housekeeper a new dining table—which I commissioned from one of the *indios* of our pueblo—and Señor Bustamente saw these things and drew his own wrongful conclusions."

"That may well be true, Padre Madura. But last night, two of my good brothers were riding near the Sangre de Cristo Mountains, and they found a little camp, and there were the two *peones* cooking the meat of a wild goat they had shot. When one of our brothers stopped to ask if they did not wish a benediction for their meal, one of the rogues angrily tried to drive him away and made a gesture of hiding a saddlebag. The movement exposed the gleam of silver. Now Fra Grigorio, who has sometimes aided me in melting down the silver and refashioning it into salable items, recognized these thieves. I have come here to tell you that I plan to have them restore the silver to the church and to go before their *patrón,* Manuel Bustamente, to warn him that vengeance will be swift and terrible if ever again he should instigate such an act of thievery."

"I do not wish to know about any violence, Fra Ignazio. And what will you do to the *hacendado*?"

The *penitente*'s grim face tightened and his lips were venomously thin as he retorted, "Show him how we punish malefactors who would steal from the dear God. Even if his hands did not touch the silver, Padre Madura, it was he who guided those who did. They will circle and go back to his *hacienda.* Tonight, two of my brothers and I will call upon them."

"I know I have no right to stop you. I shall not even ask what methods you employ. But don't forget, Fra Ignazio, that if Mexico has abandoned us and left us to our own resources and devices, that is not to say that we may take the law into our own hands whenever we please."

"Nor do I propose that, Padre Madura. Our weapons are those of morality and conscience. If it is necessary at times to scourge the rebellious or errant flesh, the fear and respect such an act engenders makes a profound impression upon other would-be malefactors."

"I cannot argue with you, nor shall I. I intend to use the silver that remains for the well-being of my poorest parishioners, who themselves are little better than *peones*."

"I know that since you have replaced our beloved Padre Moraga, you have acted in his spirit, with kindness and compassion for all, Padre Madura. I respect your feelings, although I may remind you that Padre Moraga himself was once the head of *Los Penitentes.* And we had law and order in Taos."

"Your reasoning is fallacious, if you will pardon my observation, Fra Ignazio. In the days of my predecessor, Don Sancho de Pladero was *alcalde mayor,* and Don Diego de Escobar the *intendente.* Both these men were just and kind and merciful, and they had respect for the law. Their own edicts could enforce it most of the time. Today, only Don Sancho remains, his powers waning and his health ebbing. And even the governor concentrates his troops in Santa Fe and ignores our pleas for more patrolling. So you will do what you must, Fra Ignazio. Yet I confess"—this with a wry smile—"I shall be grateful if the silver is returned, and I shall ask no questions."

"So let it be, Padre Madura. My brothers and I will pray for you when we do our work. But we shall not do it in your name."

Padre Madura nodded and again made the sign of the cross. Ignazio Peramonte, now in his sixtieth year—but strong, wiry, and as vigorous as when he was in his thirties—bowed his head and accepted the blessing, then abruptly turned and left the rectory.

Padre Madura went into his own sparsely furnished bedroom, opened another door to reveal a tiny chapel, and there he knelt upon a prayer stool. "Beloved Savior of all of us, I come to You in the humility of my priesthood. Give me the wisdom and understanding to continue my work here, and take from me the slothfulness of mind that leads me to doubt and to find fault with the motives of others whom I know to be far more zealous and courageous." He stood for a long moment looking at the cross, which one of the Pueblo Indians had fashioned long ago for Padre Moraga, and his eyes filled with tears at the exquisite craftsmanship, the fervent love that the craftsman had employed. He touched it, and then touched his forehead and his heart, closed the door of the chapel, and went back to his room.

As he sat waiting for his housekeeper to serve his supper, he thought of the Rancho de Taos, the splendid mission church of Francisco de Asis, built in the year 1710 and located three miles south of Taos. Its plain yet elegant exterior was balanced by the magnificently decorated interior, which combined fine, old *santos* with birds and butterflies handmade by his parishioners. More and more, it seemed, because of the splendor of this church, the *ricos* preferred to patronize it, rather than the little church in the town square. There were times when Padre Salvador Madura thought to himself that all too often the rich, with their emphasis on material possessions, looked upon churchgoing as though they were attending a *baile*. They only wanted to be envied by their fellows. And he remembered that the *hacendado*, Manuel Bustamente, had intimated that he might one day soon transfer his allegiance to the mission church outside the city. Disturbed by the vagaries of his mind in considering all these problems that beset the ordinary people of Taos, Padre Salvador Madura sternly set himself the penance of a dozen Hail Marys and an act of contrition that would require enough physical effort to make him conscious of even this momentary hint of envy in his nature. He loved this little church to which he had been sent, and he loved the people, many of whom he knew only by their voices in the confessional booth. Their lives were simple, their problems eternally the same. And they asked for little, except for a chance in heaven and the justice of our dear Lord.

Padre Madura, possibly more than Padre Moraga, understood the separation between Church and state. Last year, with the adoption of the new constitution, Chihuahua and Durango had become states, and New Mexico made a territory until the stipulated date of 1837. Prior to then, New Mexico had remained one of the *provincias internas* attached to the *comandancia* of Chihuahua. Now, the governor carried the title of *jefe político* and administered civil affairs, while a *comandante principal,* subordinate to the *comandante general* of Chihuahua, was put in charge of military affairs. Moreover, on the very day when Ignazio Peramonte had visited him, Padre Madura had heard that a new governor had been appointed, Antonio Narbona, who was to combine both civil and military functions. The courier who had brought him this news from Santa Fe had informed him that it was rumored that chief executives were to be appointed by the national government and would be native New Mexicans. And from this, Padre Madura suspected that, henceforth, a powerful group of local families might easily come to dominate the political affairs not only of Taos, but also of all New Mexico. Such power, if motivated by greed and a lack of compassion for the poor, could do great harm. It was just as well, therefore, that *Los Penitentes* should remain the mystic awe-inspiring counterbalance to the evil that might be perpetrated by the *ricos.* And that night, as he ate his simple supper, he said aloud, and not without some sarcasm, "God does not choose between political factions, but man too often does—to his own regret and that of many others."

Archibaldo Manquez and Juan Ibañez had ridden back to the *hacienda* of Manuel Bustamente and boastingly reported to him that they had accomplished the task he had set for them: to steal gold or silver from the church of Padre Salvador Madura to prove the *hacendado*'s premise that the church was corrupt and sought luxury for its own self and not for the people of Taos. Manuel Bustamente, forty-six, was a short, stocky little man, with a bushy, graying, black beard, thick sideburns, and a small mustache. There were pouches under his beady little black eyes, and deep lines etched his forehead. He was a widower twice over and was now surrounded by a household of over a dozen attractive young maids, most of whom he had drawn from the pueblo village. When he heard the report of his two *peones,* he clapped them on the back. "You have done well, both of you. To show you how just I am, I will let you keep two thirds of the silver and claim only the remaining third for my own coffers. And, in addition, you shall dine tonight at the feast I shall hold in your honor, and you shall have your pick of my *criadas.*"

Bustamente's estate was about seven miles to the southwest of the village of Taos itself, and he had been a crony of both former mayors, Don Esteban de Rivarola and Luis Saltareno. When he had heard the news of Padre Moraga's assassination, he had held a great feast in celebration, for it pleased him to stand as an iconoclast who defied the Holy Church and exposed its corruption. In this, his views were popular with other *hacendados* who resented giving tithes to the church and preferred, in this chaotic era that had followed the Mexican revolution against Spain, to hoard their own wealth, so as to be totally independent and as powerful as the robber barons who once flourished in the Middle Ages of unenlightened Europe.

The two *peones* fawned under their master's praise, smirking and swaggering, boasting how easy it had been to break into the church in the town plaza and to make away with the silver. They were certain they had not been traced, for they had camped last night at the base of the range of the great Sangre de Cristo Mountains and taken a roundabout way back to the *hacienda* of their esteemed *patrón.*

Bustamente strode into the kitchen and ordered his hearty, buxom cook, Marquita, to prepare a banquet. This done, he went back into his bedroom for a little *siesta* before the lavish evening repast. From this he was wakened by his frightened young mistress, Gisela Toran, a nineteen-year-old, black-haired beauty from San Luis Potosí, who had enjoyed the role of favorite for over sixteen months because of her total compliance and docility to his licentious foibles. She shook his shoulder and, in a voice taut with hysteria, pleaded, "Wake up, *por favor, patrón*! I beg of you; there are men at the door who demand to see you!"

Bustamente grumbled, slowly sat up, and slapped the pretty *criada* across the cheek: "Imbecile, stupid bitch—how dare you wake me? And what do you mean, men at the door who demand to see me? I am Manuel Bustamente, *hacendado* of Taos, and it is I who allow people to see me, never forget that."

"*S-sí, p-patrón,*" Gisela tearfully stammered. "I did not mean to disturb you, but these men frighten me. They are dressed in black, with hoods which hide their faces. And they speak in hollow voices, as ghosts do!"

That remark earned her another, even more vigorous slap, which sent her stumbling against the wall with a shrill cry of pain, rubbing her blazing cheek and staring pathetically at him. Bustamente snorted his derision: "You are more stupid than I thought, Gisela. Tomorrow I shall send you back to San Luis Potosí. Why, even an *india puta* from the pueblo here in Taos would have more intelligence than you and know enough not to annoy her master with such superstitious nonsense. Very well, you have wakened me at last, and you shall have a good whipping before you go to bed tonight, I promise you that. Meanwhile, I'll go see who these intruders are."

He donned a silken dressing gown over his underdrawers, tied the belt tightly, and, barefooted, angrily strode off toward the door of the *hacienda*. On the threshold stood three hooded monks, and their leader, none other than Ignazio Peramonte, intoned in a solemn voice: "We are of the *Penitentes*. We summon you and two of your *peones* to the justice of Mother Church."

"How dare you disturb me when I am taking my *siesta*?" Bustamente angrily countered.

"Last night, Fra Grigorio rode upon two *peones* who made camp near the Sangre de Cristo," Ignazio Peramonte calmly responded. "He saw the silver that they had taken from the church in the public square. He recognized these men as yours, Manuel Bustamente. The three of us, brothers

of *Los Penitentes* and sworn to our sacred duty, order you to
deliver these wretched thieves to us for judgment. And take
care that we do not include you when it is time to judge and
to punish."

Bustamente was almost apoplectic with indignation at
this threat: "What's this, now? You dare threaten me? I do
not recognize your order, and I have said that Padre Madura
lives in great comfort beyond his means, as the result of
milking tithes from the poor of Taos——"

"Take care, Manuel Bustamente," Fra Peramonte's voice
rang out in angry denunciation. "You are mortal like your
peones, and you will bleed like them under the lash of the
sangrador. And when the blood flows from your back, you
will call upon Him whose Son died upon the cross, but He
will not hear you, for He knows you to be a blasphemer, un-
repentant, and evil. And this will be proclaimed throughout
the village so that the humble and the poor, God's most loyal
servants, will know you for what you truly are."

At this, the *hacendado* turned pale, then began to blus-
ter: "Come now, *mi padre,* you cannot really prove that it
was I who made these stupid *peones* go so far as to ransack
the church for silver?"

Ignazio Peramonte coldly stared at him, till Bustamente's
eyes lowered and he shifted from foot to foot in obvious confusion. Scathingly, the tall, gaunt *Penitente* retorted, "You
profess to be a good *católico,* yet you would dare to argue
with *El Señor Dios* Himself as to the number of angels who
could dance on the point of a needle! You, Señor Bustamente, are worse than a doubting Thomas; you are the kind
of churchgoer who appears when it suits your fancy to do so,
so as to impress all the poor and humble—in a word, to be
seen, but never in your heart to do good works in the name
of Him who gave you your wealth and possessions. I shall
not argue with you. Deliver these men to me, so they may be
punished. And I give you an order now: you are to be in
Padre Madura's church in the front pew this Sunday, contrite
and repentant of your sins. You will wear black, showing that
you mourn for your nearly lost soul. And you will give in
tithes the equivalent of what you had your *peones* steal from
Padre Madura's church."

"You go too far—" Bustamente angrily began to argue,
but Ignazio Peramonte silenced him with a wave of his hand

and then solemnly countered, "If this is not done, I, who am a qualified priest, will issue public notice of excommunication. I have that power, and I advise you not to test it."

Trembling with frustrated rage, the *hacendado* clenched his fists, but knew himself to be defeated. The opprobrium of such an act by the head of *Los Penitentes* would be a burden of shame too great to bear and, worst of all, would dwindle his influence among the Pueblo Indians, as well as his own *peones*. In a choked voice, eyes lowered, he sullenly muttered, "I will do as you wish. And I will have the two men delivered to you."

"That is as it should be. You yourself, Manuel Bustamente, deserve the scourge. This time, I have spared you, but take care there is not a next time, for then you will surely be bound to the cross and scourged to show you what the Son of God endured to save sinners like yourself," Fra Peramonte solemnly declared.

A few minutes later, the two men whom Fra Grigorio had seen making a camp at the base of the mountain range were led out by Manuel Bustamente's majordomo, who then went back into the *hacienda* and closed and bolted the door. The two *peones* looked at each other, then sank to their knees, begging mercy. Silently, the three black-robed and hooded *Penitentes* took charge of them, led them out into a stretch of thickly wooded field to the north of the *hacienda,* and then, stripping them to the waist, made them kneel and pass their arms around the trunk of a tree. After their wrists had been tightly bound, Fra Peramonte took his scourge and flogged each man in turn, until blood oozed from the crisscrossing welts, and the *peones* sagged, nearly unconscious.

This done, the three *Penitentes* mounted their horses and rode back to Taos. Ignazio Peramonte went to the rectory and handed Padre Salvador Madura a saddlebag, which Manuel Bustamente's majordomo had given him.

"I have recovered the stolen silver, and punishment has been meted out to the malefactors," he said gravely. "The *hacendado* will appear in your church next Sunday, and he will perform his own act of contrition. I ask you to report to me if it is done with humility and without rancor. He will be dressed in black, and he will contribute in tithes the equivalent of the value of this stolen silver."

"I shall report to you, my brother. I will not ask by what means you recovered the silver, but I thank you in the name of the poor."

"It is my duty, Padre Madura. I bid you good night and ask to be remembered in your prayers." The tall, gaunt *Penitente* inclined his head as Padre Madura made the sign of the cross over him, and then went out into the night.

Eight

Carlos rode Dolor into the plaza, and tethered the mustang in front of the little church. He crossed himself as he dismounted, and then went around to the back to the rectory. The old housekeeper, recognizing him, threw her hands up in the air and beamed her welcome, gesturing to him to follow her. Padre Salvador Madura was in the confessional, she said, her voice loud and harsh because of her deafness. She insisted that Carlos seat himself at the table and wait. Then she brought him chocolate, which she was preparing for the priest, and Carlos effusively thanked her. When she left, he shook his head wonderingly at such devotion; despite her handicap, this woman, who must surely now be nearing her seventieth year of life, was a veritable paragon of kindness and thoughtfulness. If only all mankind might emulate her, he thought, how simple and rewarding life could be.

When the *padre* came in, removing his cassock, Carlos rose and knelt before him, bowing his head and making the sign of the cross. "It is good to see you again, Padre Madura," he said, after the priest had blessed him. "I have not forgotten how you helped me win back my soul when I was weary of life—"

"I know, my son," the priest gently interrupted. "And I know now"—this with a little smile—"what errand brings you to Taos. It is the Señora Teresa de Rojado, is it not?"

"Yes, *mi padre.*" Carlos uttered a sigh and shook his head. "I have come here before, as you well know, and each time, she has said that she cannot marry me. I have come to pray that this time I shall be fortunate in convincing her that I would be a devoted husband."

"Of that I have not the slightest doubt, my son. But you must give her time. She, too, had grief, as you well know. And besides, she is concerned about Don Sancho de Pladero, her father's old friend."

"What news of him, *mi padre?*"

"His health, alas, is not the best. I was told that only a few days ago, a *médico* rode in from Santa Fe to visit with him."

"That is not good news at all, *mi padre.* You know that Don Diego, my father, has often urged Don Sancho to leave Taos and come live with him at our ranch in Texas."

"Yes, my son. And he has indeed told me that he wants nothing better than to be reunited with your father. Yet he has duties here in Taos because he represents the only authority. There are still a few *hacendados* who believe themselves to be above the law. Not long ago, two *peones* broke into this church and stole some of the silver which your *cuñado* so generously gave me for the poor."

"But that is sacrilege!" Carlos exclaimed, crossing himself.

"It is, my son. *Los Penitentes* were able to recover it. I think that perhaps the lesson they taught the *patrón* of those two scoundrels may have had some valuable effect. Alas, I think the *hacendado*, Manuel Bustamente, feared more the scourge of a *sangrador* than the damnation of *El Señor Dios*. And yet, in a sense, if the fear of physical punishment keeps him from further sacrilege, one may well conclude that it was God who managed thus to appeal to his ignoble nature."

"And the Indians of the pueblo, *padre?* Are they treated well?"

"So far as I myself and Ignazio Peramonte can provide for them, yes. But as you can imagine, there are still *ricos* who abuse them, hire them for menial tasks, and then pay them only a paltry part of what was agreed upon. And there are those also who, as I suspect was done in the time of my martyred predecessor, seek out the young, attractive *indias* for their lecherous abominations. You see, my son, I studied the history of Taos before I was sent by my bishop to this church. I know how the Indians of the pueblo rebelled against oppression centuries ago. If Taos were left entirely to the *ricos*, and since the population of the *indios* greatly outnumbers them, there could well be terrible bloodshed again. I think Don Sancho knows this as well as I do, and this is what holds him to Taos, his dedication to maintaining peace, even at the cost of his own declining health."

"I am grateful that you have taken me into your confidence, and I shall not abuse it, *mi padre*." Carlos knelt and kissed the hand of the priest. "I shall go to pray now, and then if you will hear my confession, I shall be grateful. I wish to purge myself of all unworthy thoughts regarding the Señora de Rojado. I have only the deepest respect and love for her."

"I think I know that already, my son. But I shall hear your confession. When you are ready, come to the first booth. And may the blessing of our dear Lord attend you all of your days."

Carlos de Escobar rode Dolor at a leisurely pace from the church in the plaza toward the *hacienda* of Don Sancho de Pladero. Like Don Diego, the sixty-seven-year-old Don Sancho had left his native Spain years earlier to serve his country here in the New World. Much had changed in all those years, but the friendship that had begun in Taos between the two men remained steadfast.

Don Sancho's *hacienda* was on the north side of the town, a huge, one-story *casa* made of adobe and strongly reinforced with the sturdiest timbers. Built before the turn of the century, it was in the shape of a divided rectangle. In the center of this, there was a magnificent flowery *patio* flanked by a narrow, enclosed passageway that united both halves of the rectangle. Well beyond this imposing dwelling, there could be seen the huts of the *trabajadores* and the sheepherders. And beyond these was the broad stretch of rich grass on which the sheep placidly grazed. As he rode toward the stable, Carlos turned to watch the always picturesque and awe-inspiring sight of the white-capped Sangre de Cristo

Mountains, which contrasted with the almost summerlike foliage and green grass decorating the base of the mountain range. As he gazed at the blue sky, so majestic with hardly a cloud to mar its dazzling sweep toward the horizon, he remembered how he had first come here as a youth, mourning his mother who had died before they left Spain. His father, who was exiled from his beloved country, had found great happiness in his marriage to Doña Inez, the sister of his first wife. And here, thanks to the companionship of Miguel Sandarbal, Carlos had grown up in the outdoors, learning how to hunt and ride.

To see the sheepherders holding their crooked staffs and a leather flask of wine, or perhaps even *aguardiente* slung over their shoulders, made him smile as he recalled how vigorously he had protested his father's decision to raise sheep on the estate, which King Charles IV had bestowed upon the proud *hidalgo* as a kind of sop in return for the disgrace of his exile from Madrid. As he dismounted, he stared up at the mountains and again thought of the stronghold that he had left. His face sobered, and he murmured a silent prayer, then made the sign of the cross. Padre Madura had said that it was time to bury the ghosts of the past and not to flagellate himself, like a *Penitente,* over what should, or could have been. Yes, this was why he had come to Taos, to renew his courtship of Teresa de Rojado. With her, he could truly put aside the past and begin a rich, new life of companionship and love.

Now he remembered again the dream he had had upon that mountain, where John Cooper Baines had found him, after he had fled from the Double H Ranch in his agony over Weesayo's needless, cruel death. He had dreamed that she appeared to him in a vision and consoled him, telling him that she would be with him in spirit to pray for his happiness.

A young stableboy came out and, seeing Carlos, took the reins and led Dolor to one of the stables. "It is good to see you again, Señor de Escobar," the stocky, black-haired youth enthusiastically greeted him.

"*Gracias*, Paco. Your master is at the *hacienda?*"

"*Sí*, Señor de Escobar." The youth's cheerful face sobered, and he looked down at the ground. "He is not too well, alas, Señor de Escobar. The *médico* from Santa Fe came to see him—"

"Yes, Padre Madura told me. I pray it is not too serious. Look after Dolor, *amigo,* and give him all the hay and oats he can eat, but not too much water. I will see you again, and thank you for your welcome."

"*De nada,* Señor de Escobar." The stableboy grinned infectiously and touched his forehead in salute.

Carlos went to the entry of the huge house and knocked at the door. It was opened by Doña Elena herself, now in her late fifties, yet in Carlos's opinion, more attractive than when he had first met her and considered her a querulous shrew. Her hair was now entirely gray, yet there was a serenity to her features that more than eased their nominal sharpness. There had been a reconciliation, which Don Sancho himself had effected, after she had protested too much against the marriage of their son, Tomás, to Conchita Seragos, who had been a servingmaid at the *hacienda.* Doña Elena had thought the girl unworthy of her son, and had complained bitterly and had even treated the girl cruelly. Don Sancho had then exasperatedly taken his wife over his knee and resoundingly spanked her, and from that day forth, she had been the most amiable of consorts.

"What a joy to see you again, Carlos!" she smilingly exclaimed. "Do come in. I hope you will stay with us for a little time."

"If you'll have me, Doña Elena."

"*¡Ayúdame!*" she gasped, raising her hands above her head in mock horror. "Don Sancho would be furious with me if in any way I suggested that you may not stay here as long as you wish, because we both love you so very much." And then, with a conspiratorial whisper and wink, "And I know another reason, I think, why you are here. To see the Señora de Rojado."

"You know all my secrets, Doña Elena," Carlos chuckled and, putting his hands on her shoulders, gave her a friendly kiss on the cheek. "But I have heard something about Don Sancho that distresses me—about the *médico.* Padre Madura told me when I visited him just a little while ago."

Her face was grave now as she nodded, then crossed herself. "It is true, Carlos. I think this is the reason why he hesitates to leave Taos and go join your father. As for myself, and Tomás and Conchita, too, we should like it very much. Although, to be practical, Tomás is doing so well with the sheep, and he and his Conchita and their children are very happy—that I am not so sure they'd follow us if we made the decision to leave. But that depends upon my husband's good health, for which I pray to *El Señor Dios* many times a day."

"Would it tire him if I visited him now, Doña Elena?" Carlos solicitously asked.

"Oh, no, quite to the contrary! It would do him a world of good to see you again. Come, I will take you to him. I am sure he has finished his *siesta* by now."

Chatting garrulously and, as Carlos could see, forcing herself to be cheerful, she led him to Don Sancho's bedroom and, after knocking at the door, announced, "*Mi esposo,* it's Carlos!"

"Come in, come in, *¡por todos los santos!*" Carlos heard Don Sancho boom with pleasing exuberance. He entered the bedroom and found the *alcalde mayor*—for that was his title once again, the post of *intendente* having been eliminated when Mexico broke away from Spain—propped up in bed with two pillows behind his head. By now Don Sancho was totally bald, though he still boasted his elaborate mustache, which had turned white. Always corpulent, he might have emanated an air of comparatively robust health if it had not been for the telltale flaccidity of his jowls, the deep furrows in his forehead, and his slightly forced breathing, all signs that alarmed Carlos. "How good it is to see you, Carlos! And how well you look!"

Carlos attempted a bantering tone. "What's this nonsense I hear about your having a doctor all the way from Santa Fe? I swear on my hope of redemption that you still look able enough to ride out to the stronghold with me and back."

"I wish that were the case, Carlos. But Dr. Hernandín assures me otherwise. Why, do you know, he fussed over me and poked and prodded me until I felt like a newborn babe!" He shrugged and then grimaced. "These doctors, they always make it sound as if it is so very solemn, you know. But that's of course because I am older than you, Carlos. Dr. Hernandín thinks that my lungs aren't quite so clear as they might be, and he advises rest and proper diet." He turned his head to stare at Doña Elena, rolled his eyes comically, and added, "The old fool insisted that I give up my beloved *chile relleno* and *chile pasado con carne,* as well as *chivichangas!* I have eaten these all my life—or at least, since I came to Taos, which was when my life really seemed to begin."

"But you must take care and follow the doctor's orders, Don Sancho," Carlos respectfully put in. "My father misses you and hopes that it won't be long before you and your beautiful wife and your son and daughter-in-law and their children will make a pilgrimage to the Double H Ranch, where you can enjoy all the long years left to you."

"I'll say amen to that, Carlos. But it is in the hands of our beloved Savior, so I can't give you my promise today. I do feel better because now, after the doctor's visit, I know what I must do to regain my health. You'll stay with us for a time, I do hope? I look forward to your companionship at the table and all the news about Don Diego and his lovely Doña Inez and, of course, that incredible *gringo,* John Cooper!"

"It will be my pleasure. But I don't wish to wear out my welcome."

"Nonsense. It would do you good to stay here for a time. We are thinking of having the annual fair next month, in June, rather than in July. This is because so many traders are beginning to come through Taos on their way to Santa Fe. They stop here, but prefer to sell their goods in Santa Fe. By pushing up the date of the fair this year, we may be able to bring greater revenues to Taos, money to be spent for the benefit of the poor."

"You have a good heart, Don Sancho. And I know how hard you must have worked to preserve order and justice here in Taos, since the day when Mexico divorced itself from Spain."

"Yes, that distressed me. And today Mexico ignores us, and even the governor at Santa Fe pays little heed to what goes on in Taos. It is a good thing that Don Esteban de Rivarola and Luis Saltareno are no longer here to oppress the *indios,* but there are others who have taken their places, men like Manuel Bustamente, to mention only one."

"Padre Madura told me what he had his henchmen do, a sacrilegious thing. But his men were punished, and he has to make restitution and show contrition. But let's not talk of such things, Don Sancho. It will do you good to rest. I'll see you this evening at supper."

"*Hasta luego,* then, *mi* Carlos! Ah, before you go, a

thought has just occurred to me—" A crafty look glowed in Don Sancho's eyes, and a smile curved his lips. "You could be of great help to me in assisting with some of the details of the Taos fair. That would mean a rather prolonged visit with us, but—ah—that would give you ample time to court that beautiful *señora* you are so fond of."

Carlos de Escobar grinned as he came toward the bed and squeezed Don Sancho's shoulder in a gesture of devoted amity. "Do you know, you certainly are a scheming old rogue. I, for one, would testify that there's nothing wrong with either your health or your mind. I should like nothing better in all this world. Till supper, then."

At the very moment that Carlos was enjoying supper with the de Pladeros, Teresa de Rojado was giving a private supper to Alejandro Cabeza.

He had just turned thirty last month, the only son of an extremely wealthy *hacendado* and his wife, who had come to Taos, reconciling themselves to the inevitable change from the protocol of the court of King Charles IV.

They had died when Alejandro was only seventeen, and the *médico* who had come from Santa Fe to attend them had attributed their death to what he had called a mountain fever. Some had said it was from a disease transmitted by the sheep that their *capataz* had raised on their estate of over eleven hundred acres. The *capataz*, a lean, sly, and corrupt man in his late thirties, Ernesto Rojas, had become a clever opportunist who guided the youth to accept his inheritance and to lead the life of a *rico* who owed nothing to the people. He had procured young *criadas* for Alejandro and cynically taught the young heir to enjoy them as his rightful due. Ernesto Rojas had gradually been promoted from *capataz* to majordomo by the grateful youth and, in that capacity, had seen to it that his young charge wanted for nothing when it came to selfish pleasure. Many of the *trabajadores* who had respected Alejandro's parents drifted away from the estate and sought other *patrones* until, by the time Carlos de Escobar visited Taos this May of 1825, the young *hacendado*'s once-affluent estate was badly saddled with debts.

Ernesto Rojas had cunningly kept this news from the hedonistic *caballero*, his aim being to gradually dispose of Alejandro Cabeza and take over the *hacienda* himself. To this end, Rojas had sold off most of the flock, which had provided a good living for Cabeza's parents in the earlier days, and intended to see his young employer brought to ruin.

Last year, when Cabeza wanted to present a fabulous gift to his then-inamorata, a beautiful courtesan from Mexico City who had visited Taos and with whom he had fallen desperately in love, he discovered that his financial resources were abysmally low. When he had demanded an explanation from the glib majordomo, Rojas had cleverly talked his way out of the situation by setting forth a ledger—which he himself had doctored to give credence to his fabricated explanation. Then he had suggested, "*Mi patrón,* this has all come about since Mexico broke off with Spain. It is not your fault at all, and it has happened to many *hacendados* like yourself. But there is a way to recoup, and I as your majordomo feel it is my duty to make a proposal to you."

What he had proposed, which Cabeza agreed to, was that the young *hacendado* deal in contraband, sending the few still-loyal *trabajadores* of the estate into Durango and Chihuahua to buy weapons. These, in turn, were sold through Rojas's clandestine contacts with renegade bands of Comanche, Kiowa, and Toboso. These transactions brought silver and gold into the depleted coffers of the dissolute young aristocrat, who looked upon his majordomo much as the young King Arthur must have looked upon the wily Merlin.

Now convinced that his estate had been replenished and that he was as wealthy as he had been at the time of his inheritance, Cabeza surrendered himself to an unbridled life of licentiousness. Again, through the efforts of Rojas, he was provided with attractive young *indias* from the pueblo. Rojas and a group of *trabajadores* who were bribed into loyalty abducted some of the most attractive Indian girls to serve the carnal needs of Cabeza. Invariably, they selected girls from the poorest section of the pueblo, paying the parents a sum of money that seemed tempting, and justifying this transaction by suggesting that the girls would serve as honorably treated *criadas* in the *hacienda* of an important *rico*.

Once in the service of Cabeza, these Indian girls were never allowed to leave the *hacienda*. They were virtual prisoners, and they were subjected to physical coercion and degradation, which broke their spirits and compelled them to submit to the handsome young *caballero*'s most degenerate whims.

Teresa de Rojado knew nothing of this. Alejandro Cabeza, who himself was an expert horseman, had chanced to see her on her favorite mare and, following her, introduced himself with a suave assurance. He was tall and black haired, with a leonine head, dark brown eyes, a soft mouth, and elegant diction, which could not fail to impress the young widow. Rojas, that evil genius, had slyly suggested that the Señora de Rojado was not only a desirable conquest, but also extremely wealthy: if his young master were able to win her hand in marriage, he would have power and influence equaled by few in Taos.

Just two weeks before Carlos de Escobar had come to Taos to renew his courtship of Teresa de Rojado, government troops had defeated a band of renegade Toboso not far from San Luis Potosí. Two of the leaders had been captured and interrogated, and they implicated Cabeza as the man who had supplied them with weapons. The two Indian war chiefs fell before a firing squad, and a military courier rode to Santa Fe to complain to the governor that a leading citizen of Taos was suspected of furnishing traitorous support to hostile *indios*. Alejandro Cabeza was summoned to Santa Fe, where he and his majordomo told so convincing a story that they were discharged of any responsibility. Yet the handsome young *hacendado* had been frightened by this perilous accusation and turned on his majordomo. Rojas shrugged and retorted, "*Señor patrón*, I must tell you in all truthfulness that we cannot sell any more contraband to the renegades. We shall be under surveillance from now on, so your best hope to be rich is to get the Señora de Rojado to marry you."

That was why, on this May evening, Cabeza, dressed in his very finest as a *caballero*, sat at the end of the table facing the lovely widow whose fortune he hoped to appropriate, once he induced her into sharing his seemingly circumspect life.

For her part, although she lacked the snobbery of the breed of aristocratic *ricos* who ruled in Taos and Santa Fe, Teresa de Rojado had a woman's love for luxury and comfort. Out of the fortune that her elderly husband had left her and which had been deposited in the national bank in

Havana, she had arranged to transfer most of the funds to a
sound New Orleans financial institution, and what was
needed for daily use was hidden in a chest with a false bot-
tom in one of the unused guest rooms of her *hacienda*. Since
her arrival in Taos, she had contributed a considerable portion of this money to Padre Madura's church. She had also
pleased him greatly by engaging a complete staff for her
household from among the Pueblo Indians. There were many
hacendados who grumbled at her unheard-of-generosity, since
she paid each servant the equivalent of about ten dollars a
month; the average *peón* earned little more than between two
and five dollars a month and was constantly in debt to his
patrón.

The interior walls of her *hacienda* were papered with
calico and the windows decorated with crimson and blue
worsted curtains. In the larger rooms, there were massive
tables topped with white marble, several gilt-framed mirrors,
and Brussels carpets on the floor. In Santa Fe, where she had
introduced herself to the governor, she had found a dusty,
old spinet in the back of a merchant's shop. Purchasing it
from him, she had had it hauled to Taos by several Indians
who used a travois tied to their horses. She had had a spinet
in Havana and played it beautifully. Now she had one again
in the salon of her house, and this evening, after the superb
supper that her cook and servants had served to her guest,
Alejandro Cabeza, she was seated at the spinet playing music
from some of the colorful dances she had seen back in
Havana.

Cabeza stood near her, staring admiringly at her. Tall
and slim, her dark brown hair elegantly coiffed in a thick
chignon, she wore a white silk dress which flattered her sensi-
tive features and called attention to the near-olive tinting of
her flawless skin. Her fencing and horseback riding, together
with the years she had spent in Havana, had made her look
more Mexican than Spanish, yet with her slim grace it was all
the more provocative to a sensual connoisseur like Alejandro
Cabeza. He coveted her and, still more, her evident wealth
and her household of attractive Indian girls. She had, of
course, no interest whatsoever in raising sheep, but she did
exhort her maids to grow flowers, fruits, and vegetables in a
little garden at the back of the *hacienda*.

In Cabeza's clever courtship of this beautiful widow, he

had been extremely careful to give not the slightest offense by word or gesture and, still less, by any overt caress or kiss which might turn her against him. He was determined to win her, even if he must play with great conviction the role of a celibate monk.

Happily for him, no rumor of his background as a wastrel reached her ears, for Teresa was virtually isolated from the other landowners in Taos, who snubbed her because of her generosity to the poor. If the de Pladeros had known she was seeing Cabeza, they would have warned her about him; but they were unaware of his courtship.

Cabeza was also fortunate because he was an expert horseman and expert, as well, in the use of the *epée,* the rapier, and the foil. Knowing how Teresa enjoyed fencing and riding, he cleverly approached her as nothing more than an admiring fellow practitioner of these arts. This afternoon, for instance, before supping with her at her invitation, he had ridden ten miles with her.

He had worn his most elegant riding costume, one which proclaimed him as a highly eligible *caballero:* a *sombrero,* a *chaqueta* of cloth floridly embroidered with braid and fancy barrel buttons; *calzoneras* with the outer part of the leg open from hip to ankle, the borders set with tinkling filigree buttons and all of it fantastically trimmed with rich tinsel lace. This latter garment was supported by a rich sash drawn tightly around the waist and added to the picturesqueness of the costume. In addition, he wore *botas* made of embossed leather, embroidered with fancy silk and tinsel thread, bound around the knee with ingeniously tasseled garters, with a *sarape* dangling carelessly across the pommel of the saddle. This *sarape* had a slit in the middle and, in the event of bad weather, could be drawn over the shoulders or worn over the body with the rider's head poking through the slit.

Cabeza gave the appearance of wealth, not only in his costume, but also in the trappings with which he decorated his gelding. There was an embossed saddle with silver ornaments, a bridle made of solid silver, spurs with five-inch rowels, and, when they had ridden through a stretch of brush, he had taken from his saddlebag four goatskin chaps to protect the gelding's legs, a precaution that Teresa de Rojado had observed and on which she had commended him.

Indeed, Teresa couldn't help being impressed by this

dashing, elegant young man, and she believed she might be falling in love with him. It was true that Carlos de Escobar had made a strong impression on her, and her parting with him two years ago after their first meeting, when she had learned of the tragic loss of his Apache wife, had moved her deeply. His subsequent visits had, to be sure, reinforced her admiration of him as a decent, handsome, and dedicated man. To hear him speak of his children and of his life on the Texas ranch, to understand his deep regard and love for his father and stepmother, did him exceptional credit. Yet there was no gainsaying the fact that, over the past two years, she had seen him quite infrequently, and during the last several months, Alejandro Cabeza had courted her with a reserve that showed both tact and good breeding. Also, if the truth be known, in his way he was as handsome as Carlos de Escobar. In addition, there was also the fact that he was an excellent conversationalist and certainly a fine swordsman and horseman.

"I must thank you for a magnificent supper, Señora de Rojado," he suavely murmured, "but even more for this exceptional treat of beautiful music. You play like a veritable angel, and in that dress you assuredly resemble one."

Teresa turned from the spinet and gave him a roguish glance. "You are trying to turn my head, Alejandro. And I think by now you may call me Teresa," she smilingly observed as she turned back to the spinet.

"You have made my day complete, Teresa, granting me this inestimable privilege. Your name is sweet on my lips, and I say it often aloud to myself when I am alone," he said with a sentimental eloquence as he moved a step closer to her. Yet again, playing his part to perfection, he did not make the brash mistake of trying to steal a kiss or touching her in any way. It sufficed for him to be a welcome guest, and to sup alone with her. Also, he had gone out of his way to be exceptionally polite to her *criadas* and her majordomo and had insisted upon visiting the kitchen to compliment the cook on her imaginative and delicious offerings.

"You are poetic tonight, Alejandro," she observed without turning back, as now she began a little minuet by Haydn.

"I am that because the subject of my poetry so inspires me, Teresa. In all Taos, there has never been a woman with your abilities and beauty and intelligence—and this combination makes you completely irresistible."

"Oh, come now, Alejandro. The simple fact is that there are not very many women in Taos at all, because the population is mainly *indio*. It is true that I am a comparative newcomer, and that I am also young, when one thinks of the wives of all the *hacendados* in this area. But that gives me no special merit."

"Save in my eyes, Teresa," he pursued, and was rewarded by seeing the blush deepen on her olive-sheened cheeks. He smiled knowingly to himself. A few more evenings like this and, once he had her in his arms and showed her that he was as expert at making love as he was fencing with her or riding out toward the mountains, then she would be his. To be sure, he would marry her; any other kind of liaison was unthinkable with such a woman. But once she was his wife, her fortune would be his also, and once he had control of her money and her, he could lead the life of ease and total domination to which he believed fate had destined him. A true *hacendado* with the blue blood of his aristocratic forebears had no need to work; it mattered only that he live lavishly, eat the best food, drink the best wine, and have a beautiful wife to show off in public and to coerce in the bedchamber to submit to his conjugal demands. And then, of course, there would be her *criadas* for occasional diversion—discreetly, at least at first.

This delightful prospect titillated him, and he stared avidly at her. He listened attentively, too; and when she turned after finishing the minuet, she found a look on his face that she interpreted as one of rapt devotion and delight in the music she had played.

"You are a very good audience, Alejandro, and I thank you," she laughed softly. "But now, I must confess our strenuous ride this afternoon has tired me. Would you be very angry with me if I sent you home?"

"I could never be angry with you, my *muy linda* Teresa. Again, there are not thanks enough, not words enough, to express to you the joy you've given me this day. Until we meet again!" And now he bowed at the waist like a true *caballero*, took her hand, and brought it to his lips, brushing the slim fingers very lightly, and then favored her with a look of poignant distress, as might well be experienced by an ardent suitor who had just been dismissed.

When he mounted his gelding, he rode off with a smile on his face, thinking that he had taken a giant step forward toward the conquest of this delectable, desirable woman whom he intended to possess in every sense of the word—which meant access to her property and fortune, as well as to her enticing body.

Nine

On this same night when Teresa de Rojado had invited Alejandro Cabeza to ride with her and then enjoy the hospitality of her table, the deaf old housekeeper who had served the martyred Padre Juan Moraga so devotedly and bestowed the same solicitous care upon his replacement, Padre Salvador Madura, died peacefully in her sleep. Padre Madura thought she was still sleeping when he rose at dawn and, not wishing to wake her, prepared his own frugal breakfast. Then, after morning prayers, he went into the church to give the first mass of the day to a handful of parishioners and to hear confessions. It was only when he returned to the rectory and was alarmed to find her not yet up that he ventured to the little room that she occupied at the back of the rectory and found her lying peacefully, her eyes closed, a smile on her face.

He said the last rites over her, and then, greatly disturbed by the loss of this faithful old companion, went out into the yard at the back of the rectory. She had, only two days before, engaged one of the young Indian boys to weed the garden and to plant some seed, since during the last six months of her life she had been smitten with arthritis and was unable to stoop or bend.

"Donchiste," he said to the boy, "go to the village and tell Ticumbe that my housekeeper has gone to join the Great Spirit. Ask him if he will send two loyal *católicos* here at once to help me with the burial. And I wish to ask him to find me a new housekeeper who is of the faith and who will represent his people."

The tall, sturdy Pueblo Indian nodded. "I will go at once, *mi padre*. I will tell you this; my people have learned to love you almost as much as they did Padre Moraga, who was here before you. It is good that you think of one of our women to serve in the house of *El Señor Dios*."

A short time later, Donchiste arrived in the village and went to the house of Ticumbe, who was now the spokesman of all the *indios* of the village. Ticumbe's hair was nearly white, though he was only a little past fifty, and his face was grave and drawn. It was rumored that he had once been a member of the Comanche tribe of Wanderers, had captured a beautiful Mexican girl from a village across the Rio Grande, and had married her. She had given him two sons. A fellow tribesman of Ticumbe's lusted for her, and killed her and the boys when she refused to be unfaithful to her husband.

It was said also that Ticumbe had relentlessly pursued the renegade Comanche, who had fled. Ticumbe found him making camp not far from Taos, and had killed him with his bare hands. And it was also said that the then young Padre Juan Moraga had been riding his burro nearby, had witnessed this vengeance, and fearlessly approached Ticumbe to demand the reason for that brutal murder. Since Ticumbe had learned Spanish from his Mexican wife, he conversed with Padre Moraga and explained the tragedy that had befallen him. And it was also said that Padre Moraga had entreated Ticumbe to come back to Taos and become Christianized. This the Indian had done, and he had gone to live in the village of the pueblo, learned their language, and become a faithful *católico*. Since that day, he had lived the life of exemplary piety and had become a skilled blacksmith. Padre Moraga had seen to it that some of the silver that John Cooper had given him for the poor of Taos had gone to buy Ticumbe a forge and other tools needed in his blacksmith's trade. In return, Ticumbe had given back part of the money he earned to the church.

He lived in a simple *jacal* with whitewashed inner walls and a packed-earth floor, covered with a coarse wool rug. Padre Moraga had made him the gift of a mattress for his bed, and Ticumbe used this in the daytime as a seat.

He had not remarried in all these thirty years, though many a pueblo maiden had made overtures to him, admiring his stoicism and strength and having heard the story about his early days as a Comanche. Instead, he had participated in the council meetings of the pueblo tribespeople and was adjudged to be the wisest serving as spokesman between the *hacendados* and the civil authorities and his adopted people.

Because he still retained his ties with the Comanche, he would occasionally meet former tribesmen who came to the great summer fairs at Taos to exchange gossip with him. Only last week, having heard the news that the annual fair would be held in June rather than in July, a lesser chief of one of the smaller Comanche nomadic tribes had ridden into the pueblo village and there spent a day and a night in Ticumbe's little *jacal*. From this visitor, Ticumbe learned that it was known among several tribes who often raided across the Rio Grande that a certain *hacendado* of Taos was dealing in contraband and selling guns and ammunition to some of the renegade Toboso, who continued to plague the provinces of Chihuahua and Durango. And when Ticumbe asked the Comanche if the latter knew the name of this *hacendado*, the Comanche took a stick and traced on the earth the figure of a head. It symbolized the name of Alejandro Cabeza, since *cabeza* is the Spanish word for head.

When Padre Madura's gardener, Donchiste, called out and asked permission to enter the *jacal*, Ticumbe went out to meet him and was swiftly told of what had happened. "Her soul has already ascended to the sky, and the Giver of Breath, the kind *Dios*, has surely judged her and appointed her one of His holy angels," was Ticumbe's solemn reply. "I will come with you, and I shall bring Furmanti and Santoches to help with the burial. Then I will think of who will best replace this good *mujer* and who will serve the *padre* as faithfully."

"Yes, *jefe*. He is a kind man; he thinks of us as people of dignity, and he does not look down upon us because of the color of our skins, or because we live like *peones*," the boy responded.

Ticumbe put his hand on Donchiste's shoulder. "A man is not judged by his words, but by his deeds. The *ricos* of Taos who have their horses shod at my forge smile upon me and give me silver, but in their hearts they would rather see me dead as a dog from starvation, since they think me no better than that because I am an *indio*. Now then, go to the *jacales* of Furmanti and Santoches and bid them come to me. Then we shall go at once to the church."

The two strong, young Indians dug a grave for the old woman at the back of the garden, which she herself had so dutifully tended for so many years. Padre Salvador Madura, with Ticumbe at his side, spoke the simple words that consigned her to the earth, with the promise of resurrection and the knowledge of salvation through the good deeds she had done all her days. And then he turned to the white-haired *indio*, who, cupping his hands against a geranium bush, carefully drew off several of the largest flowers and dropped the petals over her. As he did so, Padre Madura prayed aloud that all of them in attendance, himself the most humble, might one day know the joy of being summoned to meet *El Señor Dios* with no more blemishes of soul or conscience than she had on the escutcheon of her own life of service to others.

Then they covered her with the earth, and Padre Madura took the crucifix from around his neck and planted it as a kind of headstone to mark where she lay.

"Tomorrow in my forge, I will make an iron cross, *mi padre*," Ticumbe said gently. "It will mark her resting place for Him whom you and I both worship, for He is the same to us, the forsaken of Taos, as to you and your flock."

"Amen, Ticumbe." Padre Madura made the sign of the cross over the grave and then solemnly thanked the two young warriors and the youth for their part in this ceremonial.

They took their leave of him then, while Ticumbe came into the rectory, and Padre Madura poured out sacramental wine and cut a loaf of bread, which the old woman had baked only the day before. And he shared this with the spokesman of the Pueblo Indians in a meaningful silence.

Finally he said, "I will have need of a housekeeper now. And I would prefer one of the *indias* from your village, Ticumbe. One who is a *católica* like yourself. In this way, I shall do what little I can to announce to those who are still smug in their wealth and power in Taos that I, as a spiritual leader of this town, am impressed more by faith and devotion than by material possessions and the insolence which people show out of false pride."

"I know such a woman, *mi padre*," Ticumbe replied. "Her name is Dalcaria. She is a widow who has known thirty summers, and her two sons and her husband died of the fever that swept our village three years ago. Our people love her because she sews for the *ricos*, and uses the money to buy food for mothers who have little *dinero* to buy good food for their little ones."

"She would truly be worthy of this post, Ticumbe. I would be grateful to you if you would bring her to me, and we shall talk."

"I shall bring her at noon tomorrow, *mi padre*. I thank you for the bread and wine, and I ask your blessing." The white-haired *indio* knelt down as Padre Madura made the sign of the cross over him.

Ten

The next morning, after having spent a nearly sleepless night, haunted as he was by his anticipation of a reunion with Teresa, Carlos breakfasted with Doña Elena, Tomás, and Conchita. Don Sancho was sleeping late, and his wife apologized for his absence: "My husband is unable to be present this morning. Dear Carlos, I hope you will not hold it against him. But I thought it best for him to sleep and rest, since he has had so many legal cases in Taos, and they have weakened him."

"There's no need to apologize, Doña Elena," Carlos smilingly said. "It's my hope to be off early this morning—on a very special errand."

Doña Elena gave him a roguish look. "Ah," she murmured, "true love. You would not believe, *mi* Carlos, that late as I am in life, my husband and I have rediscovered each other. And while I wish I could turn back the clock and go back to the days of my youth in Madrid when I was really attractive—"

"But you still are," he protested.

"Go away with you, you rascal," she teased him, holding up a protesting hand. "My mirror tells me what I am. But so long as Don Sancho finds me still desirable, I am blessed among women. And this truly is what you wish, Carlos, I know it well: to share the years with someone who understands you, who senses what is in your heart and mind, and who can respond because she appreciates those qualities which are dearest to a woman's heart. Oh, yes, for all her common sense, Teresa de Rojado has never truly, in my estimation, known love. She married a man virtually old enough to be her father; she was devoted to him; and then, in the natural consequence of things, he was taken from her. So, while this marriage was faithful and devout, it was not anything like that which has taken place between my dear son, Tomás, and my beloved daughter-in-law, Conchita."

At this, the charming orphan and former *criada* blushed and, turning to her stalwart husband, interlaced her fingers with his and squeezed them meaningfully. He turned to kiss her cheek and to whisper something into her ear, which made her blushes deepen.

"I see, and I am envious," Carlos candidly avowed.

"Well then, go to her; see her; and do not be fainthearted. But then"—Doña Elena gave him a veiled warning—"you know you have not been here very often in the last two years. And there are, of course, bound to be others who will notice, as you have, how beautiful and desirable she is."

At this, Carlos instinctively bristled: "What are you saying, Doña Elena? Are there other men who now court her?"

"None that I know of," Doña Elena admitted. "But then you must remember, there are many young *hacendados* in Taos, and they are here, and you are hundreds of miles away in Texas."

"I will convince Teresa that I would be a far better husband to her than any other *caballero* here in Taos!" Carlos hotly retorted, and his eyes were bright with mingled anger and anxiety.

Conchita now meekly put in a propitiating word, "Dear Carlos, I am sure that when she sees how much you truly desire her, she will say yes to you. Take myself—I still give thanks to *El Señor Dios* that my beloved Tomás chose me, a poor little orphan girl, who was nothing more than a *criada* on this fine *hacienda*. I did not dream such a thing could happen."

"Yes, indeed, dear Carlos," Doña Elena said, with a radiant smile at Conchita, "I myself did not appreciate this lovely girl who has made me a grandmother now and let Don Sancho and myself bask in our declining years with the knowledge that our beloved son has found himself the perfect wife. I admit that I was cruel toward Conchita—and I have often begged her forgiveness."

"*Mi madre*," Conchita smilingly responded, "I knew that I had to prove worthy of your son. And the trials that were set before me were necessary before I was granted the joy of becoming his *esposa*." Then she turned to Carlos: "Just so with you, Carlos, the time you have spent waiting for Teresa's consent must be looked upon as part of the test that you must undergo to win her. But I am certain that she knows your good qualities and will soon admit that there is no one here in Taos who could come close to you in honor and kindness."

"Tomás, this wife of yours is a treasure. Guard her constantly, and do not let her out of your sight," Carlos smilingly told Tomás de Pladero as he executed a courtly little bow of his head toward the lovely young woman.

He went out to the stable to saddle Dolor, telling himself that he must not lose heart and, on the other hand, not seem too anxious in his attitude toward Teresa de Rojado. It was as if for the first time in his life he had courted a woman and was experiencing all the frustrations and momentary periods of anguish that a lover who is not yet accepted must undergo. He thought also, with an amused smile, of how many years earlier, his brother-in-law, John Cooper, had taken the suggestion of Doña Inez and abducted Catarina and took her into the mountains to show her exactly the kind of life he led there, so that she would appreciate him the more. However, he had to admit that he did not think that kidnapping the slim, dark brown-haired widow and taking her back to Texas with him would guarantee her acquiescence. It might well estrange her forever from him, and that would be disastrous.

Mounting Dolor, he rode off toward her *hacienda*. On the way, he mentally rehearsed half a dozen speeches he meant to make to her, from one of amiable levity, to one of fervent adoration. And before he had reached her *hacienda*, he had discarded all of them and felt almost tongue-tied because he did not know what words could truly convince her that he loved her and wanted nothing more in life than to share the rest of their days together.

As he approached the clearing of her *hacienda*, he frowned and compressed his lips with a sudden surge of jealousy. There, with a mask over her face, beautiful and slim and vital, buttoned foil in hand, she was fencing with a dark-haired *caballero* who wore an elegant *camisa* of white silk and black velvet breeches and boots—exactly like a popinjay, Carlos savagely thought to himself.

He reined in his mustang and watched from a distance, seeing how the unknown *caballero* agilely fenced with her, accepting her as an equal and making no concessions. It was, he grudgingly had to admit to himself, a bout in which skill counted as paramount, and not sentimental deference to a female. Whoever this *caballero* was, he had at least some native intelligence to be able to fence with her like that, he irritably told himself.

Uttering a heavy sigh, Carlos wheeled Dolor around and, with a last look back over his shoulder, his face clouded, rode back to the de Pladero *hacienda*.

Eleven

Francisco López had taken leave of his commanding officer, Colonel Santa Anna, the day after the party he had given in the "liberator's" honor. Santa Anna had agreed to furnish a crack corps of soldiers who would be trained, armed, and mounted, ready to ride out at instant notice, once word was received from his subordinate as to the movement of the silver from the secret cache that John Cooper Baines possessed.

"With your permission—and I apologize for what I am going to say—I shall go in civilian clothes, *mi coronel.* I shall make my way to the house of Ramón Santoriaga, and I shall tell him that I have been disillusioned by your massacres and your ambition, and that I wish nothing better than to take refuge across the border and perhaps one day become an *americano.*"

Santa Anna had smiled and clapped his subordinate on the back. "Excellent, Francisco! I can see that you have the ability of a major strategist already. But understand this— ingratiate yourself; try to be taken into their conversations; or at least put yourself in the position where you can hear them. If you can find out where this silver is, how long a journey it would be for the *gringo* and his *trabajadores* to fetch it to whatever other place they wish to keep it, that would be invaluable information. And then, you see, if you can get word to me in time, it would be far better to ambush them on the trail than to let them get back to the ranch with the silver. From my own military experience, Francisco, I can tell you that the attacker must expect to lose three men to every one of the defender, particularly when the defender is fortified in a secure place, like that huge ranch."

"I shall do my very best, *mi corcnel*. I swear to you, because of my loyalty to you and my love for our country, I shall bring the silver back to your own coffers."

"Do that, Francisco, and when I am *presidente*, I will raise you to the rank of general, and there will be decorations for you besides for valor and for service beyond the call of duty to the country," Santa Anna sententiously declaimed as he put his hand upon his heart and stared smilingly into his subordinate's handsome face.

Francisco López had put his own *hacienda* into the charge of the majordomo, and issued strict orders: the majodomo was to see to it that the *criadas* did their duties and were faithful. They would not entertain any other officer, save Santa Anna. When he returned, the majordomo would give him a full report of what had taken place, and there would be severe punishments for any servant who had not been obedient and loyal to him.

This done, he had visited the homes of his own two personal aides, Teniente Benito Aguarez and Sargento Porfirio Monreal. Both men were in their early thirties, bachelors like himself, and just as profligate. When he had been in the field with his commander, both men had procured women from neighboring villages, and appropriated foods, wines, and brandies for his enjoyment. In turn, he had shared with them the spoils of war, as he cynically termed them.

"I am going into Texas," he explained to both of them, after having taken them to the largest *posada* of the town. "I go on a vital mission for our beloved country, appointed by the great Santa Anna himself. You can both be of service to me, and the rewards will be great. You, Aguarez, I will promote to *capitán*, and you, Monreal, will become *teniente* if you succeed in carrying out my instructions."

The two men leaned forward across the table, both eager and receptive to his every word. López chuckled, satisfied that he had made no mistake about them, and resumed: "I have arranged with Colonel Santa Anna to send armed troops to appropriate a stolen treasure which a damned *americano* has managed to confiscate. This treasure rightfully belongs to our great country, now more than ever because we have just achieved independence. Each of you will station yourself in a town not far from the Rio Grande, so that if I am able to pass word onto you, you can serve as couriers to Santa Anna and thus have these troops sent swiftly to wherever I designate."

"That is an easy thing to do, and both of us will take pleasure in doing it, not only for our country, but because you have always dealt so fairly with us, Colonel López," the sergeant ingratiatingly spoke up. His companion nodded confirmation.

"It's agreed, then!" López beckoned to the bartender to bring bottles of the best tequila, limes, and salt. "This evening's enjoyment is at my expense, though I must leave at once. One thing more—when you go to these towns, stop in at the busiest *posada* and tell the proprietor where you are staying. That way, I or my messenger will be able to find you."

Again both men nodded, glancing at each other, already excited by the prospect of a venture that would bring promotion and perhaps *dinero* and *mujeres* to them as well.

"*Bueno*. You, Aguarez, will station yourself in Nuevo Laredo. And you, Monreal, in Ciudad Victoria—that is a little over two hundred miles to the south of Nuevo Laredo. Thus, if you, Monreal, should receive word from the *teniente*, you will take the fastest horse you can find and convey the message onto Santa Anna himself. In this way, we can save at least a week and be prepared to ambush this *yanqui* and his men when they have the treasure with them."

"We shall go there at once, *mi coronel*," the sergeant enthusiastically declared, "and we shall wait there for word from you."

"Enjoy yourselves this evening. I have told old Felipe to provide you with attractive *putas* tonight—and this, too, is my treat. Here also, for each of you, two hundred *pesos*, which I have obtained from the regimental quartermaster, and which is being charged as a military expense. It will tide you over while you wait for word from me. See to it that you don't spend it wastefully. As soldiers, you will doubtless live off the land, and the people of these towns will welcome you, once they know that you are attached to the great army of the liberator. Make that known to them. Well then, I wish you every success, and I urge you to be faithful to me. The rewards will be great, exactly as I've promised. *¡Adiós!*"

Abruptly he rose from the table, laid down banknotes before each man, and they saluted him fervently.

Saddling a mustang he had broken in and trained, having already filled his saddlebags with provisions for the long journey, which could be replenished at any time along the way, López rode off into the night toward the Rio Grande.

On the third Monday of May, just before sundown, Francisco López rode a piebald gelding across the Frio River. On the boundary of the lands of the Double H Ranch, he questioned one of the sheepherders as to the whereabouts of the Santoriaga family, and after leaving his flock with a companion, the sheepherder escorted López to one of the separate little houses to the west of the huge *hacienda* and the bunkhouse and the huts of the *trabajadores*. López's clothes were dirtied and disheveled, and his face was lined with exhaustion. He had ridden an average of thirty miles a day for just over a month from Veracruz across the Rio Grande, and to the Double H Ranch.

His saddlebags were empty, and for the last two days, in order to lend greater veracity to the role he intended to play, he had lived on only a few *tortillas* which an old woman had given him in a little village just north of the Rio Grande and which he had thrust into his dusty jacket. During the last ten miles of his journey, he had driven the gelding almost beyond its endurance, and the animal stood, trembling, whinnying, and lathered with foam. After the sheepherder left him, López dismounted, with a heartfelt groan that was not in the least feigned.

Mercedes Santoriaga, Ramón's handsome brunet wife, in her late thirties, was outside their house playing with her little eighteen-month-old son, who had been born in this new home to which her husband had come, disillusioned by Santa Anna as Carlos de Escobar had been. The black-haired little boy was sitting on the grass, playing with a ball, when he looked up and called out at the sight of Francisco López stumbling toward him and his mother.

"¡Dios! Can it be—but what are you doing here, Colonel López?" Mercedes exclaimed as she recognized the travel-weary civilian.

"Thank God you've recognized me, Señora Santoriaga,"

he gasped. "I have ridden all the way from Veracruz to find your husband—I pray that he is home."

"Why, yes, Colonel López."

Francisco López shook his head and looked at his feet. "You see that I am not wearing a uniform any longer, Señora Santoriaga. I have left the army of Santa Anna. I can no longer endure his brutalities, his greed, his ego. And that is why I thought, since your husband was my friend, and since I knew that he had come here, that perhaps he might offer me some temporary shelter till I can make plans to resume my life. But it will not be for Mexico any longer, I fear."

"There he is now—Ramón, do come here—it's Colonel López!" Mercedes called as her tall, handsome husband appeared in the doorway.

Ramón Santoriaga strode forward, a startled look on his face as he recognized his former military colleague. "I had never expected to see you again, not in Texas, Colonel López," he exclaimed.

"I have just told your beautiful wife, Ramón, that I am no longer a member of Santa Anna's army. He is ambitious beyond belief; he loves only war and massacre and plunder. I have fled Mexico, and I do not know where I shall go, but I remember that you and I were once friends. I do not wish to presume upon your hospitality—but if you could put me up for the night, or for as much time as it will take for me to formulate some idea as to what I shall do next, I shall be eternally grateful."

Ramón glanced at his wife, who nodded as she stooped to pick up her little boy and to hold him against her bosom. "You shall be our guest, of course. I can see that you've had an exhausting journey."

"All the way from Veracruz on horseback. And look at the poor animal—it's foundering. You see, Mexico is now so poor that it was difficult to change horses along that terrible journey—I did what I could. But I shall never go back."

Ramón stared a long moment at his former military associate, and then nodded understandingly. "You know, of course, that Iturbide sent me as a liaison officer between himself and Santa Anna. It did not take me long to see that the so-called liberator had in mind personal gain, material booty, and public adoration. Yes, I think I can understand how you yourself may have found out that there is room for only one ego in all Mexico, and that is Santa Anna's. Come inside, and share supper with us. My dear one," Ramón said turning to Mercedes, "he can sleep in the little room off the kitchen for the time being, at least. Tomorrow, we'll see what can be done."

"I shall be eternally grateful to you, Ramón. I want only a chance at a new life. And how I envy you—you at least have your beautiful wife and your children, and I, as you know, am a bachelor. I left everything back in Mexico, so I must start all over again." López made his voice sound humble, and uttered a deep sigh at the end of his words.

Ramón put his arm around the younger man's shoulders. "Come in, Francisco. Here, at least, there's plenty of land and not too much interference, so that people who settle here can begin life all over again. And in the morning, you'll meet Don Diego de Escobar, the father-in-law of the *gringo*, who is known as *El Halcón*, John Cooper Baines. He has just returned from San Antonio. *Dios*, this is truly a country where one may make a fresh start. But that's enough talk for now. You are tired and hungry."

Francisco López slept the sleep of the just until nearly noon of the next day. When he wakened, Mercedes Santoriaga served him a nourishing breakfast topped off by a cup of strong, hot chocolate. Ramón lent him a pair of breeches, a clean shirt, and underclothing to replace his dirty, tattered attire. Ramón also lent him a straight razor, and López emerged, his beard and mustache neatly trimmed, his eyes again bright, and his body thoroughly refreshed.

"Now I shall introduce you to Don Diego and to his *yerno*, John Cooper Baines, who is married to Don Diego's beautiful daughter, Catarina," Ramón promised. "And you'll see for yourself what a little world we have here, with settlers and old friends from the past who have come to live with us and to strengthen this huge ranch, where we grow sheep and cattle."

"It sounds like paradise, *mi amigo*," López said, then sighed and shook his head. He accompanied Ramón toward the huge *hacienda*, just as John Cooper emerged from the corral with the wolf-dog Yankee trotting at his heels.

"¡*Hola!* Señor Baines," Ramón called out. "Come meet Francisco López, a friend of mine!"

John Cooper nodded and quickened his footsteps. Francisco López adopted a genial smile, but inwardly he was appraising this tall, sun-bronzed *gringo* of whom Santa Anna had spoken with such angry vehemence.

Yankee's ears flattened along his skull, and lowering his muzzle, he emitted a soft growl, his yellow eyes fixing the Mexican officer with unwavering scrutiny.

"No, Yankee, *es un amigo*," John Cooper rebuked the powerful young wolf-dog, and lightly cuffed him on the snout. But Yankee emitted still another growl and backed away, actually glaring at his master.

"He doesn't seem to like me, Señor Baines," López pleasantly offered. "I am sorry about that, for I come as a friend. Ramón here and I shared the same barracks at one time near Tampico, and he was kind enough to take me in last night, when I rode here exhausted from my long journey."

"Oh?" John Cooper eyed Ramón for confirmation.

The latter nodded. "It's true, Señor Baines; he and I served together. Most recently, he was attached to Colonel Santa Anna. But he has told me that he can no longer bear to serve under such a commander, and that is why he sought me out, after he had fled from Mexico."

"I see. You were an officer in Santa Anna's army, Señor López?" John Cooper questioned him in Spanish.

Francisco López made a deprecating shrug and purposefully answered in English: "Yes, I was a colonel, though my commission dated after Santa Anna's. But I could no longer endure his enormous—indeed, fanatical—admiration of himself and his belief that he was born to lead all Mexico. I consider him a tyrant, a man who enjoys raiding villages and killing innocent people. And he is a womanizer as well."

"I have heard something to that effect from Carlos," John Cooper admitted, giving the handsome Mexican a thoughtful look before speaking. "Well then, what do you wish us to do for you?"

"I abandoned everything, Señor Baines. All I have is my horse, and he is not the one I started my journey with. I've lost everything, but at least I have my life and my honor. And Ramón has told me that you were kind enough to appoint him officer in charge of your defenses against any possible attack. Since, after all, I too have as much military experience as he does, I should be very happy to serve him in a lesser capacity. I should like to prove myself and earn, as you *yanquis* say, my keep."

"You speak English quite well," John Cooper responded. "Well, Ramón, what do you think?"

"I think he could certainly be of service to us, Señor Baines, and if he is willing to place himself under my orders, I can be responsible for him," Ramón proffered.

"Well, we'll try it for a bit and see what happens. Meanwhile, Señor López, inspect the ranch, see for yourself what we have here; meet the *trabajadores* and especially my *capataz*, Miguel Sandarbal. If you are going to live among *gringos*, it's well that you begin by understanding them, what they think, what their hopes are, and how they want only peace and a chance to bring up their families on good, rich land."

"I should ask for nothing better myself, Señor Baines," López said, deferentially inclining his head.

Yankee, meanwhile, had approached the handsome Mexican and begun to sniff at him. Now, as López bowed to John Cooper Baines, the wolf-dog backed away a pace or two and, showing his fangs, growled again.

"No, Yankee, *es amigo!*" John Cooper angrily exclaimed, and came forward to rap Yankee's snout again with his knuckles. "Well, Señor López, you'll just have to get used to him and he to you, I suspect. I've trained him since he was a puppy, and he gets along with people who treat him properly. But he's got just enough wolf in him to be a little nasty to strangers."

"I thank you for cautioning me, Señor Baines. I shall try to make a friend of Yankee." With a bland smile, López held out his hands, but the wolf-dog did not acknowledge this offer of friendship. Instead, he continued to back away and finally rubbed up against John Cooper's right leg, his baleful yellow eyes continuing to fix Santa Anna's subordinate with unwavering intent.

"It has been a pleasure to meet you, Señor Baines."

"I'd like to have you meet Don Diego, as well as Doña Inez, Señor López. And I think it's time for *almuerzo*. Why don't you come along and join us all? Ramón, you're invited too."

"*Gracias*, Señor Baines. Come along, Francisco."

* * *

At luncheon on this second day of his visit, Francisco López was introduced to Don Diego and Doña Inez. Glib and self-assured, he was by now confident that his dramatic appearance at Ramón's house on a horse that he had ridden to exhaustion, and in civilian clothes, had convinced everyone of his veracity. Thus he was at his most effusive over the luncheon table.

Don Diego, glancing at his tall son-in-law, asked, "Can you tell me, Señor López, whether you think we are free from further harassment from your former commander? When my son was attached to his regiment, he told us that Santa Anna's men frequently crossed the Rio Grande to raid some of the Texas settlers, without the slightest provocation."

"As to that, Don Diego," the handsome Mexican suavely responded, "I cannot of course vouch for Santa Anna. As I've told Ramón—and he himself was in that same regiment and knows Santa Anna perhaps even better than I do—he is a dangerous man and will let nothing stand in his way of becoming either president or emperor of Mexico." López paused a moment to wipe his lips with his napkin. He was enjoying the role he was playing of disillusioned soldier, and it was quite easy for him to embroider on the theme of Santa Anna's ambition and greed. "But as to the rest, he is now in Veracruz, married and living on his estate. In addition, there is a duly appointed president of Mexico, and at the moment it does not seem that Santa Anna will pose any threat to *americanos* on this side of the Rio Grande."

"That at least is my hope," Don Diego solemnly replied. "There are many settlers who have come to us from a long distance and made their homes here. And there will be traders who will go to Santa Fe, now that the trail is at last open without prohibitive Spanish tariffs, and who will return to visit with us on their return to their homes in Missouri or beyond. We have tried to establish here, Señor López, a community that welcomes all men who wish peace. I myself, who left Madrid when Spain was oppressed by Napoleon and his brother, know very well that only generals and the kings profit from war. The people themselves are tyrannized and impoverished, if they are not slaughtered."

López respectfully inclined his head. "I share your sentiments, Don Diego." Then, with an ingratiating smile, the

Mexican turned to Doña Inez and remarked, "But I am envious of all of you here, seeing how gracefully you live and what beautiful women brighten even your dreariest days. You are indeed fortunate to have carved out this little empire of your own here in the wilderness."

"You talk like a poet," Don Diego laughingly avowed, as he signaled to one of the servant-girls to fill the Mexican officer's glass with wine from the Canaries.

"Alas, Don Diego, I hope that *El Señor Dios* will forgive the envy in my heart—I believe that is one of the Commandments, that one should not covet one's neighbor's wife, or any of his possessions—but you see, I left my estate in Mexico, my servants, even what little *dinero* I had put away from my military service, in search of freedom. That is why I am so grateful that Ramón has persuaded you to let me stay here a time, until I can reshape my life. And although it is true that I was at one time on Santa Anna's staff and planned the raids against the *gringos,* I am eager now to learn how the *gringo* lives, what his hopes and dreams are, so that I may better understand him. For if I am to live here in Texas, then I must adapt myself to my newly chosen land, which one day, I hope will be part of the great United States."

"That will be a very great day when it happens, Señor López," Don Diego at once retorted. "There would be many advantages if Texas were to become part of the United States. Not the least of these is the fact that in the United States there is no dictator or king, no military faction seeking power over another at the expense of the common people. Our country is young, true enough—I know you will smile when I say 'our country,' when you know that I am a *madrileño*—but the fact remains that I feel myself now as much an *americano* as my *yerno* here." He turned to give John Cooper an affectionate look and lifted his glass to toast Catarina's tall husband.

"You must understand, Don Diego, that Mexico was called Nueva España and was expected to become the subsidiary province of a great Spain," Francisco López declaimed. "When at last we *mejicanos* broke away from the mother country, there was bound to be chaos and a struggle for power. After all, Mexico never before had known what freedom was, and so mistakes were made. And then there were opportunists, like Santa Anna."

Catarina, radiant and seemingly more beautiful than ever in her pregnancy, interposed: "But don't you think, Señor López, that just as you have said, the fact that Mexico has an appointed president will help turn the country into a democracy like the kind enjoyed in los Estados Unidos?"

López affected a look of sober meditation and uttered a heartfelt sigh. "I wish I could be more optimistic, Señora Baines. But you must remember that the *mejicano* is governed by raw emotion, almost primitivism, I should say. I have not had much acquaintance with *gringos*, it is true, but what I have thus far observed is that they are more in control of their emotions, more disciplined and purposeful."

"Exactly," Don Diego broke in. "When the colonists came to the eastern shores of this great new country, they were in search of freedom from taxation and religious persecution and all the brutalities that the powerful nobility of Europe imposed upon them. They had to struggle against not only the elements and the unknown dangers of this new land, but against *indios* and finally against the army of George III, which at that time was considered one of the best-trained in all the world. And yet, a handful of courageous men, who, as my *yerno* tells me, were called a raggle-taggle army, made them surrender at Yorktown." Don Diego chuckled reflectively and shook his head. "These *americanos*, these *gringos* as you call them, Señor López, who had no uniforms, and who marched in winter sometimes without boots or overcoats—what must all Europe have thought, when the brilliantly red-uniformed British soldiers had to endure the ignominy of surrender to such men? I wish I might have been there to see that surrender!"

"I know that *americanos* are brave and willing to die for what they believe in," López glibly replied. "I was once willing to die for Mexico, but no longer. I hope that through the privilege of being with all of you here for what little time I am granted, I may be imbued with this same glorious spirit that all of you possess." As he said these last words, he put his hands dramatically over his heart and looked directly at Catarina with a flattering smile. She, in turn, blushed and lowered her eyes. John Cooper, from his place at the table, saw this interplay of glances, and frowned.

That afternoon, Ramón took Francisco López out into the fields to see the cattle and the sheep, and introduced him to Miguel Sandarbal. The *capataz* listened politely as Ramón explained the Mexican officer's background and decision to leave Santa Anna and seek a new life north of the Rio Grande. "I wish you the realization of your hope, Señor López," he brusquely declared. "How may I serve you?"

"If it is not too much trouble, because I know how valuable horses are, I should welcome the opportunity to ride one of your fine horses, the kind that you keep in the *remuda* when you drive your cattle to market," López smilingly requested.

"I hope, Señor López," Miguel stiffly responded, "that if I give you one of our horses to ride, you will treat it better than that poor gelding you brought to us. I'm afraid he is useless, and I do not think he will recover."

"I know; I am truly sorry," López contritely avowed. "But you see, I had come all the way from Veracruz, and I was unable to exchange horses many times along the way, as you can well understand. And this one was not too strong to begin with; but I, alas, may heaven forgive my selfishness, was intent only on crossing the Rio Grande so that I could be free of Santa Anna and any troops he might have sent after me in pursuit."

"Very well. I will have a horse saddled for you. But I will not give you a bit or spurs."

"But I shall not need these!" López tried to make amends and to win over the *capataz,* but Miguel's face was stony as he went into the corral and, with his lariat, roped one of the *remuda* horses and led him out. A *trabajador* saddled the horse, and Miguel handed López reins and a bridle but no bit.

López adjusted the reins and bridle, mounted the black mustang, and with a joyous cry, kicked his heels against the horse's belly and galloped off.

Miguel Sandarbal turned to Ramón Santoriaga and shook his head: "I've a bad feeling about your friend, may *El Señor Dios* forgive me. I think he is much too certain of the words he uses, if you will forgive my saying so. And I am not sure that I believe he gave up everything under Santa Anna to come here."

"It is quite possible, Miguel. I understand your suspicions, but remember that I myself at one time worked with Santa Anna, when Iturbide sent me as liaison officer to his regiment. I was disillusioned, and so was Carlos. It is not strange that another man, even though he is a Mexican and was in the service for a long time, should understand what a vulture Santa Anna is."

"That may be true, Señor Santoriaga, but all the same I don't trust him. And you'd do well—again forgive me for speaking out of turn—to keep an eye on him, even if he is your friend. It is possible that he might be a spy."

"Spy?" Ramón echoed, his eyes widening with incredulity. "But in what way? I am sure that Santa Anna knows about the existence of the ranch. And besides, it's as Francisco said; he's in Veracruz, enjoying his marriage, and there is a president in Mexico now. What would Santa Anna have to gain by sending Francisco here as a spy? Only to determine that we are strong and secure as in a fortress?"

Twelve

Francisco López was not a stupid man, and he had instinctively realized that Miguel Sandarbal mistrusted him. When he had breakfast with Ramón and Mercedes the next morning, the handsome Mexican had already calculated that he must be granted ample time to remain at the Double H Ranch, in order to learn what he could about the disposition of the secret silver hoard. To offend the important personages of this ranch from the very onset would be fatal to such a hope, and thus he decided to evince frank, almost apologetic sincerity.

After breakfast that next morning, he took a leisurely stroll toward the west, observing the houses of the Texas settlers like Edward Molson, who had come to settle here, both for protection and to further their own new, venturesome lives on a frontier that might well belong one day to the United States. Thirteen years ago, these men had escaped the Battle of Medina, the first major outbreak in Mexico's revolution against Spain, where rebellious Texans and downtrodden *peones* rose up against autocratic, Royalist soldiers. The revolution had been savagely put down, but Edward Molson and his friends firmly believed that Texas must one day be adjoined as a separate state to the new young country north of the Rio Grande. It could not exist as the slave-province of an embattled, chaotic Mexico, where one warlord after another would vie for total power.

That was why López made a special point of meeting the very men whom Santa Anna and his superiors had sought to decimate, in his pretentious scheme of avowing himself to be an "*americano*" in heart and spirit, if not yet in fact." Because he spoke such excellent English, he easily conversed with them, and Molson himself invited López to sup at his house.

In the mornings, Santa Anna's spy went riding on the mustang that Miguel Sandarbal had allocated to him, and he rode at a leisurely gait, savoring the magnificent spread of tall green grass, and beyond, the flowing Frio River. Indeed, it seemed to him that this region was almost untouched, pure territory whose possession should go to those who cultivate the land and bring forth its harvests. Yet at the same time, drawing from his own military experience, he was speculating on the defensive strengths of the Double H Ranch. It would take at least two hundred trained Mexican soldiers, all of them sharpshooters and experts with the bayonet. From his own experiences in the field, when he raided pitifully undefended villages, he knew what terror cold steel could effect upon people who spoke of giving their lives for freedom. The *peones* who had feebly resisted his troops had been mercilessly slaughtered—just as the Texans had been at the Battle of Medina.

When he saw Miguel Sandarbal working with the *trabajadores* building the magnificent church over which Jorge Pastronaz would preside by early fall—or so it had been planned—he humbly approached the white-haired *capataz* and vowed himself eager to lend a hand. "Of course you know that I am *católico*, Señor Sandarbal," he said self-effacingly. "I should be grateful for the privilege of taking part in no matter how small a way, to prove my devotion to Him who died to save all of us."

"You are kind to say that, Señor López," the *capataz* responded, giving him a searching look. "But you will pardon me if I do not take advantage of your offer—though I know it to be meant kindly. You see, Señor López, the *trabajadores* who followed us from Taos years ago were once *peones*, and now they are free men, almost as if they were part of one large family here. Building this church is their way of expressing thanks to *El Señor Dios*, who made it possible for them to become men of dignity. They would feel you an intruder if you helped them. I hope you can understand this and not take offense."

"I understand. I ask your pardon if I have offended in my turn."

"You have not, Señor López, because you could not possibly know. I bid you good day." Thus dismissing him, Miguel turned back to his *trabajadores* and gave them orders to bring up larger beams for the nave, and not to forget to strengthen the foundation at the back, where there would be an addition used as a rectory. One day, Miguel believed, they might also build a mission house, where Catholic nuns coming across the Rio Grande might find sanctuary from the violence and bloodshed taking place in Mexico. If such a thing took place, it would not only solemnize the church and rectory, but it would also give a spiritual enhancement to every man who toiled with his hands at the Double H Ranch.

Thwarted in his attempt to make a friend of the *capataz*, Francisco López turned to the task of ingratiating himself with the taciturn, tall John Cooper, for he realized that this *gringo* best knew the secret of that treasure which his superior officer so violently coveted.

So on this ninth day of his sojourn with Ramón Santoriaga, the Mexican officer cordially greeted John Cooper, as the latter and Yankee were walking toward the stable where the palominos were quartered. "Señor Baines, would you take it amiss if I asked to ride with you this beautiful morning?" he called.

John Cooper turned and contemplated Ramón's friend. "Come along if you've a mind to," he at last decided. "But I'd best leave Yankee shut up in the toolshed because he still doesn't like you. See how he's growling even now?" It was true: the wolf-dog, his ears again flattened against his skull, crouched low and bared his fangs at López, who grimaced with distaste and unconsciously put a hand to his waist where a brace of *pistolas* would normally be attached. Although he quickly dropped his hand and fixed Yankee with a welcoming smile, John Cooper had caught that instinctive gesture, and he frowned again, for it rang falsely against the glib humility that Ramón's friend had been displaying all this while. Abruptly he decided, "That's enough of that, Yankee; come along with me!" and rapped the wolf-dog across the muzzle with his knuckles. Yankee uttered a forlorn little yipe, plaintively looking up at John Cooper as if to say, "Why did you do that? Don't you know that I growl when there's someone I don't like or trust?"

Nonetheless, he docilely followed as John Cooper led him back to the little shed near the kennel that housed Hosea and Jude, the two Irish wolfhounds given to him by Matthew Robisard. The wolf-cub Mischief, who had been mated with the wolfhounds and who was the mother of Yankee, had been set free by John Cooper and had returned to the forests from which she originally came, though to be sure, she often reappeared on the ranch to eat the food that the cooks or the *trabajadores* left out for her. The other cub resulting from the mating of the wolfhounds and Mischief—a female John Cooper had named Luna—was also kept in the kennel, in separate quarters from the wolfhounds. So far, Luna had not given birth to any cubs of her own, but John Cooper hoped someday she would mate with either Hosea or Jude, and have a litter.

Now John Cooper gestured for Yankee to enter the shed. His tail between his legs, the sturdy wolf-dog reluctantly went inside, and John Cooper closed the door. It was not unlike the way Lobo had been incarcerated until the latter had been thoroughly trained.

John Cooper opened the door to the stable, and the palominos nickered and whinnied, delighted to see their master. Francisco López followed behind him, and his eyes greedily lit up at the sight of these magnificent horses. He thought to himself that when he had completed his mission, he must arrange to steal one of them, because no mustang in the world could match a palomino for galloping speed.

Aloud, he commented, "I really envy your good fortune, Señor Baines. These are the most beautiful horses I have ever seen in all my life."

"Yes, they're of the purest stock. One of my pleasures on the ranch is breeding them. My wife, Catarina, has a mare, and the mare can race almost as fast as Pingo, whom I shall ride this morning with you."

So saying, he led the palomino out of its stall, threw on the saddle, and mounted. López watched John Cooper ride out into the yard, and his lips tightened with annoyance. He could understand why Santa Anna hated this accursed *gringo*. What a feather in his own cap it would be to outwit the tall *americano* who thought himself a king, to take away all the silver and then, one day, to destroy this nest of *gringo* hornets!

The mustang that Miguel Sandarbal had given him was kept in a larger stable, not far from the one for the palominos; and López strode toward it, saddled his mustang, and rode out to join John Cooper. "In which direction shall we go, Señor Baines?" he amicably asked.

"We'll just ride awhile, nowhere special. I'd like to know a little more about you, Señor López."

"Why do you not call me Francisco? That is what Ramón calls me."

"That's for friends. We're not that yet. You're a guest, and we'll show you every courtesy, Señor López. But we're not yet ready to take you into our family here. At least, not on your say-so."

"What further proof can I give you, Señor Baines?" López protested with a sweeping gesture of his arm, his eyes wide with feigned innocence, "to prove to you that I have had my fill of the Mexican army and especially of that butcher, Santa Anna?"

"I'm not yet sure. I still don't know why a man who held the rank of colonel would stake everything he had on a race across the border just to see a former friend. You say that you left everything behind you, house, money, horses— that's true?"

López solemnly made the sign of the cross over his heart. "I swear it on the hope of my redemption, Señor Baines."

"All right. But words are cheap. Out here in this country, it's the way a man acts. I suppose maybe you really haven't been tested yet. Oh, sure, Yankee doesn't like you, but I'm not holding that against you. He's still young and a little wild. Anyway, I hope you aren't offended by all I've just said. I have a habit of saying what's on my mind."

Francisco López gave John Cooper a vacuous little smile and inclined his head to acknowledge that there was no offense taken. Inwardly, a murderous instinct surged within him, and if he had had a weapon, he would have impulsively used it. But at the same moment, he quelled that vindictive thought; even if it were possible, the secret of the silver would die with this infuriating *gringo*. No, he must still hold himself in check and utilize the utmost patience to learn what he had to know.

And yet, it was a dreary life here on this ranch, for his only true friend was Ramón Santoriaga. He felt himself an outsider, and he understood also that the more he tried to ingratiate himself, the more suspicious they would be of him. *Caramba*, how in the devil was one to learn the secret when those who held it never spoke of it? Still in all, he had gambled a great deal, and he must continue to gamble a little while longer.

Two days later, thoroughly bored with the monotony of being a guest on this huge ranch, Francisco López decided to go for a stroll. There was a well that the *trabajadores* had built not far from the *hacienda*, so that the *criadas* wouldn't have to carry heavy buckets to and from the river, which was some distance from the settlement. It was late afternoon; he had consumed an excellent lunch of venison and hot biscuits and a delicious flan embellished with wild berries, which Mercedes Santoriaga had prepared for him, and had a brief *siesta*. He then walked beyond the *hacienda* toward the well, his eyes facing south, where the Rio Grande lay. He thought of the two men he had stationed at Nuevo Laredo and Ciudad Victoria, relay couriers who would inform Santa Anna to send the troops whenever the word came from him. How much longer it would take to send that word, he had no way of knowing, and it began to exasperate him.

Personally, he despised these *gringos*, and even more so, Spaniards like Don Diego and Doña Inez, who fawned on this tall *gringo* and forgot all the aristocracy of their blood from the Old World, from the court of Madrid. He had often wished that he might have grown up near the Escorial and served the great monarchs of the once-powerful Spain. Now his fortunes lay in the future of a domineering, self-centered opportunist, who could as readily turn on a friend as embrace him; he had seen how Santa Anna had changed sides in the days of Iturbide's struggle for power. What was to prevent Santa Anna, once he found this treasure, if he found it, from appropriating it and then banishing him—or even having him put to death, so that no one else would know whence that fortune came?

This momentary black mood suddenly lifted: he saw a charming young black-haired *criada*, not more than eighteen, walking toward the well. She carried a bucket, and she wore a short, full, red skirt topped off with a loose, low-cut matching blouse and *rebozo*. Her feet were bare, and though the skirt's hem came to her calves, his practiced eye could detail at once the voluptuous curvaciousness of her calves and thighs and the fullness of her hips.

He moved forward slowly, a dazzling smile on his lips, and called out in a low voice, "Señorita, will you permit me to fill your bucket and to bring it back? It's truly too heavy for a charming señorita like you to carry."

The girl whirled, thunderstruck at such a romantic declaration. Her name was Paquita Cardozo, and she had come to the Double H Ranch last year. One of the *vaqueros*, Juan Duriaga, who had helped drive the cattle to San Antonio, had met her in a little *posada*, where she was working as a barmaid for her tyrannical old uncle. Seeing how the girl was constantly browbeaten by the uncle—who was also not reluctant to take a switch to her—Juan at once offered to get her a job as a *criada* at the *hacienda* of his fine *patrón*. Thus, she had come, and now she and Juan were very nearly betrothed. Indeed, Paquita was hoping that before Christmas, the good Padre Pastronaz would marry her and Juan in the great new church.

Francisco López came forward swiftly and took the bucket from her trembling hand. "Don't be afraid of me, *querida*. My name is Francisco López. I'm a friend of Coronel Ramón Santoriaga. I'm going to live here, you see. And I'm a very lonely man—I have no *esposa* or *novia*, either."

"But—but, S-Señor López, I'm already spoken for—it is

Juan Duriaga. Please, you should not speak to me this way—it is my work in the kitchen—please let me have the bucket—"

"Oh, come now, little one! What's your name?"

"P-Paquita, Señor López. But please, it is not right—I told you—"

"I do not know who this Juan is, *mi linda*," he said, with all the eloquence of an inveterate lecher, "but surely one as beautiful as you deserves a man who is *muy hombre, muy macho*. Like myself. Come now, *un pequeño beso, por favor*, to celebrate our meeting!" With this, he put his arms around her and drew her to him, kissing her forcibly on the mouth.

Paquita uttered a startled cry and put her fist against his chest, trying to disengage herself.

At this moment, Miguel Sandarbal came from around the back of the *hacienda* and stopped short in his tracks: "*¡Qué diablo!* Is that you, Señor López? What are you doing there with Paquita?"

"Why—why, Señor Sandarbal, nothing at all," López stammered. "I merely asked if I might carry her bucket to the well—"

"She is not a weakling; it is her work, and she does not need you to be her *servidor*, Señor López. You have behaved disgracefully. I suggest you go back to the house of your friend, Ramón. Go ahead, Paquita, fill the bucket and do what you are to do."

"*G-gracias*, Señor Sandarbal." Paquita, in tears of relief, seized the bucket and hurried to the well. López sent Miguel a glowering look for a moment, then turned on his heel and strode off, his face black as a storm cloud.

Francisco López quickly tried to make amends for his discovered flirtation with Paquita. That same afternoon he went of his own accord to seek out Don Diego de Escobar and found the latter heading for his study, having just said his prayers in the little chapel in the *hacienda*.

In that chapel, in a place of honor, was the three-foot statue of the *Cristo* dying on the cross, whittled by the old Pueblo Indian, Castamaguey. Don Diego had sat in judgment in the courtroom at the invitation of Don Sancho de Pladero back in Taos seventeen years ago, when the arrogant, wealthy merchant, Luis Saltareno, had refused to pay Castamaguey because this statue had been of "poor artistic quality." And Don Diego had told him, "We are taught, Señor Saltareno, that God made man in His own image . . . Is it not logical that an *indio* would see the blessed *Cristo* as like unto him and his own people?" Then he had told the Indian that he would buy it himself and keep it in his chapel. By such an act of humanity, he had endeared himself to the humble and the poor and the oppressed of Taos, and he had made of Luis Saltareno a mortal enemy.

Don Diego's face was serene as he turned to Francisco López: "A beautiful day, Señor López. I have made my peace with Him who brought all this about, and I am very grateful to be alive. How can I be of service to you?"

"If I may have a word in private with you, Don Diego, I feel I must lay my cards on the table," Santa Anna's aide glibly began. "Alas, since I came to visit my old friend Ramón, there have been some misunderstandings that possibly may put me in a bad light. I wish to clarify these before they are reported to you, so that you will trust me and believe in my sincerity."

"Come into my study. Let me pour you a glass of Madeira. It is a pleasant wine, not too strong, yet strong enough to inspire clear thinking. At least, that is my own prescription." The white-haired *hidalgo* chuckled at his own little joke as they entered his study and he took the decanter on his desk and filled a goblet to the brim, handing it to the handsome Mexican.

"I shall drink to your health and that of your beautiful wife and your children. May all of you have long, happy years."

"Thank you, Señor López." Don Diego clinked his goblet against the Mexican's and then seated himself at his writing desk, while López remained standing facing him, his head held high, assuming an attitude of great dignity and candor.

"You must understand, Señor López, that we have been through many adversities, my son-in-law and I, and indeed my entire family. What we try to do here is to carve out a new kind of homeland, where we can be strong enough to guarantee peace in years to come, peace for the *trabajadores* and their families and all who live here with us, as well as ourselves, to enjoy the benefits of an honest life of work and family love. It is as simple as that."

"I understand perfectly, and I admire your code of life. Alas, a wanderer as I now am, an outcast from Mexico, my native land, I am in need of just such an uplifting standard as yours, Don Diego."

"But you are young, certainly not more than half my age, and the world is ahead of you. Also, you are a bachelor, as you told me, and the joys of marriage and of *niños* still await you. I should say that you are indeed fortunate to have such prospects."

"That's true. And yet, I feel myself almost an unwanted guest, Don Diego. Very possibly because of my loneliness, because I've given up everything, I made an error of approaching the charming *criada*, Paquita, not knowing that she was betrothed to one of your *trabajadores*. For that I heartily apologize."

"I think that may be forgiven, since you now see the error of your ways. It is most important that one does not remain obdurate and inconsiderate of others in the society in which he finds himself."

"I understand your meaning, Don Diego. I shall try to observe all the rules. Meanwhile, I have been asking my good friend, Ramón, almost daily to help me embark on some new course of life—perhaps I could earn my way here by working on the land, or perhaps even raising horses—I have some skill with these. If I could acquire a small piece of land, build my own little *jacal*, and in time find some unattached young woman who would be happy to share my life, it would indeed be inspiration against the loneliness I now experience." Into this speech, Francisco López put all the self-pitying yet aristocratic dignity of which he was capable.

"Your sentiments do you honor, Señor López," Don Diego responded. "But I am not the one to whom you should address your request for land on which to settle. It is my son-in-law, John Cooper Baines, who discovered this beautiful stretch of land with its abundance of water and fertile grass for grazing. It is him you must convince, if you wish to remain with us as a settler and also as a defender. Even I, Señor López, if we should be attacked by, say, Santa Anna's troops or hostile *indios*, would not hesitate to take a musket, even at my age, to defend all the rest of us here."

"I should be equally willing."

"Very well, then, you have made your point. Apply to my son-in-law and let him decide if you are to remain with us permanently. I wish you a good day, Señor López," Don Diego said, concluding the interview.

López slowly went down the hill, frowning and cursing under his breath. This man who had once been an *hidalgo* had begun to think like one of the accursed *gringos*. They were living in a fool's paradise, all of them here.

As he went out into the *patio*, he encountered Catarina, who was carrying three-year-old Carmen in her arms. He effusively greeted her, bowed low, took her hand, and kissed it. At this moment, John Cooper came out onto the courtyard to join his wife, and scowled at the handsome Mexican. "Have you lost your way, Señor López?"

"Why—er—no, Señor Baines, I came out here to stretch my legs and to enjoy a little of the sunshine. Your lovely wife was here, and I wished only to pay my tribute to her."

"I see. By now I am sure that Catarina understands you have the manners of a gentleman, Señor López. But I would remind you that I am still her husband, and it is I alone who have the right to be attentive to her."

"I humbly apologize if I have offended either of you," López stammered, turning scarlet with mortification. "I shall not offend you again in this way. Believe me, Señora Baines, I had only the purest of motives in mind." With this, he hurriedly took his leave and went back to Ramón's house, this time cursing even more volubly. Decidedly, things were not going well in his attempt to ingratiate himself at the Double H Ranch.

That same afternoon, Francisco López saddled the mustang that Miguel Sandarbal had reserved for his use and went for a long ride beyond the Frio River and southward toward the Mexican border. He wanted time to think out a new stratagem to use until he had finally learned the elusive secret. Thus far, silver had not been mentioned by anyone in the household with whom he had had contact.

Shortly after he had ridden off, John Cooper went to Ramón's house and knocked on the door. Miguel had just told him of López's indiscretion with the *criada*, and as far as John Cooper was concerned, that was the last straw.

Mercedes Santoriaga opened the door and smilingly welcomed him. "If your husband isn't busy," John Cooper said, "might I have a few words with him in private?"

"But of course, Señor Baines." She hesitated, then asked, "Is anything wrong?"

"Oh, no, but it's something I'd rather talk over with him if you've no objection, Señora Santoriaga."

"I'll call him. He was out with the horses earlier, and he lay down for a little *siesta*. Just a minute, please." She went to the back of the house and called, "Ramón, wake up, *mi corazón!* It's Señor Baines; he wants to see you."

Ramón yawned and sat up, rubbing his knuckles over his eyes. "*¿Qué pasa*, Mercedes? Let him come in here; I'm awake now, *gracias*."

She went back to tell him that her husband would see him, and John Cooper thanked her. Somewhat concerned, Mercedes went into the living room with her children, while the tall American entered the bedroom and closed the door, then sat on the edge of Ramón's bed. "I didn't mean to disturb you—I'm sorry," he began.

"It's perfectly all right, Señor Baines. Is there anything wrong?"

"I don't want to offend you," John Cooper said hesitantly. "But this friend of yours, Francisco López, is not particularly liked here. There's something suspicious about him. I can't quite put my finger on it, but there's something that tells me that he's not trustworthy—that he's not always telling the truth."

"I understand what you're saying. It is true that we served in the same regiment, and we're friends on that basis, but he is not my dearest friend. And I would want to do nothing that would endanger the ranch—"

"It would be better if you would tell him that there really is no place for him here. I think you should be the one to tell him, as gently as you can so as not to hurt his feelings. I don't want to make an enemy. Just the same, if he should happen to be a spy from Santa Anna—"

"Do you really think that?" Ramón gasped. "He keeps saying how much he hates Santa Anna—"

"That's true, and I've heard him. But he says it a little too often for my liking. And then he's much too forward with the women on the ranch. The *criadas* aren't the only ones he's been trying to strike up a friendship with. He's been around Catarina and given her his flowery little speeches about how beautiful she is."

"I understand you, Señor Baines. I shall tell him this evening at supper."

"Even assuming he might be a spy, I don't think he's learned anything important so far, except how strong we are, how united and ready for any kind of attack. And you've certainly taught the *trabajadores* how to defend themselves in case we ever are attacked," John Cooper declared. Satisfied, he then rose and nodded. "I'm glad you feel this way. I didn't want to upset you or your wife,"

"Thank you for being so frank with me, Señor Baines."

"You'll tell him, then. Good." John Cooper reached out his hand, and the handsome former colonel warmly shook it. "But I must just add," John Cooper said, "that the sooner he leaves, the better."

That evening at supper, which Mercedes prepared for the two men, taking a tray and leading the children back into the bedroom so that her husband and Francisco López might be alone, Ramón Santoriaga lifted the decanter of Madeira and slowly filled the Mexican's glass. "I'm afraid I have bad news for you, Francisco," he falteringly began.

López quickly looked up, frowning. "What do you wish to tell me, Ramón? You know that you won't hurt my feelings; we've known each other too long for that."

"Well, it's just this, Francisco. Señor Baines is the head of this ranch, and he told me this afternoon that he does not really feel that you should settle here and be part of our community. And so I must, against my will, ask you to make plans to go elsewhere, tomorrow, if it's convenient for you. I will see that two of our *trabajadores* provide you with an escort as far as San Antonio."

"Well, of course, I'll leave, if that's how he feels about it," the amazed López said, the blood rising to his cheeks.

"You understand, I'm merely following orders. I have a position here, now that I'm no longer attached to the Mexican Army, Francisco. John Cooper Baines is, in a sense, my superior officer. I must obey him—you, yourself a former soldier, must understand that."

"Yes, Ramón, I understand," López said, a bitter note

creeping into his voice. "It's to your credit that you act this way. I've always known you to be a sensible, reliable officer. Well then"—he reached for the goblet of wine and took a long swig before setting the goblet down again—"I'll be off this very minute, if that can be arranged. I don't want to press on your hospitality."

"Of course it can be arranged. I'll tell the men to pack supplies at once. You can be in San Antonio the day after tomorrow, and there I'm sure you will find the new life you are looking for."

"I'm grateful for your concern, and, indeed, all you have done for me, Ramón," López said snappishly. "And of course, I do not hold it against you that you must tell me such news. You are just doing your duty—as I must do mine." With that cryptic statement, López rose, went to his room to gather his few possessions, and left the house without as much as a good-bye to Mercedes or the children.

Francisco López and the two *trabajadores* followed the trail from the Double H Ranch to San Antonio. They rode in silence, López being told he could keep the mustang he had ridden at the ranch. He was fuming with impotent rage at the cavalier treatment he had received at the hands of John Cooper and Miguel Sandarbal, and he grew angrier by the minute as he thought of how his plan had backfired. As they made camp that first evening on the trail, López could stand it no longer. He would do something to pay back that accursed *gringo* and his foreman. Then he had a thought. He would go back to the ranch and take some of the valuable palominos. At least then he would gain something for all his troubles the last few weeks. As to what he would tell Santa Anna—well, he would worry about that when the time came.

Now there was the matter of what to do about the two *trabajadores* escorting him. It was clear he would have to kill them. How foolish these men had been not to have taken away his pistols.

John Cooper had told the *vaqueros* to be cautious of Lopez, but they hadn't anticipated that he was a murderer, and thus they fell victim to his plans. While his companion slept, the other *vaquero* remained awake, watching his charge. Suddenly he saw López rise from his blanket roll and walk off into the night. The *vaquero* quickly followed him a short distance, only to be knocked unconscious by the end of a pistol butt. López then strangled the man, and returned to the campsite, where he shot the sleeping *vaquero* in the head. Freeing the *trabajadores'* horses, López mounted his own mustang and galloped back to the ranch, a few hours' ride along the trail.

But when he arrived at the outskirts of the lands of the Hacienda del Halcón, he was immediately challenged by one of the sentries on night duty. *Confound it!* López thought, disgusted with himself. *I should have remembered how carefully they protect themselves here. Now I'm in for it!* But contrary to his expectations, the sentry, a young *vaquero* who had just been assigned to his shift, did not challenge him but rather recognized him as a friend.

"*Hola*, Señor López," the young man said cheerfully. "You certainly are out late this evening."

The spy concealed his amazement at the *vaquero's* friendliness. "Yes, yes, I am," López replied warily. "But it is a very warm evening, and I felt the need for fresh air."

"Yes, it is warm," the *vaquero* agreed, and stuck his finger in between his bandanna and his neck.

"Have you—ah—seen Coronel Santoriaga this evening?" López ventured, trying to find out why this sentry hadn't summoned the other guards and apprehended him, the man who had been asked to leave the ranch in disgrace.

"No, I have not, Señor López. The truth is, I reported late for duty, having overslept, and rushed right out to my post, without first checking with the *coronel*. But you won't tell him," the young man pleaded, suddenly remembering that he was talking to someone who was supposedly a friend of his commanding officer.

So the young guard had not learned that Francisco López had been sent from the ranch in disgrace. This was a lucky night for Santa Anna's spy! "No, no, of course I won't say anything," López said with a gleeful smile. "Now you go back to your post, and I will return to the ranch. This riding has tired me."

"Yes, yes, I'll do that. Thank you, Señor López; thank you."

After this, there was nothing to stop López from riding up to the palomino barn. It was late; no one was abroad; so he left his mustang tied to a tree and stealthily approached the barn. There was no moon this evening, and there were storm clouds in the sky. He walked slowly, cautiously, making his way toward the stable in which John Cooper quartered his magnificent horses. He was at the back of the barn when he heard voices, and flattened himself against the wall to obliterate himself.

It was John Cooper, Miguel Sandarbal, and Don Diego, who had apparently come outside to enjoy the fresh air. They were talking softly, and López was some distance away, but he could make out their words, and he quickly realized that they were talking about him.

"That Señor López is well gone," Miguel Sandarbal said. "As you know, I did not like him from the start."

"I must admit I was somewhat taken with him at first," Don Diego said, "but now I see you were very wise, *mi hijo*, to send him away."

"Yes," John Cooper responded, "I'm glad I did, and now I can rest more easily. Which brings me to a subject I've been wanting to discuss with you both for some time. I have a plan that I've been mulling in my mind, a plan to bring back the silver from the hidden mine."

Francisco López caught his breath and strained his ears to listen. His heart was pounding wildly. What a fortuitous circumstance it was, and it could not have been better had he arranged it himself! He waited, his mind alert, intending to burn every word into his brain in letters of fire.

"It's asking too much of the Jicarilla to keep watching over all that silver, and yet I'll need their help to transport it back here." John Cooper turned to Miguel. "What we'll need are wagons. Can your *trabajadores* make strong wagons with false bottoms?"

"*Sí, seguramente, mi amigo.*"

"Good. I plan to ride to the stronghold to consult with Kinotatay. We'll bring the silver back here, with an escort of his braves. They can load it on travois and hide it with brush, or bags of maize and such. Then we'll keep it here in one of the stables until we go to New Orleans in the wagons."

"It sounds like an excellent idea, *amigo*," Miguel agreed. And Don Diego nodded. "Your plan to have the Indians escort it back here to the ranch sounds very sensible, John Cooper. No one would suspect that a large band of Indians would be doing anything more than hunting buffalo, or perhaps looking for a new stronghold."

"Exactly," John Cooper said, chuckling. "Then, when Miguel has the wagons ready, we can hide the silver in the wagons, and we can go to New Orleans on the next cattle drive. That may not be till next spring. Also, you remember that you and I, Don Diego, decided to purchase a bell for the new church, and when I was last in New Orleans, my factor Fabien Mallard told me that it had been ordered from Belgium. I wouldn't be surprised if it's there already, and we could bring it back on our return after the drive."

"I'll have the men start building the wagons at once, *mi amigo*," Miguel volunteered. "How many do you think you will need?"

"Several more than would be used to transport the silver," John Cooper suggested. "They could be used as decoys. If, for example, anyone should attack us and manage to divert one of the wagons, it could well be a wagon in which there is no silver."

"*Bueno*, that is very good thinking, *mi amigo*," Miguel agreed.

"To the best of my memory, there should still be about sixty or so large ingots of pure silver," John Cooper pensively declared.

From his place of hiding behind the barn, Francisco López almost emitted a startled gasp, and crossed himself. *Madre de Dios*, it was indeed a fortune! With such treasure, Santa Anna could control all Mexico! And then into his crafty mind there leaped the sly thought of how he might be and daring in coming to this ranch as a spy and learning since Santa Anna need not know the exact number of ingots. After all, did he not deserve a reward for his own courage and daring in coming to this ranch as a spy and learning what he had learned? He was sweating now with excitement.

"I'll leave for the stronghold at once," he heard John Cooper say. "I should be there in two weeks at the most. It will take the Jicarilla some weeks to construct the travois and to make plans for the army of the escort. Then figure that by the end of July or early August, we should be back. It will be up to Ramón and to you, too, Miguel, to defend the ranch while I'm gone. And of course, by then, I assuredly hope that Carlos will have returned."

"I hope things are going well for him in Taos," Don Diego anxiously put in. "Perhaps by now the good Teresa de Rojado has finally accepted him."

"Nothing would please me more than to see him married to that lovely young woman," John Cooper soberly averred. "Well, then, it's settled. And it's wisest for all of us to keep this to ourselves, and maybe a few trusted *trabajadores*. I don't think we should let the women know what we're going to bring back. I don't want them to think that there's going to be any danger—and I pray to God there'll be none."

"Do you think that Santa Anna still believes there is treasure that you have found, my son?" Don Diego worriedly demanded.

"He may guess, but I don't think he'll be able to do much about it. If what we've heard is true, that Santa Anna is back in Veracruz and settling down in his new marriage, he'll have other things to concern him. But it's getting late. I think we should be getting back to our houses."

As the men walked off in the darkness, Francisco López closed his eyes and leaned his forehead against the wall of the stable. He was trembling so violently that he thought he would faint. His mind reeled with the knowledge that he had just learned by chance. It was even better than he had hoped. An ingot of silver would be worth, say, between five and ten thousand *pesos*. Sixty bars—it was a colossal treasure, and the man who appropriated it would be wealthy beyond his wildest dreams, able to buy the power he needed. Over the past several years, Santa Anna had pursued the Teniente de Escobar, to no avail. And now, quite by chance, since he coveted the *gringo*'s palominos, he had been made privy to such incredible news as would change the fate of an entire nation!

He hid himself in the darkness, straining his ears for the sounds of their receding footsteps, and waited awhile longer after he had heard them go back into their respective houses. He must ride to Nuevo Laredo at once and have Aguarez go on by the fastest horse to Monreal, who would take the message to Santa Anna. As many soldiers as Santa Anna could spare, mounted and armed, must ride at once to the border, where he would meet them. Since the *gringo* had spoken of the Jicarilla, Lopez gathered that the stronghold was in Nuevo México. From there they would bring back the treasure. Though he had not yet learned exactly where the mine was located, that was of no consequence. With ample provisions, the soldiers would wait along the trail between Texas and New Mexico. They would make a camouflaged camp, and await the coming of the Indians with their travois and the silver. Then he would exterminate the accursed *indios*, yes, and the *gringo*, too, and he would see to it in the melee that at least one of the ingots found its way into his own saddlebag.

He decided to forego his original plans to steal some of the palominos. The information he had now was a much greater prize than any horses. Also, if the horses were found missing, suspicion would turn on him, all the more so after the two *trabajadores* were found dead along the trail to San Antonio. No, better just to ride the mustang until it collapsed of exhaustion. Going back to where he had tied it, López mounted the already weary horse and, to the surprise of the young sentry who had spotted him earlier, galloped away from the ranch, heading for the Rio Grande.

Thirteen

Simon Brown took out a red bandanna and mopped his sweating forehead, reining in his black gelding on the west bank of the Sabine River. The river was low this time of year, and he had found an especially fordable place for the settlers' wagons. All the same, it had taken them nearly the whole day to bring the wagons they had purchased in Natchez across the river. Many of these would-be inhabitants of a new, untrammeled land did not know what it was to work a plot of ground by the sweat of one's brow, to see the shoots of new plants edging above the gritty soil, and to protect those plants against the elements until they became the crops which could be harvested. They looked upon Eugene Fair's settlement across the Brazos as a land of milk and honey, as a new Eden. But Simon Brown knew the truth, and he was not certain that all of his sixty-five charges—men, women, and children—could realistically accept it. Already there were signs that the Mexican government had become somewhat weary of Stephen Austin's requests for the enlargement of his original contract: policing, provisions for schools and even hospitals, communication between local Mexican governments and the communal spokesmen who would be nominated once this party of settlers reached the new town. Idealism was good, Simon thought, but practical realism was better.

He had reason to know this from his own background. He was twenty-six, nearly six feet tall, stocky of build. He was the younger son of a New York City importer, living in virtual luxury, as compared with the arduous life on a frontier. His older brother, Daniel, had been the favored son, and he had felt himself to be little more than a parasite. New York was squalid, crowded, dirty; and the winters were miserable, the summers sticky and depressing.

After he had finished his schooling at a private academy on the Hudson and had worked for a few years as a clerk in his father's importing business, Simon Brown had been summoned to his father's study. This had been eighteen months ago. Simon was summarily told that his father was arranging a marriage between him and Julia Fowler, the spinster daughter and only child of a hotelkeeper. Julia was four years older than Simon and on the verge of dowdiness. To be sure, she was extremely rich and would bring him a fine dowry. But since Simon was suspicious of his father's motives—wanting to acquire Julia's father's hotel to add to his own wealth— he rebelled against this matchmaking.

In the New York newspaper, he read of the gradual expansion of the Southwest, of the heroic enterprise of Moses and Stephen Austin. He had also read what books he could find on the history of his young country, and understood perhaps better than most the germination of conflict between the new United States and the newly independent Republic of Mexico.

And so, the night after his father had sponsored a lavish party to which Julia Fowler had been invited with her parents, Simon had written his parents a note, taking leave of them. He had gone to a hostler's stable, bought a sturdy horse, saddled it, taken along provisions, and started out to see what he could of his own country. He had gone to Ohio, where he had worked for two weeks as a farmhand and heard more talk of Texas and the Southwest. And by stages, working here and there to acquaint himself with the burgeoning Midwest, he had at last made his way to St. Louis and been interviewed by Stephen Austin himself and then Eugene Fair.

It was his sincerity as well as his physical stamina that had persuaded Eugene Fair to hire him as a guide for this group of settlers who would go to the new town across the Brazos, some two hundred miles from the Double H Ranch. Simon Brown had been given a chit that enabled him to outfit himself, to purchase a new horse and supplies, and to have some folding money for the journey. And Fair had told him, "If you get them there safely and settle them, there'll be a bonus of two hundred dollars and more work for you. I've taken a liking to you. You're straightforward, honest, and you've got brawn as well as brains. It's true you don't know much about the trail, although you'll learn quickly enough. But you've got the guts, I think, to rectify any mistakes you make."

Before he had started out with this group of sixty-five settlers, Simon had spent about a month talking to traders and to scouts, who had taken the trail to Santa Fe past Taos. They had gone over Raton Pass and knew the hardships of severe winters and blistering summers, and they had been confronted by hostile bands of Indians and managed to survive such encounters. And thus, when he had boarded the steamer in Franklin, Missouri, to take his charges to Natchez, he had been as confident and trained a guide as could be found between St. Louis and Santa Fe.

He had appointed six of the men who had come along on the paddle-wheeler from Franklin to Natchez as a kind of tribunal who would settle any problems these travelers were certain to encounter on their trip. So far as he knew, and so far as Eugene Fair had told him, there was no established law in Texas: it was a matter of instinct and determination.

Fair had given him a map which showed creeks, rivers, and water holes along the trail. Simon had really wanted to be a surveyor, if the truth be known; maps fascinated him, but the possibility of finding a new trail or, better still, a new water hole or campsite fascinated him more.

Eugene Fair had indeed told Simon to act as a surveyor, to make his own maps, rough as they might be, so that other settlers henceforth could travel from Franklin to Natchez and then onto the settlement. Simon had taken to this task with great enthusiasm. He had remembered that George Washington himself, the first President of the new, budding country, had been a surveyor. And he had read that President Monroe, before giving up his seat in the White House to John Quincy Adams, had appointed a commission to draw up a survey of the newly opened Santa Fe Trail. Thus, before the paddleboat left Franklin, Simon spent several hours talking to some of the traders like Ernest Henson and Matthew Robisard, who were bound for Santa Fe.

This was a land of freedom. It was good to be alive and young in such a time. But at the same time, Simon Brown knew that to stay alive, one had to be alert and keep one's musket primed and ready, just in case someone decided he wanted your scalp. Eugene Fair had spent an hour with Simon before hiring him and had said to him, "You look sturdy, the sort of man who can defend himself in a rough-and-tumble fight. But what if an Indian wants to send an arrow into your back, or some Mexican soldier who hates *gringos* decides to take a potshot at you? What do you do then, Brown?" He had looked at Fair, squinted down at the floor, and then said, "I develop eyes in the back of my head, and I don't walk guard at night, unless I've got me a good knife and a pistol or musket that shoots straight." And that had been the right answer.

Eugene Fair had told him that Stephen Austin's dream was to have not only a free and independent Texas, but also a group of armed, able men who would one day be known as Texas Rangers. They would patrol the vast territory of this newest frontier, and see to it that murderers and thieves and smugglers didn't sneak into the settlements. The contract with the Mexican government made it plain that Austin and his *empresarios* were to screen the families who applied, to eliminate any possible troublemakers. But you couldn't always be sure because someone could come along on his uppers and tell you a hard-luck story, and you'd take a chance on him, only to find out that he was wanted for murder back in Kansas or Ohio or Tennessee.

Actually, it would be ten years before Stephen Austin's policing project—the Texas Rangers—would become part of America's annals; but even now, Fair was aware of the need for vigilance and bravery on the Texas frontier. Thus it was necessary for Simon Brown to spend a week with some of the old trappers and *voyageurs,* who had gotten their start in Canada and the Far Northwest, surviving everything from grizzly bears to scalping parties. He'd learned to handle a musket till he could reload it in fifty seconds, and he'd practiced target shooting with a Lancaster rifle, brought all the way to Eugene Fair by an old Pennsylvania Dutchman who had fought against the Iroquois and managed to keep his scalp. And at the end of the week, he'd been able to knock off a pinecone at a hundred yards with a Lancaster.

So far, the journey had been uneventful. They had purchased their wagons, horses, work animals, and supplies after leaving the paddle-wheeler at Natchez, crossed over by land to Natchitoches, and now they were just over the Sabine River heading for Nacogdoches. There hadn't been any trouble with Indians or outlaws, but there had been trouble enough among some of the settlers themselves. Simon Brown had already learned that he was expected to be more than just a guide; he had to be a peacemaker, a teacher, and practically a father confessor to a lot of bewildered, impatient people, some of whom would have done better to stay home back East and give up the impossible dream of carving out a new settlement on a new frontier.

Eugene Fair had told Simon that he was likely to find troublemakers in every wagon train he would guide, and that often, especially if the guide was experienced, he could recognize them even before they started out. He had already anticipated who was going to pose problems along the trail. One of them was this hard-featured, nearly bald William Mayberry, who drove one of the biggest wagons to which two of the sturdiest horses of the entire train were harnessed. What he didn't like about the man was the way Mayberry treated his wife, who looked half his age. According to gossipy old Mrs. Hornsteder, whose stolid, white-haired

Pennsylvania Dutch husband drove the wagon just behind the Mayberrys', young Mrs. Mayberry was about four months pregnant. And she didn't look the way a young wife should when she was going to give her husband their first child, or at least that was what Mrs. Hornsteder had emphatically declared.

Simon told himself that he was being unfair in his attitude toward William Mayberry just because the man was always asking questions and trying to curry favor. For example, last night, he wanted to move his wagon closest to the creek so that his wife could fetch him water in a pan for his morning shave. Simon had pointed out that the wagons traveled in the exact order in which their owners had made application to Eugene Fair, and to show Mayberry favoritism would be breaking the rules. Mayberry had got red in the face and started shouting and cursing that he was richer than anybody else and could pay his way and, besides, what the devil difference did it make if one wagon was closer to the creek than anybody else's? Simon just turned his back and walked off and hoped that he had handled it right.

Young Mrs. Mayberry had peered out at him while her husband had been giving him the dickens, and he'd caught a good look at her. That hadn't helped his feelings any at all. With her pretty, curly black hair and her sweet, heart-shaped face and dark blue eyes, she reminded him of a girl by the name of Sally Kalchen. They'd sort of been promised to each other about five years ago, and then Sally had up and jilted him and gone off with a Massachusetts shipbuilder. At the time it had just about broken his heart. He knew one thing: if he were married to a girl like Naomi Mayberry, he wouldn't be shouting at her and making her cringe away when they sat together during the day driving the horses. And another thing, if she were having his child, he wouldn't make her take the reins and manage those two big geldings, either.

There was another family he wasn't too fond of, but for a different reason. That was the Stiltons. Now the man, David Stilton, with his fancy mustache, was a pretty decent sort of fellow, considering he was as green as they came when it involved handling a team of oxen and keeping in line in the train. But at least he asked questions about what he was supposed to do and did his best to do things right. But then there was his wife, that tall, sharp-featured woman who

bossed him around as if he were her slave. And he'd caught
sight of a pretty, red-haired girl riding in the back, who, when
they stopped to make camp and to prepare meals, did all the
work.

Two nights ago, before they'd started to ford the Sabine,
he'd walked around the camp to make sure that everything
was secure for the evening and had come across this young
red-haired girl hunkering down to tend the fire under the
cooking pot. Then Mrs. Stilton had come out and given her
orders as if she were talking to a mule driver, and it was
plain as the nose on your face that she didn't think much of
this girl she called Nancy, the way she was scolding her
about how lazy and shiftless she was. And then, just as he
was going off to the next wagon, Nancy had been trying to
ladle some stew onto a tin plate and dropped it, and Mrs.
Stilton had really lit into the girl: "You can just go without
supper for that, you sly little bitch! My husband ought to
have left you in a crib at Natchez, the way I told him to. I
know your type; you'll be making eyes at all the unmarried
men in the train, and probably the married ones to boot.
Now wash that plate off good and then just hand me my supper, and then you can give my husband his—and don't you
go lollygagging around him doing it, either, or I'll thrash you
raw, you hear me?" The girl had started to cry a little and
stammered, "Yes'm." Simon tried to be a peacemaker by saying, "Come on, Mrs. Stilton, accidents will happen, and I'm
sure she didn't do it on purpose. Anyhow, I wouldn't want to
see a nice girl go without supper. If you don't have enough,
I'll be glad to share mine with her."

Cora Stilton had sniffed and then uttered a nasty little
laugh and said, "I sort of figured something like that would
happen. All right, Nancy, if you want to eat, you'd best go
off with Mr. Brown and share his vittles. Just be sure you
don't share his blanket, or we'll leave you out here for the Injuns. Like as not they'd fancy a slut like you!"

Then, of course, his face had turned red, and he'd
wished he'd never interfered, because he'd only gotten the
poor girl into more trouble. She was a bound girl, old Mrs.
Hornsteder had informed him—it seemed that she knew everything about her neighbors already, and the wagon train
wasn't halfway there yet. He thought to himself that if he
were David Stilton, he'd much rather be wed to the bound

girl than to that bony shrew who wore the wedding ring. For all he could tell, the poor little thing hadn't given anyone the least trouble and wasn't likely to, not with all the threats she was getting from Mrs. Stilton.

Matthew Robisard looked hardly a day older at thirty-seven than he had a dozen years ago, when he and stocky, black-haired Ernest Henson had come to New Mexico from St. Louis in the ambitious hope of trading in the Taos fair. Trading had been illegal in those days, and the two Missourians had been arrested and forced to stand trial before the governor on the grounds that they were military spies of the *gringos*. It had been Don Diego de Escobar who had saved them, by virtually defying the then Governor Manrique.

Both men were now prosperous, happily married, and with growing children. Ernest Henson, at thirty-nine, had lost some of his weight in making the arduous journey from St. Louis to New Orleans twice within the last two years and once to San Antonio to bring commissioned trade goods to a wealthy *hacendado*, who owned a ranch just outside the thriving town. With them now on the trail as they headed for New Mexico, rode a grizzled, thickly bearded, almost illiterate but intensely colorful prospector, Jeremy Gaige. Gaige was almost sixty and had run away from an Albany orphanage when he was a teenager and roamed through many a wilderness in his quest for gold or silver. He had lived with several Indian tribes and could speak some Pawnee, Sioux, Comanche, and Apache, as well as the dialects of a few other tribes, though he had had little schooling. Last year, when Ernest Henson had made his journey to San Antonio, he had found Gaige lying unconscious along a hilly trail not far from the Brazos. Renegades had taken his mule, his provisions, his pickax, heavy pan, and the other tools of his prospecting trade, clubbed him into insensibility, and left him for dead.

The affable Missourian had nursed him, thanks to the help of a friendly Tonkawa scout with whom Henson had struck up a friendship some years before. Pathetically grateful, the old prospector had insisted upon attaching himself to Henson's crew, and since he had turned out to be an excellent cook and, what was even more entertaining on a long dreary night, a marvelous storyteller, Henson had good-naturedly engaged him for wages and keep and was taking him along to Taos this late spring.

Over these long years, Gaige had trudged over the entire Midwest and as far northwest as the Wyoming country. At times, his pathetically eager quest for gold or silver had been gratified by an occasional small strike, which provided him with enough money to buy provisions, blankets, and sometimes a mule. Even now, nodding his head so emphatically that his beard seemed to wave like a semaphore, he was garrulously assuring Ernest Henson that there was certain to be some hidden mine, some untapped lode of gold or silver along the trail to Taos, just waiting to be found.

This evening, as they made camp, he industriously helped prepare the evening meal for the traders. As he brought Henson a plate of stew and biscuits, he squatted down with his own plate and shrewdly remarked, "You know, Mr. Henson, if I only had a mind to, I'd look for the Spaniards—they knew where all the treasure was. I remember a woman in the orphanage back in Albany who was sayin' that before the Spanish had their—what did she call it, Armaddy, or somepin' like that?—they would find gold 'n silver in what she said was the Spanish Main. But I bet when they came to this country, they found lots 'n hid it away. Now you know, I'd just like to meet a real Spaniard because I'll bet he could point out where there's lots of that treasure hidden along the Rio Grande. You mark what I'm tellin' you, Mr. Henson!"

Henson chuckled as he clapped the old man on the back. "You know, Jeremy, when we get back from Taos, I'm going to pay my respects to a real *hidalgo*, yessirree, a real Spaniard by the name of Don Diego de Escobar. You and he ought to get along just fine. Why, he came all the way from Madrid and he talked to the king and everything."

"Do tell!" Old Jeremy Gaige uttered an incredulous whistle and shook his head till his beard bobbed in the air again. "I'd sure like to meet up with that Don Diego, whatever his name is, Mr. Henson. I sure would appreciate your takin' me so's I can meet him."

"When we've finished our business in Taos, Jeremy, Matt and I are going to head back to the Texas ranch where he's living now. He's got a son-in-law, one of the bravest men I've ever met in all my life. You know, Jeremy, he started from scratch just about the way you did—except that his family was massacred by renegades and he was all by himself and just had a big Irish wolfhound. He lived with Indian tribes, too—the Ayuhwa, the Skidi Pawnee, the Dakota Sioux, and finally the Jicarilla Apache. He's a crack shot, and what's more, he helped out Matt and me when we first came to New Mexico, when it was really dangerous for us to be there."

"Golly, I sure would like to meet that one. Where's he from?"

"Came from Illinois, old Shawneetown by the Ohio."

"Land's sakes, Mr. Henson, I was through there—let's see now, must have been nigh on to forty years ago. 'Course that was a long time before this fellow you're tellin' me about was born, that's for certain. My, my, that sure reminds me of the days when there was plenty of deer comin' out of those salt licks there. I lived off one of those deer for a whole week durin' a bad winter, when I was out prospectin'."

"Well, you'll meet him, too, Jeremy. Now how about some more of that good, strong coffee of yours? Tell you what, I'll give you a good cigar out of a box I picked up in New Orleans that came in from Havana, if you'll tell Matt and me some more of your prospecting stories."

"Now that's a fair bargain, Mr. Henson, 'n I thank you kindly. I'll get your coffee in just a jiffy."

Fourteen

Carlos de Escobar went back to the de Pladero *hacienda* extremely out of sorts, and as much angry with himself as with the rival whom he had seen fencing with Teresa de Rojado. He told himself that he was acting like a schoolboy, and that if he showed pique because she had other suitors, she would be sure to brand him as egotistic. No, if it came down to a contest between himself and this rival *caballero,* it could not be a primitive duel. Besides, a woman who constantly demanded that her suitors pit themselves against one another to win her favors would be shallow and incapable of love. And she was not that sort of woman, of that he was certain.

Nonetheless, since Don Sancho told him that the Taos fair had been advanced a month, this gave him a convenient justification for prolonging his stay with these gracious people who were friends of his beloved father. And in that time, if he utilized it properly, he meant to show Teresa that his devotion was long-lasting, not merely a superficial show of romantic courtship, and that he wanted exactly what she wanted: a life that would be shared. That kind of coalescence would outlast infatuation and mere physical desire.

So this evening, at the supper table, he forced himself to be convivial and gracious almost to a fault, so that neither Don Sancho nor Doña Elena, and still less Tomás and Conchita, might guess the frustration and distress that surged through him.

He might indeed have gotten through the evening without mentioning Teresa at all, save that Doña Elena, with that inevitable feminine curiosity, smiled at him and teasingly remarked, "Well, Carlos, how did it go this afternoon with Teresa?"

"Oh, quite well. As it chanced, she had a prior engagement, so I promised that I'd see her tomorrow."

He had disengaged himself easily from the trap, but Doña Elena pressed on: "Did she seem happy to see you, Carlos?"

It was Don Sancho who hammered his fist on the table and exclaimed in a loud voice, "*Mujer,* the Inquisition does not exist in Taos! Let Carlos pursue his happiness as he thinks best, and I am sure that when he has achieved his heart's desire, he will tell you all you wish to know."

Carlos could not help sending Don Sancho a covertly grateful glance, at the same time amused by Doña Elena's show of contrition.

After supper, Carlos went for a stroll with Tomás, with whom he felt he could be much more direct than with either Doña Elena or Don Sancho. "Tell me the truth, Tomás," he urged, "is your father really seriously ill? What did the *médico* really say?"

Tomás stopped, kicked at the ground with his booted toe, and uttered a sigh. Finally, he declared, "I know it has to do with his lungs. And I have seen myself that my father sometimes has trouble breathing and that he tires easily."

"I think I know why he has not come to join us in Texas all this time, Tomás. He believes that justice must be upheld, especially for the *indios*, and he is afraid that if he leaves, someone who does not have their welfare at heart may become all powerful and send them back into a greater poverty and despair than they have known."

"You are right, Carlos. As for myself, you know that I do not have any great concern for politics, and I am perfectly happy with Conchita and my children, working with the sheep and being friends with the *trabajadores*. There are those who would say that I do not have the brains to do anything better, but I say that until I met Conchita, and until my father made me *capataz*, I know I was a milksop. That is why, when your family lived in Taos, your sister never had the slightest interest in me." He turned to give Carlos an almost boyish smile. "And it's just as well. Conchita thinks that I am wonderful, whereas Catarina would never think that in a thousand years. It flatters me; and because Conchita loves me so, I work even harder, and try to be the man she deserves."

"Do not talk yourself down like that, *amigo*," Carlos gruffly retorted as he put an arm around his friend's shoulders. "You have been a joy to your father. I can see it in his eyes whenever he looks at you and Conchita and the children. And your mother loves Conchita now, and that is a good thing. But tell me this, Tomás, if after the fair I am able to persuade the Señora de Rojado to marry me and come with me to Texas, would you and your family and perhaps also your father and mother come back with us all?"

"I have thought about that myself, Carlos, and I don't know the answer. I have heard that Texas has much more fertile grazing land for the sheep as well as for the cattle which your *cuñado*, John Cooper, raises there. Yes, I know that Conchita would be happy with me wherever I took her, and for the sake of my father's health, I hope that he will see the wisdom of what the *médico* has told him—that he must not occupy himself so intensely with affairs of state, and take more time to enjoy life. But my father is a conscientious man; he was born that way, and he will die that way, and he may insist on remaining here. Yet I pray the good God it will work out as you hope—for you and the Señora de Rojado, too—she is a beautiful woman, and I am sure she likes you very much."

"That's all very well, but this is only the fourth time in about two years that I have come to Taos to see her. And meanwhile, there are other men who live here and who see her every day—I confess it worries me, Tomás."

"You must go to her and tell her. She will know that you are sincere, as everyone does, Carlos. You do not need to take an example from anyone; you are brave and courageous. But consider how I was afraid almost of my own shadow until the day I saw Conchita being touched by that monster, our former *capataz*, José Ramirez, and then I felt no fear of him because I loved her. But you do not have a Ramirez to overcome."

Carlos responded somewhat bitterly. "No, but I do have one particular rival who appears to occupy her thoughts the most, since I last came here."

"Never fear," Tomás earnestly responded. "I am sure he cannot offer her what you can—I know of no man who could."

"I thank you for your confidence, Tomás. I feel greatly heartened. Yes, tomorrow, I shall visit her and learn what my chances are. And if they are slim, I shall stay here until I convince her that I could make her happier than any other man in Taos."

With that determination, Carlos de Escobar saddled Dolor and rode out toward Teresa de Rojado's *hacienda* shortly before noon of the next day. Tying the mustang to a tethering post near the house, he knocked at the door and was admitted by the Christianized Pueblo Indian majordomo, Novarra, a tall, impassive man in his early forties.

"Good day to you, Señor de Escobar," the majordomo gravely welcomed him, inclining his head in a token of respect. "It has been many moons since you last returned to Taos."

"Yes, that's true, Novarra. Yet I hope that I shall be welcome now. Is your mistress at home?"

"No, Señor de Escobar, she is out riding with the Señor Cabeza," was the answer. Carlos tightened his lips, then shrugged: "I wish to see her. I returned the other day from the ranch in Texas, and I shall stay with my friends, the de Pladeros, until the end of the fair next month."

"She should be back for the *almuerzo*. I am sure she would be happy to see you, Señor de Escobar, if you wish to wait."

"Yes, I think I shall do that. I do not mean to pry information from you, Novarra; that would be unworthy. But I wonder if this Señor Cabeza is a good man; if, for instance, he feels compassion toward the *indios*."

"There I can answer truthfully—he does not. We can recognize those who regard us as people of dignity and history, and those who despise us because our skins are not white. I will say no more."

"You have told me enough already. You have given me heart, Novarra. I mean to stay here until I can convince your mistress that I could make her happy for the rest of her days. And before *El Señor Dios* Himself, I swear here and now that this alone is in my heart. I thank you, Novarra. I shall wait until she returns."

He smiled cordially at the majordomo and then went outside and began to walk about the estate. He could see the *trabajadores* whom she had hired to tend the garden and the little plot of fruit and vegetables grown at the back of the *hacienda*. He went over to the stable because he knew of her love for horses and heard that she had acquired some particularly fine animals.

He spent a quarter of an hour with the horses, talking to them, patting them, and appraising them. Undoubtedly she had a superb eye for horseflesh, and he thought that if he could ever induce her to come to Texas with him, she would love John Cooper's palominos and also his own. As he emerged from the stable, he saw her riding side by side with the handsome *hacendado*, and he stiffened, drawing himself up and standing with his arms at his sides.

At the sight of her, the thick chignon of her lustrous hair neatly arranged under the trim little hat to protect her from the sun, in her riding costume, seated with elegant poise on her mare, he thought that she was lovelier than he had remembered. He moved forward a few steps and exclaimed, "Señora de Rojado, I bring you greetings from my father and Doña Inez."

"It's good to see you again, Carlos," she smilingly answered, genuinely pleased to see the young Spaniard again. She dismounted and led her mare toward the stable, where a young Indian boy no more than sixteen hurried out to take the reins from her. Alejandro Cabeza sat stiffly in his saddle, staring coldly at Carlos, a supercilious little sneer on his lips. Finally, he, too, dismounted and, with a contemptuous sort of gesture, tossed the reins toward the young stableboy. He stood with his booted feet planted widely apart and a hand on his hip, as if to question Carlos's right to be there.

"*Buenos días*, Señor Cabeza," Carlos forced himself to say pleasantly.

"And to you, señor. You know my name?"

"But of a certainty," Carlos replied, not without a touch of sarcasm. "The majordomo here was kind enough to acquaint me with you."

Teresa de Rojado stood back, watching the two men who confronted each other like angry cocks in a barnyard fight, each sizing up the other and each ready to attack. She frowned and turned to Carlos: "Please, Carlos, Alejandro is my guest. But I should like it very much if you would join us at luncheon."

"I should be in the way, Señora de Rojado. Perhaps another time. Besides, I should like to have you to myself." Carlos could not help blurting out these words.

"I hope that I shall have something to say about that, Señor Carlos," Cabeza sneered, turning to Teresa and quickly taking her hand and bringing it to his lips. "As she has told you, I am her guest. And I, for one, do not much care for the notion of sharing her company, even at *almuerzo*, with a stranger."

"The devil take you, Cabeza!" Carlos burst out, trembling with anger at seeing this garishly dressed *hacendado* adopt so proprietary an air toward the beautiful widow. "If she has given you the right to her company at all times, that is one thing. But I do not—"

"Carlos, I beg of you!" Teresa interrupted, her face crimsoning, her eyes bright with indignation. "That was unworthy of you! And certainly, both of you have no right to quarrel over me in my presence. I have given no man the right to do that yet."

"Forgive me, Teresa, but my admiration for you overcame my better judgment," the *hacendado* glibly observed. "I am all contrition. Forgive me, and I shall try my best to be amicable to this man who forgets himself before you." With this, he put his hand on his heart and bowed floridly to the young widow.

Carlos clenched his fists, fighting to master himself and to suppress the impulse to dash those fists against the sneering face of the Mexican. "I did not mean to distress you, Señora de Rojado," Carlos forced himself to say, his voice glacial as he turned to Teresa. "I apologize to both of you, then. I ask only humbly that I may have the pleasure of visiting with you when you are alone and ready to receive me."

"That is better," she said, mollified. "I will send Novarra to you at the de Pladeros."

"I thank you. I hope it will not be too long. I have much to say to you, Señora de Rojado." With this, Carlos bowed to her, gave a curt nod toward the smirking *hacendado*, and strode back to Dolor. Untying the reins, he mounted the mustang and rode back to the *hacienda* of his hosts.

Before he reached there, he had a sudden impulse to ride into Taos and to buy Teresa a present. Accordingly, wheeling Dolor's head southward, he rode toward the plaza. He tied Dolor's reins to a post near the office where Don Sancho still presided, and walked slowly along the dusty square. He looked over at the little church, and he thought of Padre Madura and of the kind old priest who had preceded him. With a sigh, he turned toward the shop of Ignazio Peramonte and decided to enter. Perhaps he would buy Teresa a pair of fine leather gloves to hold the reins of her spirited mare.

He hesitated a moment, looking up and down the square of adobe buildings. It had not changed. Taos was still sleepy and dreary. And the dust in the plaza symbolized to him the long years that had incarcerated the Indians in their village condemning them to backbreaking toil and a grudging subsistence to which the *hacendados* had consigned them generations ago. He marveled at their patience over these long years of rejection. And he thought of the valiant Indian *jefe,* Popé, who had once rallied these gentle people against tyranny and fought valiantly. But now all of that had been forgotten. Time had stood still for the pueblo. And yet, now that Mexico and Spain, once interlocking authorities whose stringent rules had given these very *hacendados* such ruthless power, had gone their separate ways and New Mexico was all but abandoned, was it possible that the *indios* would find their own strength through tribal unity and defy the corruption that must surely emerge?

He shook his head, for the philosophical ramifications that this question sent into his mind were far too deep and far too illusory for him to have any answer. Besides, the aching dismay that he had experienced when he had encountered Teresa riding with that insolent dandy of a Cabeza rankled far too much for him to think of much else.

He opened the door and went into the shop. The tall, gaunt head of *Los Penitentes* came forward and, peering at him in the semidarkness, exclaimed, "It is you, Señor de Escobar! I had heard that you were again in Taos! May the blessings of our dear Lord be with you and yours. And how are your father and Doña Inez?"

"Both are well, thank you. I must confess, señor, I do not recognize you—"

"Nor is there reason why you should," Ignazio Peramonte gently observed with a wry smile. "But the name of de Escobar is one of honor in the Holy Church, as it is with the *indios* of the village. You and your father were kind to them; you did not despise them; you did not wrong them; and your father especially strove to give them justice when he was *intendente.* For this, his name will always be remembered with prayers. And of you I have heard many good things."

"You do me too much honor, but still, I do not know your name—"

"I am Fra Peramonte. I have assumed, though I am unworthy of it, the responsibility that the martyred Padre Moraga exercised as the leader of those who work for justice in Taos."

"Wait—now I remember—was Padre Moraga not the head of *Los Penitentes?*"

"Just so, my son. And I then was one of the brothers, also the *sangrador.*"

"Then it was you who punished José Ramirez, that vile man who was *capataz* for my dear friends, the de Pladeros," Carlos wonderingly exclaimed.

"It was I, my son. Now how may I serve you?"

"I would like to purchase a pair of fine riding gloves for the Señora de Rojado. I have come to Taos to see her."

"Ah, yes, I know. We of *Los Penitentes* know much about what goes on in Taos. For instance, we know about the man who has been courting Señora de Rojado, for our brotherhood vigilantly watches Señor Cabeza. He is corrupt; he was very nearly arraigned by the *gubernador* for furnishing arms to the rebellious Toboso. He is a wastrel, and he has a concubine whom he has forced to serve him, a girl from one of the *indio* villages not far from Taos. He has a majordomo, Ernesto Rojas, who panders to all his lusts, and who persuades him that, because of his birth and station here in Taos, these things are his due."

"*Dios*, if only the Señora de Rojado knew all these things about him, she would not tolerate him around her!" Carlos indignantly expostulated. Then, with a forlorn sigh, he shook his head and added, "But I cannot tell her these things. I'm afraid she would only say that I am jealous and that I seek to blacken him in her eyes to advance my own suit."

"Do not fear, my son. God's justice will prevail, as it always does. She will learn in good time that he is not the husband for her, or for any chaste, God-fearing woman."

"I thank you for the encouragement you have given me with those words, Fra Peramonte. And I ask you to pray for me and to believe that I have only the most honorable interest in her."

"God has seen these things, Señor de Escobar. He never forgets the kindness and mercy which those who have, bestow upon those who have not. And now, I will show you a pair of my best gloves, handworked, of the finest leather, soft and supple. They will hold the reins of the Señora de Rojado's horse, and she will surely think of the one who gave them to her when she wears them as she goes riding."

The beautiful half-breed Noracia, born almost twenty-five years ago to a now dead *hacendado* and a Pueblo Indian mother, had prospered during the past two years. If she had reflected upon it, she would have given thanks for the intervention of John Cooper Baines, since through his acts of vengeance, he had made it possible for her to become wealthy and powerful beyond her wildest dreams.

At the age of twenty, she had become the mistress of the former mayor, Don Esteban de Rivarola, who had brutalized her, till she had played upon his sadistic foibles and convinced him that she could give him greater pleasure by acting as a torturer for his helpless *criadas*. Don Esteban had arranged for the murder of Padre Juan Moraga, when he had learned that he was threatened with excommunication after kidnapping a young Indian girl. John Cooper Baines, learning of the martyrdom of Padre Moraga, had shot the corrupt *hacendado* with arrows marked with the renegade Comanche sign, a fitting vengeance since Don Esteban had had his *peones* kill Padre Moraga with arrows whose markings showed the tribal signs of the pueblo in his desire to cast the blame on these innocent, peaceful *indios*.

Knowing that the merchant, Luis Saltareno, had desired her, Noracia had cunningly changed allegiance to him. She had also helped him wheedle his way into the good graces of the governor in order to replace Don Esteban as mayor. But he had been killed in a duel by John Cooper Baines, who had come to Taos to call the merchant out for having spread the word that Don Diego de Escobar, John Cooper's father-in-law, was a traitor, and for arranging with the Comanche Indians to attack the Double H Ranch. Upon Saltareno's death, Noracia had then seized her opportunity and told the man's *peones* that she would pay their wages and yet let them be free if they would work for her. And this they had done.

Thus, now she reigned as a virtual queen in the luxurious *hacienda*, with the old majordomo, Maximilian, in command of the household. Little Manuela, one of the pretty young *criadas* whom Don Esteban had often abused, had followed her to this *hacienda*, when Luis Saltareno had become her *patrón*, and now Manuela held the rank of first maid and personal confidante to the beautiful *mestiza*. Noracia was slim, her long black hair falling nearly to her hips. Her oval face and her high-set cheekbones, small insolent mouth, dainty nose, and large, wide brown eyes made her as physically desirable as any well-bred daughter of a *rico* in all Taos. She was as tall as Teresa de Rojado, with long legs and high, firm breasts, and her warmly tawny skin, which told of the mixture of her breeding, made her still more provocative.

She had been approached by several eligible *hacendados*, but she had scorned them all. She wanted for the time being, as she told Manuela, to relish the power of giving orders, rather than of having to obey them under penalty of punishment, as had happened to her while living with her two former masters. "This time, *querida*," she assured the pretty Mexican girl, "the man I choose will bow to *my* orders and please me as *I* wish, not the other way around."

Indeed, though none of the other servants knew it, to compensate for her apparent celibacy after Saltareno's death, Noracia solaced herself with her charming maid. Though Manuela had at first been horrified when she had been summoned to Noracia's bed, the *mestiza* had glibly convinced her that it was in reality no sin, since there could never be issue nor, on the other hand, would the inception of life be halted as was forbidden by the Holy Church; moreover, women were more tender in their affection for each other than any man could ever be to a woman. And since Manuela remembered only too well her whippings and violations by Don Esteban and his brutal *trabajadores*, she did not object too much and, indeed, found Noracia's amorous attentions enchantingly flattering and appeasing to her own warm-blooded nature.

Noracia had put Saltareno's appropriated wealth to excellent advantage to assure her tenure. First of all, she had come to the little church to give Padre Madura a thousand silver *pesos* for the poor, and she had meekly avowed that before he had expired in the duel with the *americano*, Luis Saltareno had tried to make his peace with God and had called out to her to see to it that a contribution was made in his name for the indigent of Taos. Thereafter she had attended mass with disciplined regularity, though it must be admitted that she did not confess her intimacies with charming young Manuela, whose compliance and silence she purchased with fine clothing and jewelry.

And since Saltareno had been a merchant, she chose several of his most dependable and literate *trabajadores* to take charge of the shop, and having perused the dead merchant's documents of sale and purchase over the years, concluded that she herself would become a merchant.

To this end, she had bought merchandise from the Pueblo Indians of the village, such as blankets, rugs, religious statues, and, from some of the skilled craftsmen, bracelets, earrings, and necklaces. She had commissioned aging Maximilian to go with four sturdy *trabajadores* into Chihuahua to buy merchandise for the shop, and had ordered silks, tapestries, and the latest fashions in clothing from Mexico City and New Orleans. To be sure, many of these articles had found their way into her own chambers, but she had been astute enough to realize the potential for profits in selling merchandise of excellent quality to the *ricos* of the area. Finally, she had seen to it that whenever she attended mass with Manuela, she dropped many silver coins into the collection plate and was often seen at the back of the little church lighting candles and making a further donation, which went to the poor.

As for the former servants of Luis Saltareno, they rejoiced in their freedom and in the wages which Noracia generously paid them. And because they felt that she was, in a sense, one of them and had overcome the adversities of her class and triumphed over the hated *ricos* who traditionally had enslaved them and their descendants almost since the first days when Taos had been built, they were loyal to a fault.

She had even sent to Santa Fe for a noted breeder of horses, and had purchased two mares, one for herself and one for Manuela. She had taken riding lessons, and encouraged the timid young *criada* also to ride—simply by telling Manuela that if she did not prove an apt pupil, there would be no more gifts of fine clothes and jewelry.

By now, thanks to her wealth and her generosity to the church and to the poor of the pueblo, she was held in high esteem in Taos. Thus, several eligible bachelors who, a few years earlier would have looked down their noses at her because of her *mestiza* origin, now courted her, sent musicians to serenade outside the *hacienda,* or had their couriers bring flowers and elegant gifts with notes begging for a rendezvous. Thus far, she had graciously declined all such invitations.

So it happened that on this day, Noracia rode into Taos by herself, leaving Manuela at home. For one thing, she wished to visit the Saltareno shop to learn when a shipment of fine wines and rich-hued taffetas was expected from New Orleans.

As she dismounted, she saw Dolor tethered outside Ignazio Peramonte's shop, and since the Saltareno shop was on the other side of the plaza, waited to see, out of curiosity, who would emerge. It was indeed a superb mustang, durable and spirited—that was obvious to her. She drew herself up haughtily, preening in her riding costume, which was in the very latest mode. To the little short-brimmed hat, which imitated the far larger *sombrero* of a *caballero,* she had added her own feminine touch of a white cockatoo feather. It had been taken from the bird she had sent to her from Mexico City, for she remembered that, as a little girl, she had a finch and then a tiny sparrow hawk. And perhaps unconsciously, it pleased her to have a bird in a cage and to be always reminded that she herself had been exactly like that when she was a concubine to Don Esteban and then to Luis Saltareno.

Carlos had purchased a pair of black leather gloves, beautifully hand-tooled, and he had persuaded Ignazio Peramonte to mark Teresa de Rojado's initials on the inner base of each glove. He emerged from the shop now and saw Noracia standing beside her mare. For an instant, so elegantly was she dressed and so beautiful did she look, he thought that it might be Teresa herself. But he quickly saw that this was not the case and greeted her with a smile and a courteous nod: *"Buenos días, señorita."*

"And to you, *caballero.* That is your mustang?"

"Yes. That is Dolor."

"But what a sad name for so spirited an animal, señor!" She laughed gaily. "Is there a reason for it?"

Carlos's face tautened. Stiffly, he rejoined, "There is, but I am not at liberty to discuss it, señorita. It is associated with an event in my life that caused me great sorrow. This faithful animal served me then as a friend when I needed him most."

"But that is most poetic. I have not seen you in Taos before, I think. I am Noracia. I occupy the *hacienda* of the former *alcalde mayor,* Luis Saltareno, peace to his memory." At this, she crossed herself.

Carlos at once remembered John Cooper's duel with Saltareno, and that his brother-in-law had told him of the woman named Noracia who took charge of the *hacienda* after her employer's death. Not mentioning that he had heard of her, Carlos politely responded, "I am Carlos de Escobar, at your service, Señorita Noracia."

"Do you live in Taos, Señor de Escobar?"

"I once did. I have come to visit my old friends, the de Pladeros. Now I live in Texas on a fine ranch, Señorita Noracia."

Noracia had eyed Carlos intently during this conversation, and she found him fascinatingly handsome. Sun-bronzed as he was, wiry and poised, there was an air of self-control and great strength to him. Here was truly an *hombre muy macho*, she told herself. "You have a wife, or certainly a *novia*, Señor de Escobar?" she boldly asked him.

"No, Señorita Noracia, I have neither. To be sure, I have hopes one day. But that is in the hands of the good God, as are our lives."

"How very true!" She gave him an affected little laugh. "If you are staying here for some time with the de Pladeros, I should like very much for you to visit me at my *hacienda*. You have only to ask anyone in town, and they will direct you to the *hacienda* of Luis Saltareno. It is mine now. And the servants he had are in my employ. But I pay them very good wages, and they are loyal to me."

"I should say they fare better with you, then, than ever they did with the former *alcalde mayor*," Carlos declared.

"You are very wise, Señor Carlos—may I call you thus—and I think we might have much in common. Will you not accept an invitation with me to have supper one evening? Or *almuerzo*, if it is more convenient?"

"I thank you for your kindness, Señorita Noracia. But I am afraid I must decline. I have no wish to offend you."

She drew herself up, her eyes flashing with sudden anger and pique at his rejection. "Perhaps you do not think that I am good enough for you, Señor Carlos?"

"Surely that isn't true! You're indeed very beautiful, Señorita Noracia. But—well, I may as well tell you, so you do not think I am trying to slight you. My wife died over two years ago, and I met someone here in Taos who herself is a widow. It is my hope to marry her if she will have me."

"Thank you for telling me." Noracia smiled graciously at him. She took a step toward him and put a hand on his wrist. "It may be that I know her. Perhaps I can do you a service—I will be frank with you, Señor Carlos. I'm a *mes-*

tiza. And the *caballeros ricos* of Taos would despise me, except that I now have *dinero* and a fine *hacienda* and *trabajadores* and *criadas* to serve me. And I have no lover, but you are the sort of man that a girl would be proud to have as her *novio*."

Carlos flushed hotly and shifted uneasily, trying to reply in a way that would not offend this candid beauty. "Assuredly, I am flattered, Señorita Noracia. But I think that I have already lost my heart—and since you have been frank with me, I shall be equally frank with you. I am here to court the Señora Teresa de Rojado."

"But I have heard of her, of course!" Noracia exclaimed. "She is a wonderful horsewoman, and she has a staff of *indio* servants. And she treats rich and poor alike with kindness and honesty—oh, yes, I admire her very much."

Carlos unbent a little, warmed by this lovely young woman's praises of the widow with whom he was in love. "It is good of you to say so. But you see, this is only the fourth time I have been to Taos in the past two years, and because I cannot court her daily, she has another suitor." With a bitter grimace, he thought of the popinjay Alejandro Cabeza.

"And who might that be? Trust me, Señor Carlos. This is the first time I have talked with you, and yet I know of your father, because both Don Esteban de Rivarola and Luis Saltareno, whose slave I was—yes, a slave to each of them, and I give thanks to the Holy Virgin that I am free of them now—both of them hated your father because he was kind and good, just as this Señora de Rojado is. Your father would not have looked down upon a woman like myself, and I see that you do not, either. I tell you honestly, and you may think me shameless, but I have had to live by my wits. My own mother told me that because she, an *india*, had had a *hacendado* as her lover, but not her husband, I would be despised. Yes, an outcast of my own people, those very people in the village whom your kind father befriended when he was *intendente*. It was she who told me to find some *rico* who would protect me. Yes, it was true that I was required to submit to such a one, and this I did to both of those vile men. But I am not a *puta* by desire."

"I believe you earnestly and with all my heart."

"You are very kind. If *El Señor Dios* had so willed it, you and I might well have become sweethearts. Even now"—this with a coy little smile as she tightened her fingers on his wrist—"if your girl should reject you, do not feel guilt or shame in coming to me. I would be good to you and for you, I know it. Because when I want a man, I will love him honestly and with all of myself, holding back nothing. And you would not be cruel to me, as those two *ricos* were."

"I swear to you, Señorita Noracia, that there is no need for you to try to lower yourself in my eyes, or to justify yourself. I am happy to see that fortune has smiled upon you. But I will tell you as honestly as you have spoken to me, I love the Señora de Rojado. I had grief for my dear wife, and I shall carry it until my death, but with the señora I think I may begin a new life, and she will be a wonderful mother to the children my dead wife gave me."

"You are a good man, Señor Carlos. May God give you the realization of all of your hopes, and long years with the Señora de Rojado. But now, tell me—you have said that she has a suitor. Who might that be?"

"I do not wish you to fight my battles for me," Carlos said kindly and, taking her hand from his wrist, kissed it as he would that of a princess.

Tears sparkled in Noracia's eyes at this display of honesty and honor. She leaned toward him and murmured, "I truly feel most sympathetic toward you, Señor Carlos. Please believe this. And I ask you for the name of this one *caballero* who seems closer to your sweetheart than you are, so that perhaps I can tell you something about him."

Carlos could not help smiling at the earnestness of this beautiful *mestiza* who had, within so short a time after first meeting him, ingeniously managed to learn so much about him. "If you must know, it is Alejandro Cabeza."

Noracia made a grimace, then hawked and spat on the dusty ground at her booted feet, exactly as a man might. "That one!" she scornfully expostulated. "All that he has in his favor is his good looks. Truly, I think you are far more handsome than he, Señor Carlos."

By now, Carlos was hugely amused at the ingenuousness she displayed toward him. "I cannot quote you a proverb, Señorita Noracia," he quipped, "but I should say rather that it is not important whether a man have good looks or not, so long as his *mujer* finds him pleasing to her and kind and loving."

"Exactly! But you see, I know more about Alejandro Cabeza than you do. He is a wastrel, that one. In his way, he would be as bad as my two *patrones*, if he had had their wealth. But he has wasted it, and his majordomo, Ernesto Rojas, has led him into costly ways of pleasure. Oh, yes, Rojas came to me some months ago and let it be known that his master would be delighted to have me spend the night with him. I sent him packing, I can tell you. If a man wants me, Señor Carlos, he must tell me so himself, not send his lackey." She drew herself up proudly, and once again Carlos was amused, but this time he strove to keep the smile from his lips, lest he offend her. "And you have every reason to expect that, Señorita Noracia," he told her.

"It is known here in Taos that the Señora de Rojado was left *mucho dinero* by her husband. And I should not be surprised if Alejandro Cabeza has his eye more on that than on her lovely face. At any rate, Señor Carlos, I am delighted to have met you. Perhaps one day we shall meet again. But remember, if you do need a friend, I am eager to be yours." Once again she put out her hand to touch his wrist, and the limpid look in her large brown eyes let him know exactly that her friendship for him would have no bounds.

Once again, he delighted her by taking her hand and kissing it, then bade her a cordial farewell.

Mounting Dolor, he tipped his *sombrero* to her and rode back to the de Pladero *hacienda*, deep in thought.

Noracia smiled to herself as, firmly holding on to the pommel of her sidesaddle, she neatly lofted herself onto her mare. "It would be very interesting," she mused aloud to herself, "if I were to take Alejandro away from the Señora de Rojado. But not to become his *criada*, never that! Instead, it would be much more interesting to make him my *sirviente*."

Five days later, to Carlos's delight, a young *indio* rode over from Teresa de Rojado's *hacienda* to ask for him, and then to convey the message that his mistress requested the pleasure of his company for a bout of foils and then supper. Carlos joyously sent back an affirmative response, and when Tomás entered the *hacienda* a few moments later for a respite of lunch with Conchita and the children, he laughingly observed, "You must have had good news, for you don't have the long face you wore yesterday, *amigo*."

"You are a very discerning man, and I can see why Conchita loves you," Carlos chuckled as he seized Tomás and shook him by the shoulders, then laughed aloud in sheer euphoria. "I shall not be present at supper this evening, and you will make my excuses—my most humble and apologetic excuses, mind you—to your beloved mother and father. The Señora de Rojado wishes to fence a little with me this afternoon, and then will have supper served to me at her *hacienda*."

"*¡Hola!*" Tomás grinned. "You need say no more. But seriously, I wish you success. And I hope that when you return this evening, you will tell us that the banns are to be spoken in Padre Madura's church."

"What I would not give for that, Tomás!" Carlos sighed. "But I'm not quite so hopeful. After all, she has seen a good deal of my rival, and not too much of me. It will take a long courtship, I'm afraid. But I am ready for it, and I do hope to convince her."

Carlos could not help admiring the lovely opponent who faced him, wearing the mask, the white blouse with the red heart, the riding breeches, and the boots. She was as agile and lithe as a man, and yet through the mask Carlos could see the sweet curve of her mouth and the luster of her eyes. But from the first engagements of the buttoned foils, he knew that she had acquired even more skill than when he had fenced the first time with her, two years ago. Indeed, he was hard pressed to keep her from scoring several hits in the very first ten minutes of their exercise together. And it was he who, saluting her with the foil swept up and pressed against the middle of his forehead, first asked for a pause to regain his breath. "You have become much more formidable in the attack, Teresa," he complimented her, "if I may still call you that?"

"Of course, Carlos. You see how I use your name as freely."

"I plan to stay here through the fair, and then I hope to persuade Don Sancho and Doña Elena to go back with me to the Double H Ranch. Perhaps Tomás and Conchita and the children will come, as well."

"I am worried about Don Sancho," Teresa confided as she removed the mask for a moment. "There are times when he has trouble breathing. You see how close we are to the mountains, and this is a strain upon the heart, and he is an old man, older than your father, he tells me."

"That's true, but surely the good God will measure out his days more generously, knowing how kind and just he has always been."

"I, too, pray that, Carlos."

"And you, Teresa? If he goes, you will have no friend here—that is to say, no one from the past who knew your father as he did. Would you still stay in Taos?" He tried to keep his voice level and casual, but it trembled all the same.

"I know what you are going to ask me, Carlos. Please do not. Yes, I am very fond of you, I will admit it. But please, let us now go back to our fencing."

"As you like. May I have just one more question?"

"Yes." She eyed him steadily.

"You have not yet pledged yourself to the Señor Cabeza?" His voice was hoarse and unsteady now.

Color flamed in her cheeks as she adjusted the mask. "I am not yet pledged to him," she finally murmured in a low voice.

"Then there is still a chance for me! So be it, Teresa! I shall be content with that—for now."

Then once again, they went *en garde*, and there was the clash of the foils under the bright summer sun, and he forgot all else, except the sheer zest of competing with this magnificent woman.

Fifteen

The traders had already begun to come into Taos for the great fair. It was the seventeenth of June, and on this very day in Massachusetts, the cornerstone of the Bunker Hill Monument was being laid, with Daniel Webster delivering an impassioned oration on the meaning of the struggle for independence against tyranny.

Many of the traders had camped at the base of the Sangre de Cristo range, so that they would have at most a day's access into Taos to set up their wagons and offer their goods to the townspeople. Matthew Robisard and Ernest Henson, along with old Jeremy Gaige, decided to pay a courtesy call on Don Sancho de Pladero, for the two Missourians knew that he had been Don Diego's good friend and had replaced the latter as judicial head of the province of Taos. As for the old prospector, he was excited at the idea of meeting a *madrileño*, since Robisard and Henson had explained Don Sancho's origin and intimated that he, too, had once been a Spanish grandee.

The two Missourians had brought with them, besides Jeremy Gaige, four apprentices in their early twenties to look after the wagons and the pack mules. So, early this afternoon, the three men rode to the de Pladero *hacienda*. In a few days, Don Sancho himself would officially open the fair, and Doña Elena insisted that he take a longer than usual *siesta* this afternoon so that he would be thoroughly rested. "You are not going to be like an old mother hen, prying into every wagon and conversing with every trader or *indio* who has come to Taos to make money, my husband," she firmly

158

declared. "I do not wish you to be a martyr. It is enough that you have stayed here longer than you should have, instead of going to Texas to be reunited with your dear friend, Don Diego. But I expect you at least to be sensible and to remember that the *médico* warned you against overly exerting yourself."

"Woman, am I never to have an end to your deciding how I shall live my life?" he stormed by way of token protest. But inwardly, he was deeply touched. Of late, the malady of his lungs seemed to have lessened, for he breathed more easily and had been able to enjoy more hours of sleep at night.

"I should rather have you call me a shrew, *mi esposo,* than be a mourner at your funeral," was her sharp retort, and he scolded her, but despite the gruff voice he used, he put his arms around her and kissed her and murmured, "*Mujer,* I am very content with you. And if *El Señor Dios* sees fit to number my days, I shall have no regrets."

Then he obediently went to take a *siesta,* much to her relief. She bustled about the *hacienda,* giving orders to the *criadas* and *trabajadores,* selecting two of the strongest young workers to accompany him to the fair and to watch over him. Two of the cook's assistants were already busy preparing food, which would be taken to the fair and offered to those in need of refreshments. Doña Elena was in her element, for if on the one hand she had amended her argumentative ways that had blighted their first years in Taos, she had now concentrated all her attentions on running the household so that Don Sancho's total creature comforts were assured.

Robisard and Henson, accompanied by Jeremy Gaige, rode into the de Pladero estate, handed the reins of their horses to two stableboys who hurried forward to take them, and then Matthew Henson jingled the little silver bell attached to the front door of the *hacienda.* The door was opened by Don Sancho's new majordomo, a genial Mexican from Durango, not quite forty years old, who had come to Taos to visit a cousin after the death of his wife and the sale of his tiny little farm. His name was Vicente Andraga, and he had already ingratiated himself with the household because of his tireless enthusiasm and his willingness to do the most menial of tasks without complaint. Don Sancho had taken a great liking to him, because Vicente had laboriously taught himself how to read and write and was very inquisitive about the history of Spain and Mexico. On many an afternoon after his *siesta*, when he was relaxing from his official duties, the elderly man would invite Vicente into his study and there, over a glass of *aguardiente*, they would converse about the days of the great Armada and the treasure galleons to and from Panama.

"Good day to you, señor," Matthew Robisard cheerfully greeted the majordomo. "May we see Don Sancho de Pladero? I think he will remember us. I am Matthew Robisard, and this is my good friend, Ernest Henson, from St. Louis. We came to Taos some years ago, when Don Diego de Escobar helped us escape a firing squad."

"Of a certainty, Señor Robisard. I will tell Don Sancho that you are here to see him. He has only just risen from his *siesta*. But a word of caution, *por favor*—he has not been too well of late, and I beg of you not to tire him. As you know, he must preside at the opening of the great fair."

"That is why we are here, señor. I promise we shan't tire him. We just want to pay our respects to him."

"If you will come this way, I will announce you, señores."

A few minutes later, Vicente ushered the three men into Don Sancho's study and, at the latter's genial order, hurried off to bring a decanter of fine French wine. After they all shook hands, with Matt introducing Jeremy Gaige to the *alcalde mayor*, Don Sancho smilingly welcomed them: "Señores, it is good to see you. I propose to drink to your health and to the success of your trading here at our great fair."

"That's kind of you, Don Sancho," Ernest Henson responded, "but you know"—this with a smiling glance at his partner—"it's been a long while since Matt and I came to Taos. And the last time, we really got ourselves into some trouble."

"How well I remember it!" Don Sancho nodded his thanks to the majordomo, and insisted on filling the glasses for his three guests. This done, he lifted his own: "I drink also to a happier understanding between Nueva España and los Estados Unidos. Oh, yes, Don Diego recounted to me in great detail the ordeals you brave men endured when you were dragged off to Santa Fe. But, as I recall, the story had a happy ending, did it not?" He lifted his glass toward Henson.

"I seem to recall that you fell in love with a charming young *criada* at Don Diego's *hacienda* and took her away with you as your wife."

"That's right, it was Carmelita, and we have four children now," Henson joyously replied. "When the fair's over, we plan to circle back to Texas and stop over at Don Diego's ranch. And we want to see John Cooper, too."

"Ah," Don Sancho answered, "I have longed to be reunited with them. But my duties here in Taos, and now of course this fair, have kept me from making that journey. And at my age, I must consider the wisdom of uprooting myself here and going that long distance. Still in all, I'll admit that I want to."

Jeremy Gaige had been listening openmouthed to this discussion, and now timidly put in, in a cracked, reedy voice, "S'cuse me, Matt, Ernie, didn't you say this fellow here, this Don Sancho, wuz a real grandee from Spain; isn't that a fact?"

"Yes, Señor Gaige, I came from Madrid many years ago," Don Sancho himself replied. "But I am only of a minor nobility. I think Señor Henson is being generous when he calls me a grandee. Now then, Don Diego was higher in the lists of Spanish nobility in the old days—but today that is all done with. Now I feel myself as much an *americano* as you or your friends do."

"You know, Don Sancho," Jeremy Gaige garrulously went on, "I've been prospectin' most of my life, and you kin tell from the color of my hair it's been a long one. I always used to think about treasure back in the days when I was a kid in an orphanage, 'n the teacher told me about the ships Spain used to send across the ocean. Them big—what wuz they called—?"

"Galleons," Matthew Robisard and Don Sancho simultaneously supplied, then looked at each other and chuckled.

"That's it, galleons!" Gaige eagerly took his cue. "I guess I've been figgerin' that maybe some of that there gold 'n silver might have been stashed away in these mountains or such—though I sure have to 'fess up that I never found much of it."

"I hardly think, Señor Gaige, that the gold and silver bullion, as well as the jewels and rare spices and other costly cargo, ever found their way so far north as los Estados Unidos," Don Sancho explained, a whimsical smile playing around his lips. "Of course, it is certainly true that when the Spanish government in the days of the old monarchy had their Nueva España appropriate this land which is called Nuevo México, they had high hopes of finding precious metals, perhaps in these very mountains, the beautiful Sangre de Cristo. Alas, thus far, we have sent wool to the Old World, but no gold or silver."

Jeremy Gaige sighed and shook his head. "That's a real pity, Don Sancho." Then, glancing at his empty goblet, he apologetically asked, "Might I have just a tech more of this drinkin' stuff? Goes down mighty fine 'n easy. Sure be obliged to you, Don Sancho."

Don Sancho laughed heartily as he came forward with the decanter and refilled the old prospector's goblet. "Do you know, Señor Gaige," he smilingly told the old man, "you are better medicine for me than the *médico* from Santa Fe could prescribe." Then, to the two Missourians, he added, "It would give my household great pleasure, and me particularly, if you, Señores Henson and Robisard, as well as your friend here, would be my guests at supper. We shall talk over old times and, if Señor Gaige wishes, about hidden treasures. But I suspect that the treasures will not be hidden once you come to the fair, and that you will take back much gold and silver, which you have earned for your arduous journey here and the fine merchandise you offer our citizens."

The wagon train of settlers had passed Nacogdoches by the end of the first week of June and was heading toward the Trinity River. Simon Brown was growing more and more concerned about several of his charges. Two days ago, he had halted the train near Nacogdoches, and he and four point riders, whom Eugene Fair had hired in Missouri to serve as armed escorts and trouble scouts, had ridden into the little town to buy supplies. There he had found quite a number of families, both Mexican and American. One of the Americans, Jed Starman, a lanky, towheaded man in his mid-thirties who had come from New Hampshire, had been in the general store when he and his four aides had entered. Jed Starman had seen the long line of wagons and oxen just north of the town, and asked Simon Brown if these were settlers coming to Nacogdoches.

"Oh, no, we're headin' for a special land grant across the Brazos. My name's Simon Brown, and I work for the *empresario* Eugene Fair out of Missouri."

The lanky New Hampshire man held out his hand. "Glad to meet you. I'm Jed Starman. Been settled here with my young Mexican wife, Rosalía, the past three years. Got me, the land's got plenty of grazin' grass and water around it, chickens and vegetables and fruits."

"I hope we'll be as lucky. But from what Mr. Fair tells me, the land's got plenty of grazin' grass and water around it, and there are quite a few farmers in my train," Simon vouchsafed. "How is the territory, any problem with hostiles?"

Starman shook his head. "No, we haven't been pestered by Injuns for quite a spell now. Most of it's the damn greaser soldiers—maybe I oughtn't to say that, 'specially seeing as how I'm married to a cute little greaser myself. But there's a passel of difference between us Yankees and them Mexes. And I think maybe that's going to cause some real trouble one of these days—though I hope not in my day."

Simon was apprehensively curious. "Just how do you mean that, Mr. Starman?"

"Well, for one thing, Yankees don't much worry about what church a man goes to, so long as he's God-fearing, if you take my meaning. But the Mexes are all Catholics, and they don't tolerate nobody else. And then, Yanks hold with the jury system—we have trials when a man's shot his neighbor or tried to steal his land. Leastways, that's what my pappy did back in New Hampshire. Out here, though, the Mexes would just as soon put you up against the wall and pull the trigger, figuring you won't cause them any more trouble, legal or otherwise. And another thing, Yanks like to run their own government, just like the United States does. You know what's been happening down Mexico way, what with all these revolutions and presidents and generals fighting for a share of the pie. It's going to come to a boil one of these days, you mark my words."

"So what you're sayin' is that the only trouble you've had is from government troops, am I right?" Simon Brown anxiously pursued.

"That's it. Just over the Rio Grande, they got this Mexican state they call Coahuila. I hear tell there's a couple of big military men down there who want to show off and prove that maybe they can be president or whatnot, one of these days. And they take a lot of pleasure in crossing the Rio Grande and picking fights with us Yankees. Why, just about two weeks ago, a sassy greaser captain with about twenty-five men rode in here and said they were looking for a murderer. We let him in here among the settlers, and damned if they didn't go through the town and haul all of us folks out of our houses and make us show papers proving who we were. Now, that's not the way to get along friendly with your neighbors who've come from across the border—to my way of thinking, anyhow."

"Thanks for the information, Mr. Starman. I'll keep my eyes peeled between here and the Brazos," Simon nervously exclaimed.

He and his four companions piled the supplies into a low, wide cart drawn by a sturdy dray horse, and returned to the impatiently waiting settlers. But Simon had been mulling over the news the colonist had just given him, and beckoned to one of the four men with whom he had become especially friendly since leaving Franklin. It was Ed Barstow, a cheerful, brown-haired young man of twenty-four, who had sought out Eugene Fair and offered to work for him. Ed had worked as a poleman on a flatboat, trying to earn enough money to buy food and medicine for his ailing father and mother in Natchez. When he returned to Natchez, he learned that his parents' home had been looted by river renegades, and his parents killed, as they tried to defend it. Ed had then determined to go farther west and start a new life. Simon Brown liked him because he was invariably cheerful and never complained about taking the midnight shift on guard duty when the train was bedded down for the night.

The other men listened now as he spoke with Ed. "Did you hear what that fellow was sayin' back in the store, about Mexican soldiers? I don't like the sound of it one little bit."

"I'm not keen about it either, Simon. Do you think we ought to tell the people to start loadin' their muskets and pistols, in case there's trouble?"

"I sure do. Not only that; I'd like to see if we can't bunch the wagons up side by side. Goin' single file makes it too easy for the first and the last to be picked off, throwin' everybody else into a tizzy so they can't fight together in case we do run into Injuns or Mexican soldiers."

"Want me to start givin' the word when we get back to the camp?"

"Good idea. Tell everyone those are my orders, Ed. What you can also do, and I'd appreciate it a lot, is to make sure all of them have got weapons, and enough ammunition too. Don't forget, if soldiers want to drive us away, they'll have guns and plenty of ammunition. And I don't know enough about our people yet to be sure whether they're up to a fight or not. Looks like you, Dave Enborg, Caleb Weston, Jack Sperry, and me might have to do most of the fightin' for them," Simon gloomily declared.

"All these people comin' here to settle in Texas, lookin' for peace and freedom . . . wouldn't it be just plain hell if they were driven off by soldiers? I thought Mr. Fair got a contract so that the families were assured of land to farm on," Ed proffered.

"He did. It goes back to Mr. Stephen Austin's contract with the Mexican government. Every family gets about four thousand acres of grazin' land and somethin' like one hundred seventy-five acres of farmland. And it's all free. They just have to cultivate it and settle down on it and use it, and not get into trouble."

Ed Barstow whistled and shook his head. "My God almighty," he said solemnly, "if Pa and Ma had heard about land like that, we'd sure have moved out of Natchez long before— Anyhow, I'll go back to the people and start findin' out what we've got by way of makin' us an army."

"Okay, you do that, Ed. All right, Dave, Caleb, Jack, let's take these supplies back and divvy them up. We got them at a pretty good price, I have to say. That storekeeper was right friendly, and he didn't have to be. Maybe that'll be good luck, instead of the bad news we heard from that tall, hungry-lookin' fellow in the store."

Jack Sperry, a sturdy, curly black-haired young man, a year older than Ed Barstow, had come with his two older brothers and father from Virginia to New Orleans over fifteen years ago, to make a fresh start in the Queen City. Then two years ago, a raging epidemic of yellow fever had killed Jack's father and brothers, and he had gone to live with a cousin in Natchitoches. When he heard of Stephen Austin's efforts to colonize Texas, he made his way to San Antonio, there met Eugene Fair, and was engaged to ride along with the groups of settlers under that aggressive *empresario*'s supervision.

Jack was naive, particularly about women, and though his brothers had enthusiastically frequented the brothels of Rampart Street, he had always been afraid of what his father called "painted Jezebels."

Just before the loss of his family, he had met a pretty seventeen-year-old seamstress's assistant, and he had almost been affianced to her. But his terrible grief at suddenly being orphaned had led him to leave New Orleans after saying a hasty farewell to her. He had almost forgotten her, until he had seen Nancy Morrison, the Stiltons' bound girl. The girl he had known back in New Orleans had had long coppery-hued hair, just like Nancy.

He turned to Simon Brown now. "I meant to ask you before, how do we get across the Trinity?"

"Mr. Fair told me there's a ferry there, has been for a couple of years now," Simon explained. "It works fine. And it's sturdy enough to handle the wagons and the oxen. 'Course, they'll have to cross maybe two at a time—but whatever, it's bound to slow us down some. Might take us as much as a whole day to ford the river.

"Now that we can defend ourselves, in case we're attacked by anybody, we'll bed down for the night. Tomorrow at sunup, we'll get a good head start. You and Caleb and Dave and Ed will see to it right after breakfast that these people get those wagons drivin' two or three alongside. The trail's not too bad till we hit the river. It'll be broad enough to bunch up our wagons. And what we ought to do is put the folks with guns and ammunition on each side, with the folks who don't have anythin' to fight with in the middle."

"You sound as if you'd been a soldier once, Simon," Jack Sperry told him with an engaging grin.

"Nope, nothing so fancy. In school, I read about some of the battles, and I tried to figure out what it would be like. Seems to make more sense, though, bunchin' up so nobody can pick off the strays, just like if you were drivin' cattle. You know."

"Sure. Anyhow, us outriders are pretty fair shots. I know I am. And I brought along my dad's old rifle from his farm in Virginia. It can shoot a long way and be right on target."

"I sure hope none of us will have to use the guns we're totin'," Simon glumly noted. "But it's just as well to be ready out here in country we don't know too much about. Especially after I heard that the Mexes aren't too friendly."

Sixteen

Capitán Juaquín Salgado had been a sergeant at the Battle of Medina twelve years ago, under the command of General Arrendondo. His superior officer then had been a slim, young beardless lieutenant named Santa Anna, and the sergeant had predicted to his companions, when Santa Anna's forgery of the general's name to a draft on the company funds had been discovered, that this brash young officer would be cashiered in disgrace. His prediction had been wrong: Santa Anna had been compelled to sell his uniforms and cavalry saber to replace the purloined funds, but the disgrace had been only temporary and taught him absolutely nothing. He was now a man waiting for the chance to seize total power over a devastated, impoverished country.

If Capitán Juaquín Salgado was embittered, he had justifiable reasons. Now, at the age of forty-four, his military progress hampered by his scrupulous honesty, he understood that his present rank of captain was as high as he could ever expect to rise in the army. His parents had been poor farmers, perhaps a grade above *peones*, but they had scraped enough money together to send him to a military school, where he had become a noncommissioned officer. It had taken him five years to rise to the rank of lieutenant, and four years ago he had been promoted to a captaincy. In the meanwhile, his attractive wife, Frasquita, whom he had married a decade ago, had presented him, after the first year, with a son. Six months later, he discovered that the son was not his, and that his twenty-year-old wife was shamelessly unfaithful to him, having secret trysts with some of the privates and corporals in his own regiment. Chance gossip around the campfire, when his men thought that he was conferring with his captain in a tent some distance away, let him overhear the truth, which he had not even suspected. And when he returned home with the intention of either killing or at least vigorously thrashing her, he found that she had taken the little boy and fled, to lose herself somewhere in a distant province with a new lover of the moment.

Thus his dreams had crumbled to ashes, and he came to the cynical realization that his dedication to the army and his scrupulous honesty had been to no avail. By contrast, he could see what Santa Anna had achieved by cunning, treachery, and violence.

Six months ago, he had been assigned to the military commander at the Presidio de Rio Grande to patrol the Texas borders and especially to investigate rumors that brigands, outlaws, and murderers with a price on their heads were infiltrating with the homesteaders to seek sanctuary in the vast Texas territory. Captain Salgado's own commander, a fussy, plump, bald colonel in his fifty-fifth year, Isidro Contrera, peremptorily dismissed his subordinate officer with an additional order: "I've no word from Mexico City as to the disposition of troops, Captain Salgado. I suggest that you patrol across the border, because these damnable *tejanos* are plotting to take Texas away from us. Yes, I know they have a contract in Mexico City for settlers, but I should wager a year's salary that there are many criminals who pose as settlers and go there to stir up trouble against us. No, *mi capitán*, take your directive from me—continue to patrol and to look for any suspect rebels or spies or outlaws. Arrest them; bring them here to me for trial; and then perhaps I can convince Mexico City that they are being much too lenient with these infernal *americanos*!"

It was onerous, thankless duty, and the disgruntled captain became more broodingly aware that no matter what deeds of valor he performed, he would still advance no farther in the ranks, while others, perhaps exactly like his fat superior, would be called to Mexico City and given the title of general or *comandante general*. Physically, he was unprepossessing, which may well have been one of the reasons that Frasquita had been unfaithful to him on so many occasions. Short and stocky, with a thick, bulbous nose out of whose nostrils black hairs profusely grew, paunchy and dyspeptic, Capitán Salgado had long since become faintly aware that attractive women would never flock to him as they did to the glorious *libertador*, Santa Anna. He remembered how Santa Anna had coerced the belles of the captured little village or town into yielding to him, and when they refused even to be taken in by the ruse of being "married" by a sergeant dressed like a priest, Santa Anna perfunctorily treated them the way a ruthless conquering general would treat the enemy women of a town just sacked, and ravished them.

Four months ago, while patrolling a barren strip of Texas territory some fifty miles south of John Cooper's Double H Ranch, he had come upon a tiny American settlement, consisting of six families. He entered the settlement and arrogantly demanded to see the *alcalde*, or headman. An elderly, crippled man in his late fifties announced himself to be spokesman for this settlement, and Captain Salgado demanded that all the settlers line up before him so that he might determine their true identities, since he was on a mission to uncover outlaws and others whose presence in Texas would be detrimental to the welfare of his government.

The old man indignantly refused, declaring that these were peaceful farmers who had no politics or military aspirations regarding Mexico, and wished only to live in peace. The stocky, mature officer then saw a teenage girl fearfully peeking out of the adobe and wood *jacal* which served the old man as home, and ordered two of his mounted troopers to seize him, while he interrogated the girl.

Gloating over her tearful terror and her winsomeness, he brutally ravished her and then, reviving the nearly fainting young victim by pinching and slapping her, coldly demanded that she tell him the names and backgrounds of all the other residents of this little settlement. When at last he was satisfied that there were no criminals or outlaws in this forsaken little hamlet, he mounted his horse, rode away a short distance, and then whirled his horse around. Drawing a pistol from his belt, he cold-bloodedly aimed it at the crippled old man and pulled the trigger. As the horrified onlookers cried out at this needless murder, Captain Salgado sneered, "This is an object lesson, *mis amigos*. Perhaps the next time you will not try to conceal anything from an officer in the army of the glorious Mexican republic!"

Those two acts of violence, the only ones he had committed in an otherwise colorless life—save, perhaps, for his murderous intentions toward his unfaithful wife, once he had learned of her adultery—had not only given him intense satisfaction, but had also gained him the respect—or at least the fear—of the soldiers under him. Thus he foresaw that if he could not rise in military rank to the acclaim of a man like Santa Anna, who had done so through corruption and treachery, he could at least engage in terror, physical brutality, and carnal domination. And finally, he rationalized that by venting all his pent-up frustrations brought about by the dead end of his military career and the destruction of his marriage, he would prove himself to be a true patriot to his country in directing all his hatred against the *yanquis*. Now that they were pouring into Texas, did they not ultimately mean to grow strong enough, one fateful day, to cross the Texas border and strike at Mexico herself?

And so, this early June morning, he sent out a Tonkawa scout to the vicinity of the Brazos and Trinity rivers with orders to report on the movement of any large body of settlers into that deserted land. He had no intention of attacking Stephen Austin's town; it was too well fortified and had too many settlers there already. But with his troop of forty able, well-armed, and mounted men, he could attack a moving wagon train, for it would be vulnerable. And the *americanos* who rode in it would be panic-stricken, when for the first time they encountered disciplined soldiers who could ride and shoot and use their lances with murderous effectiveness.

"I'd say about half the folks have guns of some kind or other," Ed Barstow reported to Simon Brown, as the smell of bacon and biscuits and coffee that the settlers were preparing for their breakfast pleasantly wafted toward the two men. "There are about five long rifles, about six muskets, and a couple of the men have pistols. There's enough ammunition for a good fight—but I sure hope to God we don't have to have one. We've got too many women and children in this train, Simon."

"You're right about that. Have you and the others been tellin' 'em how we wanted 'em to pull out after breakfast? Rows of three, and I'll want that nineteenth wagon at the head. We'll leave behind the supply cart. You and Caleb will hide in the back of the nineteenth wagon with your rifles and all the ammunition you can muster, so if we're attacked, you'll have a good place to shoot from. Dave Enborg is to drive it, hear? The folks who own the wagon should double up with another family farther down the line."

"I'll pass the word around, Simon."

"Good. Jack and I'll ride behind the train, sort of like drag riders for a herd. If they come at us from the back, we'll have a chance to warn all the rest. And be sure to tell the people with guns to load them up first thing before we pull out."

"I'll do it. Want some coffee, Simon?"

"Sure. But that's all. I'll get it myself; you've got work to do. And there's one thing more—I told you I wanted the folks who don't have any guns to ride in the middle in all those six rows, remember? Well, I want any kids or babies to be in those middle wagons, too, no matter if they don't belong to the right families. Bunched in like that, they'll be protected against stray shots. You see, this way, no matter what side they come at us from, we'll have some fire power to hold or drive them off. Now get going!"

William Mayberry owned neither pistol, musket, nor rifle. He had, however, a blacksnake whip which, some years before, he had bought at a little country fair out of an inexplicable impulse. And this morning, he was about to use it for the first time.

Naomi, ever since this journey had begun in Franklin, had grown more and more uncommunicative with him. By now, she thoroughly hated and feared him, and she prayed that the child growing within her need not grow up under his cruel, domineering aegis. She still dreamed of her lover, Benjamin Carter, ingenuously hoping that somehow the two of them might be reunited in the West. Often, when Mayberry was asleep, she wept silently.

She could not bear for him to touch her; but now that she was pregnant, his sexual demands on her had temporarily ceased, for which she was pathetically grateful. In return, however, he tyrannized her into doing all the work by herself, insisting that she drive their team of strong workhorses, cook his meals and bring them to him before she dared eat her own, wash his shirts by the bank of a river or creek, and even shave him. Yesterday morning, for example, before breakfast, she had had to fill a pan with water and lather his face with some homemade soap, then take his straight razor and, very carefully, shave away the stubble from his jaws and chin and upper lip. He had eyed her with a malignant little smile, and then he had muttered, "I know what you're thinking, Naomi. Better not try it. You cut my throat in here, they'll hang you and leave you for the buzzards, my girl. And if you want that little bastard in your belly to grow up and have a name, you'd best make sure that all you do is shave me right and proper, hear?"

This morning, again before breakfast, Mayberry sent Naomi out to fill a pan with water from the little creek, and watched with a sneering expression on his face as she humbly procured the soap and began to make a lather of it, then applied it to his stubbly jaws and chin. "Stir your stumps, girl," he snapped, "I'm right hungry for my breakfast, so don't keep me waiting!"

Naomi could not trust herself to speak, but nodded, and with trembling fingers opened the case in which the straight razor lay with its bone handle. The razor was his one luxury, having purchased it from an itinerant peddler in the Ohio town where he had run his mill. To force his young wife to shave him afforded him a sadistic pleasure, for to see her bend before him and hold her breath as she fearfully put the razor's sharp edge to the growth of stubble let him luxuriate in the feeling that she was his subjugated slave-girl.

But this morning, perhaps because of his malicious remark the morning before, or perhaps because her revulsion to him was becoming too great to bear, her hand trembled more than usual, and he uttered a blasphemous oath as she nicked his chin. "Now just see what you've done, you stupid, thoughtless bitch! You're not even good in bed; I don't know why I married you. I took you in out of charity when that no-good farmhand got you in the family way, and this is how you repay me, is it, Naomi? It's time you were taught a lesson. And before we start off on the next lap of this journey to our new home, my girl, you're going to get it. Hand me that bit of plaster—you've made me bleed like a stuck pig, damn you!"

Nearly blinded by her tears, Naomi groped for the case and produced a piece of court plaster, which he tore away from her and clapped against the bleeding nick. Then, his eyes gleaming with a vicious lust, he reached for the blacksnake whip, which he had put under the mattress, and seizing her wrist in his left hand, dragged her out of the wagon. He paused long enough to stoop to retrieve a length of tar-coated rope and then forced her to one of the huge wheels of the wagon. "Please don't—please, Mr. Mayberry, I swear I didn't mean to do it—please don't wh-whip me!" she pleaded. "At least think of the baby, if not of me—please, don't do it to me! And all these people—they'll see—"

"Aye, I mean for them to see, you stupid little bitch!" he snarled. "They'll see how a husband punishes a clumsy, inconsiderate wife who doesn't look after a man's comfort, when she ought to go down on her knees to the Lord Jehovah to thank Him for her blessings in not being cast out with a nameless bastard!" Dropping the whip to the ground, he shoved her down on her knees, took the rope length, and bound both her wrists to the top of the wheel. Then, with a lecherous snigger, he reached out to rip down the back of her linsey-woolsey dress and the coarse camisole, till she was naked to the waist. "Now you're going to learn your lesson," he hissed as he retrieved the whip and stepped back, measuring the distance. Raising his arm, he slashed it diagonally across her naked back, imprinting a bright crimson welt on the pale white flesh. Naomi ground her teeth together to keep from crying out, lifting her head and closing her eyes, her body stricken with fitful tremors.

A second stroke followed and then a third, and this time she could not suppress a strangled, sobbing groan of unspeakable torment, as her body jerked under the biting slashes that now crisscrossed the smooth symmetry of her naked flesh.

Simon Brown was moving through the little campfires that the settlers had made this morning for their breakfast, seeing that his four assistants had carried out their orders in reminding the men and women what they must do in case of attack. "I don't say this to frighten you folks," he called out, "but it's just good common sense to be prepared in a strange country. Anyhow, don't you worry, Dave, Caleb, Jack, Ed, 'n me, we're pretty good shots, and we'll take care of you. Now you men with the muskets and rifles and guns, you make sure they're loaded before you start your horses and oxen. All right now. It's clear weather and a clear sky ahead, so don't rush your breakfast, but don't dawdle over it, either. See you on the trail!"

William Mayberry had paused to contemplate his vicious handiwork, his eyes glistening and narrowed, as he watched the panting Naomi crouch against the wheel, trying to hide her naked breasts, to make herself as small as she could and diminish the cringing flesh proffered to the blacksnake whip. He raised it slowly now, licking his lips with anticipation, and delivered a fourth stroke straight down her spinal column, the tip of the whip stinging her tender nape. This time, she could not hold back her scream of pain: "Oh, my God, please, have mercy; I told you I didn't mean it! Oh, my baby, don't whip me anymore, please, Mr. Mayberry!"

Simon Brown had heard that cry, and strode into the line of wagons at about the middle, where Mayberry's wagon was. He was just in time to see the man raise the whip again, and with a cry of horrified rage, he stepped forward and sent his right fist against Mayberry's jaw, sending him sprawling on his back. "That's mean and low, Mr. Mayberry—meanest thing I ever did see, tyin' a purty girl like that and usin' that kind of whip on her. What sort of man are you, anyhow?"

"You son of a bitch, you keep your nose out of my business!" Mayberry panted as he slowly got to his feet. "I'm just disciplining her, that's all. She has it coming. She cut me with my own razor, the stupid little bitch—"

"Put that whip down, I'm tellin' you. You use it again, you'll wish you hadn't!" Simon said in a low, trembling voice, as he clenched his fists.

"Oh, sure, you see Naomi half nekkid like this, slut that she is; already she's cozened you into sticking up for her!" Mayberry snarled. He drew back the whip and slashed it across Simon's face. So unexpected had been the movement that the young scout had not had time to evade the lash, but he reached out and caught it, even as it wealed his cheek near his eye, and wrested it out of Mayberry's hand. Then he hit him again with all his strength, and as Mayberry staggered, he sent his fist into the pit of the man's stomach.

William Mayberry dropped to the ground, rolling over and over, clutching his belly and moaning in agony.

But Naomi Mayberry had slumped in her bonds, and to his horror, Simon Brown saw that there was a pool of blood on the ground under her.

"Oh, sweet Jesus, oh, no—she was going to have a baby—oh, my God!" he hoarsely ejaculated, and ran to Mrs. Minnie Hornsteder's wagon. "Ma'am, you've gotta come quick; there's a girl goin' to have a baby—I think somethin's happened to her—for God's sake, come help me," he panted. The fat, good-natured, gossipy woman stared at him a moment, then nodded and turned to her husband: "Henry, you mind the team 'n look after things. This is woman's business."

"I'll take care of things, Mother, you just go ahead with Mr. Brown," her meek little husband at once responded.

She followed Simon Brown back to the wagon, and then scolded the young scout: "You ought to have had the good sense to untie the poor thing's wrists—this is awful. I think I know what it is—how far is she along, do you know that?"

"No—no, ma'am, I sure don't," he gulped, seizing his hunting knife and cutting the rope that bound her chafed, slim wrists. She slumped onto her side, and Mrs. Hornsteder harangued him, "Men are such dumb fools—you 'n I, we gotta carry her back to my wagon. She's lost her baby, that's what, 'n she'll need lots of care. You take her arms, 'n I'll take her legs, 'n be right careful you don't jostle the poor thing. I'd like to get my hands on that nasty old man that laced into her like that." Seeing William Mayberry prostrate on the ground, still twisting and groaning and clasping his middle, she hawked and spat at him to show her supreme disgust.

As they carried the unconscious girl back to her wagon, she tried to cheer the crestfallen young scout: "Now, don't you fret, you done real good givin' that Mr. Mayberry part of what was comin' to him. Anyhow, me 'n Henry, we had five kids 'n they're all grown now, 'n off themselves to find land wherever it suits their fancy. Me 'n Henry, we're goin' on to Texas with you to meet up with Henry's first cousin. So the two of us know what to do with the poor thing that's lost her baby. But you better not start the wagons yet till we get it all settled 'n she's restin'—I could kill that Mr. Mayberry myself with my bare hands the way I feel right now!"

For the next half hour, Simon Brown performed the duties of an apprentice nurse, heating water in a kettle over one of the campfires and bringing blankets and whatever linen he could beg, borrow, or steal from the other settlers to be used as towels. Finally Mrs. Hornsteder announced, "She'll be fine, but she's weak. It could have been a lot worse if she'd been farther along than she was. We'll keep her in our wagon. I'd appreciate it a heap, Mr. Brown, if you could hold off startin' the train for about another hour or so, so the poor thing can rest."

"Sure. That's the least I can do. Anyway, I'd better go back and look after Mr. Mayberry."

"I know what I'd like to do to him, but I'm a good Christian, 'n I better not say it. You get him back into his wagon. I wouldn't blame this poor child if she never went back to a monster like that—the very idea, tyin' her and takin' a whip to her when she was with child; I never in all my born days!" Mrs. Hornsteder indignantly declaimed.

Shortly before noon, old Mrs. Hornsteder waddled over to Simon Brown, who was hunkered down before a small fire over which he was heating a pot of coffee, and when he anxiously glanced up, triumphantly announced, "She's awake now, 'n she's fine. She's lost what she was carryin', but she'll be able to git a baby next time." Then she looked angry: "Botheration, it riles me to think that low skunk of a husband of hers'll be the one to give it to her."

"I—I'm mighty grateful for all you did, Mrs. Hornsteder. I owe you an apology, too."

"What are you talkin' about, Mr. Brown? That's woman's work, ain't it? Told you Henry 'n me raised a passel of kids, and they all turned out fine." Now she guffawed heartily. "Seems like to me, Mr. Brown, you ought to git yerself a nice girl like that 'n fill her full of babies. 'Pears to me, you're a good sort; you'd make some lucky gal a mighty fine husband. Well, that's the long 'n the short of it, Mr. Brown. You kin start up fer where we're goin' anytime now. She's restin' fine."

"Thanks. But I meant what I said about the apology. I mean, when I started out in Franklin with all of you, I—

well—" His face reddened as he stood up and squirmed uneasily as her watery brown eyes fixed intently on him. "Well, to put it straight, ma'am, I just thought you were something of a—well, a gossip, likin' to tell tales and all. I was sure wrong, 'n I beg your pardon, I most humbly do."

"That was nice, real nice, Mr. Brown. Wherever you wuz brung up, I see you learned manners. I like that in you." Now her eyes seemed more suspiciously watery than ever. "What you could do, to seal the bargain, is pour me some of that coffee you're heatin'. I think I earned it."

"I'll sure say you did, ma'am!" he gratefully exclaimed as he hastened to get another cup, filled it to the brim, and handed it to her. Then he poured out his own, and stared at the trail ahead. "Well, soon as I finish this, we'll get movin'. God bless you, Mrs. Hornsteder."

"Thanks, Mr. Brown. I feel likewise about you. Reckon I'll be gettin' back to my wagon so's Mrs. Mayberry will have me there if she needs me. But she's fine, I can tell you that; and *I* know. I don't hold no truck with doctors nohow. Takes a woman to know what a woman's goin' through, I always say. But you remember what I told you; you git yerself fixed up with a nice gal and you take her in front of a preacher and you'll see you'll have a good life—if you've picked the right girl, that is." She drank down her coffee, put down the cup, and then giggled like a schoolgirl as she shot him a smiling look, turned, and went back to her wagon.

Simon exhaled a deep sigh. He hadn't bargained for anything like this when he'd signed up with Eugene Fair. And it just went to show him how much a man could learn when he thought he knew it all. About a woman like that Mrs. Hornsteder, for instance. She was kind and good and smart, and she didn't lose her head in an emergency. He'd almost done just that, and here he was the scout picked to take all these folks to the new settlement beyond the Brazos. Well, he'd make up for it the rest of the way, darned if he wouldn't!

The Tonkawa scout whom Captain Juaquín Salgado had sent ahead reined in his pinto and, cupping a hand to his eyes, squinted off to the distance. Then he grinned and wheeled the pinto back toward the troop of mounted Mexican soldiers. In the distance, he had seen rows of wagons. He'd counted about a score of them, and they were taking their time. It would be very easy for the *jefe* to ride them down, and maybe the *jefe*, after he had killed all those *americanos*, would give him one of their guns as a present for having found them.

A quarter of an hour later, the pinto snorting and lathered with foam, the scout leaped down and hurried to the Mexican officer. In part Spanish and part Tonkawan, he described what he had seen. Captain Salgado, who was taking his ease stretched out on a grassy knoll, sprang to his feet. "*¡Bueno*, Iglesias, this is good news you bring me!" Then, hoarsely raising his voice, "Sargente Bechanos, *¡ven aquí pronto!*"

A squat, thickly bearded and mustached noncommissioned officer hurried up to him, smartly saluting.

"Have the men mount up. We'll follow Iglesias. He's found a wagon train of *gringos*. We'll surround them; we'll find out who they are. If any one of those *americano* dogs fires on us, you will order the men to return the fire at once. Spare no one—except if there are any *mujeres* young and *linda* enough to amuse the men."

The sergeant grinned lewdly and nodded, saluted again, then hurried off to bawl out his orders. A corporal, already astride his black gelding, drew his bugle and sounded the call to mount up and ride. And Captain Salgado, at the head of his troops, his eyes sparkling with cruel anticipation, drew the saber from his black leather belt and flourished it, as he called out, "*¡Adelante, soldados!*"

Simon Brown posted in his saddle to look back along the route whence they had come, and called to Jack Sperry, riding alongside him, "Mebbe it's just as well we had to hold up this morning. This way we'll get to the river by sundown, make camp, and start fordin' it on the ferry at sunup. With luck, we ought to be on the other side before sundown."

Jack shook his head. "I sure hope we get some cover in case any of those Mex patrols come close. Here we are right out in the open, and we can't very well hide."

"No, but we can fight if we have to. Only thing is, we've got no way of knowin' how good the folks with guns are, in case it does come down to a fight. I don't think any of these folks were ever soldiers."

Jack shook his head again. "Not that old buzzard, Mayberry, that's for sure. He looks madder 'n a wet hornet, drivin' his team there. And his face never was purty, but it looks a lot worse from the lumps you hung on it, Simon. He sure had it comin', though."

"Yep, he did. Hey, thought I saw some dust off there to the south—hold up a second, Jack, let's see if my eyes are playin' tricks on me—no, damn it, that's a Mex patrol and ridin' fast at us, by God! You ride down the left side of this train, I'll take the right. Warn the folks we might be in for a scrap—tell 'em to get their guns ready. Remind 'em there's air holes poked in the sides of their wagons; they can get their gun barrels through 'em and be able to shoot if they hunker down. Tell 'em not to start shootin' unless that patrol starts anything, get me?"

"Sure do." Jack spurred his horse into a trot down the left side of the rows of wagons, shouting out the order the young scout had just given him, while Simon emulated him on the other side of the compact train. As Simon reached the lead wagon, he leaned to one side and called out, "Ed and Caleb, looks like the Mexes are comin' from behind and to our left. No sense tryin' to outrun 'em; we've got heavy wagons, and they've got fast horses. Maybe we can talk our way out of it. We've got Mr. Fair's contract and his map to show 'em, if they'll listen to reason."

"We're all set here," Caleb Weston shouted.

Simon wheeled his horse around and rode back to the end of the train. He reached down to the saddle sheath for his long rifle, maintaining the reins in his left hand and slackening his horse's gait so that he could turn in his saddle to see the oncoming patrol.

Captain Juaquín Salgado gestured to his sergeant: "Order those *americanos* to halt; ask them by what right they come here. You speak English better than I, but be sure to let them know they must obey the order to halt and identify themselves. Tell them, too, if they fire a single shot at us, I will give the order for no quarter."

"*¡Sí, mi capitán!*" Sergeant Bechanos saluted and rode forward. He carried a lance to which was attached a pennon of the troop, with the figure of an eagle on a yellow and red background. Holding the lance vertically, he rode forward till he had reached the last three wagons in the line, and bellowed out in English, "You are to halt, by order of Capitán

Juaquín Salgado, who commands the Texas patrol. You will halt all wagons. You will come out, and you will prove who you are and where you are going, ¿comprenden?"

Simon Brown courageously trotted his horse up to confront the sergeant. "Just a minute now. We're settlers on a land grant from your government, and I've got papers to show it. We don't want any trouble. We've got women and children in these wagons, so tell your captain we're just headin' for the Brazos to the land Mr. Austin picked for us."

"I am sorry, señor," the sergeant gruffly responded, "you must obey my officer's order. Otherwise, he will think that you are bandidos. We have forty men here, well armed, and we do not wish to kill your women and children; but you will give the order for all of these wagons to halt at once, do you understand me, señor?"

Simon frowned. Suddenly his horse reared, for in the thick grass near its front hooves there sounded the ominous buzzing of a hidden rattlesnake. As he tried to steady his frightened horse by drawing on the reins with his left hand, his right slipped down toward the rifle sheath and clutched the butt.

The sergeant took this to signify disobedience of his superior officer's order and, raising his lance, shouted back in Spanish, "The gringos will not stop. They want to fight us, mi capitán!"

Then, turning his horse's head to one side and riding off some twenty paces, he whirled round again and, lowering the lance, spurred his horse forward, the tip of the sharp lance aimed at Simon Brown's heart.

Rising in his stirrups, Captain Salgado saw what was taking place and signaled to his bugler: "Sound the alsalto! Soldados, remember, try not to kill the young women—you shall enjoy them when we have exterminated these accursed americanos!"

The sharp, crisp cadence of the bugle rang out in the still, humid summer air, and the mounted soldiers separated into two columns, one galloping forward at the left of the wagon train, the other to the right.

Simon tugged the rifle out of its sheath, but saw that he would not have time to aim and fire it before the lance reached his chest. Indian-style, he flung himself forward and to the left across his saddle, and the lance passed over his bowed back, the metal shaft just grazing him. In the same moment, Jack Sperry drew a pistol from his belt and fired it point-blank at the sergeant, sending a ball through the man's thick neck. He pitched from the saddle, his body striking the left rear leg of Simon's horse, which reared again, whinnying shrilly in its terror.

Simon swiftly dismounted, seized the lance which had fallen beside the dead Mexican, and, the rifle in his other hand, took cover beside the wagon wheel nearest him, as he cried out with all his strength, "They're attackin'! Pick your target and shoot! Watch out for their lances! Get yourselves down as flat as you can, and shoot through the air holes!"

Even as he finished his frenzied order to the now-halted wagons—for Dave Enborg in the lead wagon had instantly halted his team at the first glimpse of the Mexican cavalry flanking him at the left—a sneering Mexican private turned his horse toward the end wagon at the right and, lowering his lance, rode at Simon. Instantly, the scout lifted the rifle in his right hand and triggered a snap shot. The lance dropped from the private's nerveless fingers, and he pitched forward over the side of his horse, which threw up its head and galloped off to the west, till its lifeless rider's booted feet were disengaged from the stirrups and his inert body thudded on the ground. The recoil of the rifle had flung Simon back against the wheel, and there was no time to reload. He seized the lance in both hands as another soldier bore down on him, and parrying the lance aimed at him, he knocked it high in the air and then, drawing his back, thrust the sharp point into the rider's heart.

As the Mexican fell, he rolled over and over to lie at Simon's feet. The young scout saw a brace of pistols strapped to his belt, seized them, cocked the triggers, and taking careful aim, fired the one in his right hand. A corporal armed with a rifle had just fired into the second wagon ahead of Simon, and a man's groan responded to it, followed by the report of a musket from the wagon, as the wounded man's fifteen-year-old son sent the corporal toppling from his horse and falling to the ground, to be hidden in the grass.

A rifle ball thudded into the rim of the huge wagon wheel a few inches away from Simon's left shoulder, and he swiftly raised the pistol and pulled the trigger. The mounted Mexican rifleman jerked in the saddle, slipped forward, and lay with his arms dangling on each side of his galloping horse's neck.

In the lead wagon, Ed Barstow crouched to the right, his rifle barrel poked through one of the air holes, and squinting along the sight, pulled the trigger to send another private toppling from the saddle. Almost simultaneously, the bark of Caleb Weston's rifle rang out, and a corporal, who had thrust his lance into the side of one of the wagons on the left flank and then drawn a pistol from his belt, stiffened, his eyes rolling in their sockets as he dropped the pistol and bowed his head, both hands clasped to his bloody middle.

Captain Salgado, his face a mask of fury, brandished his saber and swore at his bugler: "By the testicles of the devil in hell, sound retreat and charge again! Then sound the *degüello*—the massacre. *Por Dios,* we shall not spare even the women, no matter how *linda* they are! These accursed pigs of *americanos* have already cost me seven men!"

Hearing the bugler's signal, the two flanking sections of the cavalry troop galloped off to the north and the south, out of range of the defenders' unexpectedly effective volleys, while the sinister notes of the bugle sounded the most terrifying of all martial warnings: no one was to be spared; there would be no quarter, even for women and children.

From his wagon in the middle, William Mayberry was clammy with the sweat of fear. Dropping the reins of his horses, he scrambled down from the driver's seat and, crouching down, began to creep along the sides of the wagons that formed the middle section of Simon Brown's train.

Meanwhile, David Stilton, who had an old musket and had fired it, though without effect, mistakenly believed that the enemy had been driven off during the first attack on the left flank of the wagons. He moved cautiously forward to the driver's seat of the wagon, and Cora was hysterical as she tried to cling to him. "Oh, please, David, I'm so frightened; oh, my God, I never dreamed it would be like this!" Then, turning back to stare at Nancy Morrison, she hissed, "Get out of the wagon, you hussy! If I'm going to die, I don't want you to be near my David, you understand me? Get out of here! Go find yourself another man in the middle there; there are bound to be lots of them!"

"Let her be, for God's sake, Cora!" David hoarsely exclaimed. But Cora's terror and her long-brooding jealousy made her deaf to his entreaty; turning back from him, she plunged both hands into the bound girl's coppery hair and dragged her, screaming in pain, to the opening of the wagon and shoved her out, so that Nancy fell to the ground. The thick grass helped break her fall, but she had sprained her ankle and lay there sobbing with pain.

David had tried to prevent it, but he had heard the bugle sounding the renewed attack and the warning of no quarter and turned to reload his musket, glancing frantically down at the young bound girl and swearing under his breath.

"They're comin' again; get ready, you folks! Make every shot count!" Simon Brown cried. By now, he had reloaded his rifle, just as the two lines of mounted Mexican troopers surged back along each side of the halted, compactly gathered wagons.

Henry Hornsteder, hunkered down in his wagon with an old Lancaster rifle, glanced back at Naomi Mayberry, who lay, her eyes closed, her face drawn and pale, on a pallet at the back, his plump wife anxiously crouching beside her and pressing a dampened cloth to Naomi's forehead. "Get down as low as you can, honey; them Mexes are comin' back!" he muttered. A rifle shot from one of the troopers tore through the heavy canvas at the wagon's side and creased his shoulder. The old man swore and pulled the trigger of his rifle, and the Mexican threw his hands in the air, his rifle dropping to the ground as he slid backward and over his horse's tail, the animal galloping off erratically until at last it burst out toward the west in a maddened gallop and disappeared from view.

A young trooper in his twenties, aiming his lance, headed for the Stilton wagon, grinning as he saw the fallen bound girl, who uttered a shriek of terror. David Stilton lifted his musket to his shoulder and pulled the trigger, but the flintlock was worn out, and the gun did not discharge. With a cry of desperation, he took hold of the barrel and, with all his might, slung it at the oncoming trooper. The heavy butt caught the Mexican in the face, smashing his teeth and nose, and he dropped his lance, which sailed harmlessly over Nancy's head and slithered under the wagon behind her. David leaped down from the wagon and retrieved the lance, shouting to the bound girl, "Crawl under the wagon—lie flat as you can—keep out of the way."

Hysterical now and wringing her hands, interpreting her husband's action as but more proof that he preferred the bound girl to her, Cora Stilton appeared at the opening of the wagon and made as if to leap down to the ground. As she did so, another trooper rode in a slanting line with his lance aimed at her. David ran forward and, both hands gripping the polished wooden handle of the lance, thrust it with all his strength into the trooper's neck. As he tried to wrench it back, he dragged the dying man from his horse to fall onto him and press him down on the ground flat on his back. With a cry of revulsion, he rolled the soldier over and, perceiving a pistol in the man's belt, pulled it out just in time to send off a shot that made a corporal, just lifting his rifle to sight it at Cora, lurch to one side and slip out of his saddle, one of his booted feet caught in the stirrup, his gelding galloping on and dragging him through the thick grass and out of sight.

William Mayberry's breeches were stained, for in his fright he had lost control of his bladder. His lips were mumbling silent prayers, promises of atonement for his crimes, as he moved along the wagons till he reached the lead wagon. Just as he straightened, looking wildly around him, a ricocheting rifle ball took him in the temple, and he dropped like a log.

Capitán Juaquín Salgado could not believe his eyes. His crack troops decimated by these stupid *americanos*! Turning to his bugler, brandishing his saber, he shouted, "Follow me; kill them, kill without mercy!" And spurring his horse, he rode toward Simon Brown and Jack Sperry. His bugler drew a pistol and fired at Sperry, wounding him in the left leg just above the knee; but the scout's assistant, despite the pain, lifted his rifle and shot the bugler down from his horse. Captain Salgado was on him now, saber uplifted, and there was just time for Simon to seize the lance and, with a prayer on his lips, hurl it at the infuriated Mexican officer. It pierced his throat, and he dropped his saber with a gurgling scream.

As the troopers saw their commanding officer fall, they wheeled their horses away from the halted wagons and, conferring among themselves, turned and rode off toward the south and disappeared. Simon staggered to his feet, his body drenched in sweat. "Praise the Lord God Jehovah," he exhaled. "Jack, you hurt bad?"

"Got a ball in my thigh, but I don't think it's too bad.

Ain't bleedin' much right now. If you gimme some whiskey and git one of those settlers who knows how to cut it out without takin' off my leg, I reckon I'll git by," Jack said between clenched teeth.

"Here, I'll make you a tourniquet to make sure the bleedin' stops, Jack. Damn, I never thought we'd beat off all those Mexes riding us down on horseback—those lances gave me the creeps—but I didn't have time to get scared; I was too busy tryin' to stay alive," Simon confessed as he tore off his shirt and used strips to bind Jack Sperry's leg. "There, now I'll go see what the damage is with the folks. And I'll find somebody who's right handy diggin' a ball out of a fellow. I'll also round up some whiskey for you. Just take it easy now, Jack."

"I sure as hell ain't goin' anywhere, the way my leg feels right now," Jack sheepishly admitted, then winced as the wound began to throb.

Ed Barstow and Caleb Weston hurried back to Simon with the news that Dave Enborg had taken a rifle ball in the heart on the very last charge of the Mexican patrol. Besides William Mayberry, a six-year-old boy had been killed by a pistol shot, when he had foolishly peered out of the wagon. Also, one of the settlers who had defended himself with a musket had been killed by a direct shot through the very air hole he was using as a sight. Henry Hornsteder had a shoulder wound, and the father of the fifteen-year-old boy who had acquitted himself so valorously was suffering from loss of blood. Two other men had minor flesh wounds.

"We'll bury our dead first, and you, Ed and Caleb, suppose you round up some of the guns and pistols these Mexes had. Just might be they'd come in handy in case any more patrols come after us," Simon cautioned.

An hour later, Caleb, Ed, and Simon had dug graves and buried the dead, and Simon Brown said a few simple words over the graves. Jack Sperry had been taken to the wagon of Hosmer Dugal, an Indiana farmer whose wife had died from river fever just a month before he and his twelve-year-old boy and ten-year-old daughter had decided to seek a new frontier in Texas. Dugal had volunteered to remove the ball from Jack's leg, reluctantly admitting that he had "patched up a few fellas back in Indiana when they couldn't settle their differences peacefullike." Fortified by half a bottle of whiskey, Jack had mercifully fallen into a stupor, and the Indiana farmer had removed the ball and then cauterized the wound by dipping a stick into tar and then holding it over a fire till it glowed, pressing it into the wound. "It'll heal just fine. He'll be sore and stiff a couple of days, but he won't lose his leg—I'll guarantee it," Hosmer Dugal announced, himself satisfied with the crude operation.

Cora Stilton turned to her husband, and there was a look of wonder and respect in her eyes. "You saved my life, David. I thought you wanted to bed down Nancy, but you saved my life. You could have let that soldier stick me with his awful spear, and then you could have had Nancy all to yourself, but you didn't," she repeated for the third time. "I've been so awful to you, but you know why—it's 'cause I can't give you a kid—oh, David, I wish we could start all over again—"

"Sure we can, honey." He patted her shoulder and drew her close to him. "Tell you what. Maybe when we get to the settlement, we might find some kids who lost their folks—maybe just like this, when those Mex soldiers tried to kill them. We could adopt them, and it would be just as good as if they were our own, you'll see."

"Why yes, I never thought of that—oh, David, David, I'll try to make it up to you—I've been so awful—"

"You could do one nice thing, though, honey, and it'll help give us both a fresh start."

"What's that, David? I'll do anything you want!" Her eyes were shining now, as she put her arms around his neck and fervently kissed him.

"You know, having a bound girl for a servant is nice and all that, but I'd just as soon the two of us build our little house and work together and do our meals without any help. Why don't we set her free and tear up her indenture? Maybe she can marry one of these scouts—to tell you the truth, Cora, I'd noticed that Jack Sperry looking at her. And I had a little talk with him just before we got to Nacogdoches. He lost a girl, and Nancy sort of reminds him of her. Maybe they'll spark together and get married when we get to the settlement."

"You know, David, that's a perfectly marvelous idea! And I'm going to apologize to Nancy, too. I know now that you didn't lie when you said you never thought of her that way—and I'm going to make it up to you, you'll see," Cora whispered.

It was nearly time to start up the train for its sundown camp near the river. And once across the river, they would come to their new homes. But before he gave the order to start, Simon Brown went over to the Hornsteder wagon. "Mind if I see how Mrs. Mayberry's doin'?" he asked the plump old woman.

"Sure, sonny, you go right ahead. Reckon you earned plenty besides our thanks for savin' our lives the way you and your friends did there," Mrs. Hornsteder beamed at him. "She's fine now; she's got her eyes open, and she's talkin'. Knows about the baby, though she's not takin' it too badly."

"I—I have to tell her—you know, about—"

"I know. Come on, Henry, let's go down and take ourselves a stroll around and see what this Texas land looks like." Henry Hornsteder cackled with laughter: "You're a born matchmaker, Ma. I get your drift. I feel like stretchin' my old legs, too."

Simon knelt beside the pallet. Naomi Mayberry's eyes fixed on him, and there was a wan smile on her lips. "I—I know about the baby. Maybe—maybe it's just as well—"

"Hush now, ma'am; you mustn't say that. You'll be fine. Mrs. Hornsteder says you'll be up and about before you know. And it's not like you couldn't have—I mean—darn it all!" He swore at himself as his face reddened, touching on so daringly intimate a topic. "Anyhow, I—I think I got more bad news for you. I don't know any other way but to come right out with it. Mr. Mayberry—well, the fact is, you know there were lots of shots fired by those Mexes who came down on us out of nowhere and—well, he took one, and it killed him. We just finished buryin' him, and I said a prayer. I'm awful sorry."

"I—I'm not. You don't know, Mr. Brown, but he was terrible to me—"

"You don't have to tell me that," he stoutly countered. "Didn't I see him take that whip to you? I—well, look now, you got any folks?"

Naomi Mayberry shook her head.

"I mean, well, I—oh, hell, I oughtn't to be sayin' this right off, but I like you an awful lot, and now that—well, you don't have a husband now, and you won't have anybody in this land—I mean, I could take the land myself and—"

Naomi put out a slim hand and weakly touched his cheek, as her eyes blurred with tears. "You can't mean it. Why, you don't even know me—"

"Yes, I do. You're brave and you're good, and he was awful cruel to you. And I wouldn't ever care what you did; no man's got a right to treat a wife like that. Well, why don't we put it this way—maybe when we get settled down, before I have to go back to Franklin to bring another lot of families out here, maybe we could get acquainted and see if we liked each other?"

Tears had begun to run down Naomi Mayberry's pale cheeks, and her voice was unsteady. "I—I'd like that awful fine, Mr. Brown. G-God bless you."

Seventeen

Before he had left on the two-week journey to the mountains of the Jicarilla Apache, John Cooper had learned of the treacherous murder of the two *trabajadores* escorting Francisco López to San Antonio. Shocked beyond measure, John Cooper saw this as definitive proof of the man's treachery, and the only solace he could take in the whole tragic episode was that at least López had been banished from the ranch. Never would John Cooper have been able to guess that the man had not only managed to return to the ranch, but had also learned of the plans for the silver—and when the *vaquero* who had seen López come and go that night learned of the man's treachery, he was too frightened to say anything.

As he rode up the path to the mountain stronghold, John Cooper breathed in the air, and he could smell the tang of the fir trees, which fringed the winding trail to the peak of the stronghold. He inhaled the rarefied air, and he turned in his saddle to stare at the sky as the sun descended in its orbit, with the incredibly breathtaking mélange of purple and scarlet and cerulean blue.

"It is good to see you again after so long, my blood brother," Kinotatay said as he embraced John Cooper, after the latter dismounted from Pingo. "It is as if you have come home, *Halcón*."

"I feel as you do, Kinotatay," John Cooper replied. "Here, high in the mountains, with the blue sky above me, and the Jicarilla here to welcome me back, I feel at peace, as if I had never left."

"The memory of you will never leave these mountains, *Halcón*. Tonight we shall have a great feast in your honor. And then you shall tell me what has brought you here—for I see in your eyes that it is not only to visit with us."

"You are still the true *jefe* of your people, Kinotatay," John Cooper smilingly retorted. "You read what is in my heart, and I would speak of it with you now, before the feast."

"Go first through the village to be welcomed by those who know and love you, as I do," the tall, mature Apache decreed. "Then come to my wickiup, and only you and I will know what words you wish to speak."

"I will gladly do that, Kinotatay." John Cooper embraced him again, and then turned to see a tall young Apache come forward to take the reins of Pingo. It was Pastanari, son of Kinotatay's predecessor as *jefe* of these mountain *indios*. John Cooper's face brightened in recognition. He would never forget, so long as he lived, the day he first met Pastanari, the young son of the former chief, Descontarti. He and Lije, fleeing ahead of the angry Sioux shaman whose son John Cooper had to kill to save his own life, had first fled to this mountain to await the attack of the six Sioux runners sent to track him down and kill him, or bring him back for a death by prolonged torture.

He had fought them off, until at last the final Sioux brave had shot an arrow meant for him, which Lije had taken in his side. The great wolfhound, before he slumped in death with the arrow in his body, had leaped across a wide gap to sink his fangs into the Sioux's throat and had killed him. And John Cooper, grief-stricken at the knowledge that the heroic Irish wolfhound—his final tie with his birthplace of Shawneetown—had perished, lifted Lije's huge body and slid down the angling side of the peak to level ground and the trail. He saw the Jicarilla Apache braves on horseback, silently watching him. He marched solemnly to the slope of the ascending hill, which merged into the peak, and there, in a hollow in the wall of the slope, he buried Lije. How long ago that seemed, an eternity! And then, as the braves had silently motioned for him to follow them to the top of the mountain where their stronghold lay, a young boy astride his father's great horse, unable to control it, had come racing around the bend in the road. With all his strength, John Cooper had snatched the boy from the horse's back, discovering that by doing this, he had saved the life of Chief Descontarti's young son. Later, he would meet Carlos de Escobar here high in the mountains, and in turn, he would meet Carlos's sister, Catarina.

The years seemed to fall away, and under the blue sky and the clear, pure air, it was as if John Cooper were a boy again, a boy forced into swift and tragic manhood.

"My brother stands on the mountaintop and his eyes are on the stars, yet he sees the shadows of the ghost moons," Kinotatay shrewdly observed. "Walk among my people. Do not look back into the shadows; do not speak those names that we cannot utter; but take pride in your welcome back with us, *Halcón*."

John Cooper turned to make the sign of friendship to sturdy Pastanari, whose lovely young wife had come to stand beside him, holding their child in her arms. John Cooper's eyes softened; he nodded, and turned to walk slowly down the rows of wickiups. From every side old men and women, boys and girls, young braves and mature warriors acclaimed him. He turned when he had come to the last row of wickiups, his wrists crossed over his heart, his palms outward, in the Apache sign of thanksgiving for returning home. A chorused sigh of approbation from the villagers told him that he was still truly blood brother to them all.

His face was serene when he finally returned to Kinotatay and again clasped him in his arms. They were silent a long moment as they both remembered their vows of blood brotherhood.

"I have given orders for the feast in your honor, *Halcón*," Kinotatay gently murmured. "There is still time for us to have words together not meant for other ears, if you so desire it."

"I do with all my heart. I follow you, *jefe* of the Jicarilla Apache."

Inside the spacious, symbolically ornamented wickiup of the Apache leader, John Cooper sat cross-legged, arms folded across his chest, waiting for Kinotatay to speak, since he was, as a welcome guest, not bidden to hold council till his host so willed it. Kinotatay nodded and said, "Now, *Halcón*, speak all that you have within you; it will reach me and no one else."

"Then it is this, my brother. Your warriors still guard the secret mine?"

"As I have pledged they would, yes. And no one yet, to this moment, has sought the way to it, save men of my tribe, *Halcón*," Kinotatay replied.

"You have done more than I could ask. But now I have decided that it is time to take the silver back to the ranch in Texas. There, it will be cleverly hidden in wagons with secret bottoms, and my *trabajadores* and I will drive these wagons and our cattle to New Orleans. Once we have arrived there, Kinotatay, the treasure will be placed in a secret underground hiding place. In this way, Kinotatay, no thief can take it, neither Mexican nor *americano*. And because it will be there in safety, I can use it to help the *indios* of the pueblo in Taos as I can your people and then my own."

"I follow your thoughts, swift as the bird of prey for which you are so rightly named, *Halcón*."

"I have another reason for coming here, Kinotatay. It is my wish to bring back Don Sancho de Pladero and his wife, his son and daughter-in-law and their children to live in peace with Don Diego, the father of my Catarina."

"I understand this."

"Just so, Kinotatay. It is in my thoughts to ask you to send your bravest warriors with me to take back this treasure. I think it can be hidden in travois, drawn by horses, and covered with brush or sacks of maize."

"I read your thoughts again, *Halcón*. Those who would

come upon us would think, seeing the travois, that we seek a new hunting ground, a new stronghold. Yes, it is very good." Kinotatay nodded his approval.

"Perhaps your older men can make the travois. While they do, I will go into Taos and talk with Don Sancho de Pladero to beg him to come back with us. Your braves will become an armed escort, so that no one will attack us. And once Don Sancho is there, he will be with his good friend, Don Diego."

"Your plan is good. I promise that I will help you."

"I am grateful to you, my brother."

"I have seen him who is bound to you by the vows you took with your *esposa*, and who is also brother to me by our sacred vows of blood," Kinotatay observed.

"You mean Carlos?" John Cooper asked.

"Yes, *Halcón*. He came to us about a moon ago, and he and the mate of Colnara, who is daughter of our shaman, Marsimaya, tried their skill at the arrow and the lance."

"Has he returned to take his leave of you, Kinotatay?"

The Apache chief shook his head. "I have heard that he is still in Taos, at the *hacienda* of Don Sancho. And I know why—he wishes to take as his squaw a woman whom he met after he rode across the Rio Grande to join with the *soldados* of the *libertador*."

"Then he will still be there!" John Cooper exclaimed with a grin. "I had hoped for just that, Kinotatay. Now then, there is one other thing I would ask of you. I told you once that when I came upon that mine, I found the bones of the *soldados* and the *padres* who had guarded it long moons before even you or I were born. And when my *perro* and I climbed the mountain and came to this hidden door, which was almost closed with ivy and lichen, I pressed myself inside and saw the dead *peones* and *indios* who had been made slaves by those *conquistadores*. Because the cave had been virtually sealed off from the outside air, and because it was very cold and dry inside, their bodies were well preserved, like mummies. Their hands were bound behind their backs with rawhide thongs, and they were wearing only breech-cloths and moccasins. As I remember now, I counted nearly forty. The monks and soldiers who had guarded them had been slain by *indios* of some other tribe whose name I do not know. The guards' bodies had turned to bones, and these I buried as best I could. Because of all this, no one came to the mountain because there were evil ghosts about it."

"I know the story, and it is true that we of the Jicarilla would not have climbed that mountain," Kinotatay replied.

"I wish to give these *indios* and *peones* who died inside the mine a burial, a burial such as your own people would provide for brave warriors, Kinotatay. They died in agony, forsaken and alone, and there is no one except myself who knows this."

"Our shaman, Marsimaya, will talk with you, and he will tell you how it can be done," was Kinotatay's answer.

"I will not break the laws of the Apache. I will do what is the custom of your people, Kinotatay."

"When the sun rises in the east tomorrow, you and Marsimaya will talk of this. I will give orders tomorrow to have my older men begin the building of these travois. How many will you need, *Halcón*?"

John Cooper pensively frowned. "I remember there were twelve times five bars of the purest silver, Kinotatay. Ten of these can be placed on each travois, and that will make six travois. Also, there are holy relics, which I propose to give to the shaman of Taos, the Padre Salvador Madura."

"It shall be as you wish, my brother. If you go into Taos to see Don Sancho and your *cuñado*, you will see that they have begun the great fair. It is held now, and not in the next moon as has been the custom."

"Then by the next moon, if all goes well, I shall ride Pingo back with your warriors, whose horses will draw the travois back to the ranch."

Kinotatay took John Cooper's hands in his and smiled. "My men will gladly go with you, *Halcón*. But now we have talked enough, and the feast begins. Pastanari has asked me if you will dance with the warriors during the feast. It will be a dance of prayer to the Great Spirit, whom we thank because our blood brother has returned to us, and it is as it was when first he came to our stronghold."

Francisco López had brutally ridden the mustang, and the horse had balked at being so mercilessly treated. But Santa Anna's spy had punished him for this rebellion by kicking his belly with his booted heels and fiercely tugging at the reins. Conquered, the mustang had submitted to the Mexican's coercion.

He had ridden all through the night, to make certain that no possible pursuer could overtake him. At dawn, he had stopped at a tiny hamlet and, tyrannically proclaiming himself a colonel under government orders, forced an impoverished farmer and his wife to give him breakfast, to provide a bucket of grain and one of water for the exhausted mustang, and then to supply all the food they could spare for his saddlebag. This done, he mounted up again and galloped on toward Nuevo Laredo.

Stabling the mustang, he went to the largest *posada* in the town and demanded of the proprietor the whereabouts of Teniente Benito Aguarez. When he had bidden farewell to his two military aides, López had instructed the lieutenant, as well as the sergeant, to identify themselves at the *posada* that had the largest patronage in the town, so that a message might find them quickly. The proprietor directed him to a little *hacienda* on the edge of the town, and López thanked him, enjoyed a glass of the best tequila the house could provide, and then went back to the stable to ride to his lieutenant's quarters.

Benito Aguarez was in his early thirties, genial of features, black bearded and mustached, almost six feet tall and a consummate profligate. He had been born in San Luis Potosí to affluent parents, but his womanizing and drinking even before he had reached sixteen had so disgusted his father that the latter had enrolled him in a school for military cadets. There, Aguarez had discovered that he enjoyed the life of a soldier, and that an officer's rank could make it even more enjoyable. Consequently, he had earnestly attempted to discipline himself so that he might become more than a lowly private.

To be sure, it had been an arduous struggle, since he was especially vulnerable to the temptations of the flesh. Twice he had been broken from the rank of sergeant because of complaints by irate fathers in the villages where he had been stationed, for, out of boredom, he had treated their daughters like *putas*. Finally, on the occasion of his second demotion, a stern-faced, ascetic captain lectured him and told him that he might well be cashiered out of the army entirely if he failed his last chance, which turned out to be an assignment as attaché to Colonel Francisco López. What a delight it was when he discovered that his new commanding officer was a sensualist also. Gradually, over the months that followed, López had come to rely upon Aguarez as a procurer, and had authorized the latter's promotion first to corporal, then sergeant, and, just last year, to the coveted post of *teniente*.

Francisco López rode the mustang to the small stable at the back of the *hacienda*, quartered it in one of the empty stalls, and then strode to the door and banged on it with his fist, calling out, "*¡Teniente Aguarez, ven aquí pronto!*"

A few moments later, the door was opened by Benito Aguarez himself, clad in a silk dressing robe and naked underneath it, reeking of *aguardiente* and scowling over the unexpected interruption during his erotic dalliance with the owner of the *hacienda*, a handsome widow in her early thirties.

At the sight of his superior officer, for all his befuddled condition, he uttered a gasp, then forced himself into an erect posture and saluted López.

"*Mi coronel*, I—I didn't know it was you—and, you see, I was with Inez—"

"Who is this Inez of yours? Some *puta*? In any case, Aguarez, now you have your orders. This moment, you'll dress and mount your horse and ride to Ciudad Victoria to find Sargento Monreal. You will make as few stops as possible for rest and food; it's vital that you have the *sargento* get to Coronel Santa Anna with all possible haste. You are to tell the *sargento* that I respectfully urge our *coronel* to send as many mounted, well-armed soldiers as he can spare."

"I—I'll go at once, *mi coronel*," Aguarez stammered, self-consciously tugging the robe closer around him and reknotting the loose belt at his waist.

"You will indeed, if you expect a captaincy from me, Aguarez. Now there's more, so pay attention. You will have the *sargento* urge the *libertador* to send these troops, who are to ride with the very fewest delays—as you yourself will ride to Ciudad Victoria at once!—to meet me on the north side of the Pecos River near the boundary of Nuevo México."

"*Sí, mi coronel*." Aguarez nodded and saluted again, rubbing his silk-covered arm over his florid, sweating face.

"You sodden fool, if you forget a single detail of this message, I'll have you demoted to private and whipped in the public square in Mexico City, till the skin is flayed from your neck to heels! Now pay attention, *hombre*. Monreal must have this from you exactly as I give it to you now, with nothing missing. Because of these enormous distances, it's important that you memorize what I am telling you. And before you saddle your horse, Aguarez, you'll repeat it back to me word for word, *¿comprendes?*"

Again the hapless lieutenant saluted and tried to stand at attention.

"Monreal is to tell the *libertador* that the reason for this is that I have discovered that the silver he seeks is somewhere near the stronghold of the Jicarilla Apache, which is in the northeastern part of Nuevo México. Tell him that the *gringo* intends to bring this silver back from the mine, which must be in that vicinity, to the Texas ranch from which I have just ridden. I heard the *gringo* say that he expected to be back at the ranch with the silver by the end of July or early August. Now, if the *libertador* can in any way detach the troops I need from a nearer point than Veracruz, much valuable time could be saved. I intend to ambush the *gringo* and his men on their way back to the ranch. Now, do you have it all, Aguarez? Repeat it to me, just as I've told it to you, *pronto!*"

Benito Aguarez had quickly sobered, and he managed to repeat most of the message to his superior officer's satisfaction. But Francisco López relentlessly insisted that he try again, and only when he was satisfied did he at last declare, "Do you see how important it is for the message to reach Santa Anna with all possible swiftness and for these troops to meet me? Of course, they will send scouts, but I myself have estimated the time of their arrival and will have no trouble finding them. This is almost the end of the first week in June. Somehow—I care not how it is done, but it must be done—Monreal must reach Santa Anna before the end of this month. That will give the troops little better than a month to reach me at the Pecos. And that, Aguarez, is why Monreal must tell the *libertador* that if he can dispatch a courier to any post closer to the Rio Grande to procure me these troops I need, then we shall have every possible chance of ambushing the *gringo* and bringing back the silver, which will make Coronel Santa Anna the most powerful man in all Mexico. If that occurs, Aguarez, you and Monreal may have even more than what I have promised you. Now dress yourself, saddle your horse, and be off."

"I—I'll say good-bye to Señora Inez—"

"I will say your farewells for you, Aguarez." López sneered and eyed the lieutenant. "She's not a *puta*, then?"

"No, *mi coronel*. I said—she—she's a widow. When I came here to Nuevo Laredo, I—well, I commandeered her *hacienda*. And because she has no man, she and I—"

"I do not need you to tell me tales that I learned when I was a cadet, Aguarez. Go now and prepare. You will ride all night without sleep. It will teach you, perhaps, that you must always be ready to take the field when your country needs you!"

Benito Aguarez saluted again and, his face lax with disappointment, hurried off into the house. López grinned to himself, entered and closed the door behind him, and strode to the bedchamber. There he found, sitting up and holding a sheet around her nudity, a handsome brown-haired woman whose eyes fixed on him with an expression of incredulity.

"My apologies, *mi bonita*," he lecherously chuckled. "I must apologize for having taken your lover from you. I am Coronel Francisco López, assigned to the regiment of the great *libertador*, Coronel Santa Anna. I have sent Benito on a mission—have no fear, he will be in no danger; and he should come back at least a captain. Meanwhile, since I must remain here for some weeks, I shall replace him."

"But—S–Señor López," she began to stammer, shrinking back against the rumpled pillows of the four-poster bed, "you must not think that I—"

He interrupted her before she could finish. "I know, you are a widow. But apparently Benito has been consoling you. And I am even better at that little game, as you will find out at once."

"Please, I beg of you—this is dreadful—I cannot let you—in all decency—" Her face was red with shame as she drew the sheet even more tightly over her ripely curved body.

But Francisco López blithely ignored her protests. He proceeded to strip down to his *calzoncillos*, then got onto the bed and brutally ripped away the sheet from the frightened widow.

"Oh, no, in the name of *Dios,* I implore you—oh, this cannot be—it is shameful—" she hysterically cried out.

But López uttered a sardonic laugh as his fingers dug into her naked shoulders and he drew her toward him. "No, Señora Inez, it is not for God; it is for Mexico—and, I am ready to admit, since you are *muy linda,* a little for myself as well!"

Eighteen

Noracia had been greatly impressed by Carlos de Escobar during her chance meeting with him in the plaza of Taos. When she had returned home, she had been pensive and silent, though pretty little Manuela, trying to cajole her into being more communicative—since the young *criada* apprehensively believed that her mistress might suddenly be vexed with her—prattled on about the inconsequential incidents that had taken place in the *hacienda* during her absence. Noracia at last regarded her and snapped, "Will you hold your tongue, you little fool! I must think. Now, to make yourself useful, draw my bath, and then tell the cook that I want something extraordinary for supper tonight. After my bath, I shall take a little *siesta.* See that I'm not disturbed, Manuela." Manuela had timidly averred that she would faithfully execute all these orders and hurried out to convey her mistress's request to the plump Indian cook. After her bath, Manuela had dried Noracia and persuaded the beautiful *mestiza* to stretch out on a long teakwood bench over which a soft, thick black merino cover had been thrown, while she massaged her with scented oil. Secretly, Manuela had hoped that this unctuous attention would alter Noracia's strange, aloof mood.

But while Noracia sighed and surrendered herself to Manuela's delicate ministrations, she preserved her brooding silence and finally curtly dismissed the fearful young servant. "That's enough; you begin to annoy me! No, no, don't snivel, you little fool; I'm not angry with you—I just want to be by myself and think something out. Just leave me here to have my *siesta*, and when the cook has supper ready, come in to dress me, *¿comprendes?*"

It was not until several days later, much to Manuela's relief, that Noracia was once again in an ebullient mood, and the two young women chattered away like magpies as they discussed the trivia of the household. After breakfast, Noracia had Manuela help her into her riding costume, and then ordered the young *indio* stableboy to saddle her horse. "I don't know when I shall be back, but it's not important. I shall just go for a good, long ride. What a beautiful day it is, Manuela! Oh, yes, I quite forgot—tell Pía that her supper the other night was splendid. I shan't forget to reward her for making such an effort to please me. Now, *hasta la vista*, little one!" With this, she chucked Manuela under the chin and left the young servant bewildered as to this sudden shift in her mistress's behavior. But at any rate, she knew she couldn't be punished, not when Noracia was so pleased. So she hurried off to the kitchen to compliment Pía. And next, to prove how industrious she truly was, she began very assiduously to tidy up Noracia's elegantly furnished bedroom.

The *mestiza* rode out at a leisurely gait toward the Sangre de Cristo Mountains, her eyes sparkling, inhaling the crisp, pleasantly cool air. Elevated as Taos was over the barren, tortured plains south of Nuevo México, the month of June was not at all oppressive. It was good to be alive, and best of all, to be free and to have money. She laughed contemptuously, remembering how some of the rich young *hacendados* courted her, as if indeed she were one of them. If she were poor, as poor as little Manuela had been before she had been forced to serve with Don Esteban de Rivarola, these same fine *caballeros* would instead have sent their majordomos to arrange for her to visit them for a night in return for a paltry few *pesos*. Oh, yes, it was because she was now a *rica* that she was being treated with such respect. And to her way of thinking, there wasn't a real *hombre* in the lot of her would-be suitors!

She had directed her mount to the *hacienda* of Señora Teresa de Rojado, hoping that she would be fortunate enough to come upon the widow out for her own morning ride. And luck favored her. A few hundred yards ahead of her, Noracia caught sight of Teresa's superb mare, and with a click of her tongue and a kick of her heels against the mount's belly, she urged it onward.

Teresa de Rojado, hearing the pounding hooves behind her, halted and turned in her saddle, her eyes wide with curiosity, as she saw the elegantly garbed *mestiza* bearing down upon her. As Noracia drew her horse to a halt, jerking violently on the reins, she turned to favor Teresa with a dazzling smile. "Please forgive me if I've disturbed you; I didn't mean to!"

"But you didn't. You've a fine horse and your costume is most becoming."

"How sweet of you to say this! I don't think you know me—my name is Noracia. But I know your name—it's the Señora Teresa de Rojado, am I right?"

"Why, yes, but I don't understand—"

"I will try to explain, señora. I have been in Taos much longer than you, so I know the people who live here better than you possibly could."

"I still don't know why—" Teresa again remonstrated.

"Please, Señora de Rojado, let me finish. I know you are keeping company with the *caballero* Alejandro Cabeza, *¿no es verdad?*"

The beautiful brown-haired widow stiffened in her saddle, her face cold and aloof. "I do not really think it concerns you, Noracia. I do not wish to be impolite, but—"

Once again, Noracia interrupted with a knowing smile. "But you take him at face value, Señora de Rojado. You will see, I shall not lie to you. I was the *puta*—there is really no other word to describe it—to both Don Esteban de Rivarola and Luis Saltareno. To put it bluntly, I was nothing more than a slave. So you understand from this that I know something more of men than you, who are so far above me in birth, in position, and in education."

"I really am embarrassed to hear such talk, Noracia; why do you confront me now, and to what purpose?"

"I will tell you. It's because I want to warn you. And because I know Alejandro Cabeza, I feel it is my duty to tell you exactly what he is and what motives he has in courting you."

"I—I'm not sure I wish to hear this. I don't know by what right you try to interfere in my life, Noracia. Please understand, I do not wish to hurt you when I say this—"

"You have a good heart, and I am not offended. But I should be doing you an injustice if I did not tell you all that I know about this Alejandro. Listen to me, please, I beg of you!"

Teresa de Rojado frowned, but she could see from the *mestiza*'s lovely face that she was being sincere. Moreover, remembering the delightful evening she had spent with Carlos de Escobar and how he had behaved with the utmost propriety, choosing words that were far less florid than Alejandro's, she felt herself compelled to hear what Noracia had to say about the *hacendado*. "Very well, I will listen to you, and I thank you for your interest."

"*Gracias*, Señora de Rojado. Alejandro Cabeza was left a great deal of *dinero* by his parents. He has by now squandered it all, and he has a majordomo named Ernesto Rojas, who caters to all his wishes. At the present time, in his *hacienda*, Alejandro keeps a *querida*, an *india* from the pueblo, who is called Leacarla. It was Rojas with two of Alejandro's *trabajadores* who took her by force from her father's *jacal* and brought her as a slave to the *hacienda*."

"But that's dreadful! Are you sure of it?"

"I am indeed, Señora de Rojado. But there is much more. By now, having wasted all of his money, he is almost *pobre*. His only hope is to marry someone who is very rich—and that is you, Señora de Rojado."

"But I can hardly believe all this, Noracia!" Teresa gasped.

"I swear on my hope of salvation, Señora de Rojado; I speak only the truth to you. And there is much worse—during the past year, he has sold contraband, including *fusiles*, across the Rio Grande. Why, did you not know that *su excelencia, el gobernador* himself, summoned Alejandro and Rojas to Santa Fe to demand that Alejandro explain this unlawful trade? By luck, he was set free, but my servants sometimes gossip with his at a *posada* in Taos, and they have told my people that their *patrón* was really guilty of the charge. This, then, Señora de Rojado, is the man who is courting you and promising to make you the perfect husband." Noracia uttered a little laugh and shook her head. "He is not capable of being truthful or faithful to any one woman for any length of time; I am certain this is so. And that is why I want to tell you, because I also know that the Señor Carlos de Escobar is truly in love with you—"

"Hush, Noracia, please don't say that!" Teresa blushed and turned away, biting her lips.

"But it's true; it's true as I sit on my horse and face you, before the eyes of *El Señor Dios* Himself!" Noracia fervently declared. "I will tell you something else. I met the Señor Carlos about a week ago, quite by accident, in the plaza. I thought to myself, how handsome he is, how noble and dignified! All that Alejandro is not. And so I talked with him, and I confess to you that, out of my knowledge of men and my own loneliness, because I now have no *novio* to watch over me, I asked him if he would not be interested in having me as his dear friend, yes, even as his *querida.*"

Teresa gasped, and turned to stare at Noracia, her lovely eyes wide with astonishment. "You—you did that?" she stammered.

"*Sí,* I'm not ashamed. A woman by herself, what chance does she have, unless she speaks what is in her heart to the man that she may desire? I tell you, Señora de Rojado, I, who have been a *puta* to earn my bread because I am a *mestiza,* have no time for all the pretty little games by which an elegant *rica* tries to hold out for the ring and the holy words in Mother Church. Yes, I offered myself to your Carlos—"

"But he is not my Carlos—"

"But he wishes to be, and he will be a far better man to you, I swear before *el Cristo* Himself, than ever Alejandro would be. You see, he told me that he was greatly flattered, that I was very beautiful, but that his heart belonged to another—and I know he meant you. Now I will trouble you no more. But think over what I have said, Señora de Rojado. Listen carefully to Alejandro Cabeza, as if you were a teacher hearing a pupil in school recite his lessons. And then listen to Carlos de Escobar. Your mind, and then your heart also, will tell you who speaks the truth. I wish you every happiness, and I envy you. *¡Hasta la vista!*" With this, the beautiful *mestiza* wheeled her horse around and rode back to Taos.

The day after Noracia's meeting with Teresa de Rojado, Alejandro Cabeza stood before the gilt-framed full-length mirror in his bedroom and preened himself, while his complacent majordomo, Ernesto Rojas, approvingly looked on.

"You are certainly *muy caballero, patrón,*" Rojas fawningly declared as he stepped back, hands on his hips, scrutinizing his dissipated, handsome master in the mirror. "*Seguramente,* there is no woman in all Taos who will say no to you."

The young *hacendado* pursed his lips and put a finger to the dimple in his chin, as he admired the reflection. He wore his elegant riding attire, with a bright green sash around his middle. This had been Rojas's nuance, and Cabeza had heartily assented to the ornamentation. "It is not too bad, I think," he said with a self-deprecating air, and turned to eye his majordomo.

"You give yourself too little credit, *patrón.* If the queen of Spain herself were to pay a visit to Taos, she would have eyes for you only; I swear it on my hope of salvation!"

Cabeza emitted a ribald little laugh. "I have lost track of what is going on at the Escorial in Madrid, Ernesto, but if memory serves me right, she is an aged relic by now, and her approval of me would count for nothing. I am much more interested in having that divine *viuda,* the Señora de Rojado, think me *hombre macho, muy hombre.*"

"And you are right, *patrón,*" the majordomo glibly agreed with a vehement nod. "Not only is she beautiful, but also she has *mucho dinero.* I think you should present her a gift—let us see, what have we in the house that would be appropriate?" He, too, pursed his lips, imitating his dissolute master, then put a finger to his forehead and scowled. Lost in thought for a moment, he suddenly brightened and exclaimed, "But I have it, *por Dios!* Do you not recall, *patrón,* that your sainted mother left you a silver cross with a large ruby in the very center? It has a silver chain that goes about the neck. It would be the perfect gift. Consider it, *patrón.* It will convince her that you are a deeply religious man, and consequently the most moral and devoted of churchgoers. From this she will surely infer that you will be the most faithful of husbands. Besides that, it is lovely, and the ruby is worth many hundreds of *pesos*. It will tell her also that you are a *hacendado rico*, and therefore that you care nothing for her fortune."

"Ernesto, you are certainly a genius! Let me have the crucifix, and I will give it to her today. And this evening when I return for supper, you may be certain that I shall tell you to summon the household so that you may lecture them on the duties befitting servants of a *patrón* like myself who is about to take unto himself a wife whose beauty and character are without flaw. You will warn them that I shall tolerate not the least familiarity in her presence, and that they must serve her as if she were a *princesa* of Spain."

Ernesto Rojas grinned as he rubbed his hands in sly anticipation. "I shall see to it, *patrón*. I shall bring you the crucifix at once, and I shall say prayers that this evening you will announce to us that your bachelor days have come to a very happy end."

"And so they will, Ernesto," Alexandro Cabeza said, giving his majordomo a salacious wink. "To be sure, you will tell my sweet *novia*, Leacarla, that as soon as the banns are announced, she must content herself with moving at once from my *hacienda* into one of the huts of the *trabajadores*. If my wife-to-be should confront her, she is to lower her eyes and curtsy, as if she were the lowliest of *criadas*. But of course, we shall explain to her, shan't we, Ernesto, that after the first weeks of marriage, and as soon as I get my hands on the Señora de Rojado's fortune, she will be compensated beyond her wildest dreams for acting like a slave."

"I shall carry out your wishes to the smallest detail, *patrón*." Rojas favored his dissolute master with a low bow and an ingratiating smile.

Alejandro Cabeza swaggered out to his stables, basking in his majordomo's flowery phrases, and certain that after this afternoon, his delectable quarry could not possibly escape him. After all, was he not of the blue-blooded aristocracy? And if the truth be known, the Señora de Rojado was really damaged goods, since she had been married to a man old enough to be her father. And yet the wedding ceremony he envisioned, and the gala *baile* that would be held at his own *hacienda* directly after they had come from the church, would be a proclamation to all the people of Taos that he held her in the very highest regard. Licentiously, he looked forward to initiating her later on their wedding day into his own particular erotic penchants.

"A word of warning to you, Rafael," he sternly told the stableboy who saddled his master's horse and led it out by the reins, "I go now to ask a beautiful and dignified *mujer* to be my wife. She is an even better rider than I am, and thus I warn you, Rafael, that when at last I bring her back here, you will no longer be quite so lazy as you have been in my service."

"But, *patrón*, that's not so; even Rojas will tell you how hard I work," the stableboy protested.

"Enough of your chatter! Open the gate, so I may ride out at a gallop," Cabeza commanded.

The boy scrambled to obey, and the *hacendado* spurred his horse in the direction of Teresa's *hacienda*. A supercilious smile curved his lips as he touched the silver crucifix in the pocket of his *camisa* and thought to himself how convincing a declaration of love it would make. Truly, Ernesto had surpassed himself!

He knew that she would be riding out before she took her *almuerzo*, and so he was confident of meeting her. What other *hacendado* in all Taos would go to such pains to court a *mujer*?

To be sure, once he married her, there would be certain alterations that he would have to effect. For one thing, she was much too forward and outspoken: a true *hacendado* should never be embarrassed by his wife, and Teresa de Rojado had a most irritating habit of speaking her mind. Of course, he would correct her very gently, at least at the outset. If she proved obstinate for any length of time, it was a simple matter to discipline her, or, more subtly, to have her watch the punishment of a disobedient *criada*.

The sun was bright, and with a cry of joy, he perceived her slim, erect figure in the saddle on her mare at a far distance beyond him. He spurred his horse again, riding at a gallop to overtake her, and then, when he realized that he was approaching so fast, slackened the gait so that she would not think he was too bold in his pursuit of her.

Teresa de Rojado had heard the pounding of his horse's hooves, and drew in the reins to ease her mare into a rhythmic canter. At last, he drew abreast of her, doffing his *sombrero* and effusively smiling: "I wish you a happy day, Teresa!"

"I thank you for your wish, Alejandro." Her voice was cool, and her glance gave him so sign of more than formal recognition.

"I'm happy I found you riding this morning, Teresa. I have a gift for you, and it will express my deepest feelings toward you."

She gave him another sidelong glance, but without halting her mare. Irked by this curious aloofness, he blurted out, "Can we not go more slowly so that I may converse with you, *querida*?"

"I am not really your *querida*, Alejandro."

"Of course, but that will come later, because I wish—"

"What exactly do you wish of me, Alejandro?" Now she did halt her mare and turned her head to contemplate him. There was no smile on her face; her eyes searched his face and showed no sign of warmth.

With an effort, he kept the ingratiating smile on his face, as with his other hand, he fumbled with the crucifix and drew it out by the chain. "This was my mother's dearest possession, Teresa, and she once said to me that if ever I took a bride, it should be hers to wear."

"But why do you show me this and tell me this story, Alejandro?"

"*¡Por todos los santos!*" he burst out. "Because I wish to make you my *esposa*! Because each of us is *católico*, and because the holy cross is the symbol of our faith and the love we shall share together."

"May I ask you a question in return, Alejandro?"

"*Pero seguramente, querida.*" He bowed from the waist, assuming his most adoring expression. All the same, her face remained cold and impersonal.

"Then I must ask you, Alejandro, if I were to become your *esposa*, what disposition would you make to your present *querida*, the girl named Leacarla?"

Alejandro Cabeza was thunderstruck, and for an instant so nonplussed that his mouth gaped. Then, lamely recovering, his face crimson, he stammered, "But—but it is traditional that a man have a mistress until he weds, my dearest Teresa. Of course, once you and I are man and wife, she will be dismissed. Oh, I will be generous to her, for that is the sort of man I am—"

"I have heard a good deal about what sort of man you really are, Alejandro," Teresa interrupted. "It appears that your character is well known to many people in Taos, but not to myself. I feel that your interest in me concerns itself with neither my mind nor my body, but rather with the legacy my late husband bequeathed to me."

"Teresa, what are you saying? This is infamous—I do not know what lies have come to your ears, but I swear to you on this cross—"

She stared at him levelly, and shook her head: "Do not add blasphemy to perjury, Alejandro. I know, for example, that you have flung away thousands of *pesos* on your own pleasures; that your majordomo, Ernesto Rojas, has procured women for you, including girls from the pueblo."

"You must not speak of such things—it is not proper for a woman of breeding to discuss such matters—and besides, all these things are falsehoods!" he angrily countered.

"I do not think so. At least, Noracia did not think so. It also appears that you asked her to spend the night with you, and she knows how you tried to make up for your wasted fortune by selling contraband."

"But *el gobernador* himself absolved me from those charges—don't you see, *querida* Teresa, someone who hates me has been spreading lies about me, so as to estrange us! Please take this crucifix, and with it my oath that I will be your adoring, faithful husband."

"If I were to take your oath, Alejandro, I would ask you to swear a counteroath, that you would support me, and that I should not have to use a *centavo* of the money my husband left me. What would you say to that?"

His face crimsoned again, and he stared incredulously at her, while his reeling mind fumbled for words.

"I see you are not ready to take such an oath. Alejandro Cabeza, I have no desire to see you ever again. As to fencing, if we should have a bout again, I might be tempted to use a foil to which no button has been placed on the point. I wish you a good day—and perhaps better luck with some more gullible *mujer*." With this, she urged her mare on and left him sitting astride his horse gaping after her, his face turning livid with frustrated rage.

He watched her recede into the distance till she was no longer in view, and then he cursed blasphemously. "Noracia, that *mestiza* bitch—she's the one who's ruined everything! Oh, I'll make her pay for it; I'll really make her pay for this! But how could she have known all these things; and why did she take it into her head to go to Teresa? I have never done anything to her. All I did was want to bed her—and that shouldn't have offended her, not when she was the whore of Don Esteban de Rivarola and Luis Saltareno!"

As his fury grew, he brutally wheeled his horse round and, digging in his spurs, galloped back to his *hacienda*. And now his thoughts were black, as he contemplated a future without wealth and luxury, for the glimmering fortune of Teresa de Rojado was gone forever.

Some ten minutes after her encounter with Alejandro Cabeza, Teresa de Rojado halted and leaned forward to stroke her mare's head and to murmur words of praise; the mare pricked up her ears and tried to nuzzle at her mistress. Her mood immediately changed; she laughed heartily and confided, "I think we shall go back now, but first we shall stop at the *hacienda* of Don Sancho de Pladero. I think a certain young man would be very glad to see us, ¿no es verdad?" At this, the mare bobbed her head and whinnied, and Teresa laughed again, her eyes shining with a joyous relief. Gently, she moved the reins to turn the mare back in the direction whence they had come; and then at a methodical canter, so there would be no danger of catching up with the rejected *hacendado*, Teresa and her mare rode to the de Pladeros.

Carlos de Escobar was in the act of saddling Dolor out near the stable when, having tethered her mare to a hitching post near the *hacienda*, she caught sight of him.

"Carlos!" she called out, and the handsome Spaniard turned as he was about to mount his mustang, his eyes widening in amazement. "Teresa—what a wonderful surprise to see you here! I was just going riding," he explained as he took Dolor's reins in his left hand and led the mustang over to where Teresa stood.

"I am wearing your gloves, as you see, Carlos," she said softly, holding out her right hand to him. Instead of kissing her hand, Carlos shook it as he would that of a man.

"Oh, that's so much better! That's the way it should be

between us, frank and open always," she exclaimed with a happy smile.

"That, my dearest Teresa, is what I have been prayerfully hoping to hear you say all this long, weary time," he observed as he stared deeply into her eyes.

A swift crimson flush suffused her cheeks. She gently disengaged her hand and lowered her eyes. "I—I owe you an apology, Carlos. That's—that's why I rode here, to find you and to tell you. I have made a very bad mistake—but it could have been far worse, if I had not had some information I did not expect to get and from a source I never would have dreamed could furnish it," she said in a low voice without looking at him. "You see, I have learned Alejandro Cabeza is not quite the honorable suitor he pretended to be."

"That gives me heart! Please, Teresa," he impulsively began, "you know I came here for the express purpose of asking you formally and honorably to be my wife and to come back with me to the Double H Ranch. I also want to have my father's dear friends, Don Sancho and Doña Elena, as well as Tomás and Conchita, accompany us. Say that you will, my dearest one."

She was silent for a moment. Then she shook her head. "Please, you mustn't try to force my answer. Please give me more time. There is no one else I think of—but I cannot yet bring myself to say yes to you. If I do, Carlos, it will be for life—"

"Yes, that is all I ask for—and my life will be yours until the day I draw my last breath, and I will devote my life to making you happy, so that you will never have cause to regret your decision," he eloquently exclaimed, and took another step toward her.

She put out her gloved hand to touch his and shook her head. "You make it so difficult for me. It would be so easy to say yes now, because I can see how you love me. It is not infatuation; you have been faithful to me for more than two years, and I believe—I know, indeed—that the memory of your sweet wife will not come between us. Indeed, if anything, it has made you a better, stronger man, a man of great courage and humility. And now that I know what Alejandro truly is. I find him insipid in comparison with you."

"Oh, Teresa, *querida, mi corazón,* what you are saying is

almost yes—by the Holy Virgin who hears us now, I dedicate myself to you—"

"I beg you not to. Please, Carlos!" Her eyes filled with tears as she averted her face from him. "I told you that I am contrite and ashamed for the way I treated you. And because I am so distraught, it would be much too easy for me now to accept you. But it would be fair to neither of us—surely you must see that. Be content with the knowledge that I respect you and admire you more than any other man I have ever known. Be content to wait until I can tell you what truthfully is in my heart." She looked up at him and almost dazedly shook her head, her eyes poignant and pleading. "When I come to you—that is, if I do, Carlos—it must be of my own free will."

"And those are the only terms on which I should want you, my beloved Teresa," he said, his voice hoarse with emotion. "Very well, then. We shall talk again. As I mentioned, I shall stay until the fair is over. It is to open in a short time, and I wish to be on hand to help Don Sancho, knowing how ill he is. And then, besides, my father urged me to do all I could to induce Don Sancho to come live with us. Teresa, it is such a magnificent ranch—for miles on every side, nothing but lush green grass, streams and rivers, trees, and the blue sky and the sun and the moon and the stars—a kind of paradise in which we are isolated, yet well defended, if any evil men should try to encroach upon our community. Our *trabajadores* and their families, and some of the Texans my father met years ago after the Battle of Medina, live with us like a huge family. And we're proud of what we do because we are neither greedy nor scheming. And you should see the palominos John Cooper owns. I would give you a palomino mare—"

"No, you must not talk on so, I beg of you, Carlos. Indeed it sounds like heaven—but I feel myself still a sinner and I have not yet the right to expect paradise."

"So be it." He bowed to her, a gentle smile on his face. "When the fair is over, and if Don Sancho agrees to come back with me to Texas, I will ask you again. Otherwise, you'll be left alone here in Taos, and every adventurer, every pampered *hacendado* who knows that you have wealth as well as great beauty and wisdom, will be around you like a swarm of vultures."

"It is not really so dreadful as that, and I can still defend myself," she said with a whimsical little smile, her
exquisite nose crinkling so that he impulsively wanted to take
her in his arms and kiss her until she accepted him. "You
forget that I am an expert with the foils. I told Alejandro
that if he continued to bother me, I would fence with him,
but with an unbuttoned foil."

"You said that to him? How discomfited he must have
been!" Carlos burst into hearty laughter, and after a moment
Teresa, brushing the tears out of her eyes, joined him.

"Now that you are here, will you not stay to *almuerzo*?"
he asked.

"I will, but only on one condition. You know that Don
Sancho was my father's friend, and he has been very kind to
me since my arrival in Taos. If you are present, Carlos, you
are in no way to continue your courtship of me. We are
agreed, you will wait until I can give you a truthful and honest answer?"

"We are agreed, *mi corazón*." He came to her now, took
her gloved hand, and, delighted to see the initials *T de R*,
which Ignazio Peramonte had cut into the superbly tooled
leather, kissed her hand with the austere elegance of a diplo-
mat.

Nineteen

Don Sancho de Pladero had been forced into virtual
inactivity by his solicitous wife for the two weeks that had
preceded the opening of the annual Taos fair, so that he
would be able to preside at its inauguration. The weather
could not have been more beautiful, with scarcely a trace of

humidity, and with the bright sun tempered by delightfully cool breezes wafting in from the Sangre de Cristo Mountains as the afternoon waned.

Accordingly, the elderly *alcalde mayor* mounted a platform that his *trabajadores* had erected two days before the opening of the fair, and addressed the throngs of eager residents, traders, and Indians, as well as many of the local Taos shopkeepers who had come. Carlos de Escobar was seated near Don Sancho at the table that had been placed in the middle of the platform, with Doña Elena between him and her husband, and Tomás at Carlos's right. Conchita had remained at home to look after the children and to supervise the household.

In his speech, Don Sancho dwelt nostalgically on the many fairs he had attended and presided over since he had first come to Taos, noting the changes that had taken place in the politics and the economy of the country since their separation from Spain. *"Mis amigos,"* he declared, turning to look in every direction, "it was always my hope that the road between our picturesque town of Taos and the capital of Santa Fe would one day be open to all comers who wish to visit here and partake of our unique culture and tradition. Thankfully, I have lived long enough to welcome old friends—yes, friends among the *americanos,* like the Señores Matthew Robisard and Ernest Henson. I recall the days when they first came here to trade, not realizing that the restrictions of the former Spanish government placed them in great jeopardy. But I knew then, even as my good friend Don Diego de Escobar did, that their presence was justified, and boded good, not evil, for Taos."

He paused a moment, cleared his throat, then continued: "I supported them, not because of any lack of loyalty to my native land of Spain, but because like them, I dreamed that we who have lived here so long, isolated behind our mountains, would one day be able to enjoy the imaginative goods that are being brought to us from the young and prospering Estados Unidos. I foresaw that these courageous and enterprising *americanos* would become our friends, bringing us goods at prices that would be within the reach of all of us, opening new horizons to us, and giving us the opportunity to establish the friendliest of relations with them. Now all this has come to pass, and I believe that, in the years ahead, there will be even greater communication and friendship between us of Nuevo México and the *americanos* from these distant regions. I open the fair at this moment, and I humbly pray to *El Señor Dios* to grant my prayer for lasting peace and growing friendship."

There was great applause, and then the murmur of voices as the people of Taos began to move toward the displays of merchandise. Farmers and shopkeepers, ranchers and traders and Indians stopped here and there and asked questions, examined the merchandise offered, and bargained—for the best part of the fair was always the good-natured haggling over price.

It was a longer speech than he had intended to make, and Doña Elena sharply whispered to him as he finally seated himself, "*Viejo*, that was foolish of you! See how tired you are, and what an effort it is for you to breathe."

"*Mujer*," he whispered back, "stop your grumbling. My time on earth is as allotted already as yours or anyone else's, and a few minutes of speechmaking will surely not shorten it. Besides, I could not let this opportunity go by without expressing my sentiments—you may not remember, my dearest wife, how many times Don Diego de Escobar and I lamented over the insularity of Taos, grieved over the arrogant tariffs imposed upon us by the Mexican government, which had its orders from Madrid. Oh, no, Doña Elena, today is especially memorable for me. If anything, letting all of the people of Taos know that I am still their *alcalde mayor*, to whom they may bring their grievances and petitions, has done me a world of good."

Teresa de Rojado had come to the fair with her *indio* majordomo, but she had graciously refused Don Sancho's offer to be seated on the platform. "I am such a newcomer to Taos, Don Sancho," she had said with so winning a smile that he could not find it in his heart to argue with her, "that the citizens of Taos would consider me overbearing and arrogant if I were to, in any way, seek to draw their attention upon myself. Besides, it is to you that it is all due, and I will not detract from the slightest part of it by sitting up there as an equal with you, which I most assuredly am not. Oh, I shall go to the fair, for, as a woman, I am eager to buy some of the goods that come from the United States. But today is your day of glory, and I shan't diminish it, dear Don Sancho."

She had dressed, too, in her simplest dress, with nothing ostentatious. She and the majordomo, who vigilantly escorted her, moved from stall to stall, and she was asking many questions about the various goods displayed for sale.

Alejandro Cabeza was there also, swaggering as was his wont, dressed in all his finery as a *caballero*, and with him was his own majordomo, Ernesto Rojas. The dissipated *hacendado* came upon Teresa while she was examining a bolt of calico brought to the fair by Ernest Henson. "Would you allow me to purchase that for you as a gift of apology, Señora de Rojado?" he politely inquired.

She turned to confront him. "It is kind of you, Alejandro, but I must decline. I meant what I said the other day. I assuredly hope there will be no unpleasantness between us. But you know my feelings—and because you do, it would not be right for me to accept any kind of gift from you."

He at least had enough good taste to realize that if he pursued the matter, she would turn on her heel and leave the fair. Consequently, he bowed, not letting her see his continued rancor, and said, "I do not wish us to be enemies. I shall trouble you no more, Teresa. And I wish you every happiness."

"That's kind of you, Alejandro. I, too, would prefer that. May you also have every happiness. And thank you for the offer of the gift. Now then, Mr. Henson, I should need about half of this bolt of cloth. If you do not make the price too dear, I can deal with you at once." She favored the Missouri trader with a charming smile, having dismissed the *hacendado* with a courteous nod. Alejandro Cabeza stared at her supple back, compressed his lips, and then strode off with his fawning majordomo at his side.

The fair was staged in a huge clearing to the south of the pueblo village, whose boundaries were marked off by isolated scrub trees. The villagers had transformed it into a colorful arena, decorating the trees with pennons and streamers of paper, while Don Sancho had arranged for stakes to be implanted here and there. To these were attached figurines made of wood and straw, painted with vegetable dyes, depicting the Indians, the priest, the *hacendados*, and the graceful *india* women who carried baskets or water jugs on their heads: these miniatures had been created especially for the fair by an artist as skilled as Taguro, the Pueblo Indian who now lived at the Double H Ranch with his adored Listanzia. And there were several long, rectangular tables conveniently set up on which reposed baskets—woven by the Jicarilla Apache women—filled with *tortillas, enchiladas,* and other tasty fare to regale the hungry visitors at the fair. It was indeed a gala occasion, and the people of Taos eagerly welcomed the traders, who had come from as far away as Franklin, Missouri, with a variety of goods that the residents had not seen for many a day, at prices that seemed extremely modest.

Noracia herself presided over her own display of taffetas, silks, handmade necklaces, and bracelets made from semiprecious stones that had been acquired by her majordomo from a talented old Toboso Indian craftsman. Not far from her stall was that of the leather craftsman and jeweler, Ignazio Peramonte, who watched the visitors to the fair, as well as the exhibitors, with attentive interest.

As he was explaining to an interested *hacendado* the workmanship of a broad leather belt such as a *vaquero* or sheepherder might wear, the head of *Los Penitentes* also observed out of the corner of his eye that Alejandro Cabeza was approaching the stall of Noracia.

The beautiful *mestiza* sat on a stool, having tied a flaming red bandanna over her head to shield her from the sun, and coquettishly smiled at the disgruntled *hacendado*. "A good afternoon to you, Señor Cabeza," she greeted him. "I hope that you are enjoying the fair?"

"No thanks to you, Noracia," he muttered as he confronted her. "It would appear that you have a loose tongue, which I suppose befits a woman of loose character."

Although her eyes momentarily narrowed at this vicious insult, the smile remained on her lips as she retorted, "You wrong me, Alejandro—"

"How dare you address me by my first name, as if we were equals?" he hissed.

"Ah, but you once sought to share my bed, which would have made us equal—if anything, it would have made me superior to you, for I do not think you are *hombre* enough to satisfy my needs. And besides, you've tried to buy my favors.

When I love a man, Alejandro, he does not have to pave the pathway to my bedchamber with *pesos*."

"You are very clever, Noracia. I know how you became rich when Luis Saltareno died. I don't begrudge you that, but I condemn the audacity you showed in discussing my private affairs with the Señora de Rojado."

"But, Alejandro, it was really in your best interests. Consider it—you are not the *esposo* for her. She is in love with the Señor Carlos de Escobar, who has much more to offer her than ever you could. She is wealthy, and you are on the verge of being very poor—"

"Keep your voice down, *mujer*!" His voice was edged with an angry anxiety as he glanced nervously around. "You have done me a great disservice. One day, I shall pay you back."

"Why would you not think of joining forces with me, Alejandro? You have already said that you know that I am rich. I am, and I shall grow richer still, because of my shop and the trading that my *trabajadores* do for me in Mexico. I have already arranged with a factor in New Orleans to furnish goods that I can sell at a great profit here in Taos and even in Santa Fe, if I so choose."

"I, consort with a *mestiza*, a *puta*?" he exclaimed, arching his eyebrows. "Oh, yes, you're most enticing, but a man would spend a night with you as he would with a high-priced *puta* and then dismiss her. You surely do not propose that I wed you?"

"I can think of far worse things that could happen to you, Alejandro," she taunted, her smile deepening. "Do not frown like that; it will leave lines in your forehead. If you keep that up, you will no longer look so handsome, and maybe even I, whom you call a *puta*, will no longer find you attractive."

"Be silent! But I shall not forget that you stood in the way of a marriage between the Señora de Rojado and myself!"

Noracia shrugged as she lifted a piece of taffeta between her hands, turned it over, and critically examined it while ignoring the fuming *hacendado*. Finally she drawled, "Consider the facts, Alejandro. If your fortune is truly gone, despite all your protests to the contrary, what future will there be for you here in Taos? Do you think that any of the eligible señoritas here will be permitted to consider you as a husband once their fathers and mothers know that you are really not much better off than the *indios* of the pueblo?"

"Hold your tongue, I told you—you go too far, *por todos los santos!*"

"Forgive me for making you angry, Alejandro. But perhaps you should consider me as a far better choice than Señora de Rojado. You see, Alejandro, if you had managed somehow to trick her into marriage, she would quickly learn what a rogue you are, what a debaucher of women. While, I, on the contrary, having been the *puta* of Don Esteban de Rivarola and Luis Saltareno, know exactly how to deal with men of your kind. I could satisfy you, Alejandro, and you could be taught in time to satisfy me. Together, we should make an ideal partnership, because one day Taos will have no authority to govern it. Don Sancho de Pladero is a very sick man. And who knows who would be appointed his successor? If he dies or leaves Taos, those who are rich and clever can become important. That is why I say you should join forces with me."

"I would sooner mate with the devil's wife, Noracia! I bid you good day!" Turning on his heel, Alejandro Cabeza strode off, while his majordomo hurried anxiously after him.

Noracia laughed softly. "How amusing it will be," she murmured to herself, "to bring such a handsome *caballero* to his knees and make him agree to be my *servidor!*"

Twenty

John Cooper Baines, with Kinotatay at his side, stood before Marsimaya, shaman to the Jicarilla Apache. Marsimaya was nearly as tall as Kinotatay, with graying hair, yet he was sturdy and wiry, his face kindly and his voice soft.

"And now you know how it was that I found the treasure, which your *jefe*'s braves have guarded for me so faithfully all this time, Marsimaya," John Cooper concluded.

"I understand, *Halcón*. When I was a boy facing the tests given to those who would become braves and warriors, my father told me of a ghost mountain, one in which the evil spirits dwelt. Surely, it must have been that very mountain which you found by chance, *Halcón*, and the treasure with it."

John Cooper gravely nodded. "I wish those poor slaves, those tortured *indios* who remain preserved inside the cave, to have a proper burial, Marsimaya. We must take the silver from that mine, and Kinotatay has already set his men to making travois that will carry the treasure back to my ranch. From there, as I have told your *jefe*, it will be taken to New Orleans and hidden in a place that is well protected so that none may steal it. And from that treasure I will take a portion to give to the *indios* of the pueblo, the poor of Taos; and I will see that the Jicarilla will never want for food or blankets or weapons, because I have vowed the oath of blood brotherhood both with him who was before Kinotatay, and with Kinotatay himself."

Marsimaya closed his eyes and pondered a long moment. "As you know," he said at last, "the Jicarilla bury their

218

dead by following ancient customs. If it is a man who is taken to the Great Spirit, his men relatives wash and paint his body. They bedeck him in his finest moccasins and leggings and jacket; they sit him astride the horse that carried him into battle, or to the hunt. His possessions are brought with him to the base of a mountain or a hill as it may be, and there he is buried, the horse swiftly slain and buried with him, that he may ride when the Great Spirit summons him forth to life at the time appointed."

John Cooper nodded, recalling a Jicarilla burial ceremony he had witnessed years ago.

"If it is a woman, then her women relatives do the same for her, except that no horse accompanies her to the burial place, unless she was skilled at the hunt and rode as her mate might, or as a brave.

"It is also our law that the man to be buried, if he had a squaw, may not be seen or touched by his *suegra,* just as when he was alive, he was forbidden to look upon or speak to the mother of his squaw."

"These things I know, Marsimaya," John Cooper murmured.

"That is how it is done with us, *Halcón.* I have thought over what you have told me. These *esclavos* in the cave have been long dead. They are not dust or bones, because the air has not reached them—did you not say this? Well, if they were taken from the cave for Apache burial, they would perhaps turn to dust. And they could not be properly prepared as is our law because no relatives still live who could care for them. It would be best to bury them at the back of this cave, for they gave their lives to preserve the treasure. And since the treasure will now be used for good instead of evil, which was not what their masters had intended—for it was the *conquistadores* who came to the land of the *indios* to plunder and to steal in the name of their Great Spirit—then these poor ones deserve at least all the dignity which we can provide them by our law. I fear there is no other way, *Halcón.*"

"You will accompany us, Marsimaya, to speak what words should be said to the Great Spirit who knows all things?" John Cooper asked.

"Yes, *Halcón,* as shaman I must purify this place where it was long ago said that evil spirits dwelt. They must be driven forth for all time. For when you have taken the treasure to this hiding place of which you have told me, then no man with evil in his heart will profane the burial place of those poor *esclavos*." Marsimaya pressed his right palm against John Cooper's heart. "Tomorrow morning, I will go with you and Kinotatay to the mountain of the dead."

"I thank you, Marsimaya."

John Cooper went back with Kinotatay to the latter's wickiup, where they smoked the calumet. During this ceremony, neither spoke. As he emptied the bowl and laid away the pipe in its ceremonial pouch, Kinotatay declared, "When the sun rises for the sixth time from this day, *Halcón*, the travois will be ready. At that time, I will give you thirty braves as an escort. I myself will lead them. Pastanari will act as *jefe* in my place, when I am gone from the stronghold, *Halcón*. The braves are well armed, thanks to your generosity." He rose to his feet with an agility that belied his age. "In the meantime, I shall order five of my men to go with us to the mountain, *Halcón*, to dig the graves for these ancient dead. And I will confess to you, my blood brother, that I am as curious as a woman to see this secret cave. It is hard for the mind to picture such a thing—in my heart is sorrow for those poor *esclavo*s who died of starvation and thirst, unable to free themselves, waiting for their oppressors to bring them food and drink. Now come, we have much to do."

John Cooper, Kinotatay, Marsimaya, and the braves left the stronghold and headed for the isolated mountain to the south. Tethering their horses to some stubby pine trees, they climbed the narrow trail to the plateau on which the mine was located.

Two Jicarilla braves were there guarding the mine, and after exchanging greetings with them, John Cooper squeezed his way into the mine itself, carrying a torch, which he lit with his tinderbox. The others followed, and Marsimaya stared at the broad wooden table around which the long-dead Indian slaves sat on benches. He murmured a prayer under his breath to the Great Spirit as he stared at the stolid, impassive, mummified faces, some of them still contorted in the agonies of death, their eyes bulging and glassy. Then he turned to Kinotatay and said in a low voice, "The tribal markings are not those of the Apache. These poor slaves were brought from across the Rio Grande as captives to work this mine."

He turned then and gave an order to the braves who would dig the graves, and they began at the back of the cave, not far from the storeroom where the ingots and holy relics were kept. They had brought blankets with them, and each body was carefully wrapped and placed in a single grave. When it was done, Marsimaya intoned a prayer that the Great Spirit would receive these lost souls, who had died so ignoble a death through no fault of theirs, into His keeping and, when the day of summons was decreed, restore unto them their pride as warriors.

Outside, the sun was sinking, and the purple glow suffused the bleak sky. John Cooper turned to Kinotatay and said, "When the travois are ready, they can be brought here. And after the silver has been loaded, I hope to bring Don Sancho and his family to a starting place at the base of this mountain. Then your escort of warriors will guard both Don Sancho and the silver and travel directly to the ranch."

"It is a good plan, and it will thus be done," Kinotatay avowed. "Till the travois are ready and you bring me word that Don Sancho is prepared for the journey, my warriors will guard this place of death, from which the shaman has now lifted the curse."

At the Double H Ranch during these last weeks of June, the *trabajadores* were enthusiastically busied in more tasks than they had had in many a day. Miguel Sandarbal had chosen twenty of the ablest workers to build the eight wagons that would be used to transport the silver from the ranch to New Orleans, once John Cooper and his escort of Jicarilla Apache had conveyed that treasure from its hiding place along the long, virtually deserted trail through Texas territory.

Before divulging the reason for this task, Miguel had taken each of the *trabajadores* aside and spent at least an hour talking with him until he was convinced that none of the men would betray this secret. On that he would stake his hope for salvation, yes, even his happiness with his beloved Bess. All the same, he had been careful not to say too much about this treasure; for having been prey to temptation in his youth himself, he understood with a kind of indulgent cynicism that even the most upright man may be tempted. He had only said that the Señor Baines had found a secret cave in a distant mountain, which contained a few bars of silver and which had been mined more than a century ago by the *conquistadores*, but that most of the treasure was in holy relics that were ultimately to be donated to the church in New Orleans. And he had gone to the chapel to ask forgiveness for this white lie, for he knew that all of his *trabajadores* were fervent *católicos* and would, therefore, be less subject to temptation if they believed that most of the treasure was to be consigned to the church itself.

He had chosen men who had already shown considerable skill in building the *hacienda*, when they had first left Taos to seek freedom in a region that would not be controlled by tyrannical Mexican and Spanish civil and military functionaries. A number of other *trabajadores* had been delegated to complete the building of the large church, which, it was hoped, would be graced in the near future by the magnificent bronze bell ordered from Belgium and now en route to New Orleans.

"The wheels must be sturdy, so that they will withstand the heavy pounding in the event the wagons are drawn through ruts or gullies or the hard, gravelly, rocky ground of a canyon," Miguel patiently explained to his men. "There are to be two false bottoms to each wagon. I will designate where these are to be placed, but when you surface them with thin pine wood and over that, nail strips of canvas, the naked eye will not be able to see any difference in any section of the flooring of this wagon. That is in case, by some ill fortune, the wagon train is attacked by *soldados* or *bandidos* or hostile *indios*."

Jorge Gonzago, a stocky, genial Mexican in his early thirties, who had come to the Double H Ranch two years ago with his two brothers, spoke up. "*Señor capataz*, what if the wagon train is attacked and the *bandidos* drive away some of the wagons?"

"It is exactly as I have told you, Jorge," Miguel patiently and smilingly explained. "We are building more wagons than we shall actually need. And we will scatter them throughout the train, those with the treasure, and those which have nothing more than the supplies and the goods we are taking to New Orleans. It is certainly unlikely, since many of you may be chosen to ride on the drive to New Orleans with the cattle and will be well armed, that any *bandido* or *soldado* will be able to steal all the wagons. I shall go also, and I am a good shot, as you all know. Especially you, Roberto Matarón, who wagered me two *pesos* last week that I could not hit a pine-cone with a rifle at a hundred yards."

There was laughter as all eyes turned to Roberto, a tall stripling not yet twenty-five, who had come to the Double H Ranch with the three Gonzago brothers, having heard that it was a sanctuary and welcoming commune for those who wanted to work free from oppression. The brothers had been his good friends, and he and they had been *peones* in a little town in the province of Coahuila. An infantry captain had ridden into their village one day with a troop of twenty armed men and demanded that the village yield up conscripts for military service. He had said that he would be back the next day and that if there were not sufficient volunteers, he and his men would pick the men of the village at random and take them off at once to serve their country. And so the four men had fled into Texas, all of them bachelors except young Roberto, whose seventeen-year-old wife, Luz, and their infant son, Pepe, had ridden with them. Once they had been fugitives; now they lived and worked and were overjoyed to be directed by so indulgent a *capataz* as Miguel Sandarbal. And by now, indeed, the three Gonzago brothers were already beginning to court some of the unwed *criadas* of the *hacienda;* and when the great church was finally completed, there would undoubtedly be weddings.

"I will wager you another two *pesos, señor capataz,*" young Roberto brashly retorted, "that if you allow me to go on the drive with you and we are attacked by *bandidos,* I will kill with my rifle two more than you will with yours!"

"I will take that wager." Miguel held up a hand to quell the burst of laughter that had followed the young *trabajador's* boast. "But," he added solemnly, "we should not tempt *El Señor Dios* to turn His face from us by making such foolish wagers that we shall be attacked and have to slay men. May He grant that our drive to New Orleans is a peaceful one, and that no one is hurt."

Now there was a chorus of "Amen!" as he waited for the workers to give him their attention once again, then continued: "These wagons will be made like the Conestogas you have seen already. We have all the materials we need, and you, Eduardo Descanso, and you also, Juan Velasquez, will go into the forest and cut down the sturdiest trees, so that we may have all the wood that we shall need. These wagons must be ready by the time Señor Baines and his *indios* arrive here with the precious cargo that will be put into the false bottoms of these wagons."

He looked around and was satisfied with his men's respectful attention and eagerness. Indeed, to heighten their enthusiasm and quicken their labors, Miguel and Don Diego had promised the *trabajadores* a bonus in their wages.

The sound of axes and saws rang out from sunup to sunset, and fat old Tía Margarita and her six helpers in the large kitchen of the main *hacienda* worked almost as valorously as the *trabajadores* themselves in preparing meals that would fill the stomachs of hungry men whose hunger was redoubled through arduous exercise and the enthusiasm for their work.

In the *hacienda*, Doña Inez was playing the new spinet, which John Cooper had recently brought from San Antonio. It was far sturdier than the one she and Don Diego had owned in Taos. Moreover, the first one had been slightly damaged during the long journey to Texas, and several of the strings had snapped and could not be replaced. This afternoon, Doña Inez, her face radiant, was amusing herself playing old English and French songs, and Bess Sandarbal stood at her side, singing in a sweet, clear soprano voice the English folk song, "Greensleeves." As the last notes died away, Doña Inez sighed rhapsodically and declared, "How lovely that was, *querida* Bess! Each day, I am so grateful for the blessings my beloved Diego and I enjoy here, away from Taos. And when I think of my blessings with our daughter, Francesca, almost a woman in the way she thinks and the consideration she shows to everyone, and then our two adopted children, Juan and Dolores—I cannot begin to thank Him who brought all this about."

"Dear Inez, I, too, have joy beyond my dreams. Miguel has fulfilled me, and I give thanks that I have kept him young. And we have Timothy and Julia and now our little Juan, named after Miguel's father. Your adopted son, dear Inez, is named after that holy man, Padre Moraga. We are blessed among women, truly."

Doña Inez reached for Bess's hand and squeezed it, tears glistening in her eyes. "Yes, Bess, some who know nothing of what is in the heart would say that our husbands are old, but we know better. And do you know, dear Bess, it seems only appropriate that we should be friends, for my Diego and your Miguel have been bound together most of their lives in friendship, yes, even when Diego was a *hidalgo* back in Spain and married to my sister. How good life is, the more so because you and I have earned it through hardship and devotion. Now, will you sing for me that Spanish song I taught you last month? It speaks of love and how love endures through hardship and even old age. And that, too, is in keeping with the way we both feel this happy day."

Young Andrew Baines had gone out after *almuerzo* to watch the *trabajadores* at work on the wagons, and had excitedly asked Miguel, "Do you think Pa will take me with him on the cattle drive to New Orleans? He's talked so much about it, I want very much to see a big city like that! Do you think he will, Miguel, really?"

The white-haired *capataz* chuckled and put his arm around the tall boy's shoulders. "I have a feeling he will. Especially after the way you behaved when we went to San Antonio, *hombre*." At this word, which signified a mature man, Andrew noticeably stiffened with pride and straightened his shoulders to stand as erect as he could. Miguel pretended not to notice this, but there was a twinkle in his eyes as he added, "Judging by the way you're growing, it won't be long before there's another *Halcón* on the Double H Ranch. And what are you going to do this morning, young señor?"

"Go for a run with Yankee," the boy promptly responded. "Pa said I was to keep training him. When do you think Pa'll be back, Miguel?"

"He said by the end of July, or early August, Andrew. It will depend on how his plans work out. It's a very long way to Taos and to the mountain where the *indios* live."

"One day, I want to go there with him, too. He's told me about Kinotatay and what a good man he is."

"Yes, he assuredly is, *hombre*. He has kept the Jicarilla at peace, and the women of his tribe make such wonderful baskets that I am sure many of them are being sold now at the great fair in Taos."

"And that's another thing I'd like to see someday soon," Andrew Baines thoughtfully vouchsafed. He watched for a few minutes as one of the *trabajadores* fitted the heavy wooden wagon wheel to a carefully shaped axle. "They will be very heavy wagons, won't they, Miguel? They'll hold a lot of supplies on a long journey."

"Just so, Andrew. That's why the men are building them from the hardest wood, so they won't break down when we go to New Orleans."

"Well, I'll tell you one thing, Miguel," the boy quipped, "if Pa doesn't take me along to New Orleans, I'll hide in one of those wagons and make sure I get there!"

"Now that is something I wouldn't try if I were you, Andrew. You have to remember your father is an officer in the army, and you're still a subordinate until you've come of age and marry and have your own children. Then you can lay down the law."

"Of course, I was just joking, Miguel," Andrew smilingly countered. "I wouldn't want to do anything Pa didn't want me to. Well, guess I'll let Yankee out and go for a run with him."

"May God be with you, young master," Miguel said, then walked over to the group of *trabajadores* who were working on the body of the heavy wagon. "That's very good. Mind you, use enough thick canvas, with peepholes for rifles and muskets, just in case there's an attack. How does that proverb go—*sí*, forewarned is forearmed."

Andrew Baines went to the shed near the kennel where Hosea, Jude, and Luna were quartered and let out the wolf-dog. Yankee leaped out and affectionately stood on his hind legs. He placed his paws against his young master's upper chest and, with his great pink tongue, licked Andrew's chin and neck and cheeks.

"That's a good boy," Andrew said happily. "Want to go for a run with me?"

Yankee let out a long, eager howl; there was nothing better in all the world that he would like to do at that moment.

"Well, that's what we'll do, then," Andrew responded. He strode off toward the north, while Yankee trotted along beside him, looking up from time to time, his yellow eyes gleaming with excitement.

John Cooper had spent many hours with Yankee and his son, to make certain that Andrew would know how to continue the wolf-dog's training in his absence. Andrew broke off a branch from a scrub tree, drew back his arm, and flung it. "Go fetch it, Yankee boy!" he commanded.

His ears flattened against his skull, Yankee crouched and then raced off to retrieve the stick and brought it back, his tail wagging.

Andrew bent down and rubbed his knuckles over Yankee's head, then gently put his left hand on the stick clenched between the wolf-dog's jaws. At once, Yankee opened them, and Andrew retrieved the stick and flung it again. This time, he threw it farther, but Yankee raced swiftly after it; and a few seconds after it hit the ground, the powerful wolf-dog found it, gripped it between his fangs, and ran back to his young master.

"Good boy!" Andrew approved. Suddenly he caught sight of a jackrabbit darting across the path some fifty feet ahead. Squatting down, he pointed to the rabbit and called out, "*Mata*, Yankee, *mata!*"

With a low growl, Yankee lowered his head and raced after the fleeing jackrabbit. Hearing the growl, the jackrabbit turned and quizzically regarded the pair, then began to run at full speed toward the sanctuary of a stream to hide among the tall reeds along the banks. But Yankee increased his speed and veered at an angle to cut off the jackrabbit.

Andrew Baines watched, his eyes sparkling, calling to Yankee, "That's it, head it off. Bring it back, and we'll have it for supper tonight!"

Hoping to throw its pursuer off the track, the jackrabbit suddenly halted, then bounded wildly for a large clump of sagebrush. But Yankee, without seeming to slacken his speed, swiftly overtook the jackrabbit. There was a piteous squeal as Yankee pounced on the furry creature and killed it with a single clenching of his powerful jaws. He stood for a moment holding the rabbit's lifeless body in his fangs, wagged his tail, and then triumphantly trotted back to Andrew.

While Andrew was occupied with Yankee, Francesca de Escobar and Carlos's sturdy young son, Diego, had gone out on their ponies that same afternoon. Grave Francesca, who her mother believed was far more mature than her dozen years, seemed to have made her peace with brash young Diego. In school, Francesca had once been in tears and complained that Diego had bullied her. But now there was a tacit truce between them, and more and more, Doña Inez's only natural child seemed to prefer Diego as her playmate. She had become an expert rider already, and Don Diego confided to his beloved wife that it would not be long before she would be given a full-grown mare. All the same, he and her mother had cautioned Francesca not to ride too far away from the ranch. He remembered with still lingering sorrow the tragic fate of Diego's Apache mother, Weesayo, when she had ridden out in search of the cinchona bark to heal little Dawn's fever, and how that act of maternal mercy had changed the lives of everyone at the Double H Ranch and for so long a time estranged Carlos from his own family.

Francesca and Diego had ridden southward, fording the shallowest bend of the Frio River, and now that it was nearing sunset, turned their ponies' heads toward home and again crossed the river.

"That was great fun, Francesca," Diego averred, flushed and perspiring from their several races. "My pony's faster than yours, though."

"It isn't, either. I let you win," Francesca proudly declared with a toss of her pretty head.

"I might have expected a girl to say something like that," Diego grumbled, glaring at her. "You're a girl, remember? And boys are supposed to be better in everything."

"Oh, you're just hateful when you say things like that!" Francesca declared. "I've read enough books to know that there are lots of women in history who have done more than men."

"Oh, well, no use arguing. You're pretty good for a girl, then," he grudgingly contributed. "Race you back to the bunkhouse!"

"We really shouldn't race our ponies so much; they're tired already. Your father loves horses, and he'd never ask too much of one, unless it were a real emergency," Francesca countered.

"Oh, well, I'd win anyway. Suit yourself. You can trot back, then."

With a boyish laugh, he spurred his pony forward and raced onward, while Francesca, with a deep sigh, bent to her pony's head and murmured, "That's all right, Beauty, we don't have to take any heed of him. I'm not going to wear you out; you're such a sweet pony, and you take me wherever I want to go. I don't care if he wins this time either, so there!"

All the same, perhaps out of girlish pique, Francesca could not resist kicking her heels against her pony's belly and urging it to trot a little faster. They neared the stables, beyond the bunkhouse, and suddenly Francesca uttered a cry and called out, "Diego, Diego, look what's in the cage—the poor thing, it's a baby trying to get to its mother! Come back here, Diego!"

Several weeks ago, Miguel had asked Esteban Morales, the assistant *capataz,* to make an ingenious cage to trap a fox that had been making raids on the small henhouse adjacent to the stables. However, a baby raccoon had been caught in the trap, and its mother had strangled herself trying to squeeze through the bars of the cage to get to her offspring.

Diego, reining in his pony, galloped back to Francesca. "What's the matter? What's in the cage? Oh, I see—but that's not a fox—"

"No, it's got fur like a fox, but it's awfully different. Oh, look, doesn't it make you cry, Diego? Look at the little baby trying to squeeze out of the cage—that must have been its mother—oh, please go find Miguel!" Francesca was sobbing now, as she dismounted from her pony.

"All right, I'll get him. Don't touch it; it might bite!" Diego called. Then, kicking his heels, he urged his pony toward the bunkhouse and called aloud, "*¡Hola,* Miguel, *aquá!*"

Miguel heard the boy's summons, and bade the *trabajadores* stop their work, for it was nearly quitting time. "You've done very well, *amigos,*" he complimented them. "In a week or two, these wagons will be ready. Don Diego will know of your industry, for I shall tell him at supper tonight, and *El Halcón* will know when he returns, and he will thank you himself. Good appetite, and get a good night's sleep, all of you, so we can be fresh when the sun comes up to continue our good work!" Then, cupping his hands to his mouth, he bawled, "I'm coming, young master!" and began to run toward the stables.

His eyes widened to see Francesca kneeling near the cage, wringing her hands, tears streaming down her cheeks, while Diego, rather more diffidently, stood holding the reins of his pony and scowling. "Why, it's a raccoon," the white-haired *capataz* exclaimed. "That's the mother—and the baby can't be more than three or four weeks old at most! Wait a bit, Francesca. I'll take it out."

"Would it make a good pet, Señor Miguel?" Francesca appealingly asked, as she looked up at the *capataz*.

"Oh, yes, a very good pet. It's still young enough—it's a male, by the by—still young enough to be trained. If you really wish to keep him, I will tell you what to do."

Francesca turned to her playmate. "May I have him, Diego? I saw him first."

He shrugged. "I guess so. I don't want a pet like that, anyhow."

"Very well then, Señorita Francesca," Miguel smilingly declared, "I will tell you just what to do. You can feed him by twisting a rag and dipping it in milk. You see, *querida,* it will remind the little one how he used to take his milk from his mother. And I'll get a basket from one of the *trabajadores'* wives with some old rags to use as a bed."

"I'll look after him, I promise. I'll feed him just the way you say, Señor Miguel," Francesca exclaimed.

"Very good. Now, well . . ." Miguel scratched his neck, somewhat embarrassed at what he was about to say, then went on. "You see, the first two weeks, you must rub your finger on the baby's tummy so that he will relieve himself—do you understand me, Francesca?"

She blushed and nodded. "I think so."

"You see, an animal like that is taught by his mother, who uses her tongue until he is old enough to attend to himself, Señorita Francesca," Miguel explained.

"I'd be afraid he would claw or bite me," Diego scornfully put in.

"No, Señor Diego, not if you tame him from the very first. I'd say in another week or two, he will be old enough to be let out of the barn to go wherever he wants. Then, Señorita Francesca, you will have to set out bowls of food for him, like milk, or perhaps a little bread crumbled in the milk, so that when he goes out, he will know where to find his food. When he knows that you have taken his mother's place, Señorita Francesca, he will come back to you."

"He has the most darling little black face, and there are

rings on his little tail," Francesca exclaimed, clasping her hands and staring at the gray-furred, wriggling baby raccoon gently cradled in Miguel's gnarled hands.

"He will grow to about twelve to sixteen pounds, when he reaches his full growth, Señorita Francesca. Now I'm going to have a little cage made for him, and by next week, remember to let him out every day, a few times in the morning and afternoon, and just before you go to bed. Once he knows his way around, he may even climb a tree and take a nap in the crotch of one of those big pine or oak trees near the river."

"You're so kind, Señor Miguel!" Francesca smilingly exclaimed. "Now I have to think of a name for him, don't I?"

"Of course, Señorita Francesca." Miguel bowed to her in as dignified a way as if she were already a mature woman. "That is your privilege."

"Let me see now—hmmm—" Francesca frowned and looked up at the sky as if for inspiration. Then she brightened. "I shall call him Chiquitico, because he is so tiny!"

"That is an excellent name, Señorita Francesca! Now, since you will want to put your pony in the stable, I will go and have one of the men make you a cage. We'll look after little Chiquitico this evening, but tomorrow when the cage is made, I shall bring it to you after you have had your breakfast, and then we will play with him a little and see how much we can teach him."

"Señor Miguel, I just love you!" Francesca exclaimed as she hurried to him and gave him a hug. Miguel beamed with pleasure, while the tiny ball of fur nestling in his big hands uttered a plaintive squeak.

Twenty-one

Benito Aguarez had ridden as if the very devil in hell were behind him, feeling guilty that his superior officer had found him in the throes of an amorous liaison at the very moment when he should have been ready to transmit this vitally urgent message to Coronel Santa Anna. By dint of flourishing the authorization that Francisco López had given him on the eve of the latter's departure for the Double H Ranch, the lieutenant was able to commandeer the fastest horses along his journey to Ciudad Victoria, so that he arrived in that flourishing Mexican town, a distance of about two hundred ten miles from Nuevo Laredo, on the evening of the sixth day.

Going to the largest *posada*, he was told at once where he might find the Sargento Porfirio Monreal. This done, he swiftly acquainted the noncommissioned officer with the details of López's message, and now it was the sergeant's turn to ride with all possible speed to the estate of Santa Anna near Veracruz.

This was a longer journey; but the diligent sergeant, who had yearned for years to win the epaulets of an officer in the glorious Army of the Republic, managed, by means of sleeping only three or four hours a day and eating only the sparsest of meals along the way, to reach the lavish estate of Manga de Clavo on the morning of the ninth day after his departure from Ciudad Victoria.

Exhausted, his uniform drenched with sweat, and his last horse foundering, he stumbled into the villa of the *libertador* and, taken at once by a sympathetic servant into Santa

Anna's presence, gasped out the news that Francisco López had discovered the secret of the fabulous treasure hoard of the *gringo,* and that Santa Anna should send out troops with the greatest possible dispatch.

Santa Anna paced the floor of his study, his brow furrowed in thought, nursing his clean-shaven chin. Then he turned to the sergeant and murmured, "Coronel López is right: to send troops from Veracruz would take at least a month. By the time they reached the rendezvous, they would be as exhausted as you, *amigo.* Thus I will take his advice. I will send a courier on the fastest horse in my stable with orders to go to Major Humberto Valdez in Ciudad Juárez. That, *sargento,* is near the border of the Rio Grande, with swift entrance into the Texas territory. From there, it would take no more than a week for a crack troop of cavalry to meet Coronel López and lay an ambush for this accursed *gringo.* Let me see now." He frowned again and turned to a map pinned to the wall of his study and, with his forefinger, traced the route. Then he turned back to the still panting, exhausted sergeant: "It is just a few days past the middle of June, is it not? *Bueno.* My courier—I shall choose my own personal aide, Teniente Bernardo Novilas—will reach Valdez by the end of the first week of July. It is a trip of eight hundred miles, and that will mean riding at least forty miles a day."

Santa Anna smiled. "Major Valdez is a dear friend of mine. Only last week, I received a dispatch from him, reminding me of the days we had spent together as cadets and pledging that in the days ahead, if I should seek the highest office in all Mexico, he would valorously support me. Well now, Teniente Novilas will call on him to fulfill his pledge, telling him of my orders to send fifty mounted, well-armed men, choosing them from the finest in his regiment. Valdez's reward will be promotion to a colonelcy—perhaps even to a general, if all goes well. As for you, *sargento,* tell my steward—he was the one who ushered you in to me—that at my order, you are to be given the best room in my villa, and that you are to rest until you are strong enough to assume your duties, which I myself will assign to you. You will have food and wine, and since my dear wife is absent for the next ten days, I shall see to it that your bed is not a lonely one, Sargento Monreal."

"Your Excellency is too kind," the sergeant babbled, swaying before the *libertador* and digging his fingers into the front of the desk to support himself, for he was bone-weary and dying for sleep.

"I shall promote you to the rank of *teniente* as a reward for having brought this news. I can see that you did not delay, and that you went without sleep and food. Mexico has need of men like you, Teniente Monreal. Now go find Costarme, my steward, and do nothing more than sleep until you have regained your strength."

His face entranced, the newly promoted courier gave Santa Anna a smart salute and hoarsely stammered, "*¡Viva el libertador; viva México!*"

He walked unsteadily to the door, turned to salute again, and then went out. Santa Anna chuckled to himself. He turned back to the map and again traced the route. "With such loyal servants to serve me, I feel that it is written in the stars that I shall be he who guides the destiny of my country. And when the treasure of that *americano* rests in the cellar of my villa here, no one will be able to block my path to either the throne as emperor, or the chair as *el presidente!*"

Several hours after he had initiated the summer fair of Taos, Don Sancho de Pladero turned to his wife and apologetically excused himself. "*Querida,*" he murmured, "I have made a vow, which I must keep. I am going to the church in the plaza, to pray before Padre Madura. Do not worry yourself about me. I will come back and we shall return to the *hacienda* at sundown. I have your permission?"

Doña Elena looked at him with tear-filled eyes. She did not reveal what presentiment she felt, but she tried to force a smile to her lips as she said in the most casual of tones, "But you are a man, *mi esposo,* and it is for you to decide what you wish to do. I shall wait here for you, as you desire."

He turned to her, touched his hand to hers, and stared at her, and all his heart was in his eyes. He, too, affected a casual tone, one of domestic bantering: "It's good of you, Elena. Do you know something? I love you very much. And now I shall go, and you will amuse yourself until I return for you."

"It is understood, *mi esposo.*"

He smiled tenderly at her, rose slowly from the table on

the platform, and descended the short flight of three steps to the ground. He prayed silently to himself that God—and Doña Elena—would forgive him his little white lie; for, in truth, he was not going to church but rather was keeping a secret appointment with his doctor. He walked, shoulders straightened, a bland smile on his face, as he exchanged comments here and there with many of the citizens whom he recognized, and continued his slow walk till he had reached the tall, wiry, black-haired majordomo at the de Pladero *hacienda*, Vicente Andraga, who had become more and more a confidant to Don Sancho.

"*Excelencia*, the *médico* Hernandín is waiting to see you," Vicente murmured so no one else might hear.

Don Sancho crossed himself and shuddered. "Take me to meet him where no one shall see us, *amigo*. You would do me a great service. And I beg of you, not a word to Doña Elena, or my son, Tomás."

"I shall be as silent as the grave, Don Sancho," the majordomo softly responded.

The aging Spanish official smiled wearily and took the majordomo's right hand between both of his and pressed it hard. "*Gracias*, a thousand times thanks. You are a man of heart, and I am grateful to you. Now take me to the *médico*."

"He is in his carriage, *patrón*. He told me to tell you he waits outside the fairgrounds."

"Very good. Say a prayer for me, *amigo*." Then, drawing a deep breath, as if he faced an arduous ordeal, he walked slowly out of the boundary of the great fair, and to a dusty little patch where a carriage waited, drawn by two piebald geldings.

Don Sancho approached the carriage and, glancing back over his shoulder, crossed himself, bowed his head, and then, straightening, made for the carriage. Forcing a smile to his lips, he greeted the doctor: "I am at your service. I trust I have not kept you waiting too long, Dr. Hernandín?"

"Of course not, Don Sancho. I had word from your messenger three days ago that you wished me to come here to the fair and to tell you what my last examination of you revealed." The doctor was a short little man, with a bushy, graying beard, a thick mustache, spectacles, and a leonine head that was nearly bald.

"As you see, I'm here, and I await your verdict, Dr. Hernandín. What you are about to tell me will decide what I am to do with the rest of my life."

"You want frankness, Don Sancho, and I am here to give it to you. The rales of your lungs are not at all sanguine. I will stake my professional reputation on this declaration to you—at most, you have one year to live. And if you wish to extend that, you would do well to leave Taos. The rarefied mountain air is not good for your lungs; it imposes a strain upon your heart."

Don Sancho de Pladero bowed his head and covered his face with his hands for a long moment. Then, drawing a deep breath, he dropped his hands and straightened his shoulders to stare at Dr. Hernandín: "You are sure?"

"No one can be sure, Don Sancho. I have been a *médico* for thirty years, and I have tried to save many men, some of whom were in better health than you, and some in worse. It is for Him"—at this, the little doctor lifted his eyes skyward and pointed his forefinger to the heavens—"to set the finite date. I beg of you; do not be panic-stricken. So far as I can determine, you will not suffer much. You will grow progressively weaker, and one night, in your sleep, you will not awaken."

"That is a blessing. For this, I should gladly settle with my Savior," Don Sancho de Pladero smilingly retorted. "Now I know what I must do, and I shall go to join my friend, Don Diego de Escobar, in Texas. You say that the height of Taos is bad for my lungs, so the low plains of Texas will assuredly be better for my health."

"Of that I am convinced, Don Sancho."

"And now, Dr. Hernandín, since we have already discussed the most important part of your news, grant me a little recreation by playing a game of cards with me."

"I—I truly am not in the mood to play cards with you, though I salute the bravery of your gesture."

"Oh, come, Dr. Hernandín, it is said that you carry a deck of cards on your person at all times," Don Sancho teased him. "At least, let us have a quick little game of *monte*. Wait—I am forgetting my manners: will you not come to the *hacienda* and be my guest for supper and stay the night?"

"Alas, I must decline with the utmost thanks, Don Sancho. I must be back in Santa Fe by tomorrow to confer with the *gubernador*. Well then, come inside the carriage, and we'll have that little game you want."

Don Sancho beamed and got into the carriage, while the doctor called to his laconic coachman, "Arturo, my friend and I are going to play *monte*. Don't be impatient. When it's over, you will take me back to Santa Fe, *¿comprendes?*"

"*Seguramente, patrón,*" the coachman replied without turning around and looking at him.

Dr. Hernandín shook his head and chuckled as he reached into the pocket of his ruffled *camiso* and drew out a deck of cards. Turning sideways on the seat of the carriage, he put the deck down on the seat and politely gestured toward his patient: "Cut for deal, Don Sancho, if you will."

At the supper table that evening, Don Sancho de Pladero smiled tenderly at Doña Elena, cleared his throat, and declared, "I should like, *con su permiso,* to make a kind of official announcement."

Carlos de Escobar and Tomás both looked up, exchanging a profound glance. Conchita regarded her father-in-law with an expectant smile, then turned to her children and put a finger to her lips, as she whispered, "Shh, *niños,* your *abuelo* has something to say to you!"

"I think it will be joyous news," Don Sancho proceeded, looking around the table with an affectionate smiling nod to his grandchildren and to Conchita. "I have come to a decision. After I left the fair, I prayed this afternoon, as I told you I should, Doña Elena. And it came to me very clearly—I propose to leave this *hacienda* and go live with my dear old friend, Don Diego. Yes, Carlos, your father. I can think of nothing that would make me happier in my last years."

"Don Sancho!" Doña Elena gasped. "Do you really mean it?"

"Very much indeed. There is a saying that man proposes and God disposes. No one knows how much time he has left on this earth, so it is wise to act quickly when one comes to a decision such as I have. Now, I must ask you, wife of my bosom; will it please you to accompany me?"

"I would go with you to the ends of the earth, and I think you know it by now, Don Sancho," Doña Elena murmured, and then turned away to wipe the tears from her eyes with her napkin.

Don Sancho was deeply moved. He pretended to have a frog in his throat, reached for his goblet of wine, and took a long sip of it. Then he coughed, patted his stomach, and smiled self-consciously, as he added, "Of course, we must ask our *trabajadores* because they have a choice; they are not *peones*. Those who wish to accompany us will be welcome. If our beloved cook refuses to leave Taos, I was thinking that we should not starve, Doña Elena. I know that Tía Margarita is famous for her cooking. On those occasions when you and I supped at Don Diego's, we came away feeling as if we had been to a Lucullan feast."

"That's very true, dear Don Sancho," Doña Elena responded, having by now regained her self-control and forcing a smile to her lips.

"I shall have to go to Santa Fe at once—perhaps tomorrow—to resign my commission here as *alcalde mayor*. And I shall ask the new governor, Gubernador Narbona, to appoint an honorable successor who will care for the villagers and the *indios* as indulgently as I have tried to do all these years."

"No one can equal you, Don Sancho," his wife contributed, and then began to sniffle again and turned away her head.

"Oh, come, this should be a happy occasion, *mi corazón*," he benevolently chided her. "Now you, Tomás, and you, Conchita, do you wish to accompany us?"

"*Mi padre*, I have thought about this ever since Don Diego first said he would like to have you live there on the ranch in Texas," Tomás soberly responded. "Conchita and I have talked it over, and we think that we should remain here. There are the sheep; they bring us a good living, and there is employment for the *trabajadores* who have been so loyal to you and to us. I am happy in this life, *mi padre*." He turned to his mother. "*Mi madre*, I hope you will not be angry with me because of what I say. And please don't believe that it's because I want to be separated from you and Father. But there's something else, too. The name of de Pladero has already become a tradition here in Taos. I am your only heir, and I bear your name with great honor, which reflects on you, *mi padre*, and on you also, *mi madre*."

"I think you have good sense, Tomás. I am proud of you. You are a man, and you owe it to your wife and children to make them happy and to see that they prosper. Yes, Tomás, I could have asked for no better son than the good God gave me in you." Don Sancho himself was affected by this speech and resorted to the wine again, after a fit of coughing.

"So, Carlos, we shall go back with you. It will not really take too much time to pack for the journey, since Tomás and Conchita are going to remain. We shall take only our prized possessions, of course our clothing, and a few of the servants who wish to remain with Doña Elena and myself. No, by all means, now that I think of it, I wouldn't dream of taking the cook along; she must continue to work and prepare the wonderful meals that have made you, Tomás, and you, Conchita, and your adorable children so strong and healthy." He nodded, as if satisfied with his decision. Then he turned to Carlos again: "When do you propose to go back?"

Carlos permitted himself a self-deprecating smile, then explained, "I had thought in the next week or two, Don Sancho. This time will be very valuable to me because you know that I am courting the Señora de Rojado. At least, she has rejected the Señor Cabeza, whom I told you about. And this gives me hope, even though she told me just the other day that she is not yet ready to give me her answer concerning our marriage. I shall pray that she changes her mind by the time you and Doña Elena are ready to leave. Nothing would delight me more than to ride beside her as part of your escort to the ranch."

Don Sancho turned to face his wife at the other end of the table. "We can be packed in two weeks, can't we, Doña Elena?"

"Sí, mi esposo. I only think of one thing—if Tomás and Conchita stay, when shall we see our grandchildren again, once we go? It is such a long way from here to Texas."

"I promise I will come there twice a year, mi madre," Tomás spoke up, and as he glanced at Conchita, she eagerly nodded confirmation, "and I'll bring the children, yes, and Conchita, too. It will be like a kind of vacation for us, and we'll stay two weeks or so. We shall arrange it in between the shearing seasons."

"That's very kind, Tomás," Don Sancho approved, though he was sadly aware that he would not be around for too many of these visits. Still, it was great consolation that once he was gone, Doña Elena would have these visits to look forward to. "Well now," he said, "I should think this is enough excitement for one evening. I shall have a last glass of wine to put me into a long sleep, so I may be refreshed when I awaken tomorrow and prepare for my journey to the governor." He made a gesture with his hand, and the smiling, pleasant-featured *criada* who was serving them at the table hurried forward to fill his glass from the magnificent Belgian cut-glass decanter.

Carlos indicated to her, with a nod of his head, that he wished more wine also, and when his glass was filled, he lifted it and toasted Don Sancho. "I drink to your long life and good health, and to that of your lovely wife, and to your son and daughter-in-law and their children—may God bring to all of you the realization of your dreams. And for myself, I pray to Him that when you go back with me to the ranch, Señora de Rojado will ride along with our escort."

"I'll gladly drink to that, Carlos. Nothing would delight me more. She's a wonderful woman, and I'm happy that that scoundrel of a Cabeza, whom you told us about, has been sent packing. But of course, I am not surprised she had the common sense to dismiss such a fop and a wastrel," Don Sancho scornfully declared. Then, lifting his glass in the direction of each person at the table, he drank slowly and smacked his lips with relish. "And now, may I beg your indulgence so that an old man may seek his bed? My errand tomorrow will be a joyous one. I shall ask His Excellency for the only reward I seek, that he will choose my successor with a strict eye to character and honor and compassion."

After a leisurely breakfast, Don Sancho took leave of his wife and son and daughter-in-law and entered the carriage that would take him to Santa Fe. It was a journey of over fifty miles, and in deference to his poor health, the *alcalde mayor* slept overnight in the little village of Almería, where he had a friend who gladly provided him with good food and wine and a soft bed in his *hacienda*.

Thus it was that, greatly refreshed, Don Sancho de Pladero was ushered into the office of Governor Narbona at about three o'clock on the afternoon of the second day of his journey. The plump, good-natured *gubernador* left his desk and came forward to shake hands, enthusiastically greeting Don Sancho. "What an unexpected pleasure, Don Sancho! What news of Taos since you sent me your last report?"

"All goes well, Your Excellency," Don Sancho smilingly averred, as he seated himself in a tapestry-covered chair in front of the governor's teakwood desk. "The fair is a great success; the *americano* traders who came to Taos are well satisfied with their profits, and the citizens are overjoyed at the variety of goods. For example, there have been many excellent buffalo robes and beaver and otter furs. Some of the wives of the rich *hacendados* will be holding one *baile* after another to show off their finery, and I foresee such ample inspiration for domestic conversation as to last all through the winter."

Governor Narbona laughed and slapped his thigh. "I have always heard that you were a man of great wit and charm, Don Sancho. You prove it to me now. I am glad that the fair went well. And the Indians, are they still peaceful and working for the citizens?"

"Certainly, Your Excellency. To be sure, there are still a few *hacendados* who treat them with contempt and even try to cheat them out of payment for their services. When I have heard of such instances, I have rectified them. And that brings me to the real purpose of my visit."

"I am all attention, Don Sancho."

"I regret to have to inform you, Governor Narbona, that I hereby resign my post as *alcalde mayor*."

"But you can't be serious, Don Sancho! Come now, you are joking, aren't you?"

Don Sancho de Pladero slowly shook his head, his face serenely impassive. "The *médico* has not yet told you?"

"*Médico?*" Governor Narbona echoed in a mystified tone. "I do not follow you, Don Sancho."

"May I recall to Your Excellency that Dr. Hernandín was to have seen you yesterday."

"And he did, yes, on a matter concerning the health of Santa Fe. There have been one or two little scares, you understand. Nothing I should wish the people of this city to know about. That is why I wished an expert professional opinion. I was relieved to learn that my suspicions were unfounded. But what does Dr. Hernandín have to do with your resignation, Don Sancho?"

"Only that he is my physician, Your Excellency, and that he told me a few days ago that I had perhaps at most a year to live. I thought he might have mentioned it to you. At any rate, since you can readily verify it when next he reports to you, you will understand one of the reasons that has motivated my decision this afternoon. I must ask to be relieved of my duties because my health is failing. And I want to spend my remaining time with my dear wife in Texas, as a guest at the *hacienda* of my dear old friend, Don Diego de Escobar."

Governor Narbona, clasping his hands behind his back, began slowly pacing the room. Don Sancho watched him placidly, entwining his fingers in his lap.

"I must, of course, grant you your request, Don Sancho. I need not tell you that not only I shall miss you, but the people of Taos, as well. My predecessors in office have acquainted me with your loyal services, first to the crown and then to the new and glorious republic. You have left an honorable name that will live long after you, Don Sancho."

"Your Excellency is much too kind. My services have been humble, and I love the people of Taos. That is why I have a favor to ask of you, Governor Narbona."

"If it is within my power to grant, you have my word that it will be granted, Don Sancho."

"It is only this, Governor Narbona: when it comes time to select the man to replace me, I ask you to earnestly study my replacement. I told you that the *indios* of the pueblo are at peace. That is true now, but a few years ago, there were two evil men who were powerful and wealthy, Luis Saltareno and Don Esteban de Rivarola. Fortunately, God saw fit to remove their blight from the province where I was administrator. As you yourself know, Excellency, when a civil authority is replaced, there is a period of transition and there are always those who are greedy to seize power. I hope you will not fail to appoint a man of patience and compassion as quickly as possible. Then I shall feel that I have not failed the people of Taos."

"Of course, of course, Don Sancho. I give you my word as *gubernador* that I shall make diligent inquiry and find just such a man. When do you propose to leave Taos?"

"I should say within a fortnight, *excelencia*. My son and daughter-in-law and their children will remain in my *hacienda*."

"May I say"—the governor's tone was warm and concerned—"that I hope with all my heart that Dr. Hernandín's verdict isn't accurate."

"I do not think there is a chance of that, *excelencia*. But if I have only a year left, I will spend it with Don Diego. I am very anxious to see the community he has built there in the south of the Texas territory." Don Sancho rose, and Governor Narbona came to put his arm around the old man's shoulders and to escort him personally to the door. "*Vaya con Dios*, Don Sancho," he murmured. "I shall keep my promise to you about a successor. When you can, do send a letter to me to let me know how you and your wife enjoy your new home. And again, may you have far longer than you think to enjoy it."

"You're most kind, *excelencia*. *Adiós*."

Twenty-two

John Cooper rode down from the mountains into Taos, accompanied by a lean and elderly but strong Jicarilla brave, Itaxa. Their horses' saddlebags were filled with the holy relics from the mine, and John Cooper planned to give them to Padre Madura, who would bless them and distribute them among the churches of Nuevo México. Then John Cooper, not knowing that Don Sancho had already decided to go to Texas to live, planned to go to the de Pladero home and entreat the elderly *alcalde mayor* to accompany his Jicarilla escort to the Double H Ranch.

It was early morning when they rode into Taos and saw the dusty plaza with the rosy dawn illuminating the soft blue sky above the Sangre de Cristo in the distance. They tethered their horses at the back of Padre Madura's church, then John Cooper knocked at the door of the rectory. The handsome *india*, Dalcaria, the housekeeper who had replaced poor old Soledad, greeted them. Itaxa at once spoke to her in the dialect of the pueblo, and she nodded and led them into the rectory. They put down the saddlebags with their priceless contents, and waited for Padre Madura, who had just finished the first mass of the day and was coming into the rectory for his breakfast.

"How good it is to see you, my son!" he exclaimed, as he held out his hands to the tall John Cooper. "Share my breakfast; we can have time together in this way. Today is a holy day, and there are two extra masses to be celebrated before sunset. It is a labor of love in the service of the dear God, who brings this village peace."

"Thank you, Padre Madura. This is Itaxa, of the Jicarilla Apache. We have brought you holy relics from that secret cave of which I spoke to you."

As John Cooper opened the saddlebags on the floor, Padre Madura came over to see the contents and crossed himself. "It is incredible! Such workmanship, and not tarnished by all these years! Rosaries, medals, crosses—the faith was strong, and yet it was cruel in those early days. That is why those poor *indios* who worked the mine and fashioned the silver died as they did. But now, blessed as they will be, my son, these relics will exalt the faith for those who have no cruelty in their hearts, but only love for the dear God and their fellow man."

"Amen to that with all my heart, Padre Madura. I told you once, and I repeat it now, that from this silver, that we take back to be put safely away in the bank in New Orleans, you will receive a share, so that your poor will never suffer as they have in the past."

"My son, you have been very generous, and God will bless you for it. These wonderful, holy articles will help the poor and the *indios* throughout Nuevo México. Many of the *ricos* will pay for these crosses and rosaries and medals, once they have been blessed. And that money will be turned over to the needy."

"That is good. And now," John Cooper said, glancing at Itaxa with a grin, "I think we could stand some breakfast, Padre Madura. We've just about lived on jerky and water the last three days. And then I want to make my confession to you and ask for your blessing, and I'll go to see Carlos."

"Dalcaria, my dear, would you prepare breakfast for my guests?" Padre Madura smilingly asked, and the handsome Indian woman responded softly in Spanish, "It will be my honor and my pleasure, *mi padre*."

The Lipan Apache war lieutenant, Minanga, whose life John Cooper had saved by killing a *jabalí* that had gored the Indian, had returned to the Double H Ranch at the tall ranch owner's urging. He had accepted this offer for two reasons. He had the fatalistic belief that because John Cooper had saved his life, it now belonged to the *wasichu*. The other reason was because his companions had seen him dismount from his horse and charge the wild boar with a feathered lance, only to stumble and be wounded by the animal. Thus they had abandoned him and ridden off. He had told John Cooper that he would be considered an outcast by his tribesmen until he had proved himself to be a worthy warrior.

Once the Lipan had been proclaimed as great warriors, but the Comanche had carried on a war of extermination against them, in order to win the rich buffalo herds of west Texas. Yet Minanga's tribe had defied the Comanche, moving in nomadic fashion throughout this vast Texas territory, and it had been on their spring hunt for buffalo that fate had put the boar in Minanga's path—thus he so believed. When he had ridden back with John Cooper to the ranch, he had explained that, in Lipan mythology, there was a legendary hero named Killer-of-Enemies, who killed or otherwise disposed of various monsters and enemies. Before he had cast off his mortal form and become a god, he had created deer, horses, and other wild animals, and taught the Lipans how to fight. And it was he, Minanga had told John Cooper, who had purposely sent the wild boar charging out of the thicket in order to test the courage of Minanga, war lieutenant of the Lipan.

His wound had rapidly healed, and within a week after his return with John Cooper to the Double H Ranch, Minanga had tried to repay his rescuer by offering to help Miguel Sandarbal with the horses of the *remuda*. The Lipan had always been excellent horsemen, and they still raided Mexican villages to steal horses when their hunting forays took them near the Rio Grande. He spoke enough Spanish, though with a guttural accent, to be understood by most of the *trabajadores*. Miguel, who had put a tourniquet around Minanga's gored leg, had agreed with John Cooper that this Indian outcast might be invaluable one day as a scout. He could ride long hours without tiring, taking but little food and water, and he could hide himself and could tell, by the signs of nature, if there were enemies at hand.

And so, for the first several weeks, Miguel took Minanga under his own personal supervision to make this new life easier for the former war lieutenant. Being a sympathetic man, he also sensed Minanga's ineradicable shame at having been rejected by his tribesmen; and when he found that Minanga could break in wild mustangs as well as any *vaquero* on the ranch, he saw to it that the *vaqueros* would applaud the exploits of this lonely man and make him feel welcome.

Aware that his appearance made him vastly different from his companions, Minanga washed the paint from his chest and back, as well as the red stripe around his neck. Moreover, he performed the tasks set to him by Miguel with great humility, and with his eyes usually averted from the watching *vaqueros* and *trabajadores*. After the first week, he made a staunch friend among the *trabajadores*, a *mestizo* named Juan Numalo, whose father was a Toboso Indian and whose mother was a handsome Mexican woman taken prisoner by the subchief and subsequently married to him. Juan Numalo was about thirty, and had come to the Double H Ranch a year ago from San Antonio, where he had worked in a stable. Several of Miguel's men, when they had gone to that town for supplies, had found him knowledgeable about horses and exceptionally friendly and communicative, since he spoke not only excellent Spanish, but also a smattering of English as well. As it chanced, he had asked his employer, a portly middle-aged Mexican, for an increase in his pitifully low wages and had been reviled for his pains. As a consequence, Miguel's men had proposed that he come back with them to the ranch, and he had quickly made friends with everyone, including John Cooper and even Yankee.

It was Juan Numalo who approached Minanga after that first week and drew him to one side behind the bunkhouse. "*Hombre*," Numalo had compassionately remarked, "I know why you have removed the tribal markings. And the *capataz,* the good Señor Sandarbal, has told me how you were cast out of your tribe. Hold your head erect. Do not be ashamed of what is in the past. The skill and yet gentleness you show when you work with horses makes us respect you."

Minanga said nothing, but he gripped the *mestizo's* hand and stared long into his new friend's eyes. And from that day forth, he began to accept this new life, after the disgrace of his tribe's rejection.

Learning that he was an excellent tracker, Miguel commissioned him to make periodic rides to all four boundaries of the Double H Ranch and report what he saw. In the month of June, Minanga observed a small body of Mexican cavalry some ten miles south of the Frio River, but they had been heading southwest and angling away from the ranch. There also was a train of six wagons skirting the Nueces River and moving northwest. Minanga followed them from a distance and reported to Miguel the curious circumstance that although these were Conestoga wagons, which settlers usually used, he saw only men riding in the wagons. They appeared to be armed with rifles and muskets, and behind the wagons was a string of about a dozen sturdy mustangs tethered to the back of the last Conestoga.

Miguel shook his head and scowled. "They are no danger to us, Minanga, but I do not like what I hear about those *hombres* with the wagons. In this lawless, vast land, there are not only smugglers of contraband and *bandidos,* but also men who trade with the Comanche. When I was in San Antonio the last time, a *vaquero* who worked on a ranch southeast of that town told me that he had once seen a group of men very much like the ones you saw, Minanga, who had ammunition and guns and whiskey loaded in their wagons. They went to meet the Comanche, and they traded those things for white prisoners whom the Comanche had carried off in their raids against the *gringos* or the *mejicanos*. And then these men would take the prisoners and force their relatives to pay them ransom. It is an ugly thing, because these men who traded in that way were *gringos* or *mejicanos* themselves, and made their *dinero* from the suffering of their own kind."

"I have heard of such men, *señor capataz,*" Minanga gravely replied. "We of the Lipan call them Comancheros."

By the end of June, Minanga's brooding loneliness had thus been solaced, not only by his friendship with Juan Numalo, as well as his obvious acceptance by the rest of the workers, but also by the easygoing camaraderie that existed at the Double H Ranch. Moreover, the Lipan Apache ingenuously admitted to Miguel that he had never eaten so well—except, of course, during the spring and the fall hunting of the fat buffalo cows. And yet, still burning within him was the stolid resolve to regain face, to prove to his fellows that he was still blessed by Killer-of-Enemies. But how to accomplish that redemption still baffled him, and on this second Saturday in July, he went at midnight to a grassy knoll near the Frio River and, lifting his arms to the sky, prayed aloud to be shown the way, a way that would not only restore him to his tribe, but also repay all these *wasichus* who had befriended him.

That was why Minanga breathed a prayer of thanks the very next day, when one of the *trabajadores* came to him in the corral and declared, "The *capataz* wants to see you, Minanga. He says it is very important and that you are the best scout on the ranch."

"I come now, if you will take this mustang I have not yet tamed," the Lipan smilingly responded. "It will take only a little more work with him, I think."

"I can see he's very gentle already, Minanga. You go see Señor Sandarbal, then." The burly young Mexican grinned at the Lipan and entered the corral, heading for the mustang, who snorted and pawed the ground with his right front hoof.

Minanga hurried to Miguel, who was standing near the almost completed church, supervising the workers. "I am here, Señor Miguel," he avowed. "You have something for me to do?"

"It's very important, yes, Minanga. I told you some weeks back that *El Halcón* went to Taos. I want you to try to find him. I think that, by the time you reach Taos, he will be

heading back here. I will tell you what trail to take, so that
you will be certain to find him. Besides, he may be coming
with a family from Taos, in their wagons, and with an escort
of Jicarilla Apache."

"I will find him, never fear!"

"*Bueno!* You are to tell him that by the time he returns
here, the wagons he ordered will be ready to be used. Tell
him that the church is almost finished, that the work goes
well here, and that we are all eager to see him and, I hope,
Don Sancho de Pladero and his family."

"I will pack provisions and water and leave at once,
Señor Miguel." Minanga's shoulders straightened, and he
stood proudly erect as he vehemently declared, "I was not
once war lieutenant of the Lipan Apache for nothing, Señor
Miguel. If I can track a distant enemy for many days and
nights and find him hiding in a cave, I can surely find *El
Halcón*, he who saved my life and brought me here. And I
will do this task with joy in my heart, Señor Miguel. I have
prayed to the Great Spirit to let me be restored to my people
with honor as I once was, and somehow I feel that He has
answered me in this task you have set me to do. It will be
done."

"And when you return, Minanga," the *capataz* smilingly
replied, "then we can prepare to welcome him. You can tell
us how many people he is bringing with him, and what escort
of Jicarilla."

Minanga immediately went to the stable and let out his
black mustang, which had not run away after he had been
gored by the *jabalí*. He had kept his saddle, which had been
made by fitting two hackberry forks to the mustang's back
and joining them together with two narrow hackberry laths
two and a half feet long. After this, two pieces of green
rawhide with the hair left on had been fitted snugly over the
wooden members, sewn with buckskin thongs, and allowed to
dry. The shrinkage of the rawhide provided a rigid and
strong saddle. He had whittled a horn on the front fork, and
fashioned his own stirrups to fit the entire foot. Undoubtedly
saddles used by the *gringos* were more elegant and comfortable, but Minanga, like most Lipan warriors, was a brilliant
horseman, and he would have found a *gringo* saddle uncom-
fortable and impractical for his needs.

Minanga had also brought along on his black mustang a

large container for water, made from the stomach of a buffalo. The bag was closed with a drawstring and hung from the horseman's left hip. Though the constant evaporation from the bag left the rider's hip damp, the water remained cool.

Fat, aging, but still genial and active, Tía Margarita, had by this time grown accustomed to the Lipan Apache's presence in her kitchen. Without his tribal paint, he seemed less savage to her, although he had always been meek and apologetically grateful whenever she gave him food. Hearing that he was about to ride toward Taos, she generously packed as much food as he could take, including dried corn, jerky, some flour and salt and coffee, and a small sack of *frijoles*.

After he had thanked her for the food, Minanga went to a little shed adjacent to the bunkhouse where he had stored his bow and quiver of arrows. Adjusting the quiver over his shoulder with its sling, he made the bow fast over the saddle horn, then mounted his black mustang, and rode back to where Miguel was still supervising the work on the church.

The white-haired *capataz* broke off his discussion with several of the *trabajadores* to impart to Minanga the most practicable route to take to Taos so that if John Cooper had already started out from Taos with the de Pladeros, they would readily be found.

"I go now; I shall bring you back good news of *El Halcón*," he fervently promised. Then, leaning forward in his saddle, kicking his heels against the mustang's belly, the Lipan Apache galloped off toward the west.

Twenty-three

Don Sancho de Pladero had a coughing fit the day after he returned from his visit to Governor Narbona in Santa Fe, and found it necessary to take to his bed for a day before he was able to make his arrangements to ride back to the Double H Ranch with Carlos and John Cooper. The arrival of John Cooper and the knowledge that a large band of Jicarilla braves was waiting to escort the de Pladeros to Texas had greatly excited the former mayor of Taos, and had aggravated his condition. While Don Sancho recuperated, John Cooper helped Doña Elena prepare for the journey. The Jicarilla brave Itaxa rode out to the isolated mountain where the treasure was hidden, to tell his tribe members who gathered there to expect John Cooper and his people in a week's time. Tomás de Pladero, meanwhile, summoned all the *trabajadores* into the *patio* of the large *hacienda* and there informed them of his parents' plans and of his own decision to remain here in Taos and to continue his work with the sheep.

Of a total of thirty servants, a fifth of whom were relegated to the *hacienda*, only eight offered to accompany Don Sancho and Doña Elena to Texas. Tomás thanked them in the name of his parents, told them that they were free from work this day, and urged them to get their own effects into order.

Shortly before the de Pladeros' departure, Carlos de Escobar rode into Taos to visit Padre Salvador Madura and to make a confession after hearing mass. As he reined in Dolor and prepared to lead him around the back of the church to

251

the tethering post in front of the rectory, he heard the clatter of hooves and, looking up, perceived the beautiful young *mestiza*, Noracia. He turned to her with a warm smile and bowed to her. "A pleasant afternoon to you, Señorita Noracia."

"You're very kind, Señor Carlos."

"I'm grateful to you, because apparently you met the Señora de Rojado and told her that Alejandro Cabeza is not a man for marriage."

"And he isn't; have faith in my judgment, Señor Carlos. If I've helped you and the Señora de Rojado come together in happiness, then I shall be happy, too. But I have a favor to ask of you."

"I owe you much, and a favor is very little. What do you wish of me, Señorita Noracia?"

The lovely *mestiza*'s cheeks flamed as, lowering her eyes as well as her voice, she murmured, "I know that you love her and want to marry her. But you will be leaving Taos soon, perhaps forever. If you will not take me as your *novia*, will you not take me for a night? Come to my *hacienda* this evening, Señor Carlos, to rest and refresh yourself, to enjoy the food of my fine cook, and then to lie with me, so I may know what a decent, good man I am missing when you leave here."

Now it was his turn to blush after so frank an avowal. "Señorita Noracia, I do not know how to say this without offending you, and I swear to you that is furthest from my wish. You are very beautiful, and it is only because I am *un romántico* that I am unable to make love to you. It is—how shall I explain it?—when I am in love with a woman, I am all hers, and I seek no other, even if she were the queen of Spain herself."

Noracia stared at him, and put out her hand and gently touched his cheek. "How I envy her, to be loved like that! What I wouldn't give to have a man like you—so decent and good, so thoughtful and considerate toward a woman—fall in love with me! Ah, I have known only the worst of men; I have been a *puta, una esclava,* but never once has a man taken me in his arms and told me that he loved me for myself and because of his own need of me. No, I cannot take offense at your refusal of me, Señor Carlos. I can only wish that I could have been lucky enough to have made you fall in love with me as you did with the Señora de Rojado. I wish you and her long happy years together and many *niños*."

"You are a very special woman, Noracia. And I, too, wish you well." Once again, he bowed to her as a cavalier would, and took her hand and kissed it.

As he went into the little church to confer with Padre Madura, Noracia stared after him and put the back of her hand to her lips and kissed it, thus kissing his lips. "It is the last time I shall have such a kiss from you, *amigo*," she murmured half to herself. And then with a philosophical shrug, she added, "But one must make do with what one has."

When he left her, Carlos was not ashamed that there were tears in his eyes, for her candid avowal had deeply moved him. There was a quiet exultance in his heart now, for this was the very day Teresa de Rojado had promised to give him her answer as to whether she would accompany him to the ranch in Texas and perhaps merge her life with his.

After he heard the mass and made his confession in the church, Carlos rode out to Teresa de Rojado's villa, full of eagerness and bright hope. But now a rude shock awaited him. Teresa was sitting in the parlor of her house, looking very grim and determined, and Carlos knew before she uttered even one word that she had decided not to go with him.

"I cannot leave," Teresa said quietly but emphatically. "Carlos, I cannot go to a strange land with strange people."

"But you did just that when you first came to Taos!" Carlos exclaimed, unable to help himself from making such an outburst. He was much too distressed to mince words any longer.

"Yes, and now after all this time I finally have a home I can call my own," Teresa explained, her own voice quavering. "I am comfortable here, Carlos, and I am content."

"Are you really so content?" Carlos persisted.

"It is enough," was all she replied.

Carlos was furious now. All the anxieties of the past two years—all the frustration and impatient yearnings—came to a head, and he blurted out angrily, "I have already told you repeatedly about the new home I am offering you. You have chosen to reject it. So be it. I cannot force you to come with me, and indeed I am growing tired of begging you to do so." He paused a moment, then forced himself to say, "I will take my leave of you. I will not bother you again." With a curt bow, and a furtive parting glance at Teresa, he stalked out of the *hacienda,* leaving behind the beautiful woman in whom he had staked all his hopes of future happiness. But he was determined not to let her see his unhappiness. No, there would be plenty of time in the future to shed tears over the loss of the only other woman he had deeply loved.

As she watched him leave the house and heard him ride away, Teresa herself was already weeping. She now realized that with Carlos's departure, her own hopes of finding someone to love were dashed. Yes, she had her house and her servants, but were they truly enough—without a husband, without a family? With Don Sancho, Doña Elena, and Carlos gone, her life was going to be very empty indeed. She looked outside through the window at her gardens and her horses in the corral: she saw her servants going about their tasks in her house, the first home she had known in a very long time. Yet all these things around her suddenly seemed totally unreal, as though they didn't have anything to do with her anymore, and Teresa began to think she had made a mistake.

The secret silver mine had finally been emptied in the year 1825. The relics were in the safekeeping of Padre Salvador Madura, and the silver ingots had been loaded onto the travois, cleverly concealed by Indian blankets, sacks of maize, and tanned hides. Some of those hides would be used by John Cooper Baines himself in fabricating the buckskin garb he preferred when he hunted or rode out with Yankee or, again, as he planned once he returned to the Double H Ranch, to ride out with his beloved Catarina for a kind of renewed honeymoon. The Jicarilla braves, some thirty in all, chosen from the younger warriors of the stronghold, were mounted and armed with bows and arrows, some with muskets, and a few with the long Belgian rifles procured from Chihuahua.

One of the braves had ridden on ahead two days ago to tell John Cooper that the escort waited for the de Pladeros. And already, on this very day, Don Sancho de Pladero and his Doña Elena, after many tearful farewells to Tomás and Conchita and their grandchildren, had climbed into the stately, old, but still durable carriage he had had made for himself during the very first year of his appointment as *alcalde mayor* of Taos. The eight loyal servants of the de

Pladero household, who had volunteered to join their master and mistress, carried their personal possessions in *carretas* attached to pairs of sturdy workhorses.

John Cooper, mounted on Pingo, rode back and forth along the processional, smiling and joking with the *trabajadores*. "By the morning of the third day we'll be at the rendezvous, *mis amigos*! No need for haste; we want your beloved *patrón* and his *esposa* to be at their ease on this long journey."

"How long will it take, Señor Baines?" Lupe Perantez, an eighteen-year-old *criada* who had become Doña Elena's personal maid, timidly spoke up.

John Cooper halted Pingo in order to take a moment to reassure the nervous servant-girl. "It's some four hundred miles to the ranch, señorita. I'd say, with these *carretas* and the carriage, if we average twenty miles a day, we'll be doing very well. And we mustn't tax Don Sancho; that's understood. Let us say three weeks, perhaps even four. But we've plenty of provisions, and I have my long rifle to bring down a deer or a *jabalí*, or some of the wild turkeys—we'll eat well off the land, just as the Indians do. Don't fear, señorita. We will have the strongest warriors of the Jicarilla Apache as our guards. No one will dare attack us with such an escort, I promise you that!"

The *criada* blushed and lowered her eyes. "So long as you are near me, Señor Baines, I shan't be afraid—but I fear *los indios*."

"Now that, señorita," he bantered with her, "is very flattering. You will see, when we get to Texas, you will soon find a *novio* from all the handsome *vaqueros* who work for me at my ranch."

Carlos was riding at the end of the processional, and it was no secret to anyone that he was totally dejected. He barely paid any attention to what was taking place around him, thinking only how Teresa had refused to go to Texas with him.

Suddenly, there was the sound of an approaching horse, and Carlos looked up, distracted from his melancholy reverie by the urgency of the hoofbeats. His eyes widened with incredulity. It couldn't be! There, galloping toward him, was that slim, beautifully costumed rider, the sight of whose face and the sound of whose voice meant more to him than he had thought possible, after having lost his adored Weesayo. Yes, it *was* true, it was Teresa!

"Teresa—my God! I never expected to see you again after we said our good-byes the other afternoon," he stammered as she halted her mare and came up to face him at a distance of some ten paces. Then he noticed she was dressed for travel, wearing a cloak, and her saddlebags were packed. "Could it be?" he exclaimed. "Have you changed your mind about going with me?"

"Wait, dear Carlos." She held up her hand, and he saw with joy that she wore the gloves he had given her. "It doesn't mean that I'm coming with you to be your wife. What I said to you before is still true—I have not yet made up my mind. But I've decided to come with Don Sancho and Doña Elena because they're like a family to me. What I plan to do is accompany them to the ranch in Texas. Perhaps then I'll go on to New Orleans, and finally go back to the *hacienda* that my husband left me in Havana."

"And your *hacienda* here, Teresa?"

"I have seen an *abogado* and arranged with him to sell my *hacienda*. My majordomo, Novarra, has a document in my handwriting, authorizing him to deal with this *abogado*. Two of the *trabajadores indios* are coming with me—there they are, riding the horses which draw the *carreta* that have my foils and some other things I don't want to leave behind me."

"I see—well then," he said, brightening, "at least while you're at the ranch, we can practice our fencing again, as we did before."

"I want that very much, Carlos. And I want us to enjoy this time together as good friends, dear friends. I love the outdoors, and I'm just adventurous enough to look forward to this long journey to Texas. Each of us can cheer up the other."

"And I'll protect you."

Her face was grave and her voice very soft now. "I know. I feel that you are my protector already. But I'm not a helpless woman, Carlos, because I can ride, fence, and shoot. I've brought along a fine Belgian rifle, which Novarra bought for me a month before you came to Taos. And I can load it in nearly a minute, sometimes a little better when I concentrate."

As she spoke, Carlos looked at her with such yearning that she had to turn away, understanding only too well the fervor and the depth of his emotion for her. Because, in his mind, home would be where Teresa de Rojado lived with him, once they were wed—and, if the dear, just *Dios* would hearken to the prayer of a man who had sinned grievously in his hope of fighting for the cause of a country torn by strife and the rivalry of selfish men for total power, then it would be as he had prayed it would be. And only then would he be content; only then would home truly mean a place of sanctuary and interminable joy.

Now the little caravan moved out. John Cooper, wiry and virile in his buckskins, rode at the head, followed by the carriage with Don Sancho and Doña Elena, and behind them the *trabajadores* and their *carretas*. Teresa de Rojado rode on one side of the carriage, and Carlos rode on the other. The young Spaniard smiled to himself to catch sight of the rifle sheath attached to her saddle; truly, she was as intrepid as she was beautiful, and her candor had only whetted his growing impatience to make her his wife.

Shortly before noon of the third day, the little caravan approached the treasure mountain. Itaxa had seen the dust rising in the air above the trail and had ridden his mustang back to the waiting Jicarilla braves to tell them that John Cooper's people were arriving.

As they approached the foot of the treasure mountain, Don Sancho and Doña Elena looked out the carriage windows, and then the latter turned to her ailing husband and smilingly declared, "*Mi esposo,* I know it will be a long journey, but I'm not afraid. I have you beside me, and we shall be together and by ourselves for the rest of our years, as *El Señor Dios* so disposes. And you see, those strong, fierce *indios* who are to escort us to Don Diego's *hacienda*—who would dare to attack them? Oh, yes, they'll look after us and see that we arrive safely."

Don Sancho turned to his wife and took her hand between both of his. "Elena, I have not said this very often, but I will say it now. *Te quiero mucho, mí corazón.* I have been happier with you these past few years in Taos than even when I courted you back in Madrid. You have made me content—you are good and kind."

She burst into tears and flung her arms around his neck,

as she buried her face against his chest. And a tiny kernel of fear gnawed at her. Don Sancho had finally told her about the *médico*'s grave warning that his lungs had been affected, and to hear her husband now declare so tenderly and youthfully his love for her made her suddenly apprehensive. It was almost as if he were summing up his life at its conclusion and taking leave of her, and she prayed silently: *oh, Blessed Mother, he is so good, so tolerant of me; he has treated me better than I ever deserved—and I was such a shrew to him for so long! Intercede, Blessed Virgin, with Your Holy Son to grant* mi esposo *some years yet to share with me! I will do penance, I will burn candles at Your shrine each day of my life, and I will be more charitable to the poor; I swear this, if only You will watch over him!*

At last she straightened, her cheeks wet with tears, and she bit her lips and tried to control the surging anguish that rose in her as he looked at her, with that irrepressible smile flickering on his lips. And then, trying to make light of this heart-wrenching moment, she forced a teasing smile and, in an airy voice, retorted, "I think, Don Sancho, the *médico* made a great mistake in his diagnosis. He did not tell you that you almost lost your vision. How can you love an old woman like me, raddled with wrinkles and—"

"Hush, my dearest one," he softly interrupted her and bent to kiss her lips. "You are still beautiful in my eyes. You are still young, and I see no wrinkles. I see instead a kind and tender *mujer*, who has cared for me. I thank God for you, my wife, my dear one, and I look forward to the ranch and Don Diego and his Doña Inez and all those loyal, good people, as a kind of honeymoon with you, *querida*."

Then Doña Elena could no longer hold back her tears. She wept unabashedly, and they clung to each other, Don Sancho soothingly murmuring words of endearment and consolation to her. Indeed, there were tears running down his cheeks as he held her protectively until she stopped weeping.

Kinotatay sat on his gray mustang, wearing the feathered bonnet that proclaimed him *jefe* of the Jicarilla. Beside him was Pastanari, the now grown son of Descontarti, the former chief of the Jicarilla. Pastanari had plucked the hair from his head and left only a scalp lock, the symbol of the war leader. John Cooper questioningly eyed Descontarti's strong young son and then turned to Kinotatay: "As you see, *mi hermano,* we are ready to begin our journey."

'I had told you, *Halcón,* that I would lead the escort of braves back to your ranch. But Pastanari came to me before we set out from the stronghold and vowed that he had a debt of honor to pay."

"But there is no debt to me, Pastanari. You must remain at the stronghold in Kinotatay's place to act as *jefe* for all of your people," John Cooper said to the younger man.

"That is what I told him from the very beginning," Kinotatay interposed. "But surely you have not forgotten how when you first came to us, Pastanari came down the road from the stronghold on his father's great stallion, and it would have killed him if you had not fearlessly snatched him from it and brought the boy back to the stronghold?"

"I have not forgotten, Kinotatay. But Pastanari has become a man and has a squaw and a child and he will one day be *jefe,* as you have told me," John Cooper replied.

"And that is so. Yet a debt of life and honor is the highest law imposed upon us by the Great Spirit, who gives us our mountain stronghold and the peace of our life," Kinotatay solemnly replied. "Pastanari has invoked it, and so I have decided that it will be he who shall lead the braves as escort for you and your friends. And he himself has chosen the men he wishes to ride with him. There are thirty of them, and they are armed with bows and arrows, some with muskets, and some with the rifles that you brought to us, *Halcón.* Yes, among these warriors are a few who remember how you helped us against the Mescalero, and they remember as do I the shadow that fell upon the life of your loved ones, while you were fighting side by side with us without heed of the danger to your own life in that battle. And they, too, have said to me that it is their debt to you as well, which they must repay now."

John Cooper turned to the young man. "Pastanari, you honor me. I told you that there was no debt, nor did I ever feel it. Yet I am grateful to you. I accept your offer, and I am proud to have you and your braves ride with us all." John Cooper extended his hand to the sturdy young brave, who gripped it and then, tilting back his head, let out the piercing war cry of the Jicarilla Apache, to signify that he was now war lieutenant.

"Let Itaxa be your scout and messenger back to me," Kinotatay declared. "When you have arrived at the ranch with all safety, send him back to tell me this, that my people and I may have a great feast to celebrate the return of the hawk to his nest."

"This I promise. I have no words by which to thank you, Kinotatay," John Cooper said.

"There are none needed between us, my brother. As *jefe*, I have given orders to the braves who ride with Pastanari. They are to remain at your ranch until you take this treasure on to New Orleans, as you plan to do. They will defend your friends and your family while you and your *trabajadores* complete the task you have set for yourself."

"*Gracias*, Kinotatay. One thing more I ask of you—and this itself concerns you and your people, as well. The *gubernador* in Santa Fe must swiftly appoint another *alcalde mayor* to take Don Sancho's place. I want to know what kind of man he is, whether he will treat the *indios* of the pueblo as kindly as Don Sancho and Don Diego did. For, if he does not, then even you and your people will be threatened. Ticumbe, the spokesman in the pueblo, whom you know, will surely bring word to you of what takes place, now that Don Sancho has left Taos forever. And Padre Madura stays on as the one certain safeguard against the evil of greedy men like those *hacendados* who were the enemies of Don Sancho and Don Diego."

"As soon as news is brought to me by Ticumbe from either what he has seen in the pueblo or from what Padre Madura has told him, I will send a courier to you, *Halcón*," Kinotatay promised.

"Then it is time to say *adiós*, Kinotatay. I will come back to the stronghold, of that you may be sure. Perhaps, when all of this is over, in the summer of next year when the sun is warm and the sky is blue and there is peace in the land, Catarina and I and my oldest son will journey back here to the stronghold and stay in a *wickiup* and dance the ceremonial dances after the feast. For your stronghold will be a home I shall never give up, so long as I live, Kinotatay. I keep alive in my heart the memories of love and friendship, of courage and honor, which I found among your people. I am proud that I have exchanged blood with you, my brother. Never will I let it be dishonored." John Cooper put his hand against his heart, and then touched first Kinotatay's forehead and then heart. They looked deeply into each other's eyes for a long, silent moment.

And then Kinotatay turned to Pastanari and brusquely ordered in a gruff voice that hid his deep emotions, "It is for you to order the beginning of the journey. Guard them well; see that no harm comes to them. Be prepared to give up your own life for theirs, and prove your courage and skill and your right to succeed me as *jefe* of the Jicarilla, when the Great Spirit summons me to Him."

Pastanari inclined his head and made a sign of obedience. Then, wheeling his mustang, he rode to the head of the braves and, in the Apache tongue, gave the order to begin the long journey to the Double H Ranch.

There were also others setting out on long journeys, men like Matthew Robisard and Ernest Henson, who had left Taos just after the fair, to go on to Santa Fe and Chihuahua to trade there, and then back to their homes in St. Louis, going by way of Texas and the ranch of Don Diego de Escobar and John Cooper Baines. Jeremy Gaige was accompanying them, for he longed to meet the esteemed grandee in Texas and perhaps learn once and for all about legendary Spanish treasure.

The three men had said their good-byes to the de Plateros, and Don Sancho had smilingly told them, "I expect we will meet again in Texas, for by the time you arrive at the Double H Ranch, Doña Elena and I will be already there, with our beloved friends."

Meanwhile, all the way across this great Southwest, another group of individuals was just concluding a long journey, preparing to arrive at a place they would now call home. It was a little before noon on a Monday in early July, and Simon Brown reined in his horse and, holding up his right arm, yelled out, "Wagons, hold!"

It had been three weeks since the attack on the settlers by Captain Juaquín Salgado and his troops. They had buried their dead and tended their wounded, and then moved on to cross the Trinity River. And now, Simon Brown had just seen in the distance—on the banks of the Brazos River—the protective circle of a tall wooden stockade. Inside were the log cabins that had been built by the first group of settlers to ar-

rive here, and they would be augmented by the new homes
that the settlers under Simon's supervision would soon
build.

What the settlers had experienced in the last few months
had taught them the importance of their dependence on one
another. Most of them had never been under fire before, yet
they had courageously fought back against the crack Mexican
troops and, what was more, routed them. And that victory
had given them a sense of confidence, since they felt that this
new land could not possibly hold any more terrors.

Indeed, they had already become a kind of community,
for all of them had had a hand in staving off disaster and
surviving the very real menace of violent death.

Simon turned back to the Hornsteder wagon, the first in
line, and smilingly declared, "Mrs. Hornsteder, your eyes are
just as good as mine—see over there where I'm pointin'?
That's Mr. Fair's settlement, and you'll find some brand-new
friendly neighbors once you get there."

"I see it, Mr. Brown!" Minnie Hornsteder enthusiastically exclaimed. She was driving the horses, her husband,
Henry, having taken charge of the Mayberry wagon. Naomi
Mayberry had protested, but the spirited old woman had
threatened to spank her if she kept on pestering her about
driving those big horses, considering what she'd been through.
"Miz Mayberry, honey, I'm older 'n you, 'n I know what's
best for a nice young woman like you, after what you've
gone through. You just rest up in my wagon. Shucks, Henry's
proud as a peacock to be drivin' that fine team your nasty
husband had."

And so Naomi had remained in the Hornsteder wagon.
She was sitting beside her protector now, and she blushed and
looked down as she met Simon's gaze.

"Only thing worries me, Mr. Brown," Minnie frowned,
"is whether I've got the know-how to build my own house.
Henry's mighty handy with tools 'n such, but mostly I tended
to the cookin' 'n raisin' our kids."

"Don't you fret any, Mrs. Hornsteder," Simon said, grinning at her. "Mr. Fair's sent along some single fellows who
hired out as carpenters, and they'll get wages for helpin' you
folks build your places. They've been cuttin' timber waitin'
for us to get here, and they've already put up a few lean-tos
for your shelter till your own houses are built."

"Well now, Mr. Brown, that's a big weight off my mind. I want to thank you; you've done a right good job of gettin' us here safe and sound the way you did."

"That's my job, Mrs. Hornsteder."

"Mebbe so. But I won't forget how you handled yourself with Naomi's hubby." Minnie Hornsteder turned and saw that Naomi's blushes were furious by now, and that she was looking away. "Now that ain't no way to act, gal," she teasingly chided the attractive young woman. "Mr. Brown here is a fine, upstandin' man, 'n you're all by yourself, 'n I happen to know he's stuck on you—"

"Mrs. Hornsteder, for Lord's sake!" Now Simon's face was as red as the back of his neck was from the hot Texas sun.

"Don't you make a fuss with me, sonny!" the plump, white-haired woman gleefully cackled as she wagged a forefinger at him. "Everybody in the train, just about, knows it. And I think that, now that we've arrived where we're headin' for, it's high time, Mr. Brown, you spoke your piece to Naomi here."

"Please, Mrs. H—Hornsteder," Naomi faintly stammered. "I—I'll never forget how you helped me. And I'll always be grateful to—to Mr. Brown. But he can't possibly want me—"

"Well, I never!" Minnie exploded. "I told you once, honey, if you kept up that notion of drivin' that team of yours after losin' your baby 'n such, I'd paddle you good. And I'll do just that right now less'n you 'n Mr. Brown there face up to facts the minute we git into that settlement."

"All—all right, Mrs. Hornsteder. I—I'll talk to him when we get there." Naomi bit her lip in embarrassment and did not look at Simon.

Naomi Mayberry had not forgotten how Simon Brown had already declared himself and suggested that they get acquainted and see if they liked each other. But since the day of the attack, when her husband's brutal flogging at the wagon wheel had cost her her unborn child, she had had recriminations. It wouldn't be right not to tell Simon how she'd carried another man's child and how William Mayberry had married her to save her from shame and disgrace. And she didn't think he'd want her after that.

David and Cora Stilton sat in their wagon and smiled at each other as they waited for the scout to give the order to drive into the settlement. They were happier than they had ever been before. And Nancy Morrison was going to marry Jack Sperry just as soon as he could build her a little house and find a preacher. Simon Brown had told him there was a fellow already working there who'd been a deacon in a church back in Indiana, and he might just be able to splice them together—and it would be legal. Or, at least, good enough in this brand-new country, where there wasn't any law except that of the gun and your own wits.

Simon rode ahead now and called out, "Wagons ho!" and the train moved on.

As they neared the wide gate of the stockade, it was open, and some twenty men and women stood there waiting to welcome them.

They were home now, and it would be a new beginning, a chance to forget the past and a chance to create a new American frontier.

By evening, cooking fires had been lighted, and some of the newcomers had already moved their possessions from the wagons into the lean-tos. They had inspected the piles of cut timber and they had met their neighbors-to-be.

Naomi Mayberry had asked Simon Brown, after the hearty supper of beef and biscuits and coffee and fresh berries, which two of the already settled wives had picked that morning, to walk with her out beyond the log cabins and the rectangular meetinghouse, which had already been erected.

"I—I'm remembering what you said to me right after— you know, Mr. Brown," she stammered, grateful for the darkness that hid her blushes. "But I told you then: you don't know a thing about me."

"Sure, I remember, Naomi. I said you're brave and good and that man of yours was awful cruel to you."

"Well, maybe—maybe he had a right to be."

"Naomi, what are you sayin' to me? I don't care what you did; you didn't deserve that lickin' he was giving you—"

"But he was a God-fearing man, Mr. Brown. You see, I—I fell in love with the hired man he had. Benjamin Carter was his name. I was—well, I'd been working for my aunt and uncle after my folks died, and they treated me like a bound girl. I couldn't help falling in love with Benjy—only you see, he ran away and left me a note and said he was going West. And I had—I had his baby in me then—and Mr. Mayberry, he said he'd marry me." She bowed her head, burst into tears, and covered her face with her hands.

"That doesn't change things at all, Naomi," Simon stoutly countered. "That's all over with. And you weren't to blame if you loved that fellow and he up and deserted you the way he did. Now look here; I don't have to go back to Franklin to pick up another group of settlers for about a month. You just let me spark you, Naomi, and I'll marry you before I go back. Then I'll tell Mr. Fair I'm goin' to settle down myself on some of this land, and you and I can be together. And I won't ever desert you; I promise you that. I—I'm in love with you, Naomi."

She was weeping now, as she put her arms around his neck, and then she looked at him, with such devotion and gratitude that he could not help weeping, too, as they exchanged their first kiss.

Twenty-four

In the palace of the governor at Santa Fe, Antonio Narbona was giving audience to Alonzo Cienguarda, for the purpose of interviewing the latter as a candidate for the post of *alcalde mayor* of Taos. Governor Narbona intended to live up to his promise to the retiring and ailing Don Sancho de Pladero that he would select a replacement who would be sure to continue the peaceful relationship between the citizens and the Pueblo Indians.

He had already painstakingly interviewed three applicants and discarded them for one reason or another. Finally, he gave serious consideration to one of his own friends, Alonzo Cienguarda, from whom he had received a letter a few weeks earlier. The governor had met Cienguarda in Mexico City nine years ago and had even courted the latter's wife some years before his friend had married her.

The man who sat attentively before him in the high-backed, scrollworked, and tapestry-upholstered chair at the front of his teakwood desk was now forty-seven, a tall, haughty man with a military bearing, whose slim waist and straight shoulders suggested an exemplary fitness and rigid self-discipline. Actually, quite the reverse was true.

Governor Narbona's friendship for Cienguarda had been based on sentiment, for he had fallen desperately in love with the young woman who had rejected him in favor of the weatlhy *hacendado*. Being idealistic, the governor had concluded that the man she had chosen in preference to him must necessarily be praiseworthy in all things. What he knew from his own observations was that Alonzo Cienguarda had been a staunch Royalist who had patriotically supported the independence of Mexico. He had, out of his own coffers, contributed money for the poor of Santa Fe and given generous tithes to the church. He had also supported Iturbide when the latter had made his ascent to the throne.

But what Governor Narbona did not know was that Cienguarda was little more than a weathervane whose opinions shifted with whatever wind was blowing at the time, for the purpose of guaranteeing his own economic and sensual well-being. By giving tithes to the church, he appeared to be a true humanitarian and a devout Catholic; by having supported first the monarchy in Spain and then Iturbide's ill-advised self-designation as emperor of Mexico, he had shown himself to be a strict traditionalist. And now that a president was administering the first uneasy attempts at a democracy in Mexico City, he seemed to demonstrate his capacity for adaptability and conformity as a loyal citizen.

But Governor Narbona would have been horrified if he had known that his respected friend had systematically and slowly poisoned his wife, so that he could acquire her dead parents' rich estate in Chihuahua, and take as his *novia* a beautiful and amoral Mexico City courtesan, Luisita Delago. His wife had been gentle and lovely, but much too chaste to satisfy his inordinate lubricity. Three years ago, when he had taken his wife to Mexico City on a kind of second honeymoon, he had chanced to meet Luisita Delago and fallen furiously in love with her. She had her choice of lovers, and they were invariably rich men who showered her with gifts, including a little villa near Monterrey. But she found in Alonzo Cienguarda a kindred spirit who could match her own insatiable lusts; however, she had stipulated that he rid himself of his wife and lavish all his attention, as well as his wealth, upon her, if she were to be faithful to him. And he had yielded to that temptation.

No suspicion had been attached to his wife's death, because the kindly old *médico* knew nothing of subtle poisons and had, indeed—only a year before Cienguarda had begun to introduce the substance into his wife's food and drink—told him that he feared she had anemic tendencies and was much too frail. Thus, when she had been found dead in her bed, the doctor had attributed it to the malady that he had suspected.

Nonetheless, Cienguarda decided to leave the area, because some of his neighbors had already begun to gossip about the suddenness of his wife's death. Besides, he had friends in Taos and Santa Fe who had apprised him that across the Rio Grande, the subordinate territory of Nuevo México was like a rudderless ship without a helmsman. Thus the opportunity for profiteering and subjugation of the poor, particularly the Indians, was a plum to be coveted. Hence, when he learned of the retirement of Don Sancho de Pladero as *alcalde mayor* of Taos, he had written his old friend, Antonio Narbona, asking for the opportunity to present his qualifications.

"Do you think you can be content to live in Taos, Alonzo?" the governor smilingly asked. Having learned of the death of the *hacendado*'s wife, he felt sympathy for the tall, haughty man who sat before him. Indeed, he had already made his choice, and this interview was little more than a formality. "I warn you, apart from the annual fair, it can be deadly dull. You would be happier in Mexico City, or even in Chihuahua, I should think."

"No, Antonio," Cienguarda replied, his years of friendship allowing him to address the governor by his first name. "I believe that it is my duty to serve in these troubled times. You yourself know how few directives we have from Mexico City of late, because it is only recently that we have had a president. And knowing the people to be restless and uninformed in the more distant provinces of Nueva España—now known as Mexico—one may wonder how long even this democracy will prevail. I pray it will, for our country has need of peace."

These fine-sounding, specious words pleased Governor Narbona. "What you say is true, Alonzo. I must make more decisions on my own authority than ever before, and I can only hope and pray that they are the right ones for Nuevo México. Still in all, we must be optimistic. If you are certain, then, that you can live in Taos and fulfill the obligations of the office, I am ready to empower you officially, yes, this very day, as *alcalde mayor*."

Cienguarda bowed his head and murmured self-effacingly, "I had not expected so great an honor. And yet, *excelencia*, I welcome this opportunity to prove my worth. I shall fulfill the duties of my office with the utmost zeal, you may be sure of it."

"I do not even question it, Alonzo. Very well." Governor Narbona dipped his feathered quill pen into the silver inkwell and scrawled his signature on a document that he had had his secretary prepare in advance of the interview, so certain had he been that the man before him was the best possible choice he could make for Don Sancho's former post. "Here, then, Alonzo, is your commission. You will, of course, prepare to move to Taos. However, I do not think that the *hacienda* of Don Sancho de Pladero will be available to you, since it is my understanding that his son and daughter-in-law with their children will continue to occupy it, having expressed a preference to continue their lives there, rather than in Texas."

"I shall acquire some modest little *casa*, have no fear of that, *excelencia*," Cienguarda said, smiling broadly as he rose. Governor Narbona had sprinkled sand upon the signature to dry and blot the ink, and when it was ready, folded the document and handed it to his aristocratic friend. "*Vaya con Dios*, Alonzo," he said. "Send a courier to me as soon as you have found a place to live."

"I must consider also a place large enough for my *novia*, Antonio," Cienguarda discreetly explained. "I mourn my María, and I shall to the end of my days, but I must remarry. I cannot bear the torment of living alone with only my memories—and I am still young enough to wish the companionship of a devoted wife—I'm sure you understand."

"A very natural sentiment. I should think that your María—" here Governor Narbona crossed himself "—may her blessed soul have eternal peace!—would want you to have companionship, especially in so remote a post as you have just been assigned. May I know the name of the woman you have honored with your suit in marriage?"

"It is Luisita Delago, excelencia. It's true that she's considerably younger than I am, but she has a brilliant mind, and she can be a real helpmate to me. She will have the woman's viewpoint, when it is necessary for me to sit in judgment upon the indias of the pueblo."

"Yes, that is a very good point. I wish you both joy. You must invite me to the wedding."

"It will be some months yet, excelencia," Cienguarda apologetically proffered. "She has property to dispose of and other matters that require her immediate attention, and naturally I must go at once to Taos to find not only a place for both of us, but also to acquaint myself with the temper of the people, their needs and hopes. I shall plunge myself at once into consideration of their problems so that I can report to you the happiest of news."

"I can see that you are a dedicated man, as well as my good friend, Alonzo. A word of caution at this point—the Indians in Taos outnumber us who are privileged to have Spanish or Mexican blood in our veins. It is, therefore, vitally essential to keep them at peace and not to arouse their enmity. You see, Alonzo, in the past, certain hacendados forced the men into working for them at less than a peón's wages, and often either did not pay them at all, or disputed that the work was poorly done and, hence, should not be recompensed. Also, I know that my predecessor, the eminent Gubernador Baca, had had reported to him several incidents of coerced slavery imposed by a few hacendados on the younger women of the pueblo. I call on you to stamp out this abusive and certainly immoral treatment. We must let the indios know that we are their friends. And of course, since they have been given the vote and are considered equals, they must no longer be made to think that they are inferior to us. They should realize that their vote will count when it comes to deciding the future of New Mexico. I think we understand each other, Alonzo."

"You and I think alike, Antonio. I shall preserve the peace, have no fear of it, without letting them think that those of us in authority have no intention of ever letting them emerge from the boundaries of their adobe *jacales* and come upon an even footing with the people who really matter, in Taos or elsewhere."

The two men stared at each other, and then Governor Narbona smiled and nodded. "I think you will fulfill my every expectation, Alonzo. Don't forget now, you're to let me know well in advance of the happy day that will unite you to this woman who will console you for the great sorrow you endured when your poor María was summoned to be among the angels."

To young Manuela's growing distress, her beautiful, domineering mistress, Noracia, seemed to have plunged herself into an aloof, uncommunicative mood ever since Don Sancho de Pladero and his wife had left Taos. She had no way of knowing that Noracia's brooding seclusion had been partially motivated by her failure to seduce Carlos de Escobar, who had graciously but firmly declined her offer to spend at least a night of passion with her so that she would have the illusion that he was her lover. It was one of the few romantic illusions she had ever cherished out of her humble beginnings, and though she could find not the slightest fault with his dignified and graciously considerate rejection of her, it rankled all the same.

But there was news that troubled her even more. One of her *trabajadores* was on the best of terms with the carriage driver of Governor Narbona, and the latter had sent back word that Don Sancho de Pladero had just been replaced and that his successor, one Alonzo Cienguarda, would soon be coming to Taos to choose a *hacienda* for his abode and to administer the civil justice of the town.

The report of Don Sancho's successor's name stirred a vague recollection in Noracia's always alert mind. On the day when the *trabajador* had brought her this news, she locked herself in her bedroom and forbade even Manuela to approach her, until she emerged. Sitting before her mirror, her elbows propped upon the table and her fists under her chin, she closed her eyes and feverishly tried to summon back what it was she had heard of that man. And then it came to her. Long ago, when she had been the *esclava-puta* of Don Esteban de Rivarola, he had entertained two friends from Mexico City, both bachelors in their fifties, debauched and sadistic men whose wealth and influence with the *junta* had given them virtual carte blanche to live as they pleased, as feudal lords who could ravish the *novia* of one of their *peones* without the least risk of reprisal. If the *peón* dared so much as to protest, he could be whipped to death or sent to one of the salt mines in Durango to expiate his insubordination. Don Esteban, who enjoyed the role of voyeur, had turned her over to these two profligates, and had avidly watched as they mauled, slapped, pinched, and whipped her before they forced her to service both of them.

And in the course of that evening, Don Esteban had asked one of his guests for the latest news from the provinces. The name of Alonzo Cienguarda had been pronounced, and one of the guests had declared, "This fellow, Cienguarda, is the kind of man you would admire, Don Esteban. He married a very beautiful woman of the very finest family, and her dowry has made him very rich. But she's much too tame for him, and unfortunately she would be horrified to learn that he has already a *novia*, who gives him the pleasure that she never would. You will see, Don Esteban; one of these days, Cienguarda will find a way to dispose of his pious *esposa* and enjoy pleasures such as I myself and my friend, Enrique, are enjoying now, thanks to your hospitality."

She exhaled a sigh of gratification at finding that her memory had not failed her. Then she frowned again. If this was true of the man who would replace Don Sancho de Pladero, he would be as ruthless as Don Esteban or Luis Saltareno, both of whom had tyrannized and brutalized her. Here she was, wealthy beyond her wildest dreams, her commerce and her shop growing with each new month. Yet by herself, being a scorned *mestiza*, she could not hope for real power in Taos, even though she was as clever as any of the men who had forced her to grovel to them. That was why the thought occurred to her that she must have as her partner a man who would be enough a scoundrel to be able to carry out her plans and yet whom she could control, without herself being subjugated.

The answer was simple: Alejandro Cabeza. He was cunning and handsome, and he had many useful contacts among the *hacendados ricos*. He was accepted as one of them and was privy to their secret conclaves at which they discussed methods to augment their power and wealth and to continue suppressing the wretched *indios*.

And now that she had personally seen to it that Teresa de Rojado would certainly never marry him, he was sure to be plunged into dire straits because he had squandered all his fortune. Once his creditors were turned loose upon him, he would lose his good name and his reputation. And then no highly born woman in all Taos or, for that matter, anywhere else in New Mexico, would have the slightest interest in him. Thus it would be to his distinct advantage to agree to her proposal.

That same afternoon, she summoned her majordomo, Maximilian, into her bedroom and bade him go to the *hacienda* of Alejandro Cabeza to invite him to sup with her. When the old majordomo returned a short time later, embarrassed and crimson faced, he stammered, "He was most insulting, Señorita Noracia. He gave me to understand that he did not care to break bread with his inferiors—those are the very words he used. Forgive me, they were not mine—"

She laughed softly, and said, "Of course they weren't, Maximilian. I don't hold you responsible for what that boor takes a notion to babble. I shall deal with him in my own way, and I think he'll have a very humble apology ready for me when I do."

And now this evening, Noracia at last unbolted the door of her bedchamber and emerged, her eyes shining with a secret malice. Manuela trembled at the sight of her, and shrank back, afraid that somehow she had erred and, by so doing, merited punishment.

But to her utter amazement, the beautiful *mestiza* purred, "Manuela, *querida*, go to Maximilian and tell him to send me Feliciano, Chico, and Corrado. Tell them that I have an order for them, and that they will make *mucho dinero* if they carry it out quickly."

"*¡Sí, al punto, señorita!*" Manuela gratefully gasped, and hurried off on her errand.

Half an hour later, the old majordomo ushered in three sturdy *trabajadores* in their late twenties, all of them with powerful muscles and skilled with weapons and horses alike. Early last month, Noracia had appointed them as her personal bodyguards, and granted them wages that represented six *pesos* a month over what they had previously been earning. As a result, they were blindly devoted to her, and each secretly hoped that, one night, as the reward for his prowess and obedience, she would summon him to her bedchamber.

"Thank you for coming so quickly," Noracia said smilingly, and gestured to the three *trabajadores*. "Sit down, make yourselves comfortable. Feliciano, if you're thirsty, you and your friends will find a bottle of *aguardiente* on the little table in that corner. Yes, that's it. Have your drinks, all of you; but then listen to me with a clear head, or you'll regret it."

She watched while each of them gulped down a small portion of the fiery Mexican brandy, and was now openly amused to see that the three of them were reluctant to take seats and were still standing, glancing nervously at one another, as if to ask what their mercurial mistress had in mind for them.

"Who of you knows anything about the Señor Alejandro Cabeza?" Noracia came bluntly to the point, without mincing words, as she eyed them. They in turn glanced at one another, not quite certain of her meaning. Irritatedly, she persisted: "Come now, *hombres,* I'm sure you've heard his name before here in Taos. Don't stand there like a bunch of *ganado estúpido*! You, Chico; do you know who he is?"

The *trabajador* called Chico, who boasted an enormous mustache and whose plump, round face was scarred from an attack of smallpox at the age of ten, scratched his head and slowly answered, "*Sí,* Señorita Noracia, I know who he is. He is *muy rico,* and I know his manservant, Ernesto Rojas."

"That's better. But you're wrong; he is *pobre,* not *rico,*" Noracia corrected. "And, Chico, if you know so much, you must know where his *hacienda* is, *¿no es verdad?*"

Chico nodded, again eyeing his companions as he uneasily shifted from foot to foot.

"Now then, the three of you," she continued, "all of you know that I have kept my promise, ever since Luis Saltareno was killed in a fair fight by that tall *americano*. I pay you well; you have your pleasure with the *criadas,* and I do not often ask too much work of you. When I do, I pay more. Isn't that so, Feliciano?"

Feliciano Servilas was over six feet tall, unusual in a Mexican, with long arms and powerful wrists, and possessed of a crisply pointed black beard, of which he was inordinately proud. Some of his companions jokingly said that he had been properly named, for his name was a derivation of the Spanish word that meant happiness, and he was rarely seen to smile. He nodded and solemnly assented, "Sí, Señorita Noracia, you have kept your promise. And we would rather work for you than for anyone else in Taos."

"Very good, Feliciano. Now pay attention, all of you. I want the three of you to arm yourselves, to go to the *hacienda* of this Alejandro Cabeza, and to bring him back to me. I am sure that he will not come of his own accord, so you will have to persuade him. How you do it, I don't care; only don't kill him. If you do this for me, each of you will receive fifty silver *pesos,* and each of you may choose one of my pretty *criadas*—excepting Manuela—and enjoy her favors for a week. Is that understood?"

The three men, with a simultaneous gasp of delighted surprise, chorused, "¡Sí, pero sí, Señorita Noracia!"

Corrado Montañez, a stocky, swarthy *mestizo* who had a Mexican father and a pueblo *india* mother and for whom Noracia felt an understandable sympathy, since the merchant, Luis Saltareno treated him with the utmost contempt, now spoke up with an insinuating grin: "Do I understand you, Señorita Noracia? You mean, if this Señor Cabeza will not go with us willingly, we are to use force, even if we must knock him down and tie him up so he cannot put up a fight?"

"Corrado, you are more intelligent than your friends there, and that is because you have *india* blood in your veins, just as I do," Noracia laughed delightedly. "That is exactly what I mean. I should think that if you could break into his *hacienda* when it is very late at night and everyone is asleep, you could do it quickly. Do not harm his servants; there is no need for that—unless, of course, you must defend yourselves. Bring him back to me and, when you have him, take him down to the *calabozo* in the cellar."

"The *calabozo,* Señorita Noracia?" Feliciano incredulously gasped with an uneasy look at Chico Ríos, who stood beside him.

"Yes, *estúpido!* When Luis Saltareno was your *patrón*, I am sure that all of you knew where the *calabozo* was. There are chains with iron gyves set into the wall, and you will use them to fix Alejandro Cabeza there, so he cannot run away till I am ready for him. And one more thing—you will take off all his clothes and leave him naked as the day he was born, do you understand me? Now go carry out my order!"

Corrado touched his forehead with the two middle fingers of his right hand and gave Noracia a sly wink. "It will be done exactly as you wish, Señorita Noracia. *¡Vámanos, muchachos!*"

It was long after midnight, and in the lavishly furnished bedchamber of the beautiful *mestiza*, the timid young Manuela lay sleeping beside her mistress, her arms clinging to Noracia and a smile wreathing her lips. She had been summoned there after her mistress had given the three *trabajadores* that startling order. Manuela had hesitantly entered, believing that she would receive, at the very best, a scolding and more than likely a whipping, in view of her mistress's previously absorbed and unfriendly mood. To her great surprise, Noracia had bidden her go to the kitchen and have the cook prepare a little late supper with a bottle of the very finest Canary wine. Then the two of them had supped together like dear friends who had survived the very worst of ordeals and whose friendship had thereby been strengthened.

And when Manuela had timidly stammered, "I—I thought you were angry with me, *querida* Señorita Noracia, and I was so afraid all this time," Noracia had laughed very softly, and then begun to undress the young servant-girl.

Now there was a soft knock at the door of the bedchamber, and then another, louder, and finally a series of knocks, till at last Noracia sat up, yawning, her long glossy hair tumbling about her face. Manuela stirred fitfully, still asleep, and the *mestiza* bent to the charming young woman and caressed her breast with a soft hand, as she called out, "Come in, and don't knock the house down when you're doing it!"

It was Corrado, his face bruised and his lower lip swollen, but with an irrepressible grin as, seeing Manuela lying on her side and with one arm flung over Noracia's body, he readily comprehended and lowered his voice to a conspiratorial whisper: "We have him, Señorita Noracia, and he is in the *calabozo*, just as you have ordered. He did fight, but we were too much for him."

"*¡Bueno!* And his servants?" she demanded.

"Chico had to break a man's arm, but that was all. We took horses, of course, Señorita Noracia, and Feliciano had them ready when Chico and I dragged the Señor Cabeza out of his bed." He grinned again and confidentially added, "He did not like being taken away from his *novia. ¡Qué guapa!* I myself would not have minded—"

"That will do, Corrado. Very well. Leave him in the *calabozo* for the night. I will see all three of you in the morning, after *el desayuno,* and you will have your reward, just as I promised."

"*Muchas gracias,* Señorita Noracia. *¡Buenas noches!*"

By now, Manuela had been wakened, and sat up, uttering a little frightened cry: "*¿Qué pasa,* Señorita Noracia?"

"Nothing, *muchachita,*" Noracia said tenderly as she bent down to kiss Manuela on the eyelids and then the mouth. "Go back to sleep. I have an errand to attend to. Don't worry, I shall be back to you before you waken again in the morning. Sleep well, *querida?*"

Manuela murmured drowsily and nestled in the warmth of the bed as Noracia slipped out of it. And then, lighting a little oil lamp on the nightstand beside the huge, four-poster bed, Noracia walked to the cherrywood dresser at the other end of the spacious room, drew out a drawer, and took from it a red silk robe. This she donned, tying the cloth belt loosely, then thrust her feet into a pair of fleece-lined moccasins and closed the door of the bedchamber. Walking swiftly down the narrow hallway, she came to a narrow door, which was standing open, and a flight of stone steps. Holding the oil lamp high, she carefully descended.

Alejandro Cabeza stood with his back against the wall, his arms extended like a cross, his wrists clamped in strong iron gyves set into the stone wall. The three men had taken the added precaution of shackling his ankles to a similar set of iron rings at the base of the wall, and he was stark naked and totally helpless.

"We meet again, Alejandro," Noracia purred.

"You damnable *puta,* this time you've gone too far!" the *hacendado* stormed. "When the governor hears of this, he will have you punished, Noracia, to say nothing of what I'll do to you before I take you to Santa Fe for trial—"

"Gently, Alejandro. You will not be able to see the governor in Santa Fe. You will remain here. You are now my prisoner."

"Why do you do this? What have you to gain?"

"An ally and a servant—and perhaps, if you are a very good servant, Alejandro, a lover as well. But that will depend on you," she said, looking him up and down with a sensual little smile. "You are *muy macho, muy hombre,* I will say that for you. Not enough to please the Señora de Rojado, it's true. But, with time, you may learn to please me."

"I would burn in hell before I would touch you, you detestable *puta,* you miserable meddler. You ruined everything for me. I would have married her—"

"Never in all this world, Alejandro," Noracia interrupted. "Sooner or later, she would have known what you were, even if I hadn't told her. It's Carlos de Escobar she loves, and she's already left Taos and gone with him to Texas to visit his father there. I'm sure they'll be married. So you may as well forget her forever, Alejandro."

"It's all your doing! But I'll pay you back!" He tried vainly to twist his wrists free of the chafing iron gyves.

"You wish to burn in hell, I think you said, Alejandro," she went on with a cruel little smile. "You have given me a very good idea. Pay attention now. And think of this, before I ask you whether you have changed your opinion of me— there is now a new *alcalde mayor* in Taos. And I remember, from what a guest of Don Esteban de Rivarola once said in my presence, that this new *alcalde mayor* will not be a good man. He will care nothing for the *indios* of the pueblo, only for his own pleasures and for his power. But if you were intelligent enough, Alejandro, to join forces with me, we could both have all the power there is in Taos and prevent this man from stealing it. Think of that for a moment, Alejandro."

With this, she set the lamp down on a footstool and walked to the end of the grim dungeon which her former master, Luis Saltareno, had used for the erotic whippings and torments he had had inflicted on his helpless young *criadas.* In one corner stood a brazier, filled with dried pieces of brush and a pile of dried grass. Beside it, on a stool, was a tinderbox, and Noracia lit the contents in the brazier. On the floor was a small pile of twigs and sundry bits of wood to replenish the fire when desired.

"What are you doing, Noracia?" he again burst out. "I command you; let me go! I swear to you, when I get loose, I'll tie you up the way you've tied me, and I'll use a whip on you to bring you to your knees and teach you manners toward a *hacendado*!"

Noracia did not reply. Instead, she reached up to take down a branding iron whose tip was shaped in the form of the letter *S*, since Saltareno had used it to brand a runaway *criada* or *trabajador*. She put the tip of the branding iron into the leaping flames of the brazier and waited, sometimes felinely stooping to pick up a handful of wooden chips and twigs and toss them in as further kindling.

And when the iron glowed ominously red, she turned and walked slowly back to Alejandro Cabeza.

"*Dios*—you would not—in the name of heaven, have you gone mad, *mujer*?" he hoarsely cried.

Again Noracia did not answer. Instead, transferring the glowing iron to her left hand, she loosened the belt of her robe with her right and shrugged it from her shoulders, letting it slip down her body till she stood naked before him.

Then, approaching the glowing end of the branding iron toward his maleness, she whispered, "Now you may choose, Alejandro. *Un beso de fuego*—a kiss of fire—either from the iron or from me. Which is it to be, *querido*?"

Twenty-five

It was four days after John Cooper and Carlos, Don Sancho and his wife, Doña Elena, and their retinue of servants, escorted by the Jicarilla warriors under the leadership of Pastanari, had left the treasure mountain and headed on the long, arduous trail back to the Double H Ranch. Fra Ignazio Peramonte entered the little church in the plaza of Taos and knelt in one of the rear pews in fervent prayer, while Padre Salvador Madura conducted the ceremonial of the mass before a handful of parishioners. He was dressed in the black robe and cowl of his order of *Los Penitentes*, and from his wrinkled neck hung a silver cross which he himself had made after having melted down one of the ingots which John Cooper had given to the martyred Padre Moraga years ago.

He waited patiently until the confessionals had been heard and the church was emptied, and then left his seat, went down the aisle, and genuflected before the altar, praying aloud in a voice that was still harsh and somber despite his advanced years. This done, he stepped onto the slightly raised platform at one side of which was the podium from which the priest addressed the worshipers, and went into the rectory.

Padre Salvador Madura, still in his robes and cassock, was instructing his handsome Indian housekeeper, Dalcaria, to prepare a brief supper.

"May God's blessing attend you always, Padre Madura," Ignazio Peramonte intoned as he made the sign of the cross in the air.

The priest turned, came to him, and, his hands on the older man's shoulders, devoutly kissed the crucifix, then straightened. "It is good to see you, my brother. Dalcaria," he said, turning to address the housekeeper, "be kind enough to set another place. Fra Peramonte will share our humble meal."

Dalcaria inclined her head in respect to the leader of the *Penitentes*. "*Seguramente, mi padre.*"

"You have something to tell me, and I am here to listen, Fra Ignazio," Padre Madura softly said as he gestured toward a chair and seated himself opposite his guest.

"Yes, Padre Madura. I have heard that Governor Narbona has appointed Alonzo Cienguarda to replace Don Sancho de Pladera as *alcalde mayor* of Taos," Fra Peramonte declared. "It is not good news for *los indios del pueblo.*"

"Do you know this man, this Cienguarda?" the priest anxiously inquired.

"I had heard of him some years before he received this appointment, Padre Madura. To the world he presents the illusion of stern, spartan discipline and sobriety in all his acts, and he is regarded with favor in the high echelon of the *junta* in Mexico City. Also, it is generally believed that he was an exemplary *esposo,* devoted to his wife and eminently faithful to her as a good *católico* should be. But as I have said, this is only an illusion."

"Do you have knowledge to the contrary, Fra Ignazio?"

The leader of the Penitent Brothers leaned back in his chair with a weary sigh and closed his eyes, as his gnarled, powerful fingers gripped the arms. Those fingers had wielded the lash on the treacherous José Ramirez, as well as on the *trabajadores* of Manuel Bustamente. He was silent for a long moment, and then he said in his harsh voice, "One of my dear friends is also of the order of Franciscans in which I took my vows long ago. He is stationed in a church in the province of Chihuahua, and he knows this Alonzo Cienguarda. It is said that his wife died most mysteriously and that circumstances point to her husband's complicity in that death. It is known also that he maintains a liaison with an infamous woman from Mexico City, who, apart from her physical beauty and her greed, is little better than a common *puta.* And my friend, Fra Porosco, has written me that this man, who will be responsible for the *indios*, considers them little better than savage animals."

"But this is dreadful, to have such a man as *alcalde mayor* in Taos, at a time when supervision by the central government in Mexico no longer exists!" Padre Madura indignantly exclaimed.

"I share your opinion, Padre Madura. That is why I think that *Los Penitentes* must assume what law there will be to govern here, since it assuredly will not be provided by either Governor Narbona or the men in power in Mexico City. And that is the reason why I have come to you this evening, to discuss this with you and to ask you to accompany us this evening to understand better what it is *Los Penitentes* consider their sacred mission and duty—the retribution of evil men for the wrongs which they have done to those who have neither power nor wealth to speak in defense of them."

"I begin to understand the mysticism and the dedication to which you and your secret order are bound, Fra Ignazio," Padre Madura observed.

"We hope that one day you will join us, for your predecessor, Padre Juan Moraga, was not only a member of our society, but also its leader, as I am now."

"I cannot yet bind myself until I know more. To be sure, I detest the ruthless oppression that these *ricos* impose upon the Indians, but I've always been against violence."

"Sometimes it is the only way to appeal to those whose minds are clouded by their own machinations of evil," Fra Peramonte dryly remarked.

"In the past, there was justice for the *indios* and the poor, thanks to the enlightened administration of both Don Diego de Escobar and Don Sancho de Pladero," Padre Madura mused.

"You are right. But because Don Sancho is old and ailing, he resigned his post in audience with Governor Narbona. And knowing Don Sancho as I did, I am convinced that he begged Governor Narbona to replace him with a man who would have the same tolerance for the have-nots of Taos, as he himself so often showed he did."

"Amen to that, Fra Ignazio."

"*Mi hermano en Cristo*," the gaunt, black-robed friar supplicated, "I have come to ask you to join *Los Penitentes* tonight. Not as a participant, but as an impartial observer.

Tonight we shall call upon one of the *hacendados* who thinks it fair game to cheat a blind old *indio* and to seize his young daughter, who is not more than sixteen. Ticumbe, who as you know is the spokesman of the *indios del pueblo,* came to my shop yesterday afternoon to tell me this. This *hacendado* has set himself up as an absolute power in Taos; and do you not see, Padre Madura, that if someone does not halt his vile career of brutality and theft and the seduction of under-age girls, he will continue to believe that there is no law save that which he sets before his own bound slaves—such they are."

"You will not hurt him too much; you will not take his life?"

"No, my brother. That is for *El Señor Dios* to do, as it is for Him to set the day when I, too, shall face judgment. But if you accompany us tonight when we confront this man— who you know generously donates tithes for your church, *mi padre*—and see him first play the role of haughty aristocrat who is beyond the law, and then whine for mercy like the veriest coward that he is, you will better understand how we uphold what law exists in Taos."

"I will go with you."

"And as we eat, I will enlighten you about our order, *mi padre.*"

"So be it, Fra Ignazio." The padre turned to the handsome Indian housekeeper and bade her serve the frugal supper. Dalcaria nodded, crossed herself, and hastened to serve a thick lentil soup with coarse bread, a small piece of fish, and a cup of strong, black coffee. This done, she knelt, received Padre Madura's blessing, and then left the dining room of the rectory.

"First, Padre Madura," Ignazio Peramonte began, after he said a prayer of thanksgiving for what they were about to receive, "you should know that neither the Spanish nor the Mexican Church has yet persuaded ecclesiastical authorities to elevate Nuevo México to a see. If this had been done long ago, perhaps the secret society of *Los Penitentes* might not have been born out of suffering, hardship, and the strict reality of the differences between a life of poverty and a life of fulfillment."

Padre Madura had broken off a small piece of bread and thoughtfully chewed it as he regarded the older man.

Then he said, "You believe, then, that our parishioners have been deprived of rituals and temporal benefits?"

"Yes, but that is only part of it. We are isolated here; we are in the mountains; and for more than a century, we have had the gradually Christianized *indios* of the pueblo, who at first savagely resisted the intrusion of *gringos*, and are now tolerant of them. What Spanish settlers there were in Taos came directly from the Old World with all its mystical powers of the Holy Inquisition and the belief that savages could be conquered by the sign of the cross. And there was bloodshed because those who came as *conquistadores*, with the priests holding the sacred symbol of Him who died to save us all, sought to win the land by force of arms, and then to convert the conquered, who had no other choice save to die as heretics. I need not tell you of the *autos-da-fé* that began with Ferdinand and Isabella and Fra Torquemada."

"I have often thought," Padre Madura pensively observed, "that it was wrong to force conversion upon people of a different world, who worshiped our dear Lord in their own fashion, and yet were damned because their theological beliefs were not acceptable."

"Take care, Padre Madura. It is well that a member of the Inquisition does not overhear us, or surely you would be called to task for what is an almost retrogressive opinion." Ignazio Peramonte permitted himself a sardonic little smile. Then, for a moment, both men fell to eating. It was the head of the *Penitentes* who resumed: "In my studies of this harsh, almost impenetrable country, I learned that Nuevo México was under the supervision of the diocese of Durango almost a hundred years ago. Yet we never had enough priests to cover so vast a territory, a territory whose population had spread into many new villages and hamlets far from the valley of the Rio Grande, leaving many inhabitants of this territory, especially the poor, to their own devices."

"I begin to see what you are driving at, Fra Ignazio."

"It was said by Pedro Bautista Pino thirteen years ago that our twenty-six Indian pueblos, and over one hundred Spanish settlements, were served by only twenty-two Franciscan missionaries and two secular priests. And he attributed many ills to the lack of a resident bishop, saying that people who had been born during the past fifty years had not been confirmed, and that the poor who wished dispensation to marry relatives could not receive it because of the great cost of traveling more than four hundred leagues to Durango. And because of this, many people lived in adultery."

"I know that we do not have enough priests for all the parishioners even here. I myself could use an assistant, but I dare not ask for one."

"Nor will you ever have one here," Fra Ignazio declared. "But I digress. You already know enough of our secret brotherhood to understand that our rituals include the bearing of the cross, self-flagellation, the singing of hymns, and praying. The idea of self-flagellation began centuries ago, when Europe was seized by the deadly plagues, which superstitious people looked upon as a sign of the wrath of God to punish sins. Yet perhaps that was not so far from the truth. And so that they might be spared the hideous death of the plague, groups of religious acolytes gathered in Spain, as in France, scourging themselves and imploring *El Señor Dios* that the blight of pestilence be lifted."

"That is a yearning for martyrdom, I perceive."

"Perhaps, Padre Madura. But martyrdom in the spiritual sense today is part of what we seek in our society. How shall I describe it to you—we have been called brothers of light and brothers of blood. The blood is our own, and it is also that of transgressors. It represents our humble yearning to experience a part of what *Jesu Cristo* knew on that dreadful day when he was marched to Golgotha and was nailed upon a cross. That is the physical suffering, but we seek to transcend this. We seek to purge our minds of sin and evil, and we realize through meditation and self-discipline that the iniquities of mankind must never be forgotten. No, Padre Madura, the Church does not seek perfection, for what man born of sin can be perfect? What we do seek here in Taos is to show the simple lesson of good against evil. If the civil authorities, if even the *gubernador* himself, take no measures against the oppression of the poor and the outcasts—who, as you know, are the *indios* of the pueblo here—then someone must speak out. And thus, here in Taos, years ago, we formed *Los Penitentes*, known also as Brothers of our Father Jesus. At Lent, we show ourselves to the people by bearing the cross and by scourging ourselves. That is the outward show, and perhaps it reminds those who have neglected attendance at mass of how *Jesu Cristo* died for the remission of our sins. But the rest of the year, Padre Madura, we observe transgressions committed by those who use their wealth and power to crush the weak and the needy."

There was a long silence as Padre Madura sipped his coffee. Then he looked at Ignazio Peramonte and said, "These patient people, destined always to be poor—except for the Christian generosity of that *gringo* to whose *hacienda* Don Sancho now journeys—live desperate lives with their humble *jacales*, their paltry wages, and their joyless work. When they turn from their pueblo village, they see the great snowcapped mountains of the Sangre de Cristo. We have Christianized them, and yet they still retain their primitive instincts upon this land of mountains and arid canyons and dusty plains—where a dry, burning sun causes thirst and blindness and death for the unwary who venture forth into the desert, and where cold winds rage on the peaks of the mountains that they try to climb to be closer to Him. Yes, Fra Ignazio, and then add to this no civil law, except the former *intendente* and *alcalde mayor*. Now both of these have gone from us, and you tell me that the man who replaces Don Sancho is venal and corrupt."

Now Padre Madura uttered a long sigh and shook his head. "Fra Ignazio, I have listened to you attentively, and I have learned much. I will come with you tonight, and you can teach me what you will. I will try to profit from it."

An hour before midnight, four black-robed and cowled *Penitentes* came to the church for Padre Salvador Madura, who, at Ignazio Peramonte's instructions, had dressed himself in a white robe and cassock. Since he was not of the order, it had been ordained that he should wear white, the symbol of purity and godliness; the black robes signified not only the agony of the Lord along the way to the cross, but also the wrath of spiritual judgment imposed on those who transgressed against both mankind and their Creator.

Fra Ignazio Peramonte drove a *carreta*, which had been attached to two sturdy burros, and his three colleagues and Padre Madura mounted into the *carreta* and stood, holding onto the horizontal tops of the sides; the back was open. In the stillness of the night, with a half-moon a ghostly wraith in a cloudy sky, the only sound was the thudding of the heavy cart wheels, as the burros moved methodically under the exhortations of their driver.

The *carreta* halted at a little adobe *jacal* on the outskirts of the pueblo village, and the *Penitente* leader gestured that Padre Madura was to enter after him and his three lay brothers.

The priest found himself inside the dwelling place of a *Penitente* where there was a tiny altar dedicated to Father Saint Francis, with an ancient frontal of blue-ribbed silk. Also in the room were a *bulto* of the Nazarene Jesus; another of the Madre Dolorosa; a wooden table, on which was posed a wooden cross of the kind used by the Third Order—which the *Penitentes* called themselves—and finally a bench on which lay a rawhide scourge.

Fra Peramonte knelt before the *bulto*, crossed himself, and prayed aloud: "Holy Son of the Virgin Mother, You and She who have known sorrow and death, we pray to You this night to look down upon us, humble acolytes to Your eternal sanctity and truth. Watch over us and guard us from the error of envy or vindictiveness in the justice we seek to bring for the oppressed and the downtrodden. We act in solemn concord for the good of the people of Taos and against the oppression of one who thinks himself beyond reckoning. Amen."

In the tiny *jacal*, the voices of the *Penitentes* responding to this prayer were hollow and low pitched, and the air of mystery was evoked in Padre Madura's perceptiveness. He crossed himself and prayed silently that he, too, might not be prone to the human failings of vindictiveness or spite in witnessing what he now knew was to be at the very least a spiritual scolding and at worst a physical chastisement for a wrongdoer. For, at the end of this symbol-fraught ceremony, he had seen Ignazio Peramonte seize the scourge and, his face dour and gaunt in the flickering light of a single candle, menacingly shake it in the air and at the ground.

They left the *jacal* and clambered back into the cart, and the head of the *Penitentes* turned the burros southward beyond the pueblo village and toward the scattered estates of the *ricos*. As he halted the burros, Ignazio Peramonte turned to Padre Madura and murmured, "Here we seek the majordomo of the *hacendado* Nicolas Abierto. He is to be punished and his master rebuked for permitting him—and I suspect, even urging him—to commit the great sin of taking a young girl by force from her father's *jacal* to be his *esclava*. You will hear his own defense, and doubtless that of his master, as well. They will both say that the majordomo gave the father *pesos* and bought the girl with his consent. It is a lie, which adds to the sins of both servant and master. Observe us, *mi padre*, and pray that we shall be guided, not in personal vengeance, for that is to substitute one corruption for another, but in the spirit of justice before *El Señor Dios*. Now we shall begin our business."

The tall, gaunt, black-robed figure moved to the door of the *hacienda* and, making a fist with his right hand, struck thrice with all his strength upon the heavy wooden door. The sound seemed to reverberate even inside the house, and now the half-moon was nearly obscured by the slowly drifting clouds, so that the eerie darkness of the night engulfed this isolated, sprawling *hacienda*.

Hearing no response, Ignazio Peramonte struck thrice again, and this time with greater force. At last, there was a faint sound of footsteps, and then the flickering light of an oil lamp, which filtered through the curtain of the window at the right of the door. Then a voice, indignant and still drowsy with sleep, called out, "*¿Quién es a esta hora?*"

And to this, Fra Peramonte answered in a sonorous voice, "*¡Los hermanos de nuestro Padre Jesu Cristo!*"

Padre Madura thought he heard a stifled gasp, and then the door was hastily opened, and an old servant, in nightdress, rubbing his rheumy eyes, stared fearfully at the black-robed figures and tremblingly made the sign of the cross as he stammered, "Forgive me, I was asleep—all are asleep in this *hacienda*—whom do you seek, holy ones?"

"The majordomo of the Señor Nicolas Abierto," Fra Peramonte sternly responded. "Bring him forth and, with him, summon also your *patrón*."

"*Sí, sí, pronto.*" The servant could hardly speak in his fear, as he turned and hurried back into the house.

In his left hand, Fra Peramonte already held the scourge, and he turned to Padre Madura and murmured, "Listen now, for it is a kind of confessional. And it must ring with the truth, or there will be retribution, even more than is planned."

Padre Madura nodded and moved to one side, remembering that he was not to be identified with these four menacing vigilantes who now, alone in Taos, sought to administer justice.

After a few moments, a portly, gray-haired man came, wearing a velvet dressing gown and slippers. He had a double chin and a paunch, and his eyes were beady and set close together against the thick bulbous nose on which there was a tiny wart. Beside him stood the same elderly servant who had opened to the *Penitentes,* twisting his hands, his face clammy with fear as he saw again the black-robed figures.

"By what right do you waken my household at this late hour?" the portly man angrily demanded.

"You are Nicolas Abierto, *hacendado* of Taos?" Ignazio Peramonte asked.

"I am. Everyone in Taos knows me. And I repeat my question: why do you disturb us? I have done nothing to incur this visit from black-robed priests. I give generous tithes to the church in Taos; I harm no one; and I resent your intrusion upon a sleeping *hacienda.*"

"I had asked your servant to bring forth your majordomo. You, as his *patrón,* somewhat share in his guilt," was Fra Peramonte's reply.

"How dare you speak to me in this way!" the *hacendado* blustered. "Josef, close the door on these beggars—"

"I should not advise that, Señor Abierto," was the stern answer. "You stand in danger of excommunication."

"Now this goes too far! But of what am I accused?"

"If you will have your majordomo face us, I will tell you the charges, which involve you as his *patrón.*"

"Oh, very well. To end this comedy, Josef, fetch Reyes Espinosa."

"At once, *patrón,* at once!" The servant bobbed his head and disappeared again. Meanwhile, Abierto fumed and glowered at the four black-robed men, who returned his stare with cold, austere, expressionless faces.

Presently, the old servant came back with the steward of the *hacienda,* a burly, slothful man in his early forties, with nearly as large a paunch as his *patrón,* fierce black eyes, and a thick mustache, together with a stubby beard at his fat chin.

"You are Reyes Espinosa, majordomo to the Señor Nicolas Abierto?" Ignazio Peramonte queried.

"That's my name, and I've done nothing."

"You call nothing, then, the forcible abduction of an unwilling girl from her father's *jacal?* A week ago, you and two of your *trabajadores* rode into the pueblo, and there entered the *jacal* of Localdi, and brought back with you, against her will, his only daughter, Genifra."

"Who says I did? I paid the old man well for the *puta;* she is mine now," the majordomo insolently responded.

"Three silver *pesos*, which he tried to throw back at you as he pleaded with you and your men to leave his daughter in peace. She was to wed a young *indio* on this very day in the church in the plaza."

"*Patrón,*" the fat steward said, turning to his master, "you said that three *pesos* would be enough for a dirty *india.* And you yourself—"

"Be silent, you fool!" Abierto hissed, with a ferocious look at his steward. Then, folding his arms across his chest and facing the four black-robed *Penitentes*, he sneeringly declared, "It's more than she was worth, the whining little slut. What would she do at the pueblo, wed with this young *indio,* except have a litter of starving *niños* who would all be dependent upon our charity."

Ignazio Peramonte's harsh voice rebuked the *hacendado's* insolence. "Her life and that of her *novio* are in God's hands to decide, not yours, Señor Abierto. You will have her brought here at once. She is to return to her father. And you, Reyes Espinosa, are to be punished for this brutal and sinful deed. The *indios* of the pueblo are not slaves. They were freed years ago by Governor Manrique, and they may vote and have a voice in the future of Taos."

"Heaven deliver us from such a future if they are given such unmerited power," Abierto angrily exclaimed.

"Seize him!" Fra Peramonte gestured to two of his companions, who advanced and grasped the steward by the elbows and dragged him out to the cart.

The *hacendado* was livid with anger and stamped his foot. "Release him; you have no right to meddle in my affairs!"

"If you do not deliver the girl to us at once, Señor Abierto, we shall have pronounced in the church in the plaza and throughout Nuevo México the sentence of excommunication upon you!" was Fra Peramonte's answer.

For a moment, the *hacendado* stared at his interlocutor, as if wanting to pursue the argument. Then, with an indifferent shrug, he growled, "Well, she's not worth even the three *pesos*. Take her back, then, for I should say my soul is worth considerably more than that."

"In the eyes of our Maker, you are not even worth the thirty *pesos* that were paid to Judas Iscariot to betray *nuestro Padre Jesu Cristo*," Ignazio Peramonte said in his most scornful tone. "How can you set yourself up to judge the worth of a girl without blemish, a good *católicá*, devoted to her father as to her vows in the Church? And you say that you are worth more than her—vain, arrogant man! Now bring her forth."

"Josef, bring that little slut, Genifra, here and have an end to this nonsense," the *hacendado* grumbled.

Meanwhile, the two sturdy *Penitentes* who had taken hold of Reyes Espinosa had already bound his hands behind his back. Now his face was ashen, and he turned back to his employer and almost tearfully blurted, "*Patrón, patrón*, don't let them do this to me—you told me that it would be all right if I gave the old fool some *pesos*—"

"I cannot help you now. Next time, at least have the cunning to take a girl whose absence will not be observed by these black-gowned meddlers," Nicolas Abierto petulantly exclaimed.

They hustled Espinosa into the cart, forced him down to his knees, and stood on either side of him, their fingers digging into his shoulders to keep him in that humble pose. The old servant now came back leading a girl who could not have been more than sixteen, her face swollen with tears, clad in only a thin cotton shift and her feet bare. On her shoulders and arms were the fading weals of a recent whipping.

At the sight of the black-hooded men, she fell upon her knees and, clasping her hands, burst into hysterical sobs: "Do not punish me—I did not sin. It was against my will—*mis padres*, forgive me, it was not my doing!"

Ignazio Peramonte's voice was gentle. "Child, no one accuses you of sin. It was the majordomo, was it not, who forced you?"

"*Sí, mi padre*—and then the *patrón* tr-tried himself— and when I could not, w–would not—" her sobs became more hysterical as she fought for self-control "—and then— he had me wh--whipped so I would obey the—the next time. Oh, save me; save my soul from damnation!"

"It is saved, my child, my poor child," Fra Peramonte sympathetically responded. "We come to take you back to your father, and to punish the evildoer. In God's eyes, my daughter, you are still a virgin. You shall marry the man you have chosen, and in his eyes also you will come to him immaculate and unstained." Then, to the fuming *hacendado*, he angrily averred: "This girl's confession damns you both from her own chaste lips, Señor Abierto! I warn you; you must atone for the evil you have done to this poor child. Nor are you blameless in that you did not violate her, as did your majordomo. Your intent was as brutal as his, as is proved by the lash marks that mar her tender young flesh."

He turned back to the men at the *carreta:* "You have heard, *mis hermanos.* Now help this poor girl into the cart. We shall have someone take her back to her father." Then he turned back to the *hacendado:* "For you, Señor Abierto, I order you to give two hundred silver *pesos* to the father of this girl, which will be her dowry. And another two hundred to Mother Church. And you will come next Sunday to the first mass and there, before you take communion, you will confess to Padre Madura and throw yourself upon God's divine mercy, which forgives even sinners like yourself. Yet, if ever again we of the *Penitentes* hear that you have forcibly taken an *india* from the pueblo for your gross purposes, I tell you that you shall be excommunicated and cast out of the Church forever and your soul condemned into an endless purgatory. Be warned!"

Nicolas Abierto stood there gaping at them, clammy sweat on his face, unable to speak, choked as he was by mingled choler and fear. Where appeals to decency and humanity would assuredly have failed, the threat of excommunication had impressed him: the consequences would make him an outcast even among the corrupt *ricos* themselves, and the people of Taos would shun him as if he were a leper. Hoarsely, he stammered, "I—I will make the restitution you demand. Now let me go back to my bed."

"Go, then, slothful, wicked sinner, and pray for your redemption. One thing more—if those tithes are not paid in full by next Sunday, I will ask Padre Madura to pronounce the

ban of excommunication from his pulpit. Remember it!"
With this, Ignazio Peramonte turned and beckoned to the
white-robed priest, and the two men clambered into the *carreta* with the others. Once again, the leader of the *Penitentes*
took the reins and drove the burros on with his firm order,
accompanied by his flicking their rumps with the reins.

Reyes Espinosa turned his contorted face back toward
the *hacienda* and tearfully shouted, "*Patrón,* don't let them
do this to me—it was you who ordered it—save me from
them—they will kill me!"

But Abierto had already slammed shut the door and
gone back to his bed. Realizing that he had been abandoned
and that he would bear the brunt of the punishment pronounced upon him by the *Penitentes,* the majordomo began
to sob like a child.

Padre Madura looked down at the groveling man with
pity in his eyes, just at the moment that Fra Peramonte
turned to look at him. Their gazes crossed, and the unflinching sternness of the *Penitente*'s look made the white-robed
priest avert his eyes and cross himself, as he prayed silently
for the redemption of all sinners.

Ignazio Peramonte drove the burros back to the pueblo
village and instructed Brother Tiburcio to take Genifra safely
back to her father's *jacal.* The tearful girl knelt to kiss the
hem of the *Penitente* leader's robe, and he touched her head
with a benevolent gesture and murmured, "Pray to Him, not
to me, my daughter. Remember, you are still unblemished in
His all-seeing, all-knowing eyes. And you will send your *novio* to me on the next Saturday, to tell me whether the Señor
Abierto has sent your father the dowry that I imposed upon
him."

"I will, I will, *mi padre.* Oh, *gracias, gracias,* I cannot
thank you enough—I was so afraid—"

Brother Tiburcio helped her rise and stood with his arm
protectively about her shoulders. Fra Peramonte made the
sign of the cross over her and gently said, "Even the bravest
must acknowledge fear. But now you know that you had no
need of fear for your immortal soul; it is still preserved. Now
go comfort your father. And do not forget to send word to
me. On Sunday following the noonday mass, Padre Madura
will marry you and your *novio.*"

She kissed his hand and then turned to go with Brother Tiburcio.

From the *carreta,* the kneeling, bound majordomo wailed out, "Forgive me, señorita, forgive me my sin; at least say a prayer for my salvation!"

She turned back then, as the tears streaked her cheeks, and she faltered, "I—I forgive you. I—I hope they will not hurt you too much, s—señor."

When Brother Tiburcio returned from the *jacal,* his face was again as stern as that of his leader. "Now to the rocky plain at the base of the mountain," Ignazio Peramonte declared as he started up the burros.

They reached the place where, years ago, José Ramirez, the treacherous former *capataz* of the de Pladero sheep ranch, had been taken out by these *Penitentes* and flogged by Ignazio Peramonte himself in the latter's role of *sangrador.* A cross already waited, upright, its base solidly planted into the earth. The three black-robed figures took hold of Reyes Espinosa and, in spite of his tearful plaints and abject pleas for mercy, dragged him to it, stripped him to the waist, and bound him so that he was crucified so as to understand the terrible mystery of Christ, who had died on the cross to save mankind.

And while Padre Madura prayed aloud, Fra Peramonte took the scourge and, rolling up the sleeve of his right arm, applied, with deliberate slowness and exemplary vigor, twenty whistling lashes of the rawhide thongs. The majordomo's cries rang out from the very first stroke, and he sagged in his bonds, his back bleeding and torn when the flogging was over.

"Repent, Reyes Espinosa, before it is too late," Fra Peramonte harshly declared. "You will be cut free at dawn. Till then, meditate upon the great sin you committed and make your vow to Him who has seen us administer justice that you will not again commit such vileness."

Then Ignazio Peramonte got back into the *carreta* and, turning the burros, headed back to Taos.

"You have seen our justice, Padre Madura," he said as they neared the plaza. "Tell me, *mi padre,* did I act with enmity or hatred, or in any other spirit save that of impersonal justice?"

"In all truthfulness, no, Fra Ignazio. I confess I did not

know that the Señor Abierto had gone so far. You know that many times the poor *indios* of the pueblo, in their superstition and lack of education, fear to bring charges against the *ricos* who cheat and abuse them, without scruple."

"Yet we have our ways of learning who these malefactors are and what sins they commit in the smug security of their wealth and position here in Taos," Fra Peramonte replied.

"I respect you, Fra Ignazio. I respect your order. I think the bishop of Durango may try to prohibit your sacred rituals, but I am now convinced that only through your order can there be just law for the poor, as well as for the rich of Taos."

Twenty-six

Don Sancho and his wife and their servants, accompanied by Carlos and Teresa and the escort of Jicarilla led by Pastanari and John Cooper, had been traveling six days on their journey from the secret mountain to the Double H Ranch. They had already covered some eighty miles, and another twenty would bring them to the Canadian River, which, after fording, meant a distance of a little over three hundred miles south by southeast remained in their journey. Carlos had been somewhat disgruntled by the slow progress they had made, but John Cooper had convincingly argued that the heavy, camouflaged travois drawn by horses militated against great speed; even more important, in his opinion, was that a faster pace would be too great a physical strain on aging Don Sancho.

So they went at a leisurely pace, stopping for the night

on the dry, breeze-swept plains, glorying in the magnificent sunsets that looked as if the sky were a vast canvas daubed with every conceivable color. Everyone slept in their blankets out in the open, all except Don Sancho and Doña Elena, for whom the Jicarilla braves constructed a little portable shelter of dried grass and branches, almost like a wickiup. Indeed, Don Sancho remarked to his wife as they bedded down for the night in their snug dwelling, "This is like the Jicarilla honeymoon I have heard Carlos and John Cooper describe, where a man and his wife live in their own little house for many days, apart from the rest of the community."

"Oh, Don Sancho," Doña Elena said, blushing, "you are like a Don Juan with all your romantic notions."

And as if to prove the truth of her words, the former *alcalde mayor* took his wife in his arms and held her to him. Thus they spent these nights of their journey, sleeping in each other's embrace.

Thus far, the travelers had encountered no delays along the journey. On the fourth day, they had seen a raiding party of Penateka Comanche at some distance to the northwest, and one of the Comanche scouts had ridden his mustang up to within a quarter of a mile of them, then turned back. In the event that this nomadic band decided to attack, John Cooper's "Long Girl" was primed and loaded as always, but Pastanari, with the eternal confidence of youth, had smilingly boasted, "Perhaps the *gringos* know us only as basket-weavers, but the Comanche have learned to respect the Jicarilla. And besides, we are too well armed for them."

At about four o'clock that afternoon, Don Sancho had suffered a sudden fit of coughing, and Doña Elena had frantically called to Carlos, who rode near their carriage, to ask the Indians to halt until her husband could recover. They were about a mile from a peaceful little creek, fringed by clumps of fir and spruce. The sun had been scorching, and the air was oppressively dry. John Cooper gave Pastanari the order to make camp and proposed that they wait to cross the Canadian, now only a few miles distant, by noon of the next day, when everyone would be rested. He had ridden ahead to find a shallow fork, which would be easily fordable, and was concerned about Don Sancho's health. True enough, the former *alcalde mayor* of Taos had been ebullient like a young man chafing at the bit and eager to reach his new home with all its new experiences and acquaintances. He had eaten well, he had made many a quip deploring his own infirmities, and he had related several anecdotes to Doña Elena, who had smilingly heard them as if for the first time.

As the Jicarilla braves industriously made camp and one of them cut firewood for the evening meal, Don Sancho sat outside the little grass house on a small footstool, taken from their carriage. His eyes were closed, there was a weary smile on his face, and it seemed to Doña Elena that he was dreaming. She leaned to him, her hand gently stroking his forehead, as she murmured, *"Mi querido,* I know I'm an old woman, but I've fallen in love with you all over again, and it's better than it was. *Te quiero mucho, mi esposo."*

Don Sancho slowly opened his eyes and stared up at his wife's solicitous face. His lips trembled as he struggled to form words, and her eyes widened with alarm. Then faintly he managed to pronounce, *"T–te q–quiero más, mi El—"* and then uttered a little cough. His head turned to one side, and his body slumped onto the ground.

"Sancho—mi Dios, Sancho—*¿qué pasa, mi esposo?"* Her voice rose to a strident cry as she cupped his face and stared down at him, willing him to open his eyes, to speak to her again. Then she uttered a shriek and recoiled, wracked by convulsive sobs: *"Oh, no, no, María Santísima,* you could not be so cruel—to take him from me now, when we are going to our new home—oh, Sancho, Sancho, speak to me, open your eyes—"

Carlos de Escobar had heard Doña Elena's agonized cries and rode to their campsite. "What is wrong, Doña Elena?" he asked.

"Look—his eyes are closed; he has fallen to the ground; he is—oh, no, not *muerto*—what shall I do now—oh, Carlos, Carlos, help me—I am lost without him!" She wrung her hands, tears pouring down her cheeks, and then she bent to her inert husband and began to cover his face with kisses as she wept.

Carlos beckoned to John Cooper, who now came up and gently leaned over Don Sancho's prostrate body, put his ear to the old man's heart, and then pressed back his eyelids. He turned to Carlos and motioned for him to come away, as Doña Elena continued to cradle the head of her lifeless husband. "He's gone," John Cooper said softly. "At least it was

swift and there was no pain. How terrible to happen before
he could reach your father, Carlos! And poor Doña Elena,
what can we do? She shouldn't come all by herself to Texas
and leave her grandchildren back in Taos—we have to do
something."

"Of course. I'll go back and stay with her. And we'd
best think of burying him here. We couldn't get back to
Taos—I know it sounds heartless, but it's being sensible. The
sun is so hot and the air so dry—"

"Don't say it, Carlos," John Cooper murmured. "I'll go
tell the *indios*."

Mounting Pingo, he rode up to Pastanari, who was
directing the braves to prepare the evening meal and to make
a shelter in the event of a sudden storm. Quickly he told the
sturdy young Jicarilla what had happened. Pastanari frowned
and shook his head: "If she wishes, two of the men will ride
back with her and her *trabajadores* to Taos. I will divide
some of the food the men have with them. Doña Elena must
have enough for the return journey."

Doña Elena turned to Carlos and, weeping hysterically,
clung to him with all her strength while he tried to comfort
her.

At his sign, two of the Jicarilla braves unobtrusively
came up to them and carefully lifted Don Sancho's body
from the ground.

"Dear Doña Elena," Carlos tried to soothe the distraught
woman, "he had no pain. It was swift and merciful; God was
good to him."

"And he deserved it, truly, my husband did." Doña
Elena lifted her tear-ravaged face to the handsome young
Spaniard. "He never did an unkind thing in his life—he loved
me so, and I was such a bad wife to him for so long—that is
what I regret most of all, that I did not make him happier—
and now we shall never share this life on the ranch in Texas
with our old friends, Don Diego and his Doña Inez and—and
you, *mi* Carlos!"

"You certainly were not a bad wife! Often he told me,
when you were in the kitchen or elsewhere in the *hacienda*,
Doña Elena, that he was blessed to have you. He said that
you had become a joy in his declining years," Carlos murmured.

She fumbled for a handkerchief and tried to dry her

tears, then stared at him with widening eyes. "He—he told you that, Carlos? Do not lie to me now—please, I could not bear it—"

"Before God as my witness, Doña Elena, he thought you the most wonderful of women."

"Oh Carlos, Carlos, how I miss him—how shall I live my life without him now?" She burst into another flurry of sobs and buried her face against his chest while she clung to him with piteous anguish. He stroked her shoulder, not knowing what else to say, sensing the burden of her grief. And once again he thought of the agonizing hours when he had first learned how Weesayo had been taken from him, and the madness that had seized him, the powerless, helpless rage. But now there remained the widow who must be consoled, who must be given some purpose in her life, distraught and helpless as she now was. He tried gently: "Doña Elena, we must bury him here, you know that."

"Oh, no—the church—"

"Please, Doña Elena. Listen to me. It is summer; the sun is scorching, and before you could get back to Taos—I do not wish to say things that will hurt you—but believe me, it is best. We shall bury him near a tree along the trail, at a high place that will overlook the long plain that stretches toward the ranch of my father. And it will be as if he is waiting there to be reunited with all of us when that final day comes, Doña Elena."

"Why—yes, yes, perhaps you are—you are right, Carlos. How kind you are to help me now—I am so alone—"

"But there is your son, Tomás, and your sweet *nuera*, Conchita, and your grandchildren, too, Doña Elena," Carlos softly reminded her. "You will want to go back to them because they need you, and they will need you all the more now. That is where you will be happiest, back in Taos with them, watching the children growing up to be strong and healthy and happy, as you and Don Sancho were."

"Oh, yes! Yes, with all my heart. I will go back to my children. I could not bear it to be at Don Diego's ranch all alone; it would be as if I were taken in out of charity and pity. No, I must go back to Taos!"

"You must rest first, Doña Elena. I will bring you a little brandy. And then a little something to eat—yes, you must. Do not shake your head—you must. Don Sancho would not want you to neglect yourself. He is up there in heaven already smiling down at you and wanting you to love him as you always did and to obey his wishes so that you may live a long life with Tomás and Conchita and the grandchildren."

She wept again, but this time they were tears of poignant tenderness and resignation, and Carlos breathed a silent prayer for having had the inspiration to say words that would comfort this unhappy, aging woman who had found the mellow beauty of a renewed and restored marriage.

At last Doña Elena had fallen asleep, Carlos having seen to it that she drank several cups filled with *aguardiente* to numb the agony of this sudden, tragic loss. When she woke, it was close to noon of the next day, and the sun was even more pitiless, a red ball of fire in the cloudless blue sky. By then, four of the Jicarilla braves had dug a grave and wrapped the body of Don Sancho in blankets. The grave was near a giant saguaro, on an elevated knoll just off the flat stretch of arid plain that ended at the bank of the Canadian River. The *trabajadores* of Don Sancho de Pladero stood respectfully near the grave, behind Doña Elena, who watched, dabbing at her eyes with her handkerchief, as the four braves gently lowered the blanket-wrapped body of her husband into the grave. Then she looked helplessly at Carlos and John Cooper, and her lips formed a word so tremulous and faint that they hardly heard it, except that they understood its meaning: "Pl—please—"

"Let me, *amigo*," Carlos whispered to John Cooper. "I know the mass very well, and because I am Don Diego's son, perhaps it will have more meaning for poor Doña Elena."

"Of course."

Carlos advanced to the head of the grave, cupped his hand against his forehead to shield his eyes from the sun as he quickly glanced upward, and then sent a compassionate look at Doña Elena, who was supported by two of her *criadas*, and began: "*Nuestro Señor Dios*, we commend to You the body and the soul of Don Sancho de Pladero, who was *alcalde mayor*, then *intendente*, and once again *alcalde mayor* of Taos. Born in Madrid, he came to this Nuevo México with his beloved wife and son, Tomás, and he poured his energy and his life and all of his honor into this harsh land. He, who was an aristocrat, gave justice to the poor and the *indios*. In

all my days never did I hear him speak an ill word of anyone, and there was never any malice in his heart." Doña
Elena began to sob softly, burying her face in her hands,
while the young maids anxiously encircled their arms around
her waist.

"He stands before You, *Señor Dios,* to await that final
day of judgment by which You would judge us all. We here
gather now to pay tribute to him and to pray unto You to
lessen his purgatory and to receive him at last into Thy
blessed sanctuary of heaven." Carlos sank down on his knees
and clasped his hands in prayer, and then, in the stillness,
said the word solemnly, "Amen."

At the base of the tall saguaro, a gilded flicker was busy
digging a nest-hole. Now it turned, showing its brown crown
and gray face, and fluttering its yellow wings and tail linings,
as it emitted a soft chirp, then went back to preparing its
nest-hole.

The *criadas* gently urged Doña Elena to the carriage, as
Pastanari gestured to two of his youngest companions to ride
back with her and the *trabajadores* to Taos. But before she
entered the carriage, she turned and held out her arms to
Carlos de Escobar and sobbingly declared, "May God bless
you, Carlos, for your words comforted me. I shall mourn him
until *El Señor Dios* calls me to be reunited with *mi esposo,*
but your words have warmed me in the cold loneliness of
what I have lost." And then, seeing Teresa de Rojado standing not far from John Cooper, she called, "Teresa, *querida,*
come give me a kiss and pray for me and pray for him whom
I loved with all my life."

The slim young widow hurried forward to her, and the
two women embraced each other, and tears ran down Teresa's cheeks as she said farewell to Doña Elena de Pladero.

But Doña Elena had not taken leave of all of them yet,
and just as she was about to enter the carriage, she turned
back a last time and said, in a voice choked with emotion,
"Teresa and Carlos, each of you has mourned your own dear
one as I now mourn mine. The lesson of death is that life is
the more precious. I will pray for you back in Taos that the
two of you may one day join your lives and know life instead
of the sorrow of mourning. My life will be with my son and
Conchita and my grandchildren, and it will be rich, even
though my dear husband is gone forever from me. Remember

my words—love each other one day and be blessed by Him who looks down upon us in this hour. *Adios, vaya con Dios.*" She got into the carriage, and the two *criadas* sat on each side of her, whispering soothing words, trying to solace her as she wept softly.

The *trabajadores* had climbed back into their *carretas* and taken up the reins of their horses, and the two sturdy young Jicarilla braves trotted their mustangs to the head of this small processional.

John Cooper watched as they began the return along the same trail they had come. And Carlos de Escobar stood near John Cooper, but his eyes were on Teresa de Rojado, who knelt before the grave of Don Sancho de Pladero, crossed herself, and bowed her head in prayer.

Twenty-seven

⊁————————————————————⊰

Minanga crouched over his black mustang's neck as the wind sliced through the air. He had named him Esarti, meaning "swift one" in the Apache tongue, after he had bought him at the Taos fair four years ago. The mustang had long since earned his name. Minanga had ridden five days now, stopping only to let Esarti eat from a sack of dried corn tied to his saddle horn, or to graze and take water, but sparingly, since he did not wish the horse to founder in this unusually dry summer weather. But Esarti was wise. He was now just over five, Minanga judged, and it seemed that he knew where to graze and what poisonous grasses or growths he should not eat; and he had never yet had to be rebuked for drinking more than was proper after a long run.

As he rode, Minanga saw the patches of mesquite,

chaparral, and, here and there, large, grotesque forms of the giant cactus on the sun-baked earth. He knew this land as he knew the palm of his hand, for he and his tribesmen had often roamed it in search of buffalo or, at other times, when they crossed the Rio Grande to raid Mexican villages for horses and women.

Thanks to this, he knew where he could find water when it seemed that there was none available for miles around. Nor did he have to worry if his provisions ran out. He knew where to find the agave, whose leaves could be roasted over coals for a tough but tasty food. Even the flowers, especially the bulb, would satisfy a man's hunger after a long journey. He remembered how the women had taken the sotol and ground it into coarse flour, from which they made small ash cakes, a substitute for the bread of the *gringo*. And there were the tunas of prickly pears, mesquite beans, datiles, and nuts, as well as wild fruits to be found if one knew how to look for them.

Thus far, Minanga had seen no one along the trail. There had been only the twittering of birds and the occasional ominous rattle of a poisonous snake sunning itself near a rock. At night when he camped, he sometimes heard the quavering whistle or series of short notes emitted by a gray screech owl perched in an oak or fir tree.

On this fifth evening of his journey, he placed his blanket in the thick grass and tethered Esarti inside a little clump of trees. Back in the tepee, in the days when he had been war lieutenant, beds were made by piling grass or cedar twigs several inches deep and covering these with dressed hides. There was nothing warmer than that, nothing that even the *gringos*, clever as they were, could devise.

He knew he wasn't far from the Pecos River. From the Double H Ranch, Minanga had traveled northwest, following the route that John Cooper himself had taken to meet with Kinotatay. If he estimated correctly, he should encounter John Cooper on his return journey with the silver in about two, or at most two and a half days.

He ate his simple supper, then extinguished the tiny campfire. And just as he rubbed it out with his moccasined foot, turning southward, he thought he saw a man on horseback. A man in uniform . . . it was much too distant for him to be certain, but he had always had keen eyesight, and he could have sworn by his hope of becoming war lieutenant again among his people that the rider had worn the colored uniform of a dragoon of *soldados mejicanos.*

He crouched low, for he thought he heard, very faintly but audibly all the same, the trampling of a horse's hooves, moving eastward and a little to the south.

Perhaps it was an advance scout for a patrol of *soldados.* But why would they come to this isolated spot near the Pecos, where once he and his tribe had hunted the buffalo? Minanga moved toward Esarti, untied the reins from the trunk of the sturdy scrub tree, mounted, and rode noiselessly in the direction of the sight and the sound he had just observed.

One year ago, when the Lipan Apache had had a pitched battle against a small renegade branch of the Comanche Honey-Eaters, Minanga's battle plan had gained for him a glorious victory, and nearly all the Comanche war party had been killed. There had been much booty of fine horses and weapons and ammunition. *Ayiee,* but it was hard to think of those days of glory and remember that he was now an outcast, dependent upon the charity of a *gringo;* and, worst of all, he owed the *gringo* his life. It was a double debt, which somehow must be paid in full before he was gathered up to the sky, or he would never again set foot in a camp of the Lipan Apache.

But tonight, luck favored him. He caught sight of the uniformed dragoon riding back to what looked like a camp. He swiftly dismounted, tethered Esarti's reins to a tree stump, and crouching low, went swiftly forward to learn what he could.

There were tents, and beyond those he could see the light of a small campfire. Two *mejicanos* in full-dress uniform stood talking beside it. He counted the tents swiftly, and there were almost fifty of them. It was a sizable force—and they had fine horses, he could see that at once. A noncommissioned officer led one of the strong roan geldings near the officers, saluted, and stopped to exchange words with them, then disappeared from view.

The tents meant they were camping here. But why would they choose so abandoned an area between the Double H Ranch and the Jicarilla stronghold? There were no settlements, no *haciendas* anywhere for miles in every direction, that he knew.

Minanga did not like the looks of things. He began to crawl closer. Perhaps he could hear what the officers were saying . . .

"You have made better time than I thought you would, Capitán Mora," Francisco López cheerfully declared. "It was fortunate that our great *libertador* remembered that he had a friend so close to the border."

"Yes, my commanding officer," replied the captain, a tall, heavily mustached man who would be thirty in November. "At Coronel Santa Anna's order, my fifty men and myself, armed with sabers, lances, muskets, *pistolas*, and a few rifles, together with provisions and our tents, rode to the Pecos with all speed. I was instructed to bring at least half a dozen fresh horses, not only to transport the tents, but also to draw two light *carretas* filled with provisions. I myself chose the scout, and there is none better in all Mexico, Colonel López."

"I agree with you. He followed the Pecos at about the point I had indicated by my courier to the *libertador,* and he was able to find me without excessive delay."

"We are at your orders. Moreover, your rank outweighs mine, and therefore my men and I are at your complete disposal."

"You are a good soldier, Capitán Mora. I congratulate you. You may be certain that when I report to *el libertador,* I shall speak in glowing terms of your cooperation and the speed with which you and your men rode here for the rendezvous. Now it's becoming late, and it would be an admirable idea for all of us to get what sleep we can."

"I thank you for your praise, *mi coronel*. How long do you estimate it will be before this *gringo* and his treasure come back along this way, bound for his ranch?"

"I cannot give you a precise date, Capitán Mora; but I can tell you that the conversation I overheard between the *gringo* and his companions was that he proposed to return to the ranch, which is about a hundred sixty miles from here, by the end of this month or the first week in August. Now, since I can only conjecture how long it is taking the *gringo* and his men to transfer the treasure into conveyances that can be drawn by horses, and since there may be some delays of which we cannot possibly have any knowledge, I suggest that your forces always be on the alert so they may mount up and attack as soon as we sight the return of the *gringo*. It is my plan to kill him and his men before they are any nearer than a hundred miles to the ranch. By the time scouts are sent out to learn why they are not yet arrived, you and I and your men will be long gone across the border and on our way to *el libertador*."

"You may count on my fullest cooperation, *mi coronel*." Capitán Rafael Mora stiffened and saluted his superior officer. Francisco López negligently returned the salute, then clapped the captain on the back: "I have already seen the fine discipline of your men. And they're certainly well armed for a real battle. But it won't come to that. We'll take that damned *gringo* by surprise. You're not to spare anyone—unless, by some chance, your men find a *mujer linda*. You may count her as part of the spoils of war. And this, Capitán Mora, is a war in which cunning and imagination will count for much more than sheer numbers and brutal violence."

"I understand perfectly." The captain grinned cheerfully and averred: "I truly envy you, *mi coronel*, to have the ear of Santa Anna himself, and now to find that you have been commissioned on a private mission for that great man. Be very certain I shall exceed myself in this project."

"See that you do. By one means or another, none of those *gringos* is to come back to the *hacienda* to be able to report what happened to the treasure. Yes, we understand each other, Capitán Mora. Now let's turn in. Then you'll send out your scout in the morning to see if he can locate the man whose treasure will assuredly make Coronel Santa Anna a man capable of achieving even his wildest dreams. And so I bid you good night, Capitán Mora."

Minanga had listened, having crept on his belly up to the edge of the camp, but at a safe distance from the dragoons so he could not be seen. But suddenly, he felt a prickling along his spine. Instinctively, he rolled over, his right hand plunging to the sheath at his belt, which contained his knife.

It was a sentry who had discovered him and who, dagger in hand, was trying to kill him.

Minanga feinted to one side and then leaped at his opponent, his left palm pressed against the sentry's mouth to prevent any outcry. In almost the same movement, he drove his blade to the hilt in the man's heart, and only the faintest sigh was heard as the body stiffened and then was lax in the final agony.

Very carefully, Minanga wiped the blade on the thick grass, then crawled back until he could safely rise and run to his mustang. Untying the reins, he leaped astride him and, his heels kicking the mustang's belly, headed back along the trail.

Even if the sentry's body should be found tonight, he did not think they would abandon their ambush for the *gringo* to whom he rode. He had heard them speak of treasure, and now he began to understand. Somehow he had the feeling deep within him, as he urged Esarti onward at full speed, that he would have his opportunity to pay off a burdensome debt.

Twenty-eight

John Cooper rode alongside Pastanari, with the Jicarilla braves behind their war lieutenant and, behind them, those braves who rode the horses to which the camouflaged travois were attached. Carlos de Escobar and Teresa de Rojado brought up the rear of this now shortened processional, riding about twenty feet apart.

The sudden tragedy of Don Sancho's unexpected death, the profound ceremonial of the burial service, and then Doña Elena's tearful farewell, had cast a pall upon them. They had gone on now for about two hours after Don Sancho's carriage had turned back toward Taos, taking his widow back to be reunited with Tomás, Conchita, and their children.

From time to time, Carlos stealthily glanced to his right at the slim, beautiful young woman riding sidesaddle on her spirited mare, and there was much in his heart; yet he said nothing. He knew that she had heard Doña Elena's sobbing last words, praying that both of them might find a new life together and build upon it so as to inter the ghosts of their dead. Carlos secretly blessed Doña Elena for having spoken in so forthright a manner; he did not have the nerve to do so. And as he glanced at Teresa from time to time, he wondered what she must have thought of that agonized farewell.

He tried to comfort himself with the thought that they still had many long days and nights on the trail back to the Double H Ranch, and that there would be occasion, whether by chance or out of spontaneous inspiration, to propose once again.

Suddenly he found what he thought would be a subtle and yet effective means of drawing her into that acceptant frame of mind which might entertain his proposal without a summary rejection. "I'm happy that Doña Elena went back to Taos, truly, Teresa," he said aloud without looking at her as he slackened his mustang's gait to a leisurely trot. "Her grandchildren will make all the difference. They'll keep her occupied, and she won't have time to think how much she's going to miss Don Sancho. Though," he added, still without looking at her, "we have many children at the Double H Ranch, Teresa. It's a wonderful thing. Children need so much love, and grown-ups mustn't ever forget that, though they're inclined to be selfish and think only of themselves."

She flashed him a swift look, and there was a hint of tears. But then, quickly mastering that weakness, she drew in the reins a little more tightly and stiffened in her sidesaddle, as she called a soothing endearment to her mare. Finally she answered, "It sounds as if you and John Cooper have created a private little world all your own at this ranch of yours, Carlos."

"Yes, and all our *trabajadores* and their families are sharing this life with us. That isn't what we had back in Taos, with the *rico* and the *peón*. Anyway, I think that system is dying, Teresa."

"I agree. Still in all, progress is always slow, and there has already been a revolution in Mexico. I should not like to see another. Innocent people, the old and the sick, the women and the children; these are the ones who pay the highest price for this revolutionary freedom that is supposed to be so essential."

Now they rode in silence, and occasionally Teresa considered Carlos from under lowered lashes. If she married him—*if* she did—it must be a union born of love and respect, and not simply because he offered her shelter and comfort at a time when she had never felt lonelier.

Don Sancho's death had cut the ties that had bound her to Taos. She had known at that moment that she could not return with Doña Elena to Taos, that a period in her life had come to an end, a period that had begun when she first left the convent school. Young and impressionable, she had been wedded, through the manipulations of her solicitous father, to an elderly husband. She had accepted the obligation that her father had imposed upon her, and though she was ashamed of the thought, it was just as well that her husband had died in Havana. Their marriage had been based only on duty and obligation, not real love.

As the sun began to set and the sky became a magnificent canvas of somber red and faint purple and the hint of a waning pallid gold, Carlos looked over at her and thought to himself: María, *Madre, I pray to You to let this woman know that I have love and admiration for her. I am lonely; I have never been lonelier in all my life. I have my children, and they make me lonelier still because they need a mother. Let her be the one in whom they will confide, in whose eyes they will see the pride of their maturing and their giving of joy to both of us. And if it be Thy will, let her give me a child of her own flesh and spirit, for it will be a priceless heritage for both of us. I will dedicate my life to her; I will never cause her pain nor sorrow; and I will do whatever she wishes to give her the happiness and the honor she merits. Madre, María, You of mercy and grace, hear me now. I wish to wed her in the new church at the ranch, and I will pledge her all of my love and my strength to grant her joy.*

His eyes misted with tears, and he was gruff with himself, blaming the angular rays of the dying sun and the hot, faint gusts of summer heat, which burned the dreary rock-covered plain and dried up the gulches and creeks.

She, in her turn, secretly glanced at him, and she, too, prayed: *Most Holy Virgin*, María Santísima, *he has done so much for me, and yet I cannot marry him simply because of my gratitude or my loneliness. Do You not understand me, Holy Mother? I cannot tell yet whether he is the one for whom I am destined, or that I should marry him. No, Holy Mother, show me the way that I must take. I do not want to hurt him; it is so easy to love him; he is good and kind, and how his Weesayo must have loved him! I know the torture of his heart when he learned of her death in so cruel a way, and if I were a man, I would have ridden side by side with him to avenge that horror. And yet I cannot tell what is right for me. I have wealth, more than I need for my frugal comforts. I can go back to Havana, or even across the Atlantic to live in Madrid. I do not know. Help me, Holy Mother!*

It was the middle of the third week of July, and the weather had been swelteringly hot, though dry. Hardly a gust of wind stirred the rocky, uneven terrain beyond the mounted Jicarilla Apache drawing the travois, and the three *gringo* riders at the back of them, Carlos, John Cooper, and Teresa de Rojado. They were moving southward, slowly veering to the east, a five- or six-day journey to the Pecos River. Once along that familiar, winding tributary, they would head for Uvalde and the area of fertile valley that would take them to the Double H Ranch.

Pastanari held up his right arm to halt his riders, and John Cooper trotted Pingo up to the sturdy young warrior. "What is it, Pastanari?" he asked.

"You know this land better than I, *Halcón*. Is there water ahead of us?"

"Yes, a freshwater creek about ten miles southeast," John Cooper responded.

"That is good. I'll tell you, it is easier to go without the carriage and the *trabajadores* of poor Doña Elena. Still, it is rocky ground here, and we must go more slowly, or else upset the travois."

"So far, we've had no trouble. There is no great hurry to it, Pastanari. Nor do I wish to have your horses foundering in this heat. We cannot replace horses till we reach my ranch, that you already know."

"I do, *Halcón*. Yet, the mustangs we keep in the *remuda* of the stronghold are as strong as my braves. They do not complain, and they have courage and strength. All the same, it will be good to drench oneself in the stream and to cool off from the hot sun." Shading his eyes with his left hand, Pastanari scowled up into the bright blue sky with its red ball of fire at its zenith. "Perhaps that is why we Jicarilla love the mountain stronghold. There are always cool winds, even in the worst days of the summer."

"Tell your braves that I am grateful for their loyalty. I ask of them no more than I do of myself, Pastanari."

Pastanari boyishly grinned at his friend. "You would have made a great warrior for the Apache. Sometimes I find myself wishing you had taken a mate like Colnara. You would have lived your life with us, and you could have been our shaman. Your days would have been long, and your tongue, which speaks straight and is not forked, would have been held in respect by us who live high in the mountain."

"I have often thought that, too, Pastanari," John Cooper philosophically averred. "Yes, I would have been happy with you to the end of my days. But with my Catarina, my children, and the friends at the ranch, I find myself in a world that, in its way, is as secret and private as your stronghold, Pastanari."

"Yes, the Great Spirit tests us and sends us into new adventures to learn how we can manage to face His tests."

"What you say is not unlike our own philosophy, we who are *gringo* and yet who sympathize with you. I wish that the blood brotherhood between you and me and Kinotatay could be extended to every *gringo* who lives in Taos and in Santa Fe. It would make both our people stronger."

Pastanari sighed and shrugged. "How simple it is, and yet no one is ready to admit it." Then, intently looking at John Cooper, the young warrior vouchsafed, "I am glad, *Halcón*, that I asked Kinotatay to let me ride back with you—and to stay at your ranch when you take your treasure on to that *gringo* city you call New Orleans. I envy you. You have traveled over so much of this country I shall never see, and you will go on traveling, seeing the country push back its frontiers until there are settlers and homes."

"I think of that, too, Pastanari."

"I think of it with sadness, *Halcón*. The more the *wasi-chu* occupies the land of this great country, the less land there will be one day for the *indios*. We do not hunt the buffalo as we did in the old days. The tribes on the plains hunt it, and yet it seems that the great herds move northward, and the *indios* follow. But as the settlers push forward, they will take these lands, and then there will be war between the *wasi-chu* and *indio*. This is what I most fear."

"There will be many suns and moons before that day takes place, Pastanari. You and I may not see the rising of the sun when it comes."

"But while my people and I fear the *wasichu* and his coming like locusts upon this land, which once was for all the *indios* of the hills and of the plains," Pastanari continued, "I see that you and your people will one day become the enemies of the *mejicanos*. They think that because they were here before even you, they own the land."

"That I know, and *that* you and I will see before our days are done, Pastanari. But I hope there will not be war between the *mejicanos* and the *wasichu*."

"Wait a moment—I see a rider coming toward us from the east. He rides his horse as if he cannot wait to reach us."

John Cooper pulled "Long Girl" out of the saddle sheath and tested it for priming, then patted it as he would a friend's shoulder and thrust it back into the sheath, his hand resting lightly on the butt in order to pull it out swiftly if need be.

"You're right, I see him, too. Wait—the black mustang—I recognize him now; it's Minanga! He is a Lipan Apache who lives on our ranch. Miguel Sandarbal must have sent him to us to see how our journey is progressing."

"His mustang races with all its speed," Pastanari observed. "He has driven it hard and for many suns."

"By the Eternal," John Cooper cried, "he must have an important message from Miguel, or Don Diego—I'll ride out to meet him, Pastanari!" Kicking his heels against Pingo's belly, John Cooper galloped the palomino toward the oncoming Lipan Apache, who slackened his own horse's speed as he saw the *wasichu* approach. Esarti was already winded, his eyes bloodshot and rolling, and he snorted from the merciless pace at which the former war lieutenant had ridden him.

"Minanga, rest your mustang! Good Lord Almighty, you've had a ride for yourself—when did you start from the ranch?"

"Six days ago, *Halcón*." Minanga slid down from his saddle and held the reins of his mustang, patting the horse's head and murmuring to it. "I come from the Señor Sandarbal, but there is also something else I must tell you. The *capataz* bids me tell you that the wagons are ready when you return."

"And that's good news! But what's the other thing, Minanga?"

"I was making camp after sundown not far from the Pecos River, *Halcón*. I saw a *mejicano* in the uniform of a *soldado*, and I followed him. He rode back to his camp, and there, *Halcón*, were the tents and horses of many *soldados*. I crept forward and listened to two men, two officers—one whose name was López, I think. They spoke of ambushing a *gringo* and his treasure when they return from the Jicarilla stronghold."

"My God, I'll bet that's Francisco López!" John Cooper hoarsely ejaculated. He beckoned to Pastanari, who rode quickly up to him and leaned forward, his keen face taut with curiosity. "This is Minanga, Pastanari. He says that he crossed the Pecos River and saw a *mejicano* in uniform. He followed the man and was near their camp, and he heard two officers talking of how they would wait in ambush to rob us of the silver. I'm pretty sure I know who one of those men is—he came to the ranch this spring, but we didn't like him from the start, so we sent him away."

"You think it is one and the same man, *Halcón*?"

"I'd be willing to bet 'Long Girl' that he came to the ranch to spy on us for Santa Anna, and somehow learned about the treasure." He turned back to Minanga: "Did they see you or hear you, Minanga?"

"No, *Halcón*, but they had a sentry who found me, and I had to kill him with my knife. I put my hand over his mouth when I struck the blow, and he died without a sound. But by now they must have found him, and they may ride after me. I heard this one man say that he knew you were planning to come back to the ranch by the end of this month or the beginning of next—those were his words, *Halcón*."

"Well, that pretty much settles it—it has to be Francisco López," John Cooper declared. "I don't know where he heard about my plans, but that's what I told Miguel Sandarbal and Don Diego just before I left the ranch."

He pondered a moment, lost in deep thought. It suddenly came to him that López must have sneaked back to the ranch after he had been asked to leave. Yes, that was it, and that explained why he had killed the two *trabajadores* escorting him. Now addressing Pastanari, John Cooper said, "We'll have to figure out how to throw them off the track, Pastanari. That silver must never fall into the hands of Santa Anna. He'd use it for his own power; he'd make himself president or emperor of Mexico, and then there'd be revolutions and lots of innocent people would die. That money has to go for the poor and the Indians."

"Do you think they will follow you, Minanga?" Pastanari now asked the Lipan Apache.

"If they found the sentry so close to their camp, they would guess that the man who killed him had heard the officers talk," the Lipan Apache reasoned. "And perhaps they would also think that this man would come to warn *El Halcón*."

"Well, we have to make a plan, and in a hurry, too, Pastanari—just in case they're riding after us. Minanga, could you tell how many soldiers there were?"

"I counted tents—I think there are fifty men. And they have many horses."

"They have a sizable force against ours. And we sent back two braves with Doña Elena," John Cooper mused aloud. He scowled for a moment, pondering a possible solution to this unexpected dilemma. Then his face brightened: "Wait a minute, I remember now. Along the trail, there are a series of hills on each side and a canyon through them."

"Sí, Halcón," Minanga excitedly spoke up. "My people call it the Cañon de Muerte—the Canyon of Death. Long ago, when I was only a boy and not yet ready for the puberty rites of my tribe, there was a battle between the Comanche and the Lipan. The war chief tricked the Comanche to ride into the canyon, and the bowmen of the Lipan sent their arrows down from the tops of the hills and defeated them, so that they lost almost all their braves."

"That's it!" John Cooper exulted. "Look, Pastanari, while

we've still some time, let's have some braves take the silver off the travois. They can load the travois with rocks and cover the rocks with blankets, and then I and maybe five or six braves will pull the travois through the canyon, to act as bait. Then the rest of your men and Carlos will wait at the top of the hills, and when the soldiers are lured into the canyon, you can fire down and take them by surprise."

"It is a good plan! What shall we do with the silver, *Halcón?*" Pastanari asked.

John Cooper squinted down at the ground as he thought for a moment. "The braves can bury the ingots right here and now while we make camp and unload the travois, Pastanari. They'll put a special marker so we won't forget where they're buried. And once we beat off those Mexican troops, we can take our time getting back home safely to the Double H Ranch."

"I will tell my men to start digging a pit into which we can put the ingots and also to unload them as you have proposed and to bury them," Pastanari said. "There are rocks enough on the ground to put into the travois so the *soldados* will think the treasure is under the blankets."

John Cooper declared, "I know it's a gamble, but after what Minanga told me, I've got a feeling that López will be riding at the head of the troops to intercept us before we get much farther back home. And if that's the case, we don't have time to lose. I'll lend a hand unloading the silver. Minanga, you rest—you've earned it."

Twenty-nine

An hour after Minanga had knifed the dragoon to death, the Toboso scout, Guapaldi, attached to Major Valdez's detachment that had been sent to meet with Colonel Francisco López, discovered the body. He had hurried at once to the pompous young Captain Mora in charge of the detachment, to report his discovery. And that officer at once informed Francisco López.

Santa Anna's spy had sworn vitriolically, and then, his face tightening with a cruel expression, had declared, "I see more than a coincidental parallel in this murderous act, *mi capitán*. You will see where Private Mendoza's body was found, quite near the clearing in which you and I discussed our plans to ambush that damned *gringo* with his silver treasure. To me, that suggests that Mendoza's killer must have overheard us speaking. Nor would it surprise me to learn that the killer was one of the *gringo*'s *trabajadores* or *vaqueros*."

"What are we to do then, *mi coronel*?"

"If what I suppose to be true is true," Francisco López slowly averred, "then that man has ridden off to warn the *gringo* that we are here waiting for him. So the element of surprise will be eliminated—unless we create another one out of our own ingenuity."

"And what do you have in mind?" the captain pressed.

López's look was both sneeringly triumphant and contemptuous. "We shall go forward to intercept him, and attack him without warning the moment we see him!"

The captain solemnly nodded. "I have been told by Major Valdez that I am to follow your orders."

Francisco López's voice was harsh with a sadistic anticipation. "Have your noncommissioned officers confirm for you the amounts of ammunition available; inspect their weapons. Then order your men to mount their horses, clear this camp, and ride northwestward. I do not think, if my suppositions are correct, that we can reach the *gringo* before this spy of his does."

"I agree that we should attack, Coronel López," the captain gravely nodded. "I will give the orders to break camp."

"If we succeed, *capitán*, Santa Anna will himself reward you. As for myself, I ask nothing better than to serve *el libertador*!"

There was something that Minanga had told neither John Cooper nor Pastanari when he had narrated his unexpected encounter with the Mexican detachment lying in wait for the tall *wasichu* and his secret treasure hoard. Some four hours after he had mounted Esarti and ridden at all speed to overtake John Cooper, he had suddenly drawn in the reins and halted the snorting black mustang. The moonlight was bright enough to show him what lay along the trail, and the black mustang now pawed the air with his front hooves and tossed his head as he found himself a few feet away from the carcass of a buffalo. It was a cow, from which the hide had been stripped, the liver and most of the forequarters removed, and already, even in the dark night, there was the whirring of a buzzard's wings and then the hideous flapping noise as it settled on the ground near the carcass and waddled toward it.

Grimacing with revulsion, Minanga had fitted an arrow from his quiver to his long bow, drawn it, and sent the shaft whistling into the buzzard's heart. But his eyes had fixed on a feathered arrow that still remained deeply embedded in the neck of the buffalo carcass. He recognized the marking of the feathers: they proclaimed that a Lipan Apache of his own tribe had loosed that shaft during the hunt. His tribesmen were somewhere in this deserted territory, perhaps even this very night feasting on the tasty meat they had carved from the dead cow.

Superstitiously, Minanga had seen this as a sign that

Killer-of-Enemies had smiled upon him at last, telling him that the braves, whose leader he had once been, were still nearby. And as at last he directed Esarti forward at a gallop, he swore a vow that he would aid the *gringo patrón*, if these *soldados* should attack him. Here at last was the opportunity he had so long awaited: a chance to count coup, to prove that he was still a powerful warrior with much magic. Then at last the shame and dishonor would be lifted from him, and he would be once again the war lieutenant of the Lipan Apache.

There was no need, he was sure, to tell the *gringo* that his people were nearby. And when it was over, when he had fulfilled his mission, he would ride back here to find the bones of that carcass picked away by the birds of prey and look for signs that would direct him to those who had cast him out of the tribe and belittled his prowess.

So when he saw John Cooper talking with Pastanari, he led his mustang over to a scrub tree and tethered him by the reins, then walked a distance away till he was out of sight of the Jicarilla braves. Then, falling onto his knees and crossing his arms over his wiry chest, Minanga invoked Killer-of-Enemies, as he looked upward at the sky and spoke softly in his own tribal dialect to the omnipotent deity of his people: "Hear me, O Killer-of-Enemies. I, of the Lipan, scorned by them, forced to live as I can by a servitude, which is a debt of honor and repays the *wasichu* who saved my life when my own people would have left me there to die; hear me! Grant me a coup, which will absolve my debt in two ways and will prove my own manhood to those who doubted it. When my mother brought me forth from her belly, You in the form of both lightning and a whirlwind entered my body through my throat. You have kept me warm and alive, and yet You have withheld from me the final warmth of a manhood that You took from me. Yet I am no coward, and if there is to be battle between these *mejicanos* and the *gringo* with his Jicarilla companions, I swear I shall take part in it. I shall sacrifice to You an enemy, and I will take his scalp back to my tribe to show them that Minanga is no coward, no old man who whines for scraps at a dying campfire. Grant me strength for the battle, O Killer-of-Enemies!"

He knelt there a long time silently, his head bowed, pressing his arms tightly against his chest till it pained him.

In the distance there was a low rumble of thunder and, with it, the plaintive hoot of a desert screech owl.

His bleak face brightened, his eyes glistened, and he sprang to his feet, flinging his arms up toward the sky: "I have a sign from You, O Killer-of-Enemies! I have a sign, and I am grateful. I shall earn it, and I shall sacrifice to You. My arrows will drink blood, and I shall be without fear when I loose them!"

And then, very slowly, he walked back to the camp of the *gringo* whom these Jicarilla called *Halcón*.

Returning to his mustang, he lifted his bow from the saddle horn to examine it. It was four feet long, made of seasoned mountain mulberry. The bowstring had been fashioned from split deer sinews tightly twisted together. He put the bow back on the saddle, then unstrapped the quiver of arrows from his neck. Thrusting the quiver upright into the sandy soil, he drew out an arrow and stared at it. It was made of hardwood; three feathers were tied on with sinew, and the tip was made from an iron point which had been derived from a barrel hoop.

Satisfied with the arrow, he put it back into the deerskin quiver. There were two dozen arrows in the quiver. They would drink blood.

Minanga walked up to the others now, his face impassive. John Cooper glanced at him and gave him a smiling nod, then turned back to Pastanari: "I'd say we are a day ahead of them. Don't forget, Minanga rode alone, and that mustang of his is bound to be faster than the horses of troops who'll be carrying weapons."

"I have been thinking about this Cañon de Muerte," the young warrior slowly responded. He hesitated a moment, and then resumed, "It is dangerous for you, *Halcón*. There'll be just yourself and six of the braves drawing the travois—but if all fifty of these mounted *soldados* come at you with their swords and lances and guns, you could be killed at the first attack."

"Yes, I could, Pastanari," John Cooper admitted. "But the minute they get into that canyon, your men will start shooting arrows down at them. They'll be so flustered they won't have time to think about shooting straight. I'll be fine, don't you worry about that. The only thing is that we'll need braves—who will be armed, of course—to volunteer to come through the canyon."

"I have already had volunteers who wish to try this trick of yours, *Halcón*," Pastanari responded.

"That's excellent. Now, what we'll do is get a good night's sleep, and you post guards around the camp. I'll tell Carlos and the señora what to expect tomorrow."

"The travois are all ready, and they look as they did before we took away the silver," Pastanari declared. "Two of my men have already buried the ingots and marked the place in a special way so that, when it is over, we can put them back on the travois and go on to your ranch."

"That's fine." John Cooper held out his hand, and Pastanari shook it, flushing lightly under the intense scrutiny of his blood brother.

By dawn of the next day, Pastanari's braves had already tethered their mustangs out of sight in a small forest of cedar and scrub trees not far from their camp, and then prepared for the expected attack by Francisco López's troops. Of the twenty-eight braves who accompanied Descontarti's stalwart young son (two of their original number having left with Doña Elena), six were to draw the travois. They waited not far from the mesa and its imposing canyon, which Minanga had called El Cañon de Muerte. Minanga had asked John Cooper's permission to accompany the braves into the canyon and John Cooper had reluctantly agreed, well understanding the Lipan Apache's need to salvage his honor by counting a coup in a pitched battle against the enemy.

Half an hour later, the twenty-two remaining braves of Pastanari's armed escort had climbed their way up the gently angling rocky hills that flanked the short, narrow canyon. It extended for barely half a mile, and from a height of two hundred feet the Jicarilla could look down on the trail below and cover every foot of it with their bullets and arrows. At Pastanari's order, eleven braves had mounted each side of the canyon. Teresa and Carlos ascended with the eleven Jicarilla on the north side. She had taken her rifle out of its sheath, slung over her shoulder a leather pouch that contained balls and powder, and gripped in her left hand the ramrod used for loading. Carlos was almost beside himself with joy at this nearness.

He had said to her before they had begun the ascent of the canyon walls, "Teresa, this is not your fight. I don't want you to risk your life. You know that Minanga said he counted around fifty *soldados*. They'll be well armed, and they outnumber us."

She had given him a brief smile and, assuring herself that the leather pouch was secured around her slim neck, had retorted, "I would have been much worse off if poor Don Sancho and Doña Elena had been here now. Anyway, I've perfect confidence in these wonderful Apache who are John Cooper's friends. They will be more than a match for a troop of Mexican soldiers. And you forget that I'm a very good shot." With this, they began their ascent up the slope, and soon were at the top, on the opposite side of the canyon from where Pastanari and eleven of his braves were stationed.

Everything was in readiness. Rifles were primed; bows and arrows were drawn. From his vantage point atop the hill, Pastanari put his left hand over his forehead and squinted southward. In the distance was a cloud of dust, which slowly grew larger. It was the Mexicans, Pastanari was certain! He now gave a sign to John Cooper below, who in turn gestured to indicate he understood Pastanari. Then John Cooper called to the six braves who drew the travois: "Let's start now! We're going through the canyon!"

The Toboso scout, Guapaldi, had ridden slightly ahead of Captain Mora's men and caught sight of the Jicarilla braves slowly drawing the travois and coming through the canyon. He wheeled his mustang back and rode up to the Mexican officer to tell him what he had seen.

Francisco López, who had armed himself with a brace of *pistolas* in his belt and a saber, rode up alongside the pompous young captain. "The fool!" he jeered, pointing in the direction of the Jicarilla. "A handful of *indios* and the *gringo* with the treasure—this will be child's play. Kill them all without mercy, and then the treasure will belong to our glorious *libertador*!"

Captain Mora saluted, turned in his saddle, and shouted, "¡*Adelante, soldados! Es por México y el libertador*, Santa Anna! *Muerte por todos, ¿comprenden ustedes?*"

The fifty dragoons leaned forward over the necks of their horses, as they veered northwestward toward the opening of the canyon ahead. The first eight carried lances to which were attached pennons designating their regimental colors, as well as those of the newly independent republic, and these men, like Colonel López, had the supplemental arms of a brace of *pistolas* at their belts. Behind them, the other dragoons were armed with muskets, a few with old Belgian rifles, pistols, and sabers. Captain Mora himself led the charge, while the Toboso scout galloped alongside of him, unstrapping his own rifle out of the shoulder sling.

Beyond them, Pastanari's braves waited, flat on their bellies, arrows already fitted to the bowstrings. Those with rifles trained them down on the oncoming troops.

Besides "Long Girl," John Cooper had his Spanish dagger around his neck, a hunting knife strapped to his belt, and his ammunition sack with its powder horn over one shoulder. He leaned forward over Pingo's neck, for he was proceeding at a trot, which the braves behind him emulated with their heavy travois. Quickly glancing up, he made a sign to Pastanari, and the Jicarilla war lieutenant nodded, then notched an arrow to his bow and waited. John Cooper had seen that the inner walls of the canyon were not steep and that if need be, he could readily climb to an elevation where he could lie concealed on an overhanging boulder and shoot down into the dragoons.

As he and his men entered the canyon, Captain Mora sheathed his saber and lifted the well-balanced lance with its regimental pennon. He had had an attractive seamstress (whose lover he had once been) sew onto the pennon his own personal escutcheon. Gripping the top of the smooth wooden handle, he lowered the murderously sharp tip to his waist, as he saw John Cooper and the six Jicarilla horsemen approach from the other end of the short canyon. Almost gleefully, glancing back over his shoulder, he bawled, "There are only a handful of them; kill them all, no quarter!" And then he galloped forward.

Rising erect on the peak of the canyon wall, Pastanari took careful aim and sent the shaft winging toward the Mexican officer. The arrow thudded home into Captain Mora's left shoulder, a deep, agonizing wound that made him jerk in the saddle with a hoarse cry of pain. At the same moment, John Cooper fired from the hip, his strong wrist being able to manage the recoil of the old Lancaster. A lance-bearing corporal behind the Mexican captain slumped forward, his lance dropping to the dusty ground, and slid off his galloping mustang to roll over and over near the wall of the canyon. Minanga, halting his mustang, drew his bow, and sped an arrow through the air. Captain Mora stiffened, then toppled from his saddle, the arrow having pierced his heart. The scout, Guapaldi, having himself narrowly escaped an arrow, now wheeled his mustang around and rode back in the direction of the Rio Grande and Major Valdez.

Meanwhile, Colonel López hoarsely cried to the dragoons, "The *americano*! Cut him down; that's an order!"

The six Jicarilla braves pulling the travois had halted their mustangs, four of them drawing their bows and fitting arrows to the strings while the other two, armed with muskets, nimbly dismounted and ran to the sides of the canyon, crouching down and firing as they took position. One of the dragoons was wounded in the shoulder but, grimly ignoring the pain, rode after the brave who had shot him, and transfixed him with the spear, whose point emerged from the Indian's naked back. At almost the same moment, an arrow aimed by one of the Jicarilla at the top of the north wall of the canyon took the dragoon in the back of the neck, and he plunged from his whinnying horse to lie atop his victim in a union of death.

Francisco López ducked in his saddle as an arrow whizzed past his face, and he hoarsely shouted, "It's an ambush! Take cover, *soldados*!" He wheeled his horse back to the mouth of the canyon, while the troops behind him halted their mounts and began to follow his example. A flight of arrows and the bark of rifles from the top of the canyon dropped three of the dragoons with fatal wounds and a fourth with a flesh wound in the left arm before Santa Anna's spy could guide his troops back out of the canyon.

Livid with fury at the way he had been tricked, the Mexican colonel shouted orders to the soldiers: "Never mind the *gringo;* we can finish him when we want! Ride out of range of those *indios* on the top of the canyon. By all the devils in hell, how could we have fallen into such a trap?" The troops, demoralized by their captain's death at the very first engagement, cantered out of the canyon and drew off to one side.

John Cooper had swiftly dismounted from Pingo, led

him to the side of the canyon, and bade him stay with a gesture he had used in training the spirited palomino. Later, he would have to compliment Pastanari on the way he had directed the attack from above on the unsuspecting dragoons.

Minanga had halted his mustang, too, and now ran toward the inert body of the fallen Captain Mora. From on high, Teresa stared down and then, with an incredulous gasp, turned to Carlos beside her and exclaimed, "What is he doing with the knife, Carlos?"

"Scalping him, Teresa," was the laconic answer.

"How horrible!" She closed her eyes and bowed her head.

"Don't think about it, *querida*. At least, we've beaten off their first attack. But they still outnumber us by at least fifteen men, and they are very well armed."

"They will attack us again?" She looked at him, and his heart quickened at the intent, comradely look she gave him, as if she had accepted him as her equal and confidant.

"They've ridden back out of arrow range from the top of the hill, and I think they've seen that Pastanari's men are on both sides of the canyon. I'm sure they'll try to shoot them down. We may be in for a long siege, Teresa *querida*. But—I must say this, forgive me if it offends you—I want nothing better than to be here beside you, to protect and defend you."

Again she gave him a long, searching look. "You are truly *muy hombre*, Carlos," she murmured at last and then quickly turned away, but not before Carlos had seen a crimson flush stain her sun-bronzed cheeks.

He felt an almost unbearable tenderness toward her. As he cradled his rifle against his shoulder, having reloaded it after that first attack, he thought to himself that, truly, there was no other woman in the world as courageous and noble.

Francisco López had ordered his men to take cover about two hundred feet from the mouth of the canyon in a grassy knoll where a few sparse scrub trees grew. The dragoons with rifles flung themselves on the ground and began to aim their rifles at the top of the canyon. At his sign, they opened fire, and the brave next to Pastanari slumped forward without a sound, shot through the head.

John Cooper carefully edged toward the mouth of the canyon, flattening himself against the rocky wall. Kneeling down, he took careful aim at Francisco López who, waving his saber, was directing the volleys up at the Jicarilla. Just as he was about to squeeze the trigger, the Mexican officer moved to one side, and as "Long Girl" fired, the bullet grazed the hand of a soldier who was crouching behind López.

Swiftly reloading, John Cooper edged even closer to the mouth of the canyon, while Minanga, drawing his bow and notching an arrow to it, moved to the other side, near the entrance. Drawing his bow to the maximum, the muscles of his right forearm bulging with the tremendous exertion, he at last released the arrow, and a dragoon sergeant staggered backward, dropping his rifle and clutching at the arrow in his neck, his eyes glassy and huge with agonized terror, before he fell like a log and lay still.

One of the dragoons fired his rifle at Minanga, but in his angry haste to avenge his companion, his bullet ricocheted off the rocks. By now, John Cooper had reloaded and quickly fired. A bloody hole appeared in the center of the dragoon's forehead, and the man was flung back as if by an invisible hand. A cry of rage broke from López, as he turned to his disorganized troops and savagely commanded, "On your horses! Flank them on each side and shoot upward. Major Valdez sent word by your captain that you are among the best marksmen in all Mexico—prove it now! Will you let this *gringo* dog murder so many of your comrades? Are you weaklings unfit to wear the uniform of your country?"

His forceful orders served to recall the dragoons to discipline, and they mounted their horses and drew back, while John Cooper called up the canyon walls to Pastanari, who had come down part way to meet him, "They'll attack us from the outside! Turn your men and be ready to meet them!"

Now he reloaded, while Minanga fitted another arrow to his bow and watched as the dragoons broke into two files, with about twenty men to each flank, and then, as Francisco López raised his saber and descended it, began to gallop forward. They veered off from the entrance of the canyon, and lifting pistols, muskets, and rifles toward the top of the canyon hills, fired as they galloped. One of the Jicarilla, who had been in the act of drawing his bow, threw up his arms, dropped the bow, and tumbled lifelessly down the angling side till he reached the level of the mesa and lay sprawled, not far from John Cooper. Pastanari sighed. Another of the Jicarilla was wounded and another shot through the heart, but in retaliation, Pastanari's warriors shot down with their arrows two dragoons, and with their rifles, shot down three more of the enemy.

The remaining dragoons turned around and returned to join López to the south. López told them, "You call yourselves marksmen? You couldn't hit a *piñata* at a Christmas party with your bare hand!" he tiraded, his face red with anger. "Choose your target and don't worry about their fire—do you want to be old women and die in bed, or do you want to win that treasure for *el libertador*?"

The dragoons, their faces taut with the stress of combat, eyed one another, then awaited his signal. As his saber flashed down, they galloped back, flanking the canyon and, crouching low over their horses' necks, fired.

Teresa de Rojado squinted along the sight of her rifle and pulled the trigger. One of the dragoons jerked back, dropping the reins as her bullet broke his left wrist. But in the same movement, he fired his musket, and the ball, glancing off a rock near the top of the canyon wall, grazed Teresa's arm. Carlos uttered a cry as he saw the blood ooze from the wound. Grinding his teeth in anger, he followed the dragoon as he galloped away and, holding his breath, remembering all that John Cooper had told him about lining up a target in the sights for greatest accuracy, pulled the trigger. The dragoon dropped his musket and toppled back off his horse, his boots free of the stirrups. He thudded on the ground, and rolled over and over, while the riderless horse galloped away.

But as Carlos had turned to fire, a dragoon who had brought up the rear of this galloping enfilade aimed his rifle at the handsome Spaniard and pulled the trigger. Carlos uttered a stifled groan as the ball embedded itself into the fleshy part of his left shoulder. The numbing shock of the wound made him drop his rifle and roll onto his right side. Immediately, Teresa uttered a sobbing cry: "Oh, Carlos, Carlos, you're hurt! You're bleeding badly! Carlos, can you hear me? Is the wound bad?"

"It—it's in the shoulder—no, it's not too bad—"

"Oh, *querido* Carlos, yes, I do love you—I know it

now—I saw how you shot at that man whose bullet grazed me—"

"I thought I heard an angel speak to me then—Teresa, do you really mean it—do you love me?" he gasped as he looked up at her.

As he did so, a drop of blood from her grazing wound fell onto his shirt, and he stared at it, then at her again.

It was a symbol. He, who had been blood brother to Descontarti and husband of Weesayo, saw that this merging of blood bespoke his longed-for union with Teresa more than anything else could do. It was the sign *El Señor Dios* had given him. Now he could be content. And she had said, moreover, that she loved him. Oh, blessed day; he did not even feel the throbbing pain of the ball in his flesh.

There were tears on her cheeks as she knelt beside him, reaching under her riding skirt to tear away a piece of her petticoat to bind his bleeding wound. She made a tourniquet, and saw him wince when she tied the knots tightly. "There, it should stop the bleeding. Oh, Carlos, *mi* Carlos, you risked your life for me—that's something no man has ever done for me!" Her voice trembled with sobs. Then suddenly she stiffened and cried out, "Lie down flat, *querido;* they're coming back at us again!"

Francisco López only had about half his troops left after these ineffective attacks against the Jicarilla defenders. With his men once again drawn south of the canyon, he tried to rally them for a last time: "One more time, *soldados,* we'll do it this time; I know we will! *Caramba,* think how close we are to the treasure! But one thing I swear to you; I will kill that *gringo* with my own hands, while you go past the canyon and kill those savages, those accursed *indios!*"

He could see that John Cooper still crouched at the mouth of the canyon, with Minanga at the other side of the opening. Blind fury at his frustration made him dare a hand-to-hand encounter with the tall American. And his vindictive courage was infectious: his disorganized and decimated troops stiffened, drew breaths, exchanged looks among themselves, and nodded. "*A sus órdenes, mi coronel,*" a beardless young *teniente* said, and saluted.

"I will promote you to *capitán* to replace your gallant superior, Capitán Mora," López told him. "Lead the attack; go!"

He watched the mounted dragoons again move into two flanking lines, bend low over their horses' necks, and then spur them on to a gallop. Grinding his teeth, his eyes blazing with rage, López seized a lance and rode full tilt into the mouth of the canyon.

John Cooper gasped, grudgingly admiring the courage of this tall Mexican officer. He calmly reloaded "Long Girl" and waited. Slowly lifting the rifle, he squinted along the sight, and his right forefinger began to nudge the trigger. At that very moment, Colonel López swerved his mustang in the direction of Minanga, just as John Cooper pulled the trigger. The ball sped past López's head, and John Cooper uttered an exasperated cry as he flung down his rifle and ran toward the Mexican officer. Minanga had drawn his bow but, taken by surprise at López's sudden maneuver that brought the lance leveling at him, loosed his arrow too quickly. It struck the horse in the neck, and the maddened animal screamed in pain and reared with its front hooves high in the air, while López toppled from it. Quickly retrieving his balance as the dying horse thrashed and kicked, he seized the lance and tried to thrust it first at Minanga, then at John Cooper.

John Cooper seized one of his pistols, leveled it, and pulled the trigger, but it misfired. With all his strength, he flung it at the maddened colonel, who seemed miraculously protected from harm. The butt struck López in the forehead, but it only stunned him, and he came doggedly on.

As John Cooper reached for the other pistol, López swung his lance and knocked it out of the American's hand.

Momentarily cornered, John Cooper drew the Spanish dagger from its sheath around his neck and warily moved to one side as his adversary came at him, his eyes narrowed and blazing with a demonic fury and bloodlust. Minanga, dropping to one knee, had fitted another arrow to his bow; but as if he had seen him out of the corner of his eye, López swung the lance and knocked the bow out of the Lipan Apache's hands.

On the top of the canyon, Pastanari, seeing this duel, put an arrow to his bow and loosed a swift shot. The arrow grazed the colonel's left arm, and blood stained his shirt. Meanwhile, the troopers on each side of the canyon were firing their last volleys up at the Jicarilla, and three of the

Indians toppled and fell to the floor of the canyon, while two others were badly wounded.

The young lieutenant who had survived the return fire of the defenders had wheeled his horse back to the southern end of the canyon and saw his superior officer holding off Minanga and John Cooper.

"*¡Mi coronel, aquí!*" he shouted.

Panting, trembling in reaction, Francisco López crouched, the lance gripped in both hands, as John Cooper, the Spanish dagger in his right hand, kept a respectful distance away from the point of the iron lance. Minanga had his hunting knife and drew it, balancing it to throw. The young lieutenant drew his pistol and fired a snap shot, which grazed Minanga's right hand and caused him to drop the knife to the ground.

"Get on my horse, *mi coronel, por amor de Dios!*" the lieutenant urged, almost hysterical with grief at the death of so many of his comrades.

López warily moved back, still threatening his two opponents with the lance, then glanced up at the lieutenant: "Is all lost, *teniente*?" he asked.

"Yes, yes, I beg of you; get on my horse, save yourself! There'll be another time for the *gringo!*"

"Yes," López muttered as he shot John Cooper a baleful look. "May God grant me the chance to kill you, you *yanqui* dog!" He drew back the lance in both hands and flung it at John Cooper, who leaped to one side so that it went clattering against the rocks. Then swiftly, Colonel Francisco López swung himself up behind the lieutenant, who wheeled his gelding and galloped at full speed out of the canyon and rode southward.

The Jicarilla braves sent arrows and rifle bullets after him, but the lieutenant was a brilliant horseman and constantly veered the direction of his mount so that, at last, he and his superior officer were out of range.

Only five mounted dragoons galloped after their commanding officer, the rest of them having fallen to the defenders.

It was over. And the bodies that lay on each side of the canyon justified its grim name: the Canyon of Death.

Thirty

Pastanari spoke solemnly: "My brother, my debt to you for saving my life so many years ago is paid. Now you must help me send those warriors who have given their lives for us to the Great Spirit. I wish that our shaman were here, but we who live must do for the dead what must be done."

"I am your blood brother and proud of it, Pastanari. I will take part in this, if you will allow it."

"Yes, *Halcón*, and then we shall resume our journey back to the ranch. But I am afraid that we shall not have enough to guard your ranch when you take the silver onto New Orleans—we have lost many men."

"You will have enough, Pastanari," John Cooper gravely replied. "For each Jicarilla brave is worth at least five or six *soldados mejicanos.*"

"This I think, too." Pastanari permitted himself a fleeting smile, and then his face was sad again. "And your *cuñado* and the señora?"

"They are still at the top of the canyon, and one of your braves told me they have been wounded, though not badly."

Pastanari turned to a sturdy, middle-aged brave named Nizami. "Bring the horses of those who are lost to us, Nizami," he ordered. Nizami lifted his hand in salute to his young *jefe* and turned to run, but John Cooper interposed, "Take Pingo and ride to the horses, Nizami."

"As you wish, *Halcón.*" The mature brave inclined his head in respect to the blood brother of the Jicarilla, as John Cooper led Pingo out by the reins. The spirited palomino had learned his lesson well from his master's tutelage: during

329

John Cooper's duel with Francisco López, he had remained beside the wall of the canyon, waiting patiently for his master to give new orders. John Cooper stroked the palomino's head and murmured a few words in the Apache tongue, as Nizami mounted. And Pingo, despite the weight of a new rider on his back, obeyed the brave's directions and raced toward the little forest where the Jicarilla had tethered their mustangs.

Not quite an hour later, Nizami returned on Pingo, leading the horses of the slain braves in a doleful line. Pastanari solemnly walked to the south side of the canyon, and gestured to his braves who had survived the Mexican dragoon attack to tend to the wounded. The braves knew what to do and lifted the bodies of their slain comrades and carried them to the base of the rocky hills. Then, taking the bladder pouches which had been attached to the saddle horns of the horses of their dead companions, they laved the bodies of the dead. When this was done, they lifted them astride their horses, adjusting them so that they would not topple off, and led them to the canyon for burial where they cleared the ground to make gravesites large enough to accommodate the horses as well. The bodies of the dead would be covered with earth and rocks, and the resulting mounds would be a testimonial to those who had given up their lives to defeat the Mexicans.

Teresa de Rojado and Carlos, their arms around each other's waist, slowly descended from the top of the rocky crags and stood, silent and awestruck, to witness the burial rites of the Jicarilla Apache, exactly as their shaman had explained it to John Cooper.

When the huge gravesites were ready, the braves took their bows and arrows and sent arrows through the horses' hearts. And then, slowly and laboriously, they buried each horse with a dead rider in a separate grave, covering the graves with dirt and rocks, until there were several large mounds appearing on the mesa.

"I have done what our shaman would have done, *Halcón*," Pastanari murmured, looking up at the darkening sky. "Let us go back to where our camp was last night, and before it is dark, I shall have the braves dig up the silver and put it back on the travois—unless you believe those few *soldados* will dare to attack us again?"

"No, Pastanari," John Cooper said, shaking his head.

"Colonel López may be a treacherous spy, but he also is wise enough to know that if he could not defeat us with fifty dragoons, he has no chance with the few who survived your heroic defense. I feel it in my bones that we haven't heard the last of him, but I think we will be safe for the night. I will help the braves dig up the ingots and put them back in the travois. Some of your men can return to the wounded and bring them to our camp. Also, I want your braves to take the weapons and the few remaining horses of the Mexicans. Your men are entitled to them after the way they defended us."

Pastanari nodded, and put his palm against John Cooper's heart to signify that he understood.

They rode to the other end of the canyon, where they had camped the previous night and where the ingots had been hidden. Now the mesa was quiet, with only the faint sound of an occasional bird and, from a greater distance, the forlorn wail of a coyote. A cheerful fire rose to dispel the shadows of the night and the memories of bloodshed and death.

Carlos de Escobar and Teresa de Rojado sat side by side in front of one of the small fires. The bullet in his shoulder had been removed, and his wound had been washed and poulticed by herbs that one of the Jicarilla braves had found near the forest where the horses had been tethered. Teresa, her slight wound already forgotten, looked at him and smiled understandingly, and the silence between them was more eloquent than words. John Cooper busied himself with Pastanari in preparing the evening meal of jerky and biscuits and coffee. From time to time, Carlos's brother-in-law glanced surreptitiously back at the couple, and he smiled to himself. They had shared the struggle for survival; it had welded an unbreakable bond between them. John Cooper knew that these two were destined to belong to each other and to share the oncoming years—yes, and to have children, to whom Teresa de Rojado would be a fond and devoted mother, as she would to Weesayo's children.

But he could not help thinking, with a certain troubling foreboding, of Colonel Francisco López, remembering his own initial reaction to their meeting in the canyon. He had been far from surprised to see that suave, smirking face, that military bearing, that arrogant self-assurance of this man whom both he and Yankee had distrusted from the very first moment of his arrival at the Double H Ranch. And John Cooper knew almost with a certainty that he had not seen the last of Francisco López.

A shadow fell across him from the firelight, and he looked up from his supper to see Minanga standing before him. The Lipan Apache had bandaged his hand, though there was no serious injury. "*Halcón*, I come to you now to ask if my debt to you is paid."

John Cooper put down the remnants of his simple meal and rose to face the courageous Indian. "There is no longer any debt between us, Minanga. You worked at the ranch, and I know that our *capataz*, the Señor Miguel, was pleased with you and trusted you, or he would not have sent you out to us. And what you did by learning of that *mejicano*'s plans to attack us saved many lives. Finally, Minanga, you bore yourself with great courage in the canyon, and your bow and arrow helped turn back the enemy with his superior numbers. Yes, there is no debt between us, except that I am in yours for what you have done for us all."

Minanga's dark eyes were bright now. "If that is so, *Halcón*, I ask your permission to go back to my people. As I rode here, I saw the signs that they had hunted the buffalo. They cannot be far from here, and my mustang will help me find them."

"I understand you. One day, you may be chief of the Lipan Apache, but even then, Minanga, I will always look upon you as a friend."

"It is good to hear such words after all this time, *Halcón*. I have counted my coup—you saw me take the scalp of the *capitán mejicano*. They will show my tribe that I have come back as a warrior."

"And I want you to take with you also one of the rifles we got from the Mexicans. This too, will be a sign of your bravery. But if your people still are not convinced, Minanga, come to me again and I will write picture bark for them to read, to learn how you stood beside us and did not turn away from the muskets and the rifles and the lances. I will tell them how you did not fear the lance of Francisco López and would have killed him with your bow and arrow if the knife had not been shot from your hand, injuring you."

John Cooper went to get one of the rifles, and when he

handed it to Minanga, the Lipan put his right palm over his own heart first and then over John Cooper's. "*Gracias, Halcón.* I will also tell my people how the tall *wasichu* killed the *mejicano* dogs with his long stick that speaks with thunder and spits fire, and how he was willing to fight with dagger against lance. You are already known to our people, *Halcón;* your name will soon be known throughout all the land. It is known to the Comanche, as it is to your Jicarilla brothers, and to the Navajo and the Ute. May the Great Spirit, He whom we call Killer-of-Enemies when we come to battle, protect you and those who love you and are loved by you. And now I say farewell to you, and you have my thanks for having given me this chance to count my coup of honor."

He inclined his head toward John Cooper, who made a similar gesture of respect, deeply moved by the Lipan's almost mystical fervor. Minanga turned, went into the shadows beyond the campfire, and led back his black mustang. He mounted it, adjusting the quiver of arrows and the bow at his back. Taking the reins in his left hand, he raised his new gun in his right hand and uttered the long eerie cry of the Lipan warrior as he rode off into the night.

After he said farewell to the man who had saved his life from the *jabalí*, Minanga kicked his heels against his mustang's belly and rode off in the direction of the buffalo carcass that he had seen on his way to warn John Cooper. He had no fear of the few remaining Mexican dragoons who might be in the vicinity; he was Minanga, war lieutenant of the Lipan Apache.

When he found the carcass, he dismounted, letting the reins dangle while the mustang snorted and pawed the ground in distaste at the rotting, mutilated animal. Two buzzards, disturbed from their feast, had indolently flapped their huge wings and flown off when they had seen the mustang racing toward them.

Crouching, his eyes narrowed to note the slightest sign that would lead him back to the tribe that had abandoned him, he saw again the feathered arrow emerging from the neck.

Straightening, he trotted on his moccasined feet about a hundred yards northward, and then again stooped down and studied the ground. He could see the hoof marks, many of them, indicating a hunting party. And here there were droppings—perhaps a week old, but not more. Again straightening, Minanga followed the tracks for a quarter of a mile, till he was satisfied that here, by a dense thicket of chaparral, the men had made a brief camp and cooked some of the buffalo meat. There had been no travois, so they must have cut large strips of the meat and thrust them into their water bags. That lone buffalo had evidently been a stray; doubtless the hunters had been hungry and gorged themselves to regain their strength, then taken after the herd itself.

Satisfied, he trotted back to his mustang, which awaited him, mounted it, and rode off in the direction of the tracks.

Two days and two nights later, having changed his direction slightly to the northeast, for the tracks were plainer now and there was no doubt that the hunting party was still after the herd, he saw in the distance the tiny glow of what was assuredly a campfire.

His mustang had valiantly carried him without slackening, though he had contented himself with only a few hours of sleep each night. Now, his heart exultant within him, he crouched over the horse's neck and murmured Lipan words to Esarti, urging a last burst of speed to bring him closer to those who had cast him out and scorned him. His debt was paid to the *gringo* and to the friends of the *gringo*, as well; now there remained for him to regain his honor and to belong once again to the proud, nomadic Lipan whose war lieutenant he had been. He could almost hear the chant of the shaman, acclaiming his prowess, telling the story of how he had fallen from grace and then proved his true courage and cunning. He tilted back his head and let out a wailing cry, akin to that the shaman would make to signify that he, Minanga, was no longer an outcast. And his eyes shone with pride and impatience; Esarti could not go fast enough for him now.

The campfire grew brighter and larger as Esarti's hooves pounded on the dry ground, and then suddenly a challenge rang out from the high back of a stagnant little creek, where the Lipan hunting party was camping for the night: "Who are you to come upon us without sign or warning?"

"It is I, Minanga, the Lipan!" Minanga cried.

He dismounted at once and stood beside his mustang, head lowered, to signify that he came in peace.

The creek was fringed with dwindling scrub trees, and he could see by the bright fire that there were thirty braves gathered around it, chewing strips of the meat which they had dried and pounded, and the man who had challenged him came forward now with a lance in his hand. He recognized him as Noraldo, who had once been his best friend and who now, by the markings on his chest and arm, had replaced him as war lieutenant.

"Your name is not spoken at the fire; you are not welcome," Noraldo told him.

"I know the law. I come to prove I have counted coup over an enemy, an enemy to all of you as to me. Behold these!" Minanga held up the scalp and the epaulets and the rifle for all to see.

A tall man, perhaps fifty, yet giving no sign of that advanced age in the alertness and dignity of his bearing, came forward from his place of honor at the campfire. He wore two eagle feathers that had been dipped into red dye—the sign of the Lipan *jefe*. "I know you, Minanga. You were a warrior of courage among the Lipan. How came you by these trophies?"

Minanga told briefly how the *wasichu* had killed the *jabalí* and taken him back to the *wasichu's hacienda*, where he had been put to work tending horses. And then he related how the *capataz* had sent him as a scout to find the *wasichu* who had gone on to Taos to bring back a great treasure. And how he had found the Mexican dragoons camped near the Pecos, waiting for the *wasichu* and his men. And finally, he told of the battle of the Cañon de Muerto, how he had killed Capitán Mora, and how *El Halcón* had given him one of the Mexican rifles as a present.

"You have never spoken with a forked tongue, and I recognize the signs a *mejicano* officer would wear." The Lipan chief turned to look at the braves who squatted on their haunches and listened impassively. "I, Sotolma, *jefe* of the Lipans, say that Minanga has proved himself. He is once again a warrior. Come share the buffalo meat with us."

"It was by the slain buffalo that I found you, Sotolma," Minanga smilingly vouchsafed.

"You shall be as you were before, our war lieutenant. But Noraldo, who helped us find the buffalo herd, has equal right to this rank."

"I do not dispute it. Why can we not have two war lieutenants, so that our tribe may be the more feared by our enemies?" was Minanga's diplomatic reply.

At this, there was a shout of laughter, and one of the braves handed him a flask of *tiswin,* and the others drank to celebrate his return to them, as if he had come back from the dead.

Minanga looked back toward where he had left the *gringo,* and he murmured a silent prayer of gratitude to John Cooper, and then, looking up at the dark sky, one to Killer-of-Enemies.

Francisco López, his face contorted with rage, his arms clasped around the waist of the intrepid young lieutenant who had saved him from death at the hands of John Cooper Baines and Minanga, at last hoarsely commanded, "Teniente Sotomayor, we're safe now. In the name of all the devils in hell, rein in your horse before my guts are shaken out of me!"

He and the other five survivors of that battle in the canyon had come about ten miles southeast, and as he glanced over his shoulder now, Colonel López saw that there were no pursuers.

The lieutenant obeyed, and Santa Anna's spy slipped down off the horse with a groan of relief as he rubbed his lower back and thighs. *"Madre de Dios,"* he swore, "you might at least have thought to bring me a horse, Teniente Sotomayor!"

"There wasn't time, *mi coronel.* What do we do now? Are we to report back to Major Valdez in Ciudad Juárez?"

"No. *¡Holá todos aquí!"* López shouted.

He stood there fuming, and then looked back in the direction whence he had come, his eyes narrowing and his lips sadistically compressing. "I'd give a year's wages to find the filthy dog who spied on our camp and got word to that *bastardo* of an *americano* that we were trying to take his silver from him! I'd tear him apart with my hands, beginning with his *cojones!"*

"We outnumbered them almost two to one, *mi coronel*," the young lieutenant almost petulantly complained, shaking his head. "And we had more and better weapons than they did."

"I'm well aware of that, *estúpido*!" López snapped. "To answer your question about what we're going to do—I will tell you; I don't propose to go back to Santa Anna. He'd have me shot, or maybe even hanged, because I failed this mission. Think of it; a fortune in pure silver in our grasp, and we couldn't take it from those damned *indios* and that meddlesome *yanqui*!"

The five dragoons sat astride their horses, eyeing him with curiosity and uneasily glancing at one another, as they waited for their commanding officer to give them an order. The virtual massacre of their comrades had dazed and bewildered them as much as it had young Teniente Fernando Sotomayor.

Francisco López had loaded his *pistolas* as soon as he had dismounted from the lieutenant's horse. They were in his belt now, and he slowly appraised the five dragoons who sat staring at him, their faces drained of emotion. No, he told himself, these men were little better than *peones*, probably all louts from the provinces who had enlisted because it meant a few *pesos* a month and food and tequila and once in awhile a *puta*, and because perhaps they could ride horses, which they had learned on the farms where they had been born. How could they grasp the enormity of that treasure which had been there for the taking and now was on its way to the *gringo*'s ranch?

Yes, all that treasure would go to the ranch near the Frio River, and it would stay there until the *americano* took it to New Orleans. Had he not said that it might not be until next spring? A plan began to formulate in López's cunning brain.

"*Amigos*," he began, with a frank smile, "let us take stock of the situation. I entreat you to hear me out and, since I believe you all to be intelligent men, to help me decide what we should all do."

"But, *mi coronel*," the young lieutenant stammered, "I remember Capitán Mora told us that when this mission was over, we were to return to our post at Ciudad Juárez."

"But don't you see, *mi teniente*," López said in a whee-dling tone such as he might use to a child, "that what has just happened countermands all that and, to my way of thinking, calls for an appraisal of what action we should take. There is still great treasure to be had, so much that it staggers the mind even to think of it."

"But Major Valdez explained that our purpose was to aid you, *mi coronel*, and to bring back the *gringo*'s silver for Coronel Santa Anna," Lieutenant Sotomayor protested.

"Be patient with me a moment, *mi teniente*. If we go back to Mexico and report that there are only seven of us out of fifty, it is very possible we may be court-martialed, per-haps even shot for cowardice. And Coronel Santa Anna does not easily forgive those who fail to carry out his orders. Think of that a moment, I beg of you all." He looked stead-ily at the five mounted dragoons, who again glanced uneasily at one another. A faint smile curved his sensual lips. "On the other hand, consider the possibilities. That treasure is being taken to a ranch where I spent a little time. I had a friend there, Coronel Ramón Santoriaga, who is in charge of de-fenses. I was able to see how well defended it was; but I think that, with the right sort of force, it could be successfully besieged and the treasure recovered. But, you see, to do that would require more men."

The lieutenant was puzzled. "I do not follow you, *mi coronel*. Are you proposing that we try to raise more troops and attack that ranch?"

"I will recruit an army. I know men who deal with the Comanche, and I know some outlaws who camp near them. I can raise an army large enough to burn that ranch to the ground, and there will be young *muchachas* for the taking, as well as the silver."

He could see greed begin to show itself in the looks the dragoons were giving him now, and he heard them mutter among themselves and saw one of them nod. Four of them were privates, one a corporal. He raised his voice a little, to appeal to them still more: "*Amigos*, what future do you have since you are not officers and not likely ever to be? You have not had the education, nor the proper political and social connections to win a rank such as mine, or even that of Ten-iente Sotomayor here. But what if I were to tell you that if we could take that silver from the *gringo*, there would be enough to share with all of you."

"But the silver is to be delivered to *el libertador!*" Lieutenant Sotomayor protested. "What you are saying amounts to treason. It would make us deserters—"

"Amigos," López blandly continued as he faced the five dragoons, "I ask you as men of judgment and intelligence; would you look upon that as treason?"

"No, *por Dios!*" the corporal swore, a burly man with an enormous mustache.

"I am happy to see that I have found men with good judgment and the ability to make decisions, even if they are not officers," López chuckled. He saw Lieutenant Sotomayor drop his right hand toward his belt, and he had anticipated just such a movement. A pistol appeared in his right hand in a lightning-fast draw, and his forefinger squeezed the trigger. Lieutenant Sotomayor stiffened, his eyes widening, fixing on López's face with incredulous horror, and then he slid down from the horse and rolled over until he lay facedown.

Francisco López blew the smoke away from the barrel of the pistol. "How very kind it was of the *teniente* to let me have his horse," he sardonically observed as he mounted it. "Well now, *amigos,* shall we gather our own army and take the silver for ourselves?"

"I'm your man, *mi coronel,*" the burly corporal shouted. "And these *soldados* are in my platoon. They feel as I do."

"Then let us ride on. Great wealth awaits us!"

Thirty-one

Eleven days later, John Cooper, Carlos, and Pastanari, with Teresa de Rojado riding alongside Carlos, saw in the distance the outlines of the large *hacienda* of the Double H Ranch, the bunkhouse, and the houses of the settlers who had come to join this commune. Behind them came the seventeen surviving Jicarilla braves and the travois into which the silver ingots had been replaced and camouflaged. And since it was still early August, John Cooper was convinced that his plan for conveying the ingots on to New Orleans and hiding it with a huge cattle drive might be accomplished right away, this fall, not next spring, since the heavy wagons with their false bottoms were ready for travel.

And there was another reason now to speed this project. John Cooper was sure López would be back. The man now had nothing to lose, and John Cooper had already guessed that López would not return to Santa Anna with a tale of failure, that he was opportunistic enough to seek the treasure for himself. That meant that the sooner the treasure was in the bank vault in New Orleans, the safer it would be.

Carlos and Teresa had spoken very little on the last leg of the journey. The handsome Spaniard had sensed that her spontaneous avowal during the fighting that she did love him had been a finite declaration. It would not do to press her into setting any date for their marriage; he was content with the way things were, for he felt that it would not be long before they would be married in the newly built church at the Double H Ranch.

And as for Teresa, it was not that she had doubts or

self-recriminations over the impulsive, emotionally charged declaration she had made when the Mexican dragoons were firing at them. But rather it was an awareness that her admission of love for Carlos might seem too sudden after she had told him back in Taos that she had not yet made up her mind and that she was not certain yet of her future. She knew very well that the dramatic and perilous attack in the canyon had made it all too easy for her to see exactly how he was willing to defend her with his own life, if need be. But she was still enough of her own woman to want to wait for a time when they could talk openly of their feelings for each other.

And yet, from time to time—during the meals, and as they rode along the prairie trail that led back to the magnificent valleylike terrain of the Double H Ranch and the swiftly flowing Frio River to the south of it—they exchanged significant looks that said more than words.

As they slackened their pace now, easing themselves in their saddles, John Cooper and Carlos rode alongside each other and waved their *sombreros* to attract the sheepherders. At the western end of this huge ranch, there was plentiful grazing land for sheep, and John Cooper had learned from Miguel that at least in so fertile an area, with its spacious expanses of nutritious grazing fodder, sheep and cattle could graze side by side. The sheepherders saw them and began to cheer, and one of the youngest of them ran to tell Miguel Sandarbal the good news that the Señores Baines and de Escobar were home at last.

The sheepherder was out of breath as he reached the bunkhouse. "Señor capataz, they're back home! Come see them; it's the Señor Carlos and Señor Baines, too, and there's a young *mujer* riding with them and many *indios*!"

"God be praised!" Miguel joyously ejaculated. He was already in a buoyant mood, his wife, Bess, having told him just last night that she was again with child. This would be their fourth, and Miguel thanked God for allowing him such joys in the latter years of his life. He beckoned to some of the *trabajadores* with whom he had been chatting, and said heartily, "Come, *amigos*, let's welcome them back in style! And one of you go tell Tía Margarita to get ready for a big feast tonight to celebrate their safe return!"

"*¡Sí, mi capataz!*" The grinning worker touched his hand to his forehead and hurried out of the bunkhouse to the kitchen of the sprawling *hacienda*. It was good news indeed, for whenever there was a feast, the *patrón* always saw to it that the *trabajadores* got plenty of good food and *aguardiente* and, sometimes, even some of the excellent wine. It was no wonder that the *trabajadores* on the Double H Ranch would have said, to a man, that they preferred to work for no other *patrón!*

Tía Margarita flung up her hands and joyously and stridently acclaimed the return, then turned to her young assistants and began to give orders: "Gisella, go tell Enrique that we shall need at least six sheep for the feast tonight! Have him kill them at once and bring their carcasses around to the shed just outside my kitchen so I can start cutting the meat and preparing it for cooking! Magdalena, go to the supply shed and have one of the *trabajadores* bring in a barrel of flour, *¡pronto!* Lupe, you go to the garden and pick all the ripe apricots you can! And you, Amalia, pick the sweet peppers and the *frijoles* we'll need, and mind you take along a basket so you don't crush the peppers—I want them firm so I can cut them properly!"

This done, the fat, gray-haired cook hurried out of the kitchen to tell Don Diego and Doña Inez the happy tidings of the return of his son and son-in-law.

"Our prayers have been answered," Don Diego exultantly exclaimed as he turned to Doña Inez. "And let us hope that we will have Don Sancho and Doña Elena to sup with us this evening to celebrate their arrival in the new home I hope they will enjoy for many long years to come."

With this, an arm around his handsome wife's waist, he walked out of the *hacienda* to greet the new arrivals, who were now surrounded by the ebullient Miguel and his *trabajadores,* welcoming them home.

"Look there, *mi* Inez," Don Diego exclaimed as he gestured toward the oncoming riders, "there is a young woman riding near my son—that must be the Señora de Rojado. Oh, blessed day, and what a happy thought it is that our church is finished so that perhaps Fra Pastronaz can marry them as soon as possible! Inez, you do not know how relieved I am that she has come to the ranch with my son."

"I know how you feel, *querido*," Doña Inez put a hand on his arm. "I have prayed for that, too. But they may not yet be betrothed, and I think we should wait before we begin to congratulate them."

"Of course, of course, dear Inez! How sensible you always are."

Doña Inez blushed with pleasure and put her hand on his shoulder as her right arm curved around his waist.

Catarina, who had just left the new church after attending afternoon mass, had heard the uproar in the kitchen and went outside the *hacienda* just in time to see John Cooper descend from Pingo and hurry to greet Doña Inez and Don Diego. "Coop, *mi corazón!*" she ecstatically cried and ran to meet him. He turned, grinning like a little boy in his undisguised pleasure at seeing her, and took her in his arms very carefully, realizing she was five months pregnant. But Catarina fairly crushed him with her arms and covered his face with kisses: "It's so good to have you back—I've been so lonely without you, *querido*—oh, there's Carlos, too!"

"Now I know I'm back home," John Cooper said laughing, as he at last released his beautiful wife from his embrace. Then, seeing Don Diego and Doña Inez cling to each other, his face saddened as he turned to Don Diego: *"Mi suegro,* I'm afraid I've got very bad news about the de Pladeros."

"Why, what do you mean—? They are not here—didn't they come with you?" Don Diego anxiously demanded.

John Cooper shook his head. "Don Sancho and Doña Elena began the journey with us in their carriage, along with about ten of their *trabajadores* who wanted to come along with them. But on the way, a few days out of Taos, Don Sancho died very peacefully in his wife's arms. We—we buried him on the way, and we marked his grave—and Carlos said the words over him. And then you see, *mi suegro,* Doña Elena decided that there was no point in her coming here because she would feel so alone and almost as if taken in out of kindness—so she went back to Taos to stay with Tomás and Conchita and her grandchildren."

"¡Qué lástima!" Don Diego uttered a groan and then, making the sign of the cross, turned to Doña Inez: "And I never had the chance even to say good-bye to him, my dear old friend Sancho—I'll miss him dreadfully!"

Carlos now approached his father, with Teresa de Rojado beside him. *"Mi padre,"* he said, as he took Doña Inez's hand and kissed it, *"y mi madrastra querida,* I have the honor to present to you the Señora Teresa de Rojado. She has ridden with us and she has helped defend us against that traitor Francisco López."

"*¡Madre de Dios!*" Don Diego cried, aghast. "Do you mean to tell me that after he left our ranch, he tried to steal the silver?"

"He means exactly that, *mi suegro*," John Cooper put in with a grim smile. "I don't know how he did it, but there was a body of about fifty well-armed dragoons on horseback who attacked us. And Carlos and the Señora de Rojado were wounded, but not badly."

"Carlos, *mi hijo*," Don Diego said in a worried voice as he grasped his son by the shoulders, "do not lie to your old father—and do not try to play the hero, either! How serious was your wound?"

Carlos grimaced a little as he put his hands to his father's wrists and gently removed them. "I took a ball in my shoulder, *mi padre*. But one of the *indios* took out the ball and found some medicinal bark to poultice it. It is just a little stiff; and you are still a very strong man, so when you held me just now I felt a little pain."

Don Diego rolled his eyes upward. "May heaven forgive me, to hurt my own son! That is the very last thing I want to do. And here you have made me forget my manners—Señora de Rojado, I have heard so much about you—our *hacienda* is honored if you will remain with us for a time."

"That's most kind of you, Don Diego—if it causes no inconvenience."

Don Diego looked almost pleadingly at his wife, but Doña Inez came to his rescue. She moved forward, put her arms around the young woman, and kissed her on the cheek, then warmly said, "Do not even talk of inconvenience, Señora de Rojado! We have plenty of room here, and everything will be done for your comfort, you will see. But I heard Carlos say that you were wounded, too."

"It was nothing, Doña Inez, only a scratch. I am grateful to God our lives were spared."

"Amen to that!" Don Diego broke in, reassured by his wife's gentle welcome to the young woman. "Now there is to be no more talk about wounds and attacks and soldiers, and that is an order from me!" He clapped his hands, and a young *criada* appeared at the doorway. "Rita, *por favor,* show the Señora de Rojado to the best room in the house. And have the other *criadas* prepare my son's room, so that he will have a good long sleep this night, after we have had our feast of celebration!"

Catarina turned to John Cooper, who had been holding her hand all through this discussion. "And you, dear Coop, were you hurt?" she uneasily murmured.

"No, I was very lucky, *querida*. I am just fine. And now, how do you feel? You really should take good care of yourself now, Catarina; you're going to have another child—"

"You silly, it won't be for at least a few months yet! And now I'm so glad I have you home!" She laughed softly and put her arm around his waist, tendering him her mouth.

"Just the same," he whispered after a long and satisfying kiss, "you must take good care of our baby. And I'm afraid you'll also have to do without me for awhile longer, dearest."

"What are you saying to me now? You've hardly just come back, and you're talking of going away again?" Catarina flared up.

"Hush, darling, it's for the good of all of us," John Cooper softly explained. "We've brought the silver back from the mine, all of it, and given the holy relics to Padre Madura in Taos. But now it wouldn't be wise to keep all of this fortune at the ranch, and that's why, in the next few days, now that I know that the big wagons are ready, I'm going to drive some cattle to New Orleans and then take these silver ingots to my bank."

"I—I know you must do that, Coop, but can't we have some time together?" Catarina pleaded.

He cupped her face in his hands and gently kissed her. "No one wants it anymore than I do, especially after the journey we've just made. But it is very important that we get the treasure far away from here, and where it's going to be safe for all time to come. But don't you worry, Catarina; the Jicarilla braves who escorted us home are going to stay here to defend the ranch. And I think I'll take Andrew with me—"

"Oh, no, Coop, he's still only a boy, and it's such a long trip to New Orleans and back!" she protested.

"It'll be good for him, darling. And to tell the truth, after the way he handled himself on the drive to San Antonio, he's become a valuable member of the team." He kissed her again before she could protest further, and then taking her hand, he said, "Now, come. Let's go in to see the children."

The Jicarilla braves and their leader, Pastanari, were quartered in the bunkhouse, where they were treated as honored guests. Miguel and his *trabajadores* arranged for a great feast. A festive barbecue with sides of cattle and pigs was roasted over a large fire outside. The Jicarilla brave, Itaxa, would get a good rest that night, then go back to the stronghold in New Mexico and tell Chief Kinotatay that *El Halcón* had returned to his nest safe and sound.

Meanwhile, at the *hacienda*, it was also a memorable evening, and Tía Margarita had surpassed herself. The servants, too, in awe of her unflagging energy, flattered the weary travelers by showing them attention and making them feel thoroughly at home.

Don Diego filled in his son and son-in-law on the events at the ranch over the past few months. The big news, of course, was the completion of the church, for which there would be a dedication ceremony as soon as John Cooper returned from New Orleans with the bell for the steeple. Then he was quiet for some time, reflecting on the loss of his dear old friend, Don Sancho de Pladero. He promptly proposed a toast to the latter's memory in which all joined, rising from the table and holding aloft their goblets.

There were several times during the evening when Doña Inez had to send Don Diego a warning look, lest he embarrass Teresa de Rojado by making pointed remarks about his hopes for her forthcoming marriage to his son. Carlos had purposely seated himself on the other side of the table so that his proximity might not be looked upon as such an avowal here in the bosom of his family. For this, Teresa was very grateful and sent him a long, affectionate look.

After supper, the men retired to Don Diego's study for fine French brandy and some excellent Havana cigars. Teresa spent a very pleasant hour chatting with Bess Sandarbal, Doña Inez, and Catarina. And though she, too, was eager to see her brother find happiness after the tragedy of Weesayo, Catarina refrained from casting any allusions to a union between her brother and the beautiful widow.

"So the treasure is safe at last," Don Diego philosophically exclaimed as he sipped at his glass of brandy. "And you want to take it on to New Orleans? How soon do you intend to leave?"

"That's for Miguel to say," John Cooper answered, turning to the *capataz*, who was seated with them. "Miguel, do you think we've enough cattle now for a drive to New Orleans? A large herd would help conceal the wagons with their false bottoms. And how many of the *vaqueros* and *trabajadores* could you spare me to drive the herd and also to act as defenders, if we're attacked again?"

"You feel certain, then, that this traitorous López will try again?" Don Diego interjected.

John Cooper had a serious look on his face, and he tried to choose his words carefully. "I do, Don Diego. The last I saw of him, he and his lieutenant were riding southward. I believe he will be back again, and that is why I just don't feel right about keeping all this silver on the ranch. If it's gone, if it's put in that vault in the bank at New Orleans, then López will have the devil's own time getting hold of it, no matter what tricks he tries."

"And the Jicarilla braves will stay at the ranch to defend us, in case there should be an attack against us—is that your plan?"

"Yes, that's exactly it. The *trabajadores* and the *vaqueros* and the settlers here, as well as Carlos and Ramón de Santoriaga and the Jicarilla, ought to be able to hold off any sort of attack."

Now Miguel spoke up. "To answer your question about the cattle and men, *mi amigo*, I'd say we have four thousand head." Miguel paused a moment before continuing. "In all, we have some sixty *vaqueros* and *trabajadores*. I can spare you thirty. And I'll draw half the men from the *vaqueros*, the rest from the *trabajadores*."

"That's fine. I'd like to leave by the end of this week. Let's now see, four thousand head of cattle and thirty *vaqueros*, and myself—but you'll come with us, too, won't you, Miguel?" John Cooper demanded.

"It would be an honor for me to do so—if my *patrón* permits it." Miguel looked over to Don Diego, who nodded, smiled, and waved his goblet in token of consent. "Well then, since he's willing, as I said, it will be an honor and a privilege to ride with you, *Halcón*."

"I should like to ride along with you, *mis amigos*," Car-

los spoke up. But Don Diego turned on him almost fiercely:
"Now then, for once, let a father have some rights around
this *hacienda*! You know perfectly well, you young scoundrel,
that Doña Inez and I were worried to death all those two
dreadful years you went away from us. Of course we know
why, and yet you are hardly back after that harrowing trip
and the attack by the traitorous López and the *soldados*, and
now you want to traipse off on another expedition. *Hombre*,
here you have brought the Señora de Rojado back, and I
should think you would want to stay here so you can continue your wooing of her."

Carlos lowered his head, unable to reply. He did indeed
want to be with Teresa, now that they had come so far together and had reached an understanding. But he also felt it
his duty to do his share in getting the silver safely into the
bank vaults.

John Cooper understood what his brother-in-law was
feeling, and interposed, "Anyway, Carlos, as I said before,
you're needed here at the ranch. You will look after things in
my absence. It is essential that one of us be here, in case of
any problems."

Carlos looked up and smiled. "All right, it is agreed, *mi
cuñado*. I will stay here and keep an eye on things."

"Including the Señora de Rojado, I have no doubt," Don
Diego said with a chuckle and a wink at John Cooper.

John Cooper now turned to Miguel. "We've the wagons
and the four thousand head of cattle. Thank goodness we've
got oxen enough to draw the wagons. And we'll use the oxcarts to carry back that big bronze bell ordered from Fabien
Mallard for our new church. But how much time do you
think we can make with a herd like that, Miguel?"

The white-haired *capataz* pursed his lips and thought for
a moment before replying. "If the weather stays decent, you
can figure on really not much more than twelve to fourteen
miles a day. Cattle are skittish animals. You have to think
about the possibility of a stampede if there's a storm, or even
if, by accident, a Mexican patrol comes by and fires a warning shot—that could send them into a headlong rush, and it
would take us days to get them back into the drive. Well
now, that would make about two months, give or take a week
one way or the other."

"I think that's about right," John Cooper mused aloud.

"Naturally, once we've disposed of the cattle in New Orleans and put the silver in the vault there, we can make much faster time coming back. It's true we'll have the big bronze bell and the oxcarts, and we'll fill some of the wagons with supplies; but since we won't have cattle to worry about on the journey back, we ought to be able to cut at least two weeks off our return time. Don't you agree, Miguel?"

"Yes, I think you're right, young master."

"I'd like very much on the way back to stop off at that new settlement of Eugene Fair's near the Brazos and see how it's working out," John Cooper added. "Well, with God's help, we should all be back here safely by the middle of December, well before Christmas and the time Catarina is to have her baby. Carlos, you can do me a favor by having Catarina become very good friends with the Señora de Rojado. That should keep her from brooding too much about my being away. And I think, too, when the Señora de Rojado meets your children and sees how mature and companionable they are, she'll be very much impressed with your qualifications as a husband and father."

Carlos's face reddened, as he saw Miguel and his father give him an affectionate look. "Fortunately," he said as he poured himself some more brandy, "I haven't yet let my oldest, Diego, know that I really want Teresa to be his new mother. Otherwise, I'd live in fear that, one day, he'd blurt out something about my feelings, and then I really should be embarrassed. And she would think that it was a very deceitful trick on my part."

"No, Carlos," his father said as he came to the handsome Spaniard and put his arm around Carlos's shoulders, "I'm sure she'd never think that of you. You're not capable of deceit. You're a true de Escobar. I'll drink to that—and to the successful cattle drive and the deposit of the silver in the bank vault. Heaven knows that once it's beyond the reach of a scheming rogue like that Colonel López, we can all breathe a sigh of relief. And now, let's go back and make sure that we haven't neglected our lovely ladies."

In the next few days, the Double H Ranch was bustling with activity, as John Cooper prepared for the second and final stage of the silver transport. One of his first acts the next morning was to confer with Ramón Santoriaga, and to tell the former liaison officer to increase the number of hours spent in military drills. That way the *trabajadores* and *vaqueros* who remained behind would be better able to defend the ranch in the event of an actual attack.

Also, he revealed to him the treachery of Francisco López, and Ramón was consternated: "I swear to you, Señor Baines, that I myself was taken in. And I can only hope that my error of judgment has not made you think me unworthy of remaining here to defend the ones you love and all the settlers and the workers while you go off on such a dangerous mission."

"I've never been in doubt about your loyalty, Ramón," John Cooper said, putting his hand on Ramón's shoulder.

"I pledge you my word that I'll keep everyone alert," Ramón promised. "I'll station guards at night and change them in shifts."

"That'll do it fine. Naturally, if there should be an attack—and I'm praying to God there won't be—you'll see to it that the women and children are hidden away in a safe place, where they won't be exposed to any danger."

"Absolutely. And your idea about increasing the defense drills is exactly what I intend to do, Señor Baines."

"Thanks, Ramón."

Miguel had appointed Esteban Morales, the assistant *capataz*, to replace him during his absence. "You'll give him the same obedience and attention you've given me, *mis amigos*," he told the workers. "And Coronel Santoriaga will be in military charge of all of you, and you'll obey his orders without question."

The workers eyed one another, murmured among themselves, and Esteban Morales stepped forward and said in a loud voice, "Respected *señor capataz*, the men have asked me to speak for them, and all of them have sworn by all they hold sacred that those who remain here on the ranch will fight to the death to defend it and their beloved *patrón*, Don Diego de Escobar."

"I thank all of you; you are *mis compañeros*." Miguel was deeply touched, and made his voice gruffer than usual to hide it. "And now, I'm going to ask for volunteers, but I'll be the one to decide who goes and who stays. I know all of you, as well as your wives and children. And I know some of you are just eager for adventure, but that won't necessarily make you the best *vaqueros* on a long drive that will take at least two months. So I'll be the one who decides who's going to go along with us."

An hour later, Miguel had chosen the thirty *vaqueros* and *trabajadores* who would accompany John Cooper and himself on the arduous journey to New Orleans.

Then the silver ingots were loaded in the false bottoms of the wagons, and Miguel made a secret marking on the hub of the left rear wheel of each wagon to indicate where the silver was and which wagons contained only supplies or were empty.

Carlos insisted on aiding Miguel in choosing horses for the *remuda,* so that the *vaqueros* would have extra mounts. Other workers hitched up the sturdy oxen to the carts. When they reached New Orleans, Miguel explained to John Cooper, three of the six carts would be joined together, and the top front frame of each would be lifted out of its pegs so as to make a single long conveyance for the great bronze bell ordered from Belgium.

The Saturday morning before they left, John Cooper took his ten-year-old son, Charles, aside, and promised him that when he was a little older, he, like his brother, Andrew, would also go along on the cattle drives. "But in the meantime," John Cooper continued, as he put his arm around the boy's shoulders and walked with him down the path leading from the main house, "you've got to look after your mother and your sisters. Oh, yes, there's one other very important thing you have to do while I'm gone."

"What is it, Pa?" the boy eagerly asked, looking forward to any tasks his father assigned to him.

"I want you to take charge of the training of Yankee. He's going to stay at the ranch to look after everybody, but I want you to look after *him*."

"Oh, I will, Pa, I will. Yankee and I get along real fine, don't we, boy?" Charles said to the wolf-dog, who was trotting alongside and now licked Charles's hand. Charles stopped walking long enough to rub Yankee's head with his knuckles, just as his father had taught him to do.

"You two make a good team," John Cooper put in. "Now I want you to see to it, Charles, that Yankee gets a good long run every day. And I also want you to see to it that he behaves himself and gets along with everyone on the ranch."

"You bet I will, Pa," Charles said, and disengaging himself from his father, the boy and the wolf-dog happily ran on ahead down the path.

John Cooper then went to speak with Pastanari, who was out in a field with some of his braves, practicing with bows and arrows and rifles.

Taking aside the youthful war chief, who had dismounted from his mustang, John Cooper said solemnly, "You, along with your father and his successor, Chief Kinotatay, have been as much my family as those here on the *hacienda.*"

"And you are the same to us, *Halcón,*" Pastanari replied. "That is why my braves and I will look after your home as if it were our own."

"That is all I could ask of you, *mi amigo.* Now I can leave on the cattle drive with no fear in my heart." With this, the two men clasped each other's forearm, a gesture that served as a silent pledge of their brotherhood.

Finally on this Saturday, the *vaqueros* chosen for the drive mounted their horses and rode into the valley where the cattle had been rounded up. All of them had been marked with the special double H brand of the ranch, and Miguel had selected a giant steer to lead all the rest. Good-naturedly, Miguel had named the docile animal El Primo, since he would indeed be first.

It was a tremendous processional, the oxcarts at the very end and the silver wagons at the front, with John Cooper and Miguel riding on each side of the wagons. In his buckskins, the tall ranch owner glowed with enthusiasm for the intrepid venture that lay ahead. He had already said his good-byes to Catarina, to Don Diego, and to Carlos, and had promised Teresa de Rojado that he would try to bring back a fine new pair of matched foils, with buttons and a guard-mask, smilingly telling her, "I've always wanted to have fencing lessons, ever since I once had to fight a duel for my life. I won, Señora de Rojado, but it was just by luck and the fact that I was much younger than my opponent, who had eaten too much before he tried his skill against mine. But, from what Carlos tells me, you're as good as Miguel."

To this, the lovely young widow had expressed surprise. "Do you mean that your *capataz* is a swordsman?"

Seeing that this chance comment had prompted a keen interest, he emphatically nodded: "The fact is, señora, that Miguel Sandarbal took over his father's fencing school in Madrid and was actually one of the finest blades in that city. It's quite a story, and I'm sure he'll tell it to you. I don't want to spoil it, because it has a very romantic flavor to it. He was a good friend of Don Diego's, and so, when Don Diego was banished from the royal court, he followed him to Taos."

"But that's fascinating, Señor Baines!" Teresa had excitedly replied. "I would very much like to ask him about it."

John Cooper had ingenuously shrugged with a guileless smile on his bearded face, and said, "Why, then, señora, you'll have to wait till December, because we won't be back from New Orleans till then." This was as far as John Cooper had dared to go in his attempt to further Carlos's suit. But he was aware that if Teresa was indeed still here in December, it would mean she and Carlos had probably set a wedding date.

Teresa was well aware of John Cooper's subtle intimations about the future, and it was hard to tell who was blushing more—she or John Cooper. But the lovely young widow quickly relieved any embarrassment by saying, "I wish you all a safe trip. And yes, I do indeed hope I get a chance to hear more about Señor Sandarbal's fencing experiences."

"I'll tell Miguel, and he'll look forward to it. Well now, I wish you a peaceful and restful stay as our honored guest at the ranch, Señora de Rojado," John Cooper had diplomatically declared, as he respectfully inclined his head toward her, then mounted Pingo.

He had one last farewell to make, and he rode to the houses of the six Texans, which formed a western boundary on the outskirts of the great ranch. By now, the brothers John and Henry Ames, Edward Molson and his cousin Ben Forrester, Malcolm Pauley, and Jack Williams, had become an integral part of the Double H Ranch; married, with children, they had escaped the harassment of Mexican patrols and the repressive governmental orders that had made their lives in the little settlement near San Antonio almost intolerable. Then it had seemed to them—all survivors of the Battle of Medina—that they were destined to be eternally at war for survival against the Mexicans; but here, in this fertile valley near the Frio River, they had enjoyed the freedom they had dreamed of when they had first come to Texas.

Dismounting from his spirited palomino, John Cooper knocked in turn on each door, and the six Texans emerged, to stand in a little group facing him. "I'm just about to leave for New Orleans, and I look to you to guard the ranch just as ably as you did when the renegade Comanche chief, Sarpento, attacked us," he told them. He went on to explain all that had taken place with Francisco López, and told them to be vigilant.

"If it's one of Santa Anna's own," Edward Molson said as he bared his teeth in a humorless grin, "we'll save some extra balls for him. Thanks for the warning, Mr. Baines. We'll be watching. I don't think any Mexican officer, especially one who works for Santa Anna, is going to make much headway against this ranch, not if we six have anything to do with it."

"That's what I thought you'd say. God bless you all. Well, the best to all of you, and Don Diego and I are proud to have you as our neighbors and friends." He shook hands with each of them and then rode back to where the herd had been rounded up. Miguel gave the signal, and the *vaqueros*, flourishing their *sombreros*, exhorted the huge herd to move southeast toward San Antonio. There would be good grass for the cattle to graze on and plenty of fresh water as they crossed the Colorado, the Brazos, and the Sabine rivers on the long trek. Young Andrew Baines rode a roan palomino gelding, two years old, which his father had carefully trained for him. And in his saddle sheath there was a long rifle, not unlike "Long Girl," that John Cooper had bought from a Pennsylvania trader in Taos. He gave the rifle to Andrew as a present to reward the boy for the valor he had shown on the spring trip to San Antonio.

Teresa de Rojado had watched the long processional of cattle flanked by riders, the wagons, the oxcarts, and she had sighed. She would have enjoyed a visit to New Orleans, but she knew that it would have been impractical. Already she had been shown so much gracious hospitality by Doña Inez and Don Diego, as well as by Catarina and Bess Sandarbal, that she had begun to feel very self-conscious. She had already made friends with quite a few of the children, including the motherly Francesca, and also Diego, Carlos's firstborn by his gentle Weesayo. And Diego, much to Carlos's relief, had acquitted himself with the utmost politeness and discretion, and without a word in his father's behalf. Nonetheless, precocious for his years, he had already guessed that his father was very much interested in this tall, slim, brown-haired señora. And when he had learned from Francesca that the señora rode horseback as well as a man and could shoot a musket or rifle and handle a rapier, he was extremely impressed and determined to be on his best behavior around her.

Thirty-two

In the village of the Pueblo Indians of Taos, Ticumbe was holding council with the headmen, the elders from the oldest families. Indeed, they had demanded this meeting, for the news they had just received from an emissary of the new *alcalde mayor*, Alonzo Cienguarda, had filled them with apprehension.

"We do not understand this, Ticumbe," said old Maguay, a dignified, white-haired *indio* nearly seventy but still erect and proud, as in the days when he had fought against raiding parties of Comanche and Kiowa Apache. "Was it not said by the good *jefe* of Taos at the fair before he left us that the man who would take his place would leave us in peace and let us decide on matters that concern our village? And now suddenly we are told that each ablebodied man who works for any *hacendado* in Taos must pay a tax of a *peso* a month. This was never done to us, so long as I can remember."

"It is doubtless because the new *alcalde mayor* has to build himself a fine new *hacienda*," Piminanda dryly observed. Now fifty, with three sturdy sons and two daughters, all of whom had found mates among the daughters and sons of other old *indio* families, he was highly regarded as a maker of sacred *bultos,* which many *hacendados* had purchased to adorn their chapels. "And it is also said that he has a highborn *puta* to keep him company in this fine, new *hacienda* he has built not far from that of Don Sancho de Pladero. Probably, these *pesos* will buy her many fine clothes and ornaments."

"I know only that the *gubernador* at Santa Fe chose this man because they were old friends. And because of this, it will not be easy to protest against his acts," Ticumbe pessimistically replied.

"I have also heard that he has no liking for *americanos,* most of all those who come to the fair to trade," another elder remarked. "Must we pay the tax, Ticumbe?"

Ticumbe nodded his head and sighed. "If we do not pay it, the *alcalde mayor* will report to his friend the *gubernador,* and then perhaps the *gubernador* will send his *soldados* from Santa Fe to come into our *jacales* and force us to pay. But if this *alcalde mayor* is as greedy as I fear he may be, then after we have paid this tax of one *peso* each month, he may well call upon us to pay even more, like two or three *pesos* each month."

Rocaldi, a stout, genial *indio* in his mid-forties, who was more skilled in the weaving of blankets than any woman of the village and had made the almost unheard-of sum of twenty-six *pesos* selling his ornately designed blankets at the great fair in June, rose to his feet to address Ticumbe. "I was in the plaza," he angrily declared, "and I saw the carriage of the *alcalde mayor.* His *puta* rode in it, with a *mejicano* coachman. And old Marsida, who tries to make a few *centavos* to buy medicine for her ailing daughter from that evil old apothecary, Barnaba Canepa, offered to sell her some of the mountain flowers she had just picked. This *puta* laughed at her and took the flowers and flung them into the dust and then told the coachman, 'Drive on, and do not stop for beggars again, or the *alcalde mayor* will have you whipped!' Is this what we have come to after these good years when we were treated like men by Don Sancho and by his good friend, the *intendente,* Don Diego?"

"Rocaldi, all of this is because times are changing," Ticumbe gravely replied. "Ever since the *mejicanos* declared their freedom from Spain, this land of Nuevo México has been left to itself. And if it had not been for Don Sancho and Don Diego, the *ricos* would have ruled and driven us out of our village long ago. We are many and they are few, and yet they see to it that we are kept poor, that we have no weapons to defend ourselves. And the *hacendados* steal our daughters to make them *putas* and *criadas*. And now, because we have this new *alcalde mayor* who begins by taxing us on our work, we come upon evil days in Taos. But I tell you, my brothers, it will do no good to fight against the tax. The *gubernador* would send soldiers, and he would call upon the provinces near Santa Fe to cross the Rio Grande and to come destroy us. There is no hope for it. We must make do as best we can."

There was a heavy silence as the elders listened to Ticumbe's gloomy words. Yet they knew in their hearts that they had no recourse. Surely not when this new greedy *alcalde mayor* was a friend of the *gubernador* himself.

Near the end of summer, with snow capping the towering peaks of the Sangre de Cristo Mountains, the newly appointed *alcalde mayor*, Alonzo Cienguarda, had indeed demonstrated his intention of being a virtual feudal overlord in Taos.

Not content with levying a tax of a *peso* per month on every male and female inhabitant of the pueblo village who sold wares or services, he had now decreed that he believed it necessary to establish a local militia for the protection of the citizens throughout the environs and the town proper. He had speciously argued that, in view of the far-distant separation of Mexico City from its subsidiary provinces, Taos could expect no civil or military support from the Mexican government. Though he paid a hypocritical tribute to the creation of a democratic republic for what had been Nueva España, and was now Mexico, Cienguarda declared that, in his opinion, there was no guarantee of longevity for such a government and that, in any case, the affairs of Nuevo México would be totally disregarded.

Accordingly, he had sent to the city of San Luis Potosí for a longtime friend of his, a certain Ferdinand Mondago, to take the post of *jefe de policiá* at a salary of two thousand *pesos* per year. In order to meet this annual expenditure, as well as to provide funds for the maintenance of a local militia, he decreed that every *hacendado* in Taos should contribute the sum of a hundred *pesos* every six months, and since the *indios* of the pueblo would also benefit from the protection that his newly appointed head of the civil guard would provide for them, an additional tax of fifty *centavos* per month was to be imposed on every pueblo dweller, including children. Thus, if an *indio* household consisted of a husband and a wife and six children, the husband, as head of that household, would be required to pay four *pesos* a month. Alonzo Cienguarda appointed his own majordomo to the post of collector of tithes, benevolently explaining that since the majordomo was in his own employ, he would charge the people of Taos not a single *centavo* for the majordomo's services.

This majordomo was one Armando Díaz, a fat, indolent man in his mid-forties, who had worked on his employer's estate during the fatal illness of Cienguarda's wife. He was a complacent man who wanted nothing more in the world than security and physical comforts, and although he guessed that his master might well have been responsible for his wife's untimely death, he preferred to ignore what he had seen and heard. For this, Alonzo Cienguarda had doubled his wages.

Last Sunday, the new *alcalde mayor* of Taos, and his paramour, Luisita Delago, had appeared in the church of Padre Salvador Madura to have their banns publicly announced, with their wedding day to be exactly three weeks from that day.

Sanctimoniously, Alonzo Cienguarda had bestowed upon Padre Madura a handsome donation of five hundred *pesos*, saying, "It is for your poor, *mi padre*." And there were those who, upon learning of this act, looked at one another and whispered, "Truly this is a generous, good man, who will be caring about the people of Taos, as if they were his own kin."

There were many others, however, who did not believe this and who, indeed, were fearful . . .

On the very morning that marked the day that John Cooper Baines and Miguel Sandarbal and their thirty *vaqueros* began the arduous cattle drive to New Orleans, the beautiful *mestiza*, Noracia, was breakfasting with Alejandro Cabeza. Lovely young Manuela was serving them, having resigned herself to playing only a minor role as the *confi-*

dante of her imperious and mercurial mistress. For on that never-to-be forgotten night when Noracia had her *trabajadores* kidnap Alejandro by force and bring him to her *hacienda,* she had compelled the dissipated, penniless *hacendado* to accept luxury under her yoke. She had come to a tacit understanding with this handsome roué, and they had joined forces. He was in servitude to her, but in truth, after having followed her orders and dismissed his pandering majordomo, Ernesto Rojas, he was quite content with the bargain he had made. When it pleased her, she accorded him greater carnal pleasure than any of his most attractive and compliant *criadas* had ever given him; she provided him with fine clothing and many luxurious little gifts, and she had even granted him a monthly allowance out of the growing profits from her shop and from the importation of luxurious merchandise sent on from Mexico City, Chihuahua, and New Orleans.

She had even playfully intimated to him this morning, as they breakfasted on roast chicken and rich hot chocolate, diligently served by Manuela, that if he continued to please her in this way, she might deign to marry him. "Do not look so unhappy, Alejandro," she twitted him. "Be realistic enough to know your situation in life and to make the most of it, as I have always done. A word from me, and my servants will throw you out into the street. You will be penniless, your creditors will descend upon you like locusts, and no sensible and eligible young woman from any of these aristocratic families of Taos will have anything to do with you. Continue to please me as you have done so far, and you and I can take power away from this ambitious scoundrel of a Cienguarda. I have heard that he is about to marry his slut. And you and I have both heard about the taxes he is now imposing, which will hurt the poor *indios.* Even if I did not have you here to be my ally, Alejandro, I would fight Cienguarda for impoverishing my people—for such they are. What I propose is this: we shall go on paying back to the *indios* all the money that our greedy *alcalde mayor* takes from them with his ridiculous taxes. But you will see, we shall raise our own little army, and it will be stronger than this civil guard, as Cienguarda calls it."

"My dear Noracia, I've already begun to admire your quick mind and your grasp of things," Cabeza chuckled as he reached across the table to squeeze her hand. Manuela, about to pour more chocolate into their cups, saw this amorous gesture and turned her face away, making an unhappy grimace, which her mistress, fortunately for her, did not see. "I have come to realize that even though you are not of aristocratic birth, you assuredly have more intelligence than the empty-headed pretty young daughters of *hacendados* whom I used to court. Very well, then, I'll agree to marry you."

"You won't be sorry, Alejandro," Noracia said smiling, and sent him a sultry look from beneath lowering lashes. Once again, Manuela made a wry face and busied herself with tidying up the room, while waiting for new orders. Thus far, what she feared most had not happened: the dissolute *hacendado* had not been permitted to demonstrate any amorous interest in her, for when she had tearfully besought Noracia not to let Alejandro Cabeza possess her, the *mestiza* had laughed softly, patted her cheek, and murmured, "Never fear, little one; he's all mine. He's my slave, and I don't propose to share him with anyone, not even you. But since he pleases me so far and is quite *macho* in bed, I hope you will understand that I cannot summon you quite so often as in the past. But I shan't forget you, little one, and we are still the dearest of friends, remember that."

Noracia finished her chocolate and beckoned to Manuela to fill her cup again. "Alejandro," she murmured, "you and I will go this afternoon to the pueblo village, and we will ask Ticumbe, who is the leader of all of those *indios*, to let us speak to his people. I propose to offer posts as servants in my household to the strongest young men of the village. But in reality—and don't look at me that way, you've no reason to be jealous!—they will become my own civil guard. With the *indios* on our side and with their ablest young men here in my household, we shall have nothing to fear of Cienguarda."

"That's a brilliant idea, Noracia," he enthusiastically commended her. "The Indians will know who their real friends are, and if this *alcalde mayor* tries to interfere with us, we shall be much stronger than he is when it comes to a showdown."

"Now that is the way I like to hear you talk, Alejandro," Noracia purred as she came to nestle in his lap and to link a satiny arm around his neck, lean forward, and give him a stinging kiss on the mouth. And the unhappy young Manuela, seeing this once again, suddenly turned away and closed her eyes, which had begun to fill with jealous tears. "You see, Alejandro, what happens when you use your mind to think of something besides *criadas* and *putas*? You will really become indispensable to me, *amigo*. And now, go to your room and bathe and trim your beard, and dress in your finest. We shall visit the pueblo this afternoon."

"Fra Ignazio, I wish to join your order," Padre Salvador Madura said softly as the leader of the *Penitentes* rose from his knees after making confession in the booth. Through the cloth that separated them, these words had come with conviction and fervor, and Ignazio Peramonte's eyes widened. Taken by surprise, he stammered, "We must talk of this alone and in your rectory, not while you preside here as *padre*."

"Come then to the rectory and break bread with me, Fra Ignazio. I am troubled with myself, for a week from this very day I must unite in marriage the *alcalde mayor* and the woman who has already made herself detested in Taos for her contempt of the poor and the *indios*."

A little later, having doffed his cassock and the robe he had worn during the celebration of the mass, Padre Madura and the tall gaunt head of *Los Penitentes* sat at the table in the rectory. Dalcaria brought them bread and some dry wine and a little broth, and then, crossing herself and inclining her head respectfully to each of them, left the room.

"You know what you are asking, Padre Madura?"

"Yes. I know it will involve physical suffering for the initiation."

"Justly so. But you must do this of your own free will, and you must have a sponsor. I will sponsor you gladly, but I wonder if you are ready for the penance."

"If in my own humble way I can suffer and thus understand His martyrdom for the remission of our sins upon this earth, I may better understand my priesthood," Padre Madura responded.

"That is a good answer, *mi hermano en Cristo*. Very well, then. Here is what will be done. Think well of it, and if when I have finished, it seems repugnant to you, we shall not speak of it again." So saying, he leaned forward over the table and spoke in a low voice. And when he had finished a long time later, Padre Madura stared at him and, with a smile on his lips, murmured, "I am willing and eager for it; I swear it on the cross on which our Lord was crucified."

Thus on the next Friday night, after fasting all day, Padre Salvador Madura mounted his burro and rode out toward the Sangre de Cristo range. When he neared the base of the mountains, he saw a hut, and knew it to be the *morada* of the *Penitentes*. He dismounted and approached, making the sign of the cross. Then, looking up at the white-capped mountains, he prayed silently a moment before knocking three times. And then he asked in a loud voice that showed no sign of faltering. "*¿Quién vive en esta casa da luz?*"

From the inside, a resonant voice replied, "Jesus."

"*¿Quién la llena de alegría?*"

Again from the inside came the response, "María."

Next, Padre Madura asked, "*¿Quién la conserva en la fé?*"

"José," was the answer from inside. And thus this invocation of the Christ, the Virgin Mary, and her husband, Joseph, signified that the *morada* was a kind of holy dwelling place, a place of life and not of death.

The door opened, and Fra Ignazio beckoned for Padre Madura to enter. There was a table, and seated on a long bench were members of *Los Penitentes*, who wore black *capuchas* to denote humility.

The head of the order turned to the hooded witnesses and intoned, "Here comes a novice to take his vows. He is humble and willing to be instructed."

As a chorus, the hooded men responded, "So let it be shown unto us and to our Father Jesus."

Fra Ignazio Peramonte nodded, and Padre Madura removed all his clothes, then donned a pair of white *calzones*, the symbol of the novice-penitent. Kneeling, he recited a creed, and repeating the words spoken by the leader of the order, he swore an undying oath of allegiance.

"It is time for the seal of obligation," Fra Peramonte observed. He took a piece of flint and laid it on the edge of the table as Padre Madura continued to kneel. Then, in his role as *sangrador*, he began to massage Padre Madura's back with the palm of his hands, numbing the muscles on both sides of the spine. This done, he lifted the razor-edged piece of flint and made three surface cuts into the flesh, lengthwise on each side.

Padre Madura sustained this without even a grimace, closing his eyes and praying silently. When he opened his eyes, he saw the stern face of Fra Peramonte confronting him, and remembered what he must do. "I ask humbly for lashes equal to the three meditations on the Passion of Jesus, the five wounds of *Cristo*, the seven last words, and the forty days in the wilderness. For the love of God, I ask humbly that they be given me."

Fra Peramonte gravely nodded. Then, from the table, he lifted a short whip made of sizal and slowly applied fifty-five strokes to Padre Madura's naked back. The wounds left by the seal of obligation assured a free flow of blood so that the scourging would not cause lasting welts and bruises. Padre Madura closed his eyes at the beginning, sucked in his breath at the first strokes, and then, as the whipping progressed, opened his eyes to fix them on the hooded men at the table, while his lips moved in prayer and he clasped his hands tightly together. "For the love of God, harder," he groaned at the fiftieth lash.

It was done. Shuddering, his eyes now closed, his face damp with sweat, Padre Salvador Madura had endured the rigorous initiation of *Los Penitentes*. There was a murmur of approbation from the hooded brothers at the tribunal table. Fra Peramonte turned to them: "Shall we accept this penitent?"

"For the love of God, he is truly *un hermano*, worthy of the mysteries. He has courage and devotion," came a voice from the other end of the table.

"It is done, Padre Madura. I am proud to have been your sponsor. Wait now, the *coadjutores*, those who are now your brothers, will help me wash your back with silver-sage tea, which acts as an astringent so that you will not have ugly sores from the penance."

"I am grateful to my brothers, for the love of God." Padre Madura's voice trembled, but now he opened his eyes and, with a joyous smile, stared at the black-hooded men at the tribunal table.

"We do not ask you to drag the cross, for what you have done already shows great humility and love of God and of the people you serve, Padre Madura," Fra Peramonte observed. "Each of us, at many times during the year, during Lent and on holy days, asks one or another of his *hermanos de nuestro Padre Jesus* to scourge him. We do this in obedience to the authority of tradition, in which there is no room for secular compromise or false principles. We believe that our mortification is a total surrender, a self-sacrifice that helps us fulfill our duties both as citizens of a community, and as the children of our blessed Lord."

"And this I understand with all my heart and soul," Padre Madura murmured.

Two of the brothers held him now to support him on his knees, while Fra Peramonte sponged his back with the astringent liquid. He sucked in his breath and ground his teeth, but let no sound of suffering escape him, except heavy breathing. And again there were murmurs of approbation from the brotherhood.

In this *morada*, with its spotless, whitewashed walls, its clean, packed-earth floors, and its white lace curtains, there was an aura of intimate domesticity and communal brotherhood. Fra Peramonte said to Padre Madura, who was now being helped to the bench beside his brothers—for now he was one of them—"When we come again, each of us will knock upon the door and from inside the brothers will ask, 'Who knocketh upon the doors of this *morada*?' and from the outside we others will answer, 'These are not the doors of the *morada*, only the doors of your conscience.' Thus you understand our rituals, serving God with humility and serving man also that he may follow in the teachings of our dear Father, Jesus Christ."

"It is a beautiful symbol, Fra Ignazio. I am grateful to you and to all of you, my new brothers, for having accepted me as one of you. I shall not forget my oath of allegiance."

"We knew this long before you asked me at the confessional to become one of us, Padre Madura," Fra Peramonte said, his voice gentle. "And now there is the business of the world, and not of the spirit, which we must discuss. If we have said that we knock upon the doors of our own conscience, it is even more true today than it was in the earlier days of Taos. Now we have among us a ruthless, greedy, and evil man as *alcalde mayor*, who taxes the *indios* beyond reason, and then boasts that he will create a civil guard to protect us all. It will be a kind of private army, I tell you, and it will be used to enforce the cruelties and the plundering of which I know this man to be capable. To this end, my brothers, we must think wisely and plan with caution. If he will use force and wealth, we must use prayer and our own vigilance."

Fra Peramonte turned to Padre Madura: "You are to marry this man in your church. He cannot be denied the privileges of the faith until he is excommunicated. And yet, you should somehow let him know that the people he has been sent to govern are terrified of his power and his greed and his contempt."

"I can preach that in my sermon before the marriage ceremony," Padre Madura replied.

"Good! He will probably not heed it, but it will serve as a warning, a warning that we, who are vigilant in the night against all manner of evildoers, are resolved to protect the people from oppression."

A low murmur of assent came from the others. Fra Peramonte held out his hand to Padre Madura, who took and shook it. "We look to you, Padre Madura, from the pulpit of your holy church, to tell us of the inequities and the cruelties that are inflicted upon the helpless of Taos. We have sworn the oath of brotherhood, and we are brothers to all."

"I shall take the oath that I shall watch for the true light, and purge evil by blood, as is meant in our order," Padre Madura said in the ritualistic language of the *Penitentes*.

Unaware of all the intrigue going on around them in this remote, oppressed province of Taos, Doña Elena, her son and daughter-in-law, and her grandchildren, adjusted to a new life without the presence of the good and kind Don Sancho. It had been a sad reunion when Doña Elena returned home from the aborted trip to Texas, accompanied as she was, by her maids and the *trabajadores*. But in that sadness there was also the love and joy that family members were able to provide each other, knowing that even though Don Sancho would be sorely missed, they at least all had one another. And so the de Pladero sheep ranch continued to prosper, and Doña Elena enjoyed her latter years in the company of her son, his wife, and their children. She spent many happy hours reminiscing with Tomás, embroidering with

Conchita, or reading wonderful fairy tales to the children. And this warm and loving household was a bright oasis in the otherwise bleak surroundings of a corrupt and chaotic Taos.

Thirty-three

The first week of the great cattle drive to New Orleans went by without incident. By the time John Cooper, Miguel, and the *trabajadores* bedded down the lowing cattle for the night the first Saturday after they had left the Double H Ranch, they had traveled eighty miles. It was somewhat slower than John Cooper had anticipated, although he realized that the size of the herd, as well as the cumbersome, heavy wagons and the *carretas*, hampered any greater speed. They had passed the little village of Pearsall, and were within about fifteen miles of the sluggish San Antonio River.

Each night, John Cooper posted guards on four-hour shifts, for they ran the risk of encountering an armed and mounted Mexican patrol. But the nagging feeling of Francisco López's vindictive scheming was uppermost in John Cooper's mind. After the attack in the canyon, he feared that Francisco López would somehow try an even more daring and brutal assault to gain the treasure. At least there was solace in the fact that the ranch was well protected and that the silver was on its way to the bank vaults. Indeed, that was the reason John Cooper had hastened the preparations for the drive.

Young Andrew insisted on doing his own share of guard duty, and his admiring father granted him the opportunity, making sure that he was being shown absolutely no favoritism solely because he was the *patrón*'s son. In this way, none of the *vaqueros* could ever complain that Andrew had accompanied his father simply for a pleasurable outing. Moreover, the boy possessed traits that John Cooper himself admired: a wary reticence, until acceptance was cordially proffered; a dutiful and totally unselfish devotion to tasks and chores appointed; and the ability to endure hardship without self-pitying complaints. Already Andrew had shown himself to be far older than his years, which enormously pleased his father.

On this Saturday evening, before the tiny fire, John Cooper sat with his hands on his knees, watching tall, lean Andrew on duty about fifty feet away, holding his long rifle at the ready. At the sudden call of a night bird, he could see Andrew turn alertly to the direction from which the sound came, and he smiled to himself: the boy had been properly taught, and now he was beginning to think for himself. That was as it should be. Perhaps in ten more years Andrew would be ready for an important post of responsibility on the Double H Ranch. He might even replace Esteban Morales, who merited promotion to the rank of *capataz* when Miguel decided to retire to the life of a rustic gentleman and watch his children grow under the tutelage of his beloved Bess. That Miguel could die, John Cooper did not even conjecture: white haired though he was and now sixty, the *capataz* seemed indomitable, hewn out of granite, and yet with as rich a sense of humor as he had had back in Taos, to which he had come with Don Diego to begin a new life far from the intrigues of Madrid.

They crossed the San Antonio River two days later. One of the heavy Conestoga-style wagons got stuck in the mud at a shallow fording place; it took nearly two hours to drag it out. It required the efforts of six *vaqueros*, who tethered sturdy lariats to the front of the wagon, and drove their geldings to aid the foundering dray horses pulling the wagon. The situation could have been far worse, for after the wagon had been safely drawn to the eastern bank, Miguel concluded that it had actually foundered in a patch of quicksand, of which there had not been the slightest advance warning.

The cattle had watered and grazed and were already showing signs of fattening. The weather was warm and sultry, and both Miguel and John Cooper often glanced anxiously up at the sky. With so large a herd, a sudden squall or the rumble of thunder or the flash of lightning could easily cause a frenzied stampede.

It took them eight days more to reach the Colorado River at a little village called Brenham. Here the water was deeper and swollen at many points, but Jamie Cordoban, a likable young *vaquero* in his late twenties who had once worked for a Mexican rancher some miles south of this area, pointed out a shallow ford, and the lowing cattle moved through the water, driven on by the tireless *vaqueros*.

John Cooper and Miguel sat beside their campfire. Young Andrew, at his father's side, listened spellbound to Miguel's anecdotes about Madrid, when he had taught fencing and then fallen so desperately in love that his sweetheart's aunt had contemptuously arranged to send him to prison on a trumped-up charge to punish him for daring to climb so high on the social ladder. John Cooper, observing Andrew's intense interest, related some of his own adventures with the Skidi Pawnee and the Dakota Sioux, which he had not previously told his son. In the distance, they could hear one of the *vaqueros* strumming a guitar and singing a lullaby to the drowsy herd. There was a warm camaraderie among all of the *vaqueros* and Miguel, John Cooper, and his son, as they shared the drudgery and monotony and loneliness of the trail. It was, John Cooper thought, invaluable experience for young Andrew.

Four days later, they had crossed the meandering Trinity River, driven past Silsbee nearly two days after that, with only the powerful Sabine River as their last major obstacle. That was fifty miles off, and marked the boundary of Louisiana Territory. From there to New Orleans was about two hundred miles, through dreary swampy wasteland, with the ever-present danger of outlaws and bushwhackers.

They found a little trading center near Silsbee and replenished their stores of flour and beans, and purchased some jerky, salt, and coffee. Where they had chosen to ford the Sabine, they had had to wait a full day until the rain-swollen water subsided. Fortunately, they had missed the brief storm that had brought a torrential deluge two days earlier.

Young Andrew had shot a deer, several jackrabbits, and a young boar, which added pleasing variety to the otherwise repititious provender of the evening meals. John Cooper critically observed his son, showing him how to allow for wind and to estimate distance, using the rifle sight to its maximum efficiency. The memory came back to him of how his father had once told him that it would be a good many years before he would be capable of using a rifle like "Long Girl," and Andrew was delighted that his father had changed his mind.

Even now, eighteen years later, "Long Girl" was as reliable a firearm as John Cooper had found. In Taos, he had bought several new Belgian rifles, but "Long Girl" could not be surpassed for distance and for accuracy. He saw to it that it was always oiled and cleaned, and he had shown Andrew how to care for his own rifle. "Maybe you'll fret a bit when you're polishing the stock or cleaning out the barrel, boy," he had told his son. "But then again, when you get into a tight fix, you'll be mighty grateful you took enough pains to make sure it'll work when it has to save your life. Don't ever forget that. But I'll give you this, boy; you've shown you can shoot much better at your age with that rifle I got you than I could with a musket when I was the same age. I'm proud of you, Andy."

"Thanks, Pa," Andrew Baines had murmured and looked quickly away. All these years, even as a very little boy, Andrew had secretly studied his father, deeply respected, and admired him, and he understood that the praise John Cooper had just given him was the highest he could expect from him.

The day after they crossed the Sabine and headed the herd in the direction of New Orleans, Miguel and John Cooper reined in their horses just before sundown and stared up at the sky. There was an unnatural haze around the setting sun, and the air was oppressively still. From the southeast, they could just make out the sight of dark storm clouds moving toward them.

"I don't like the looks of that, Miguel," John Cooper muttered. "It appears like we're in for a real squall. We'd better get the cattle bedded down in as sheltered a place as we can find with lots of trees, and hold on tight."

"You're right, *patrón*," Miguel solemnly agreed. "So far we've been very lucky, and I've said my prayers every night to thank *El Señor Dios* for such an easy journey. I'll go tell the *vaqueros* to get the cattle settled as quickly as they can before that storm is on us."

"Good idea," John Cooper said, frowning as he glanced

up at the sky again. "We might need more than the usual guards tonight, Miguel."

They had chosen as the campsite this evening a stretch of elevated ground framed by copses of scrub and live-oak trees. It was as good protection as they could hope for in this desolate country, and the *vaqueros* worked diligently to earn their supper by making certain that the cattle were bedded down. They had grazed abundantly and had water when they crossed the Sabine and, a little farther on, more water from a freshwater creek.

Now the men relaxed from their labors, looking forward to the evening meal, when they would relate anecdotes around the campfires, and listen to the love songs the young *vaquero* strummed on his guitar.

They had just begun to eat when suddenly John Cooper looked up and scowled. "Listen, Miguel," he muttered under his breath. The *capataz* was chewing on a biscuit prepared by the cook, an overworked forty-year-old Mexican named Roberto Pasanara. Turning his head, Miguel swallowed the rest of the biscuit and shook his head. "I don't like the looks of that at all, *patrón*. There's going to be trouble; I feel it in my bones."

"First the stillness, and then from that distance in the southeast, a kind of—well, it sounds like whistling and moaning, if there's such a thing."

"Once," Miguel reflected, "I was in the Mediterranean when I was a very young boy; my father took me on a vacation to the islands where we might enjoy the sun. And there was what they call a *sirocco,* a tempest which made the water very dangerous. I remember hugging my father's leg and crying and praying to *El Señor Dios* to put an end to it, to save us both."

"I can't imagine you crying, Miguel," John Cooper playfully teased him.

"Laugh all you want, *patrón,* but I was only about six, and I had never been in such a storm. But this sounds as if it might be the *sirocco.* I think that in the Estados Unidos it is called a tornado, and I tell you now that I am worried."

John Cooper sprang to his feet as the curious sound grew louder. In this eerie darkness, illumined by the flickering of the campfires, it seemed to him that far to the southeast he could hear the grass, the trees, even the sky moving. And now, to increase his anxiety, he could hear the herd stirring restlessly.

"It's a real storm—whatever it's called, Miguel—and we're in for trouble!" he hoarsely exclaimed. Then, cupping his hands to his mouth, he called, "*Vaqueros*, be alert; a storm is coming; look to the cattle!"

He strained his eyes to see what he could in this unearthly darkness, and the howling sound was stronger now, and then he uttered an astonished cry, for it seemed to him there was a giant black cloud—not in the sky, but in the air and headed directly for their camp. "Is it a tornado, Miguel?" he demanded. "I've heard of them but never seen them before."

"It is, *patrón*!" Miguel shouted, for that was the only way he could be heard over the sound of the wind. "It is a tornado! I have been told that wind like this can lift a ship from the ocean and fling it onto the rocks. And here, it can take a house and uproot it—I pray *El Señor Dios* this same storm is nowhere near the *hacienda*!"

"So do I, amen to that!" John Cooper was also shouting. Then he turned to his son, "Get down low, Andrew, flat on your belly on the ground! It's going to hit us—look out, it's coming—"

Now the droning and whistling sound had combined into an almost ghastly screeching, as the cloud seemed to envelop them, and in an instant there was panic.

The herd began to bellow and to run off in all directions, crashing through the smaller trees and felling them in their heedless path. There was a sudden crash as the wagons were overturned, and the fires were extinguished, as if a giant thumb had pressed down upon them and blotted them out, without leaving even an ember.

Young Andrew had stretched out beside his father and Miguel, imitating them by placing his arms over his head. John Cooper was suddenly jostled, lunging and rolling over his son, and then, as quickly as it had come upon them, the ominous black funnellike cloud swept beyond. Dazed, blinking his eyes, John Cooper stared after it. Trees were torn from the earth and whirled about in the air, in a kind of dervishlike movement.

And then suddenly there was the rumble of thunder and the downpour of warm rain beating into the earth.

"Are you all right, boy?" he panted.

"S-sure, P-Pa. That was sure something! I never in all my days saw anything like that!" Andrew's voice was awed.

"Then we're even, because I didn't either!" John Cooper smiled wryly. "But we're alive. Let's be grateful for that." Then he turned to Miguel, who was slowly rising from the ground: "I'm half afraid to see what the reckoning is, *capataz*."

"The herd has stampeded. I hope none of the *vaqueros* was hurt." Then Miguel bawled out, "*¡Vaqueros, vengan aquí!*"

As some of the *vaqueros* came toward him, tottering, dazed, and pale from the fright that the hurtling storm had so swiftly evoked, Miguel called, "You, Roberto, is everyone all right?"

"*Patrón,* José Echániz—may God rest his soul—he's dead," the *vaquero* said in a muffled voice, and rubbed his eyes with the back of his hand. "His neck is broken—one of the wagons tipped over on him—"

"Light some campfires, if we can now that the rain has suddenly stopped," John Cooper directed. "Andrew, go see if you can be of any help to the *vaqueros!*"

Miguel managed to improvise a torch, by dint of winding a strip of dry cloth from one of the wagons around a broken branch and, striking tinder into the wood shavings and dry leaves in his tinderbox, kindled it. As he lifted it, he uttered a cry of disbelief: six of the wagons had overturned, and he could see some of the silver ingots strewn on the ground. Or the four thousand cattle, not a one was in sight. Two of the *vaqueros* lay on the ground, their faces bloodied, but one of their comrades, kneeling over them, hoarsely assured Miguel that they were not seriously hurt.

"We'll have to go after those *ganado,*" Miguel told the men. "That's the first order."

"I'll see that you have a bonus added to your wages, *amigos,*" John Cooper called to them. "And we'll have some good food and hot coffee ready as soon as you come back."

"Let me go help round the cattle up, Pa," Andrew volunteered as he ran up to his father and Miguel.

"Not on your life, boy!" John Cooper said turning to him, his face stern. "You're not experienced enough to ride alongside stampeding cattle. You stay here, boy, and make yourself useful. If you want to, you can start heating up some coffee. The men will be coming back in shifts, depending on how far away the cattle have gone by now."

"I'll do it, Pa," Andrew promised.

Miguel gloomily shook his head. "He was a fine man, that Echániz. This will delay us by at least a week, *patrón*. We'll have to repack the silver, and of course there's the matter of rounding up all the cattle. Four thousand of them, scampering off to the four corners of the earth—"

"Echániz was indeed a fine worker and loyal and kind. I'd willingly give up a wagonful of silver to have him still alive. Come, Miguel, we'll bury him—the *vaqueros* can't do it, not after riding after the cattle all night. Come along. I can remember enough of the words to pray over him."

Miguel and John Cooper walked wearily over to the wagon which six of the *vaqueros* had righted, and Miguel crossed himself at the sight of the dead *vaquero*. John Cooper reached into the wagon for a shovel and began to dig a grave.

When it was finished, he and Miguel gently lifted the *vaquero*'s body into the grave, and then John Cooper covered it with earth. "See if you can break off some wood that isn't too wet, and I'll make a cross as a marker, Miguel," he softly proposed.

Taking a strip of cloth, he bound two pieces of wood securely and thrust the cross into the moist ground at the head of the grave. Then, kneeling, he prayed aloud, "Almighty Father, receive the soul of José Echániz. He was a loyal man, with no enemies, and a host of friends. May he be with You among the angels. Rest his soul; he had no time to shrive his sins. Receive him, Merciful Father, and grant him eternal salvation and the hope of resurrection on the Day of Judgment. Amen."

Then he crossed himself and rose, and Miguel emulated him.

From afar, they could hear the shouts of some of the *vaqueros*. "Perhaps the cattle haven't spread too far," Miguel hopefully proposed.

"For the men's sake, I hope so with all my heart. Andrew, I think we can use a cup of coffee, as strong and as hot as you can get it." He turned to look at the white-haired *capataz*. "Andrew's seen death now, and this rounds out the molding of a man. I wish he hadn't, but I'm proud of him, Miguel."

"As you have every right to be, *Halcón*. One day, he'll soar as you did." Miguel smiled admiringly at John Cooper, then turned to take the mug from the boy's hand. "*Gracias*, young master! Ah, there's nothing like good, strong coffee to revive an old man's spirit!"

It took five days to reassemble the herd, and when the tally was made by Miguel, the *capataz* announced, "We have lost sixty-two head, and from all reports, they've crossed the Rio Grande."

"We've lost a fine *vaquero* and sixty-two head," John Cooper soberly corrected. "And I wish it had been a thousand head if only we had him riding back with us. But now, *vámanos* to New Orleans!"

As if nature itself sought to recompense the *vaqueros* and Miguel and John and young Andrew for the frightful, unexpected obstacle it had put in their path, the weather now remained sunny and hot, without the slightest trace of a storm. The lowing cattle moved docilely to the *vaqueros'* orders, and the heavy Conestoga-style wagons lumbered onward, leaving deep ruts in the earth. There still was no sign of any Mexican patrol all the rest of the way.

On the eleventh of October, they came to the outskirts of New Orleans, and the *vaqueros* hoisted their *sombreros* and let out an exultant cheer. It had been a heroic trek, and now it was over. John Cooper himself exhaled a sigh of relief at the thought that this incredible fortune, which fate had unexpectedly put into his possession, would soon be safe from thieves, including Colonel Francisco López.

As they rode down the muddy street through the center of New Orleans and on to the riverfront stockades, young Andrew Baines was goggle-eyed. It took the better part of a day to transfer the shuffling, snorting Texas longhorns into the stockades. From there, they would be loaded into cattle boats bound for the West Indies and the East Coast.

Armed with his receipt, John Cooper walked down the long dock to find the office of his factor, Fabien Mallard. The elegantly dressed, mustachioed and bearded Creole, a week away from his fortieth birthday, was just about to close his office for the day as the tall American in his buckskins sauntered toward it. The two men shook hands energetically.

"I'm glad I caught you, M'sieu Mallard," John Cooper genially exclaimed. "Here's the receipt for nearly four thousand cattle, penned up and ready for shipment. It's for you to sell them for me."

"It comes at a very good time, M'sieu Baines," the Creole factor graciously declared. "I think by tomorrow I can dispose of them for about twelve thousand American dollars. That, of course, will be net to you, the rest being my commission."

"I'll take it, without any argument or haggling, M'sieu Mallard."

"And as Señor Cobrara in San Antonio requested in your behalf, I have reserved some short-horned pedigreed bulls for you from the East. They'll be here next spring."

"And I should be back in New Orleans then to get them, if all goes well," John Cooper replied. "Well, now I'm going to get my men tucked down for the night, get them a good meal and some whiskey, and I'll be back tomorrow. I've another piece of business to transact at the Banque de la Nouvelle Orléans."

"That's right, you've your account there. How would it be, M'sieu Baines, if I met you there tomorrow afternoon and brought over a draft, which you can deposit at once? That would save you time."

"That's most thoughtful of you, M'sieu Mallard. And then I'll buy you your supper at the best restaurant in all New Orleans."

"And I am gourmet enough to take you at your word, M'sieu Baines. Till tomorrow, then. Will four o'clock be satisfactory for you?"

"Couldn't be better." John Cooper looked around the dock. "This is quite a harbor. I was just thinking of the old Ohio River in the days when I was a boy growing up. If we saw a couple of pirogues and maybe an old flatboat every couple of weeks, we thought we had a harbor."

"New Orleans will soon be one of the greatest ports in all of these beautiful États-Unis," Fabien Mallard enthusiastically avowed as they shook hands again.

"Good Lord, I almost forgot, M'sieu Mallard, about the church bell I ordered from Belgium."

"Ah, *oui*, I, too, had forgotten—but it's here already, M'sieu Baines!" the factor said beaming. "I've already transferred it to my warehouse, and you may pick it up whenever it is convenient for you."

"Fine! I brought along some *carretas*, and we'll go to your warehouse, secure the bell to them with all the heavy rope we can, and take it back to the ranch when we leave. Oh, yes! Señor Cobrara also asked you to find dress materials for the women at the ranch, isn't that correct?"

"Yes, M'sieu Baines, and I have a very nice selection indeed."

John Cooper offered his hand. "That's excellent. So I'll see you tomorrow then. *Au revoir*, M'sieu Mallard!"

John Cooper, his son Andrew, and Miguel had taken a suite of rooms at the City Exchange. At a newly constructed villa about two blocks away, the hidden silver had been stored, at the suggestion of the affable Creole manager. Four of the *vaqueros* stood armed guard through the night. John Cooper awoke at dawn, realizing that he was within a few hours of accomplishing the long-planned and difficult mission of transporting the secret silver hoard out of the mysterious mountain, all the way to Texas, and thence to New Orleans and ultimate security.

When they had reached the outskirts of New Orleans the previous day, he had stopped the drive long enough to have the *vaqueros* transfer all the silver into a single wagon. All the wagons were now in the carriage house of the newly built villa. But John Cooper was understandably restless, fearing that during the night someone might break in and discover the wagons.

Happily, his fears proved groundless. After a hasty breakfast with Miguel and his son, he walked over to the villa and found the *vaqueros* standing armed guard over the wagon that contained the fortune for which Santa Anna was willing to sell his very soul to the devil, and for which the cunning opportunist, Francisco López, was willing to betray his superior officer and make it a terrible power for evil and corruption.

The bank would not open until ten o'clock in the morning, and so John Cooper, Miguel, and Andrew waited in the courtyard of the villa, chatting with the *vaqueros* and planning their return to the Double H Ranch.

"We'll go back by a different route this time," John Cooper declared. "We'll stop by Eugene Fair's new settlement, and maybe we'll be lucky and find the *empresario* himself there. One day, that settlement will be a kind of addition to our own security; the people there can make Texas strong against Santa Anna's bullies."

Thus far, everything had gone off without a hitch, and John Cooper glanced up at the sky and murmured a silent prayer of gratitude. Now his loyal Jicarilla friends would no longer be constrained to guard the mysterious mountain. The silver would repose in the vault of the bank, to benefit the poor of Taos and the hardworking settlers who had come to fortify the Double H Ranch. Some would be kept in reserve for the Jicarilla Apache, and some of it would be used, of course, to buy weapons for the defense of the great ranch and comforts for the wives of the *trabajadores* and *vaqueros*, as well as for Don Diego and Doña Inez, Miguel and his Bess and their children. But mostly, this fortune would grow in value over the years and be judiciously administered.

All of them rode in the wagon to La Banque de la Nouvelle Orléans, and John Cooper and his son strode into the bank where its president, Eduard Beaubien, saw them from his office and came out to welcome them.

"It's good to see you, M'sieu Beaubien. I think you know why I'm here—we talked about my plan to bring bars of silver from the mine I found some years ago. They're outside in the wagon, and I'd like to put them into your vault."

"I'm honored that you've chosen my institution, M'sieu Baines. I'll have several of my clerks assist your men in putting the bars where they'll be quite secure. Since the last time you put several on deposit here, I've purchased an accurate scale. And because I know exactly what the current price of silver is, I can enter in your account not just so many bars of silver, but also the weight and the current market value. Thus your receipt will show to the penny what you are depositing today."

"That's very systematic, M'sieu Beaubien. I'll be glad to have your men assist mine."

"And this must be your oldest son, Andrew? He's tall and strong—"

"And almost twelve years old," John Cooper proudly broke in, as he put an arm around his son's shoulders. "He's learned a lot on the trail, and one day he'll be a better shot and tracker than I ever was."

"Oh, no, Pa," the boy flushed self-consciously, "I could never be that good! But if I'm only half as good as you, I'll sure be satisfied!"

The banker and John Cooper burst into affectionate laughter, as Eduard Beaubien solemnly shook hands with the wiry boy. Then the banker summoned three clerks to help move the silver ingots down to the vault.

A little over an hour later, the transaction was completed. John Cooper looked at the receipt, which stipulated that on this day of October in the year 1825, he had deposited with La Banque de la Nouvelle Orléans, the sum of $196,875 in silver at current market value.

"I'd now like to withdraw ten thousand dollars of that amount in silver pesos," John Cooper said, for as soon as he returned to Texas he meant to give the money to the people of Taos and to the Jicarilla. "I'm also going to meet my factor here later today, M'sieu Beaubien," John Cooper continued, "and I'll have a draft for the sale of the cattle I brought here yesterday. I'll deposit about half of that and take the rest in cash to pay off my *vaqueros* and to buy a few things I'll need for the ranch."

"I shall be at your service. If you like, I can arrange to be here until six this evening."

"Oh, no, I'll be here well before that," John Cooper smilingly promised as he shook hands with the affable banker; Andrew imitated his father.

Miguel, John Cooper, and Andrew spent the next several hours visiting cafés and shops in the city, buying little gifts to surprise their families. The men bought lovely silver grooming sets for their wives, as well as for Doña Elena in Taos; and John Cooper also decided to surprise Carlos with a fine new hunting knife made of the highest-quality Spanish steel. John Cooper also bought some new rifles and ammunition as well as hunting knives to give as presents to the Jicarilla, and he did not forget his promise to Teresa to purchase new foils and a mask. In addition, he bought large quantities of powder and lead, for they made their own bullets at the Double H Ranch, and he purchased new muskets for the *trabajadores* and *vaqueros*. Finally, he bought tobacco to give both to his workmen and to the Indians, many books for the school, and new oil lamps; and for the loyal cook Tía Margarita, he saw to it that they stocked up on spices, coffee, and chocolate.

At four that afternoon they returned to meet Fabien Mallard. The genial Creole smilingly handed John Cooper a draft in the amount of twelve thousand American dollars. This done, he eagerly remarked, "You know, M'sieu Baines, if you have any palominos to sell, I can get you a fine price for them. There are many Creoles who race horses in this city and wager large sums of money. To have a palomino, one of the finest breeds in all the world, and invariably a swift racer, would be a mark of great social success for such gamblers."

"I hadn't thought of selling any of my palominos, M'sieu Mallard. But perhaps next year I might be able to spare you one or two."

"I'd look upon that as a real favor, M'sieu Baines. Will you be staying long in New Orleans?"

"Probably just another day, M'sieu Mallard. I want to get back to the ranch as fast as I can, because for one thing, my wife's expecting a baby. I almost missed being on hand for Andrew's coming into this world"—he turned to his sturdy young son and gave him a playful nudge in the ribs— "and if I had, I'd have never heard the last of it, you can bet your boots on that." They all laughed at this, and then John Cooper said, "Before I start off tomorrow afternoon, I'll bring the carts down to your warehouse, load up the bell, and pick up the dress materials."

"I'll have some stevedores help your men."

"I'm much obliged to you for everything. And thanks again for the bank draft." John Cooper shook hands with the factor, then arranged to meet him that evening at Le Poulet Rouge, a fine Creole restaurant. After Fabien Mallard left the bank, John Cooper deposited the draft, drawing out about half the money in greenbacks, a large portion of which he handed to Miguel: "You'll pay the men, and you'll give them bonuses for the work they did on that stampede. And when I get back to the ranch, I want to send poor José Echániz's folks some money—he earned it, and I want them to have a little extra to help them get along."

"That's good of you, *patrón*," Miguel murmured.

The *vaqueros* were quartered in a large inn about a mile away from the City Exchange, and that evening John Cooper and Miguel and Andrew called for them to take them to supper at Le Poulet Rouge. Fabien Mallard was there already to join them in this celebratory feast.

At a table nearby, there sat a tall, pleasant-featured man in his late twenties, who eyed John Cooper repeatedly through the supper. The tall ranch man, in his buckskins, with the Spanish dagger hanging in its sheath around his neck, had been the cynosure of all eyes wherever he went in the Queen City.

Finally, the stranger, catching John Cooper's eye, apologetically said, "I hope you don't take offense to my staring at you, mister. But that knife of yours fair interests me. My name's Jim Bowie."

"Glad to meet you, Mr. Bowie. I'm John Cooper Baines, and this is Miguel Sandarbal, the *capataz* of my Texas ranch, and this is my firstborn, Andrew."

"A fine-looking lad, takes after his father for a fact," Jim Bowie said, nodding an acknowledgment to young Andrew. "You mentioned Texas, did you?"

"Yes, I've a spread near the Frio River," John Cooper replied.

"You know, I'm from Tennessee myself, and I'm living at Bayou Boeuf in the Louisiana Territory. But I've got a hankering to see what Texas is like and have wanted to go there ever since I heard about Moses and Stephen Austin. Seems they're opening up settlements there with the approval of the Mexican government."

"That's correct, Mr. Bowie."

"Call me Jim. My friends do. Anyway, one of these days, the way I see it, we're going to have trouble with Mexico. Real trouble. That's why I'm thinking about Texas, because it's a stepping-off point, and if we could get enough settlers there, we could take it into the United States and fend off anything the Mexicans had to give us by way of protest."

"I share your view, Jim. You said you were interested in my Spanish dagger. Well, it's a fine knife for throwing when you're in a fix and your gun misfires, or you're out of powder and ball."

"You know, John Cooper, I'm sort of partial to knives

myself. My brother, Rezin, and I invented one. It's called the Bowie knife in these parts. Maybe you'd like to take a look at it." From his belt, the affable, fair-haired young man drew a heavy sheath knife with a long single-edged blade, about nine inches in length, superbly fitted to a skillfully carved bone handle. He handed it handle-first to John Cooper, who balanced and hefted it, and whistled in admiration: "That's really a fine knife! Feels good to the hand."

"Tell you what, let's see how your Spanish dagger does against my knife," Jim Bowie smilingly proposed. "Loser stands the winner a drink."

"Fair enough."

"We can go to the back of the restaurant where it's not crowded. Lucien won't mind—he's a friend of mine."

John Cooper chuckled and nodded, then rose from the table. Having overheard some of the conversation, a few of the *vaqueros,* as well as Miguel and Andrew, followed him.

There was a wooden puncheon wall in the right wing of the restaurant, which had only about four or five tables in it. Jim Bowie took his stance at the back and pointed to a highly ornamental clock hanging on the wall, and turned to his companion. "I'd say this is a distance of about fifty feet, John Cooper. Let's see how close you and I can come to that peg from which the clock is hanging. Mind you, if either of us is clumsy enough to hit the clock, we'll have to pay for it, and it's an heirloom."

"I'll do my best," John Cooper smiled. "You go first."

"No, you. I know what my knife can do, but I want to see what your Spanish dagger does."

John Cooper drew the dagger from its sheath, balanced it, took careful aim, and let fly. The point of the dagger dug into the wall about an inch to the right of the round wooden peg from which the clock was suspended.

"Not bad at all. Now let's see whether my knife's up to it," Jim Bowie humorously remarked. Squinting, his blue eyes narrowed and intent on the target, he balanced the sheath knife in his hand, then suddenly flung it.

The *vaqueros* cried out with admiration: the point of the knife had buried itself exactly in the center of the wooden peg.

"Now that's the best I've ever seen done," John Cooper admitted. "You just name your poison, Jim. And I don't care if it's French champagne; it'd be worth it just for having seen you make that throw."

"Mighty neighborly of you. But my taste runs more to mountain whiskey. Lucien knows what I like, and he keeps a jug in back for me when I visit town. I'll stand you one, too. And if you'd like, if I ever get to Texas, I'll make you a present of one of these knifes."

"I'll just take you up on that, Jim. Maybe we'll be neighbors one day."

"I'd like that. Well now, let's go find out what you think of mountain whiskey."

Thirty-four

Francisco López and the five dragoons who had survived the canyon attack on John Cooper and his Jicarilla escort had ridden across the Rio Grande into the province of Coahuila and headed for the thriving little town of La Babia, located at the mouth of the river of that same name. It had taken them a week to reach that refuge, and they had camped at night near little Mexican villages whose occupants were mainly poor farmers. They were, in some ways, far worse off than the *peones* who worked for the wealthy landowners of this province: the latter, at least, had only to work in exchange for their food and *jacales*. But the free villagers, who answered only to themselves and not to any lordly *hacendado*, gleaned a scant living from the grainy, arid soil and were constantly at the mercy of renegade Indian or outlaw bands.

Santa Anna's spy knew this country well. For two years, shortly after having been appointed *teniente*, he had been sent to the garrison of Nueva Rosita, some eighty miles from La Babia. Once his regiment had been ordered to ride out to exterminate a renegade band of Comanche who had raided the town of San Carlos near the Texas border. It had been an unsuccessful venture, because the Comanche raiding party, after attacking the town of Ciudad Acuña, had gone back over the Rio Grande and left no trace. When the regiment had returned, crossing the Rio de la Babia, the *alcalde mayor* had ridden out on a spavined mare to implore them to give protection to his townspeople, who were plagued by raids not only from the Comanche but also by the rebellious Toboso and *gringos* who seemed to be in league with these fierce *indios.*

Francisco López had remembered this all these years, and his reason for riding to La Babia with his five recruits for the avenging army he intended to form was that his hand had been forced by the tall *gringo.* He knew perfectly well that he could expect no further military aid from Santa Anna, who, if anything, would at least reduce him in rank or perhaps even have him shot for having failed in the attempt in the canyon.

What he knew he had to do was to raise an army of ruthless mercenaries, men who would act for the gain of *dinero* and *mujeres,* not out of any great patriotic love for their country. It would take time, and it would also take money to attract such men, López knew. In a word, Francisco López planned to create a little band of *bandidos,* who would strike quickly and raid isolated villages along the outskirts of the province, until he had enough *pesos,* and perhaps jewelry and precious metals besides, to attract volunteers to the force he would use against the Double H Ranch.

And so, between the time that he and the five deserting dragoons had ridden away from the Cañon de Muerte and crossed the Rio Grande, until nearly the end of October of this year of 1825, López, the four privates, and the corporal, plundered half a dozen towns that they knew to be vulnerable and without any military protection whatsoever.

It suited López's purpose to retain his military uniform and to have his five aides wear theirs as dragoons. Thus, when they entered a village, their victims were duped into believing that here was a patrol of inspection who came to learn of conditions in the area—and then, with rifles and pis-

tols leveled at the head of the *alcalde mayor*, the villagers
found themselves taken by surprise and compelled to surrender their valuables.

During these months of banditry, Santa Anna's spy had
become obsessed by the defeat that John Cooper and the
Jicarilla had administered to the crack troops under his command. He had forgotten his villa near Veracruz and his
criadas who were forced to submit to the carnal service of
Santa Anna and the latter's associates. He thought only of revenge, the death of that tall, fair-haired *yanqui* and, above all
else, the recovery of the treasure. And he remembered what
he had overheard when he had hidden against the side of the
stable of the palominos after being a guest of Ramón Santoriaga at the Texas ranch: that the *gringo* would leave the
treasure carefully hidden away on the ranch, and would not
attempt to take it to New Orleans until the following spring.

That was why, he told himself, he must be able to raise
at least a hundred men who could engage in an all-out attack
upon the unsuspecting people of the ranch. It should be an
attack at night, which would create the most panic among the
defenders. And because they would be fortified within their
bunkhouses and *hacienda* and houses, fire must be used to
smoke them out so that his men could shoot them down from
their shelter in the protective landscape of trees and tall grass
and reeds and bushes along the Frio River. He would attack
from the south. He had stayed there long enough to know almost every physical detail of the great sprawling ranch: its
church, its stables, the houses of the settlers, the bunkhouse,
and the great *hacienda* and cottages of the sheepherders and
the *capataz*. He remembered how many workers he had seen
there and their women as well, and he knew that he could
promise rich spoils to those who would accompany him. But
first, of course, he must show these potential recruits sufficient *dinero* to whet their appetites for the fabulous treasure
that could be theirs for the taking at the ranch of the detested and cunning *gringo*.

There was a strategic reason for his choice of La Babia
as headquarters from which to launch the formidable attack
he planned: the town was only about a hundred thirty miles
from the Double H Ranch. It would take four days at most
to ride northeast. And there was no danger that any legiti-
mate Mexican military patrol would be anywhere in the area

between himself and the *gringo,* when the time came to strike.

By mid-October, Francisco López had amassed some five thousand *pesos* and a small sack of rings, bracelets, brooches, and watches, as well as a few objets d'art in gold and silver. But the aggregate worth of the contents of that sack was not enough, he knew, to rouse the greed of a hundred unscrupulous men who would ride with him on the venture he proposed and be loyal enough to his orders to complete the destruction of John Cooper's ranch, the death of the meddlesome *yanqui* himself, and the abduction of the most attractive women of quality and *criadas.* What he needed, he was sure, to convince such rogues to accept him as their leader in such a venture was an object not only of great monetary worth, but also of great historical or sentimental value.

And since he was after a fortune in silver, what would better serve to illustrate his quest than a crucifix of pure silver, the large, magnificent crucifix one would find on the altar of a church? Such a theft would convince the most skeptical viewers that he, Francisco López, was a man who feared neither physical death nor spiritual damnation.

There was an old Franciscan church in Nueva Rosita, and it was reputed to have a great silver cross nearly two centuries old. It would be a journey of about eighty miles from La Babia, where he had meanwhile taken over, under an assumed name, the rental of an abandoned *hacienda* on the edge of town. Already, he had met a few bandits and a Comanchero named Felipe Santorcia, had bought them tequila at a small *posada* not far from his *hacienda,* and hinted that one day he might have a scheme whereby they could profit beyond their wildest dreams. And they had seemed interested. Now, if he could avail himself of that great cross, he could talk to them of a silver treasure at least a hundred times greater.

Throughout these months that had followed the thwarted attack in the canyon, Francisco López had occasionally had the nagging thought that Santa Anna might be searching for him, not having had a report in all this time of his attempt to glean the *gringo*'s silver. Actually, he had no cause to worry on that score. When the Toboso scout, Guapaldi, had seen Minanga kill Captain Mora with an arrow through his heart, he had wheeled the head of his mustang around and ridden back across the Rio Grande to Major Valdez. There, he had reported that the entire detachment had been wiped out. And Major Valdez had sent a courier to Santa Anna on his estate at Manga de Clavo. The *libertador* had sworn a blasphemous oath, then curtly dismissed the courier. As the latter had saluted and turned to leave Santa Anna's study, he had heard Santa Anna say aloud, "That treasure must surely be cursed! I must plan again one day to take it, when I have learned to avoid the pitfalls set in my path by my bad luck!"

The meeting with Felipe Santorcia made up López's mind. For that matter, the Comanchero leader had been struck by his new friend's appearance. By now, the once crisp, pointed beard that López had tended so narcissistically had become shaggy and thick. His curly black hair had grown, and he had not bothered to trim his sideburns. But most of all, the change was in his eyes: the once soft, cajoling brown that had made such an impression on young women became narrowed and burning, almost feverish. His eyes glittered, and his ripely sensual mouth was more often than not, compressed and thinned as he brooded over his failures. It was the Señor John Cooper Baines who was responsible. It was he and that ferocious mongrel pet of his, half dog and half wolf, who had forced him to leave the ranch, completely mistrusting his suave pretense of sharing Ramón Santoriaga's views on Santa Anna. The damned *gringo*'s fiendish cunning in having the Jicarilla lie in wait atop the hills of the canyon to kill crack Mexican troops that was an affront not so much to Santa Anna as to him personally.

He would not rest, he would not smile again, until he killed the Señor John Cooper Baines with his own hands. And again and again, in his dreams, he relived the moment in the canyon when with his spear he had tried to kill first the *gringo*, and then that accursed *indio*. Yes, there would be another time, a better time, a time when he would have this fine *americano* completely at his mercy. And then he, Francisco López, would inflict a mortal wound, but one that would make the Señor Baines suffer and agonize for long hours until death at last became a blessed mercy.

Thus it was that three days following the meeting with

Felipe Santorcia, Francisco López and his five deserters started out for Nueva Rosita, reaching that quiet, prospering little town shortly before midnight.

His followers had tethered their horses to a post a few steps away from the church. López ordered them to remain vigilant: he alone would steal the cross.

The night was dark, the sky cloudy, and the quarter-moon scarcely filtered through the thick cumulus. It was an ideal time for his sacrilegious theft. Trying the door of the rectory, he found it locked; but it was a simple matter to thrust his body against it and lunge forward with all his strength until suddenly the lock would give way. Finding himself inside a deserted rectory, he tiptoed down a narrow corridor and entered the wing where the priest emerged to say the mass. And there the great cross stood, set into a thin circular base of silver, which in turn reposed in a round bowl of the finest teakwood.

Lighting a candle that he took from the altar, he stared covetously at the cross. And then, his eyes shining with an unholy light, he reached out his hand and seized the crucifix at the base, wrapping it in a woolen blanket he had brought with him. As he turned to retrace his footsteps, the old sacristan emerged from the other wing. Catching sight of what was in López's hand, he uttered a hoarse cry.

Francisco López wheeled, taken by surprise. "Go back to your bed, old man!" he snarled.

"The people of this town worship at that cross—do not steal it from them. It is very old. The *conquistadores* brought it. Godless one, would you dare profane His holy altar?" The old sacristan's voice was shrill with indignation.

"Out of my way—the cross is mine—I will use it in a good cause, have no fear of that!" López contemptuously declared as he tried to walk past the sacristan. The old man, intrepid beyond his years, grappled with the tall officer and managed to drag the cross back down to the altar.

"Take care; I don't want to hurt you, but I will if I need to," the tall officer snarled as he retrieved the cross and tried to walk out of the church.

But again the sacristan, with all his failing strength, tried to tug it out of López's grip. At last, letting go with his right hand and drawing his hunting knife from its belt sheath, López buried it in the old man's chest.

The sacristan's hands dropped from the uplifted cross; he staggered back, and fell heavily at the side of the altar. One hand clasped to the bleeding wound, he stretched out the clawlike other hand toward the officer and, in a failing voice still touched with horror and righteous anger, denounced him: "God will curse you, *hombre*! It is sacrilege—you will not die, but you will be damned through all your life and after it—*Dios*, I commend my spirit to Thee— You are doomed to fail in all that you do from this moment forth, and you will fear death—because—because—" his voice began to trail off, and he coughed, and blood oozed from his lips "—because of the hell that awaits you, wretched *hombre*!"

His lifeless hand fell to the floor, and he lay still. López bent down and wiped the bloody knife on the sacristan's monastic robe, and then crept out of the church through the rectory, to where his companions awaited him.

Two nights later, in a back room of the Posada del Toro Rojo, the burly, beady-eyed Comanchero leader, Felipe Santorcia, lifted his glass of tequila and tilted back in his chair with a bored expression, as López lifted a hempen sack onto the table. "You've talked of treasure this evening, Señor López, but you've shown me nothing except a few trinkets and a few thousand *pesos*. Why should I have my men risk their lives on a fairy tale?"

"By the devil's horns, Santorcia, do you think I left the army as a *coronel* because of a fairy tale? Use your eyes and look at this!" Santa Anna's former spy lifted out the great silver cross from the church of Nueva Rosita.

The black-bearded Comanchero tilted back his chair till it crashed on the planked floor, and his jaw dropped as he stared incredulously at the holy symbol. Then instinctively he crossed himself and muttered, "Where did you get that, Señor López?"

"My comrades and I appropriated it from the church of Nueva Rosita. I did this to prove to you that I mean every word I've told you, Santorcia. This ranch is near the Frio River in the Texas territory, ¿comprendes? It's at most four days' ride from here. And this *americano* brought back at least five dozen bars of silver as pure as this. He had the Jicarilla Apache warriors with him; and when we tried to secure it from them, they took us by surprise from the top of the canyon. But this time, with the help of your band and the others I know you can bring in with you, we'll strike at night. We'll use fire the way the Comanche do. With torches and with wagons filled with lighted pitch, we will destroy the *hacienda,* the bunkhouse, and the houses of all the *americanos* who have come to live there with this *gringo.* Give me an army of a hundred men, Santorcia, and you and I will take the silver and the women and the horses— Oh, yes, I saw with my own eyes the most beautiful palominos I've ever seen in all my life."

"You stole this cross, and you risked eternal damnation to prove your words to me," the Comanchero wonderingly muttered as he stroked his beard and continued to stare fascinatedly at the gleaming silver cross. "How you must hate this *americano!*"

Francisco López's brown eyes narrowed and glinted with an almost maddened intensity. "Yes, Santorcia, I hate him. If I had him here before me, I'd kill him with my bare hands. He treated me as if I were a *peón,* I, friend of *El Libertador,* Santa Anna himself! And he tricked me when I led my dragoons against him. And because he did, I cannot go back to Santa Anna; my military career is finished." Now his lips twisted in a savage grimace. "But he'll pay for all that, and you and I will spend his silver while his bones lie rotting under the sun near the ashes of his *hacienda!* Look, Santorcia, I've sacrificed my villa near Veracruz with nearly a dozen lovely *criadas* who obeyed my every order— I've lost everything, do you understand me? And it's all because of that damned *yanqui!*"

"I must talk with my people. I think, *amigo,* that if there is all the silver you say, it will be worth going after."

"Of course it will!" López's voice was exultantly hoarse. "I'll draw a map of the ranch, so you and your men will know where every building is, and you'll know how to attack."

"*Bueno.* Come back here a week from now. There is a *jefe* of a tribe of Comanche whose braves have broken away from the Wanderers. He would do much to have some of those fine palominos. I will talk with him." The Comanchero rose, downed the last of his tequila, and belched. "With that much silver, there'll be enough for me to buy some decent tequila instead of this swill. Come back next week, and you'll have my answer."

Thirty-five

Having heard how little Ruth had asked Carlos to bring her back a bird for her from Taos, and equally aware that Carlos had forgotten it during his ardent courtship of Teresa de Rojado, John Cooper had purchased a little brown finch in a lovely cage, as well as food for the bird, from a New Orleans shop owner. He intended to take it back to the ranch and give to it Carlos without Ruth's seeing it, so that she would not be able to say that her Uncle Carlos had not kept his promise. He secured the cage by a thong passed through the ring at its top and made both ends of the thong fast to a sturdy hook that he had screwed into the archlike top of one of the supply wagons. And since the weather was extremely warm for November, the vivacious little bird would be able to hop about on its perch and enjoy the scenic return journey home.

The Belgian church bell had been packed carefully into the joined *carretas,* which were harnessed as a single elongated unit to four sturdy oxen. When he had begun the drive to New Orleans, John Cooper had feared that the oxen would slow the pace, but they had pleasantly surprised him. Now, with no cattle to drive back, he had estimated that he should make some twenty miles a day. He wanted most of all to be home well before Christmas, and certainly before Catarina's child would be born. All the same, it was important to swing northwest to reach Nacogdoches, where he would pause briefly for fresh supplies, and then visit Eugene Fair's new settlement near the Brazos River. Even though this settlement was nearly two hundred miles from the Double H Ranch, he looked upon it as a vital link between two growing communities. If they could establish some sort of regular communication, it might very well stand as a powerfully protective influence against future harassment by either nomadic and hostile Indians, or plunder-minded Mexican troops.

The more successful Eugene Fair's settlement could become, the more defensive strength they could all count on against any future harassment. More than that, John Cooper foresaw an interchange of ideas between his ranch and Eugene Fair's new colony. They would discuss new ways of raising cattle and sheep and produce, as well as sharing ideas on the best methods of defense. And all of this, he enthusiastically believed, would help bring the vast Texas territory sooner under the aegis of the United States as a permanent part of this magnificent country, which would celebrate next year the fiftieth anniversary of its founding. He well remembered his father's stories of how British-based landlords had tyrannized the Irish farmers, and he had thrilled as a little boy to hear Andrew Baines tell how General George Washington's raggle-taggle army had defeated the crack British troops to the amazement of all the civilized world.

The *vaqueros* and *trabajadores* were in high spirits, having received their wages and a considerable bonus for the risk they had taken during the tornado. They visited the New Orleans shops to buy presents for their wives and children, and they treated themselves to the best food and drink during their stay.

Young Andrew seemed to have grown a full inch, and he was sun bronzed like his father, as well as alert and tireless. He had already endeared himself to the men by sharing the long hours in the saddle, the capricious assault of the elements, and the often monotonous meals that ended a long day's journey. He had also shown himself to be a fine marksman with the rifle his father had given him.

They reached Nacogdoches by mid-November, spent a short time loading fresh food supplies onto the already heavily laden wagons, and then headed toward the Brazos.

Ten days later, they came in sight of the settlement, where the Stiltons, the Hornsteders, and Simon Brown were building their own cabins. They were met by the sentries, who welcomed them after John Cooper introduced himself and his men, and they were escorted into the stockade. Only the day before, Naomi Mayberry had been married to the young scout by a kindly Franciscan friar from Nacogdoches who, hearing of the arrival of new settlers, had gone to the settlement to offer his prayers for the success of the community. Finding a number of Catholics among the families who had come all the way from Franklin, the friar had stayed on to say mass and hear confessions and, finally, to marry Simon and Naomi. Jack Sperry and Nancy Morrison had induced him to make it a double wedding; and when John Cooper and his men arrived, the settlers were still celebrating the happy occasion. They were having an outdoor barbecue, with sides of mutton and beef, and many of the women had picked berries and baked pies.

Some of the younger men of the settlement were earning their share of the feast by extending the sturdy wooden stockade around the community to protect it from attack, and others were building a large rectangular meetinghouse where the affairs of the community could be discussed. This would be a democratic community where all landholders would have an equal vote. Yesterday, also, along with the wedding, the settlers had elected, by voice vote, Joseph Benyon, a tall, middle-aged schoolteacher from St. Louis. Saddened by the death of his wife and two children from river fever two years earlier, Benyon had decided to begin a new life on this vast frontier. One of his ex-pupils, a shy girl of eighteen, whose parents had died when she was ten and who lived with a spinster aunt, had startled Benyon by telling him that she wanted to go with him. They had been married before they left St. Louis, and now he was the father of an eleven-month-old son and rejoicing in this new beginning.

The settlers had chosen him to draw up a kind of constitution, "just like the one our Founding Fathers signed, you know, schoolteacher," said elderly David Burroughs, a Wisconsin doctor who had retired from his practice when his wife had died, and impulsively decided to come out to Texas to offer his medical services to those who would need them.

John Cooper and Miguel were delighted with the settlement. As Ed Barstow put it, "We started out hatin' every other feller's guts, Mr. Baines, but then when we had to pull together to keep those Mexes from shootin' us down, we found out that we made a pretty good army ourselves."

After John Cooper had read the rough draft of the constitution, he smilingly declared, "Mr. Benyon, I'd say you've a good thing going here. If you carry out all these ideas, you'll grow and be prosperous—and that's good for all of us out here. I'd like to send one of my *vaqueros* over to you maybe every other month or so, to find out if you need anything. Also, maybe my ranch can put to use some of your ideas—we can trade notions back and forth. And if there are any soldiers or Indians giving you trouble, you send one of your riders to us lickety-split, and we'll come to help you out."

"I hope we won't have to take you up on that offer as regards having to fight off any hostiles," Joseph Benyon good-naturedly chuckled. "We had our fill of that sort of thing coming out here." Then, his face solemn, he added, "It was a good lesson for all of us, and God was on our side."

"Well, it's been good meeting you, Mr. Benyon. And it was mighty neighborly of you to invite my men and Miguel and me and my son Andrew here to have a bite to eat and help celebrate those weddings you had yesterday. I'm just sorry Eugene Fair wasn't here so I could pay my respects to him."

Meanwhile, the Franciscan friar had seen the Belgian church bell and took this opportunity to bless it, while the *vaqueros* and *trabajadores* knelt in reverence. And then, on the first day of December, John Cooper, Andrew, and Miguel rode ahead of the *vaqueros* and the oxen-drawn *carretas* and wagons back toward the Double H Ranch. With any luck, they would arrive there in ten days. "And that way," John Cooper smilingly told Miguel, "I can be sure of having a say in naming my next-born!"

On October 26 of this year of 1825, the great project of the Erie Canal had been completed, connecting the city of New York with the Great Lakes. For the travelers and traders of that area, it was a boon. But for those in the vast stretches of the still uncharted Southwest, there were no such time-saving boons to travel. On horse or by mule, through gulches, rocky canyons, and sometimes arid stretches of great desert, whose challenges offered death by poisonous snakes and spiders—these were the experiences of those who sought to conquer this limitless territory and expand the frontier.

Ernest Henson, Matthew Robisard, and Jeremy Gaige had gone on from the June fair in Taos to the province of Chihuahua. What goods they had not sold at the fair, they had disposed of at a fine profit in the town of Chihuahua, and the officials there had asked them to return next year with more wares. The traders promised they would, rejoicing in the warm hospitality that their Mexican hosts had shown them. And on their long return to St. Louis, they decided to stop once again in Taos, to pay their respects to Don Sancho de Pladero, only to learn of his death from the lips of a tearful Doña Elena. They expressed to her their great sympathy and gave her daughter-in-law, Conchita, a bolt of gay red calico as a gift—which had pleased her husband, Tomás. And they promised they would convey the greetings of Doña Elena, Tomás, and Conchita to Don Diego de Escobar, at whose ranch they planned to stop as a break in their wearily long journey back to Missouri.

They brought along the four young apprentices who had helped drive the wagons and unload the trade goods. Henson and Robisard also sold their burros in Chihuahua, and bought fresh horses. They were of the opinion that nothing in the world could beat a Missouri mule for sheer stubbornness and dogged stamina, but they had taken a fancy to some of the lean Mexican mustangs, which could go a good thirty miles a day without tiring or wanting too much food or water.

As they passed the Sangre de Cristo range and turned their horses and wagons eastward by southeast, Robisard said to his partner, "Ernie, I can't wait to see how those Irish wolfhound pups I sent John Cooper Baines turned out for him."

"I can't either, Matt. What a shame Don Sancho had to die before he could get out there and have some great years swapping yarns with Don Diego!" Henson said, sighing and shaking his head.

Both men missed their families, having been absent from them since early April of this year. And both men expected to have additions to their families when they finally returned to St. Louis. Perhaps that was why, as they crossed the Pecos River and headed on toward the Double H Ranch at the beginning of December, they remembered the warm alliances of family ties that they had observed when both of them, far younger and still bachelors, had come brashly to trade in Taos and Santa Fe against the prohibitive restrictions of the Mexican government and had been rescued from possible long-term imprisonment by the courageous defense of Don Diego de Escobar. "You know, Ernie," Robisard nostalgically declared as they forded the Pecos River and headed on toward the Double H Ranch a hundred miles distant, "folks like that Don Diego and John Cooper Baines and his Catarina, they'd make swell neighbors in St. Louis. They'd get along just about anywhere because they're honest and they're ready to fight for what they believe in, and they don't look down on either Injuns or people who didn't get born on the right side of the tracks."

"You're right about that, Matt," Henson observed. "That's the whole point about this country. When a person goes out to live where there hasn't been much civilization before he came, he's likely to have a straightforward way of looking at things and not worry about who to say hello to and who not to, and what fork to use and trying to impress his neighbor next door with how much he's got in the bank and such."

"Damned right," Robisard emphatically nodded, and then fell silent.

On the unseasonably warm afternoon of December 9, Matthew Robisard and Ernest Henson reined their horses and turned to Jeremy Gaige to point out to him the distant sight of the huge *hacienda*, the settlers' houses, the bunkhouse, the stables, and the corral of the great Double H Ranch. The old prospector drawled, "That shore 'nuff is the best sight I've seen since we left Taos, boys. I'm just hopin' there's something cool with a mule's wallop I can tie into once I ease my sore butt off this bony critter." He looked reproachfully down at the wiry mustang he was riding and uttered a doleful sigh, at which the two bearded Missouri traders burst into amused laughter.

"No doubt about it, Jeremy," Henson answered, "they'll treat you just fine. Remember, I told you this Don Diego came from Madrid, and he's the one who can talk to you about buried treasure."

"That's right, I plumb remember you tellin' me about

him!" the grizzled old prospector excitedly exclaimed. "I hope
we git to stay a couple of days there so's this Don Diego 'n
me kin swap some tall yarns. I'd like that mighty fine."

"And you'll also like the way that cook of theirs, if she's
still around, let's see—oh, yes, Tía Margarita!—fixes chow,
Jeremy. My, they've certainly got a spread for themselves
here! See over there, Matt? Guess they must have had lots of
settlers who came out to live around them. Practically a town
all by itself, wouldn't you say?"

Robisard leaned forward to look at the little huts of the
sheepherders, erected on the perimeter of the western boundary of the Double H Ranch. "That I would, Ernie. That's
mighty rich land for grazing cattle and sheep and for growing
crops, I'd say. My Lord, if we weren't getting old, I'd almost
have a hankering to come settle down here and try my hand
at running a farm or a ranch the way they do."

"I know. It's beautiful country. All the same, we've done
right well for ourselves back in St. Louis, and somehow I
don't think our wives and kids would cotton to the idea of
moving way out here with hardly any neighbors around for
miles and miles. Hey there, see? They've got a church—now
that's a good sign they're getting along with one another and
fixing up just the sort of life they want to lead for themselves."

Quickening their mounts, the two affable Missouri traders and the old prospector cantered toward the ranch.

Catarina had gone to the chapel this morning to pray,
for she felt that her time was soon upon her. Doña Inez and
Bess Sandarbal, who herself was in her fifth month of pregnancy, had breakfasted with her and tried to cheer her up
with the assurance that John Cooper would be back any day
and in time to see his child born. Catarina, with a hysterical
little laugh, had retorted, "If everything were properly on
schedule, I shouldn't be concerned, my dear ones. But I'm
afraid this child inside me is anxious to come into the world,
and I think he or she is a week early. Oh, dear, I surely
thought Coop would be back by now from New Orleans!"

The sheepherders out on the range had waved a greeting
to the Missouri traders as they rode on toward the two tall
gateposts at the entry to the huge ranch. Surmounting those
gateposts was a large wooden sign in the shape of a hawk, on

which Taguro—the young Pueblo Indian who, with his wife, Listanzia, had escaped the cruelty of Don Esteban de Rivarola—had etched the double H insignia of the ranch: on the one side of the sign was written Hacienda del Halcón, and on the other side, Double H Ranch. The Texan, Edward Molson, who was standing on the veranda of his house with his lovely wife, Margarita, their two young sons and two-year-old daughter clinging to their mother, espied the riders and excitedly said to his wife, "*Querida*, we've got visitors. I'm going over to the main house to tell Don Diego and Carlos."

"It is not the Señor Baines, is it, *mi corazón*?" comely, black-haired Margarita Molson asked him as she leaned down to stroke her little daughter's head and, then with the other hand, encouragingly pat her sons and whisper to them, "We'll have our *almuerzo* soon, Pablo, Eduardo."

"No, they'd be back with wagons and oxen and that bell they had ordered from Belgium for our new church," Molson said. He kissed Margarita quickly, rumpled his sons' hair, took up his little daughter and kissed her on the cheek, and then set her down again and hurried off to the house.

Don Diego and Carlos, apprised of the visitors' arrival, hurried out to greet them. Don Diego's face beamed with recognition as Ernest Henson and Matthew Robisard dismounted and came toward him. "*¡Por todos los santos!*" he exclaimed. "How good it is to see you again, *mis amigos!*"

"Likewise, Don Diego," Robisard said, grinning as he energetically shook Don Diego's hand. "Ernie and I have never forgotten what you did for us in Santa Fe. We still could be growing white beards in a Mexican jail if it hadn't been for you. And I want you to meet Jeremy Gaige; he's been hankering to meet up with you ever since I told him that you're a real *hidalgo* from Madrid."

"I have really almost forgotten that part of my life, *mis amigos*," Don Diego genially replied. "The Spain I knew when I was a young, ambitious man eager to follow in my father's footsteps is no more. I have learned that true nobility is the way one acts toward one's friends and neighbors and family, not one's birthright and the acquisition of a legacy and a title. Well now, Señor Gaige, why would you want to meet a doddering old man like me?"

The bearded old prospector slapped his thigh and then

gingerly proffered his callused hand to John Cooper's father-in-law. "Say now, Don Diego, Matt 'n Ernie told me you could set me straight about all the hidden treasure them Spaniards put away back in the old days, 'n I'm a darn sight older 'n you, if it comes to that!"

"Señor Gaige," Don Diego said with a twinkle in his eyes, "if I knew the whereabouts of all the treasures buried since the days of the great Armada, I assure you I would be one of the wealthiest men in all this world and far more powerful than any king or emperor. The fact is, Señor Gaige, back in Taos, apart from the stipend that the then king of Spain was kind enough to give me as *intendente,* my only income came from the raising of sheep."

"Sheep," Jeremy Gaige disgustedly ejaculated, "never had much use for 'em—mebbe a slice of mutton once in a while, but when I was prospectin', I was lucky if I had me a little hardtack 'n some jerky 'n a canteen full of water. But mebbe we kin palaver some about where you used to live—I mean, there was gold 'n silver in them palaces in Spain, wasn't they?"

Don Diego laughed uproariously and put his arm around the prospector's stooped shoulders. "Señor Gaige, you are a marvelous tonic for me, as good as the finest brandy. Now then, you, and you also, Señores Robisard and Henson, let me have our majordomo show you to your rooms. You are my honored guests, and I shall tell Tía Margarita to prepare as tasty a supper as you could enjoy in the Escorial in Madrid!"

Indeed, Don Diego's promise was not an idle one, for that night the plump, good-natured *cocinera* had provided a mouth-watering assortment of palatable dishes for the Missouri traders and the old prospector. Besides *enchiladas, poblano,* and a sumptuous *guisado de cerdo,* she had prepared such appetizers as *tostadas con chorizo y con pollo,* and her own special *flan* with rum as a dessert, as well as fruits and cheeses and biscuits and rich, strong coffee. At the end of the supper, to which the old prospector had done full justice, he looked over at Don Diego, who whimsically asked, "Well now, Señor Gaige, do you find our table to your taste?"

"Wal now, Your Grace"—Jeremy Gaige was hardly familiar with titles, but Don Diego took not the slightest notice of this misapplication—"I'll jist say this—if I'd known about grub like this when I was out in the desert, I might jist have given up prospectin'!"

Afterward, in Don Diego's study, there was brandy and some excellent port and more strong coffee, which the Missourians and Jeremy Gaige enjoyed. Carlos joined them also, and the traders listened with great interest to his description of the military situation he had experienced while he had been a lieutenant in the forces of Santa Anna. Ernest Henson was of the firm opinion that it would not be much longer before the United States and Mexico came to serious grips over the disposition of Texas territory, and Carlos warmly supported this view: "I for one, Señor Henson, would like to see this great country become a part of the Estados Unidos. From what I learned last year riding through many of the provinces, the Mexican government still continues to instigate great class differences between the *ricos* and the *pobres*. It would never really come to a democracy such as we know it here. Yes, I was born in Madrid like my father, but I feel myself almost an *americano* now—thanks to John Cooper, who, you know, is my brother-in-law."

"It's a darned shame he isn't here tonight. We'd really like to say hello to him and ask him how those wolfhound pups we sent him are getting along," Matthew Robisard ventured.

"Well, señores," Carlos smilingly replied, "he should be home anytime now; but in his stead, I'd be happy to take a walk with you after our coffee and show you Hosea and Jude, and Luna and Yankee as well."

"I'd like that a lot!" Robisard said. "Of course, we're anxious, both of us, to get back to St. Louis and our families. But if you think there's a chance that Mr. Baines will be returning any day now, and if you've no objection, we'd like to stay over an extra day or two, just for the pleasure."

"Of course, of course; you're my guests and it's understood!" Don Diego beamed.

"Most gracious of you, Don Diego." Robisard lifted his glass of brandy to toast the elderly *hidalgo*.

"And I think that's my cue to go to bed, gentlemen. I am far older than you—"

"Not me, you ain't, Your Grace," Jeremy Gaige irrepressibly piped up, and this time there was gently amused laughter from his host, as well as from the others.

"All the same, I'll take my leave of you now and see you at breakfast. Enjoy your stay at the Hacienda del Halcón, señores."

"Thanks again, Don Diego," Ernest Henson enthusiastically spoke up, "and when you see that wonderful cook of yours, tell her we're going to send her a present when we get back to St. Louis—I've never in my life had better food than that!"

After Don Diego had left the study, Carlos took them outside and walked to the kennel to see Hosea and Jude, as well as the female wolf-dog, Luna. The wolfhounds, fully grown now, were thoroughly preoccupied chewing on marrow bones that one of Tía Margarita's helpers had given them, and they took no heed of their visitors. "Well, that's gratitude for you," Matthew said, chuckling. "Here Ernie and I found such a good home for those dogs. You'd think the least they could do is say hello to us." As the four men laughed heartily, Carlos showed his guests Luna, who was quartered in a separate compartment and was also busy working on a bone. Then he led them to the shed where Yankee was housed. Hearing familiar footsteps, the wolf-dog uttered a joyous bark and began to scrabble at the door with his paws.

Carlos unlocked the shed and called out a warning, "Careful now, Yankee, these are *amigos*! Be good now, the way your master would want you to, ¿comprendes?"

Yankee bounded out and, at first, seeing the two Missourians and Jeremy Gaige, with whom he was not familiar, uttered a soft growl, stopping dead in his tracks and regarding them with baleful yellow eyes. But Carlos at once put out his right hand and rubbed his knuckles over Yankee's head, murmuring, "I said, they're *amigos*! Now be good!"

Yankee began to wag his tail, and Robisard, shrewdly appraising the strong young wolf-dog, remarked, "I can see the wolfhound in him, all right. Those are good lines."

"John Cooper has taught him how to attack enemies. But there's no need for me to show you, because there are none around us tonight," Carlos smilingly proffered. "I can show you how he'll retrieve a stick thrown to him, and if it weren't so late, I'd take my Belgian rifle and try for a rabbit and let Yankee retrieve it."

"Perhaps we can see that in the morning after breakfast. Thank you. He's really a superb creature, isn't he, Ernie?"

Thirty-six

It was half an hour until midnight. The countryside was quiet, and from the distance, only the soft, continuous flowing of the Frio River could be heard, as well as the twitterings of some of the night birds and, occasionally, the warning hoot of an owl preparing for its dinner foray of a rat or mouse.

Catarina's labor pains had begun, and Bess Sandarbal had anxiously come from her own house to help out. It was common practice now on the ranch never to leave the children untended, and Bess's three children had come to the *hacienda* with her, and were now sleeping in rooms adjacent to those of the Baines and de Escobar children.

"You must relax, *querida*," Bess told the anguished Catarina, who lay on her bed with her head propped up on two pillows, her exquisite face contorted and damp with the pain of her oncoming birth. "It will be easier for the *niño* if you do not try to force it."

"The pains come more quickly now, Bess. *Dios,* how it hurts—Coop, where are you? I wanted you here to know about the baby—ohhh, Bess, it really does hurt now; the pains are coming ever so quickly—"

"Hush, dear one," Bess comforted her, as she leaned over to pat Catarina's perspiring forehead with a cloth dipped into cool water. "I'm here. I'll help you. Now don't you

worry; everything will be fine. Your other children have come
very easily, and this one will, too, you'll see."

The *trabajadores* had gone to their huts and to the bunkhouse. Two young sheepherders—part of the guard duty that
night—remained with the flock, which had settled down for
the night, and were just beyond the houses of Edward Molson and his Texas companions who had come to live on the
Double H Ranch. To the southwest, there was a long stretch
of fir and spruce trees, as well as thick mesquite, which
fringed the trees. A dark shadow disengaged itself from behind a tree and, crouching very low, slowly approached one
of the unsuspecting sheepherders. He reached him from behind, his left hand over the man's mouth, as his right drove a
dagger to the heart. He wiped the bloody knife on the dead
man's shirt front, then turned and put two fingers to his
mouth to emit a long, melancholy whistle.

From inside the forestlike growths of trees, a similar
sound told him that his signal had been heard.

A few moments later, another dark shadow moved
stealthily from behind a towering spruce tree and came
crouching through the tall grass toward the other sheepherder. The latter straightened, perhaps some presentiment of
danger warning him, and turned just in time to see a lanky,
black-bearded man in an American army uniform leap at
him and topple him onto his back. Kneeling astride his stomach, his left hand over the sheepherder's mouth, the
uniformed renegade—he had deserted a year ago his post as
corporal in the nation's capitol and, lured by the prospect of
booty and women, had become an outlaw in Texas—at once
palmed his victim's mouth and gloatingly lifted his hunting
knife high in the air. The sheepherder writhed ineffectually,
his eyes rolling in their sockets, trying frenziedly to cry out,
his nostrils dilating and shrinking as the knife swept down.

The deserter turned, and he, too, sent the same whistle
toward the darkened woods.

Francisco López crouched beside the Comanchero *jefe*,
Felipe Santorcia, and grinned wickedly: "So much for the
guards on the west side of the ranch! You've talked to Quintana?"

"I told you I would," the Comanchero growled. "What
he wants is all the palomino horses for his Comanche braves.

What do you care? You'll have a good part of the silver and some of the women—that should content you."

"How many braves did Quintana bring with him, and did he remember to bring the fire wagons?"

"Teach your grandmother to suck eggs, *mi coronel*," the Comanchero sneered. "I am not a boy in need of lessons. Thirty braves, armed with bows and arrows, lances, some muskets, and a few rifles I myself sold him. And yes, he has eight wagons filled with straw and pitch. It needs only a moment to plunge a torch into them. One of the braves will ride a horse-drawn wagon as close to those *casas* as he can get, then leap off into the grass. Quintana will probably sacrifice a few of his own horses that way, which is the reason for his wanting all the palominos."

"I won't quarrel with that. But remember, leave that *americano* with his long rifle to me! I owe him a slow and agonizing death!" López hissed.

Santorcia rose from his place of concealment and moved back deeper into the woods. There he conferred with a group of his own men, all of them outlaws, some with prices on their heads, from Kansas, Missouri, and even as far east as Pennsylvania and Maryland. In all, Santa Anna's former spy had been able to recruit one hundred ten men to launch an all-out attack against John Cooper Baines and his people.

A few moments later, the Comanchero *jefe* crawled back to him and muttered, "My men will start heading toward the *hacienda* itself any moment now, and they'll start firing. Everyone's asleep—I see almost no lights, except one in the bunkhouse and the other at the back of the *hacienda*. It should be over quickly—and once the fire reaches those buildings, they'll come out into the open, and we can pick them off like sitting ducks!"

"All of them, mind you, except the Señor Baines!" López growled. He put his right hand to his hunting knife and drew it out, examining it in the faint reflection of the quarter-moon. "I'll cut out his guts slowly, inch by inch, and I'll watch him die, and I'll hear him beg for mercy!" His voice was hoarse and trembling with an ungovernable fury.

"He's yours; I've no interest in the bastard," Santorcia said, shrugging. "Now I'll give the signal!"

He cupped his hands to the sides of his mouth and emitted the call of the coyote: once, twice, three times.

Hardly had the last sound died away when a volley of musket and rifle fire crashed out in the still night.

Bess Sandarbal uttered a cry of terror as one of the rifle balls shattered the shutter and glanced harmlessly against the wall behind her. "My God, it's a bandit attack or a Mexican patrol! Catarina, poor darling, can you be by yourself for just a minute? I have to go warn the others—"

Catarina groaned and arched herself as a new spasm seized her. Once again, a volley rang out, and one of the shutters snapped as a ball shattered it. Catarina put her hand over her mouth, her eyes dilating with fear and pain as she stared at the window. Then, gingerly shifting herself and groaning aloud at the pain it cost her, she blew out the oil lamp on the little table beside her bed so as to extinguish the target of the hidden marksman.

Bess ran into the kitchen, and there found the plump cook and Concepción Morales, who was helping Tía Margarita clean up. "Get Esteban, Concepción—did you hear the shooting? I don't know who's out there, but it sounds like a lot of men with guns—can you go to Colonel Santoriaga? I have to stay with Catarina. She's going to have her baby any minute! Oh, thank God, Señor Carlos!" At this moment, Carlos appeared. He had been wakened by the volleys and had already run down the corridor, banging on the door to waken his father and Doña Inez, telling them to gather all the children and take them to the chapel, which, since it was a windowless room, would be a place of safety.

"The children and my parents will be out of danger, Bess. Now I'll go for Santoriaga. You take care of my sister—is she very close?"

Bess wrung her hands. "She's going to have her baby any minute—what a terrible thing to have happen at such a time—"

"I'll come; I know something about babies, after all," Concepción said, uttering a nervous giggle as she hurried back with Bess Sandarbal to Catarina's bedroom.

Carlos ran to the study and, opening the closet, buckled on his rapier, thrust a brace of pistols into his belt, and seized his Belgian rifle. Swiftly priming and loading it, and slinging the pouch of gunpowder and balls over one shoulder, he hurried out of the *hacienda* and toward the direction of Ramón Santoriaga's dwelling.

Mercedes Santoriaga had heard the shooting, and her first thought had been of her children. She had gone to their bedroom, wakened them, and ordered them to crawl under their beds and stay there without a sound. She had soothed them, for the youngest one had begun to cry. To the oldest, she uttered a stern maternal command, "I'm counting on you to look after the baby, and mind you do!"

"*Sí, mi madre*," the youngster gasped.

Meanwhile, Ramón Santoriaga had hastily donned a pair of breeches and a *camisa*, tugged on his boots, and seized his rifle. Assuring himself that it was already primed and loaded, he hurried out of the house with it, warning Mercedes to remain in the bedroom with the children and to stay as close to the floor as she could, so that no stray balls would find any living targets.

The *trabajadores* in the bunkhouse and the Jicarilla as well, had also wakened. Colonel Santoriaga had already conducted many practice defense sessions with them, and they knew just what to do. Pastanari gave swift orders in his Apache tongue to the seventeen braves. A dozen of them nimbly clambered onto the roof of the *hacienda* and stationed themselves with bows and arrows, several with rifles and muskets, while the other five followed him around to the east side of the bunkhouse where they took position to await a charge from that side of the Frio River.

Meanwhile, Esteban Morales, acting as *capataz*, led his *trabajadores* to the west and north sides of the bunkhouse, and they took up defense positions there. Matt Robisard and Ernest Henson, who were residing in the main house during their stay, had come out with their rifles to help, and Esteban directed them to take up places with the workmen. Jeremy Gaige had remained inside his room at the *hacienda*, and was vociferously directing the campaign from there, even though there was no one to listen to him.

When Carlos had put Yankee back into his shed, he had forgotten to make the lock fast. Excited by all the sounds of voices and weapon fire, Yankee whined, then barked, and finally hurled himself at the door. It gave way, and he bounded out, his yellow eyes gleaming in the darkness, his fangs bared. He ran swiftly toward the *hacienda*, then doubled back toward the shed, then stopped, nonplussed. His beloved master was nowhere in sight, nor was there any scent of him. He lifted his muzzle toward the sky to utter a long, soft growl and waited, quivering.

Teresa de Rojado sat up straight in her bed, already wakened from a deep sleep by the sounds of musket and rifle fire. Carlos had just stopped by her room and implored her to get down on the floor, but before she could do so, a ball crashed through the window and bent one of the shutters. With a frightened cry, she sprang out of bed and swiftly put on her riding habit. In her closet, she had her rifle in a sling, and crouching low, she drew it out and loaded it. Then, crawling on her knees toward the window, she carefully opened the shutters with the barrel of her rifle. Squinting along the sights of the rifle, she waited, her eyes fixed on the dark woods beyond. She saw two shadowy figures come forward out of the woods, each carrying a musket. Holding her breath, shifting her rifle, keeping one of them fully in her sights, she squeezed the trigger. There was an agonized shriek as the Comanchero dropped his musket, his knees buckling and giving way under him, and then collapsed, lying facedown.

Teresa hastily reloaded her rifle, then thrust its barrel back out through the window to wait for another attacker.

Quintana and his Comanche braves had killed the guards at the southeastern part of the woods, and now the chief gave an order. Ten of his braves mounted their mustangs and, brandishing muskets and rifles, rode toward the back of the *hacienda*.

Pastanari's bowmen, watching the racing figures, notched arrows into their bows and drew them back to maximum. As the horsemen neared them, they sped their arrows. Three of the Comanche riders dropped from their saddles, and a fourth clutched his left arm, an arrow having pierced the flesh in only a superficial wound. Another Comanche fired into the bunkhouse and the *hacienda*, and then, seeing one of his comrades drop with an arrow in his back, looked up to see the Jicarilla bowmen lying flat on the roof. He triggered a rifle shot that caught one of Pastanari's men in the act of rising to take better aim, and the brave dropped his bow and pitched forward onto his face, his body writhing in the convulsive throes of death.

Now Felipe Santorcia uttered a shrill whistle, and ten of his riflemen began to crawl on their bellies toward the *hacienda*, pausing to reload their rifles. When they reached a distance of about four hundred feet, they took careful aim against the shuttered windows and squeezed the triggers.

Teresa de Rojado uttered a gasp as a spent ball dropped at her booted feet. There was very little light to shoot by, but she could see the dark, ominous shadows moving slowly forward. She cuddled the rifle butt to her shoulder, rested her cheek against it, following the sights as best she could, and then pulled the trigger. With a hideous screech of agony, one of the Comancheros stood upright, dropped his rifle, and pitched forward to lie inert before his companions.

Carlos had reached Colonel Ramón Santoriaga, and the two men hastily conferred. "Your Texas friends to the west of me, *mi compañero,* are lying beside their houses, like true marksmen," Santoriaga told Carlos. "It's a murky night, and there's not much moon to see by, but by God, we'll make out."

In her bedroom, Catarina seized a towel that Concepción had handed her and, wadding it, bit into it to stifle her agonized cries. By the dim light of an oil lamp she had brought with her, Concepción examined Catarina and smilingly nodded: "All is well, *querida,* don't worry. I'll have it out and bawling for its mother in a few more minutes, you just wait and see! Now don't try to sit up again, and don't even think about what's going on out there—I'll see that your baby's born safely so when the Señor Baines comes home, he'll be ever so proud!"

"*Gracias, muchas, gr-gracias,*" the half-fainting young woman breathed.

On the western side of the ranch, the Ames brothers, as well as Ben Forrester, Malcolm Pauley, Jack Williams, and Edward Molson, had seized their rifles and crept out of the houses, instructing their women and children to lie on the floor and to show no sign of light in the windows.

Now the Comanchero advance guard knelt down and fired in a bevy at the *hacienda.* One of them fell to a Jicarilla arrow, another to a lance that sailed from the roof and unerringly into a Comanchero's chest. But in return, two of Pastanari's men stumbled, dropped their bows and arrows, and rolled off the edge of the roof, their bodies thudding on the ground below.

The two American deserters who had knifed the sheepherders now crept toward the houses of the Texas set-

tlers, with long rifles primed and ready. Crawling on their
bellies, they stationed themselves opposite the house of
Ramón Santoriaga, and one of them leveled his rifle to his
shoulder and fired. The ball crashed through the shutters and
whizzed by the four-poster bed under which Mercedes and
her children lay in hiding. The children began to weep, but
she soothed them, telling them, "Your father is outside; he
will drive away the bad men. It will be all over soon, *mis
niños!*"

Yankee had been barking furiously all this time, and
now, racing through the courtyard of the *hacienda*, he saw
one of the Comanche braves climbing the wall, a scalp knife
between his teeth. Yankee crouched low, growling softly, and
just as the brave leaped down, Yankee hurtled through the
air at him and went for his throat. With a hideous scream,
the Comanche regained his fallen knife and tried to stab at
the wolf-dog, but Yankee's fangs had already found his jugu-
lar vein. The knife scratched his fur and drew a little blood,
but there was no force behind the wound, for the brave was
already dead. The wolf-dog lifted his bloody muzzle and
emitted a baleful howl.

Francisco López ground his teeth as he watched from
his hiding place. "Damn you, Santorcia; tell Quintana to send
the fire wagons against the *hacienda!*" he cried, beside himself at seeing his obsessive goal once again about to be
denied.

But the Comanche renegade chief had already anticipated his wish: the tall, glowering *jefe*, his head shaved bald
except for a scalp lock, and with yellow and red war paint on
his chest and arms, lifted his tomahawk and swept it down.
At once, three braves sprang forward, each jumping into a
wagon to which two mustangs had been harnessed. The
braves were carrying kindled branches, and they began to
race the wagons toward the ranch buildings.

Pastanari, seeing the sudden glow of light from three
different sources which began to move toward the ranch,
understood what was happening. He called out in Apache:
"Bowmen, strike them down before they can set fire to these
wooden buildings."

The Jicarilla bowmen notched their arrows, waiting as
the thundering of the mustangs' hooves grew louder. Then, as
the wagons broke out of the woods into the clearing of tall

grass at the back of the ranch, they drew their bows back with all their strength. The foremost rider, calling out to his mustangs to gallop faster, turned and flung the torch behind him into the pitch-soaked wagon, which at once began to burn. He steered the galloping mustangs with both hands now at the reins, veering them toward the side of the *hacienda* itself. There was the twang of an arrow, and he dropped the reins and fell over the side, sprawled on the ground dying, as the panic-stricken horses, smelling the fire behind them, tried to turn. The left wheel of the wagon collided with the wall of the *hacienda*, and the maddened mustangs broke free of the vehicle and galloped eastward. The flames mounted and began to assail the wooden beams at the back of the *hacienda*.

Carlos, who had joined Yankee in the courtyard, saw a Comanchero clamber over the wall and, before the latter could draw his pistol, impaled him in the throat with the point of his sharp rapier. The man's body fell heavily beside him. Yankee ran up growling, but Carlos waved him aside with a curt command.

"They're using fire," he said hoarsely to himself. "My God, we'll need water to put it out!"

Another Comanchero, taking advantage of the noise and confusion created by the racing mustangs with their fire wagons, crawled on his belly to the back of the house and straightened near Teresa de Rojado's window. She knelt there, rifle loaded and ready, and as the outline of his head appeared before her, pulled the trigger. He plunged over on his side, half his skull blown away by the velocity of the ball at such short range.

Don Diego and Doña Inez had taken all the children into the chapel for safety, as Carlos had instructed. Little Dawn sobbed aloud at the sounds of gunfire outside the *hacienda*, but young Diego, seeing that Francesca's grave eyes were on him, fraternally comforted her and told her not to cry, because he was there to protect her. And the aging *hidalgo* and his handsome wife looked at each other, tears in their eyes, as they thanked the dear God for uniting them in such unshakable faith and devotion, which would be a bulwark against the vilest of enemies.

Bess and Concepción labored over Catarina, for the child was being born. The smell of smoke reached the two women, and Concepción crossed herself and prayed aloud. When the baby was finally delivered, Concepción wrapped the baby in swaddling clothes after Bess had cleaned away the afterbirth. Catarina lay still now, very pale, but at least her ordeal was over. It was a tiny son, perfect in every limb, with black hair like his mother and blue eyes like his father, *El Halcón.*

Suddenly, Bess heard a noise at the window and whispered to Concepción, "Be very still. There's a loaded musket in the closet—I know Catarina keeps one there. I'll get it, and you keep down with the baby. I wish we could move Catarina—" On her knees she crawled to the closet, opened it, and took out the musket, then crawled back toward the window. A hand reached in, the shutters having already been broken open by some of the balls that had whistled against the *hacienda* from the clearing. Bess leveled the musket, steadied herself, and pulled the trigger. There was a gurgling shriek, the hand twisted and clawed at the windowsill, and then disappeared.

Meanwhile, the second Comanche rider drawing the fire wagon escaped the first flight of arrows from the Jicarilla bowmen on the roof of the *hacienda,* and sped his wagon toward the bunkhouse. There, one of the *trabajadores* drew a pistol from his belt and sent off a snap shot. The brave grunted, clapped a hand to his ribs, then slowly fell off the wagon, which plunged against the side of the bunkhouse. The mustangs reared in the air, screaming in terror as the flames reached them, for they had spread quickly as the horses drew the flaming wagon at galloping speed. One of the *vaqueros,* cursing under his breath, pulled out his pistols and shot both mustangs through the head to end their suffering. Hardly had he lowered the smoking pistols when an arrow sent by one of the Comanche bowmen, who with five other braves had run forward to fire at the *trabajadores,* struck him in the chest.

He fell backward and lay still, with his arms crossed, his sightless eyes staring up at the cloud-obscured quarter-moon.

The third Comanche was more successful with his wagon than his two companions: he managed to steer his galloping mustangs toward the newly finished church, arrows and balls missing him—for the flames in the wagon had mounted high and obscured him as a target from both workers and Apache bowmen. Feeling the flames singe his naked back, he leaped from the wagon and, like a cat, landed on all fours as the wagon crashed into the side of the church and began to set it afire. As he crawled back to the safety of the tall grass and then the woods, Yankee, who had raced out of the courtyard and toward the bunkhouse, saw him. His ears flattening, and uttering a hideous low growl, the wolf-dog jumped on the back of his neck. With an inhuman shriek, the Comanche's knees jerked forward, his hands desperately groping for Yankee's throat to tear away those murderous fangs. His eyes bulged and then were glassy, as the wolf-dog growled, without relinquishing the pressure of its sharp fangs. The Comanche fell over onto his side, his dead hand still clutching Yankee's throat. At last the wolf-dog shook off that moribund grasp and turned, barking at the smoke rising from the side of the church. The *trabajadores*, seeing the smoke, rushed toward the well, dipped buckets into it, and tried to extinguish the fire, without concern for their own lives. Two of them were shot down by Comanchero rifles, but the other *trabajadores*, setting down their buckets, fired their guns and killed three of the Mexican and white renegades.

Now the bunkhouse had caught fire and could not be saved. Esteban Morales had hoarsely directed the *vaqueros* and the *trabajadores* to various vantage points to repel the attackers, as they had practiced earlier with Ramón Santoriaga. Now a Comanche on horseback came at the *capataz* with leveled lance, and Esteban took aim and fired his musket, but missed. Leaping to one side and swinging the musket by its barrel, he sent the heavy butt thudding against the Comanche's naked back. With a shriek of pain, the rider tumbled from his mustang, and groping on his knees, wincing with the pain of the savage blow, drew out a hunting knife from his belt. But before he could rise and encounter his adversary, Esteban had swung the musket again and killed the man with a blow to his head. Panting and shuddering, he flung the useless musket aside and seized the Comanche's lance. Another brave came riding at him just as he did so, and Esteban, standing with his back to the oncoming rider, would have been killed save that the brave, in anticipatory triumph, let out the war whoop of the tribe. Instinctively, Esteban flung himself to one side on the ground, as the mustang rode by. Leaping to his feet, he raced after the warrior, and as the latter turned in his saddle to try to spear him by jabbing the lance at short range, Esteban lunged from a crouching position and sent the point of his lance into the Comanche's belly, skewering him off the mustang as one harpoons a fish.

The five remaining Comanche now drove the last of the wagons toward the ranch, tossing in their torches to set the wagons aflame and then, crouching low over the reins, urged their mustangs forward at full gallop. One of them dropped to a Jicarilla bowman, another to the rifle of a *trabajador*. Edward Molson, at the site of his house, had shot down three Comancheros who had come skulking around that perimeter of the ranch. Suddenly, Felipe Santorcia appeared out of darkness, brandishing a knife, fiendishly grinning. "*¡Tejano, muerte a ti!*" he snarled.

Molson's rifle was empty, and there was no time to reload. He had a knife in his belt and, fearlessly dropping the rifle, drew his knife and circled the Comanchero *jefe*. Santorcia tried the old ruse of feinting with the knife and then quickly kicking up dust with his right foot. But his boot struck a rock just under the grainy soil, and he stumbled. Molson leaped forward and plunged his knife into the Comanchero's heart, then drew it out and leaped back, lest, in a dying reflex, he himself be stabbed.

Felipe Santorcia stood, his eyes huge with amazement and disbelief, contemplating his killer. "*Bastardo* of a—" he began in a feeble voice, and then his eyes closed, and he sank down on his knees, rolled over, and was still.

The younger of the Ames brothers had been killed by a direct rifle shot to the temple as he was reloading his rifle to fire at some of the shadowy forms emerging out of the tall grass. His brother avenged his death with a quick pistol shot.

Teresa de Rojado had coolly reloaded her rifle, praying under her breath that none of the people she had come to care for so much on this ranch would be hurt, and most of all Catarina, who was giving birth. "Holy Virgin, spare them all, I pray You," she murmured as she loaded the rifle with her ramrod and then knelt in wait, the barrel of the gun thrust through the open window, the torn shutter pulled to one side so that she could choose a target. She saw one of the fire wagons coming past her and, in the instant illumination of the flames, saw its hideously war-painted driver. The rifle recoiled against her shoulder, bruising her, and she gasped, but she saw the Comanche jump to his feet, as if propelled by lightning, and then fall backward and disappear. But the wagon, with the mustangs frantically galloping to try to break it from them—for the fire was beginning to reach them with its searing heat—swung toward the stable of the palominos and the flames began to lick along the sides of the entrance. The mustangs reared, and they galloped off, squealing and snorting in their fright and pain.

Esteban Morales saw the wagon ignite the side of the palomino stable, and uttered a blasphemous oath. "You, Pedro—you, García—get those buckets and put out that fire. I'll cover you. Sanchez—load your rifle and come with me. We'll cover the *trabajadores* while they put out the fire— *pronto!*"

The two workers dipped their buckets in the well and ran to the stable. Sanchez, a burly Mexican *trabajador* in his late twenties, and Esteban, moved forward to cover them. A Comanche wearing a warbonnet and brandishing a spear rode at them. It was Quintana himself, believing that now that the ranch had been set afire, victory was in sight. As one of the *trabajadores* tossed the contents of his bucket against the burning side of the stable, Quintana speared him in the back. But Sanchez dropped to one knee, squinted along the sight of his Belgian rifle, and pulled the trigger. Quintana flung his hands up in the air, releasing the spear, and toppled off his mustang.

There was an angry shout from the woods, where the remaining braves under his command saw the death of their chief. Francisco López had seen it, too, and gnashed his teeth, balling his right fist and driving it with full force against the trunk of the tree behind which he was hiding. His knuckles were bloodied and bruised, and he swore vitriolically: *That damned americano, the spawn of a cross-eyed pig and a scrofulous deer—may he burn in hell—if I had him in my* calabozo, *I'd cut off his* cojones *and feed them to my dogs and pour red-hot peppers on the bleeding wounds—by all the devils in hell, how does he manage to escape such an army as this? His buildings are burning, and yet our men drop like flies—does he have some special magic?* And then, his mind almost completely gone in the dementia of his frustration, he shook his fist at the sky and bellowed, "*Señor Dios,* I renounce You! Do You hear? I call upon Lucifer, the

Evil One, to aid me against this *gringo* whom You protect so well!"

But now the attack was over. The Comancheros and the Comanche alike had lost too many men. Ten of the deserters had been killed, and the Comanchero leader and the Comanche chief had perished. Those who remained muttered among themselves that there was no one to guide them now, and that these demons who guarded the ranch seemed invincible. Even though those buildings were aflame, there was not force enough to take the silver and the women—better to escape. And so, López, calling on the devil to bring him better fortune than he had known thus far against John Cooper Baines, saw the shadowy forms of what remained of this supposedly invincible army skulk off to the woods and disappear, to go their various ways into the unsettled wilderness of Texas and farther south into nameless Mexican hamlets where they would wait another time for another chance to plunder—but never again against the Hacienda del Halcón.

Francisco López stalked to the place where he tethered his horse south of the little forest. All was lost. And even the five soldiers who had deserted with him to form the nucleus of his bandit band had died, the corporal from a Jicarilla arrow, the four privates by gunfire—and two of these had fallen to Teresa de Rojado and Bess Sandarbal. Mounting his horse, he dug in his spurs and galloped off to the south, continuing to shout imprecations at the silent sky.

Esteban Morales, tireless, his voice cracking from continuous shouting, dipped a bucket into the well and rushed toward the palomino stable, directing his workers to do what they could to save the *hacienda* and the church.

The *hacienda* had been very badly burned, one wing almost entirely destroyed before the fire could be extinguished. Fortunately, no one was in the rooms, but the chapel was very close to that wing. As Don Diego turned to Doña Inez, he said wanly, "*El Señor Dios* has answered our prayers. He stopped the fire before it could touch this holy place, which we dedicate to Him in our humble gratitude for His good works and kindness to us all."

"Look, Pa, I see smoke!" young Andrew Baines cried out as he pointed westward.

Miguel Sandarbal rode up, his face grave with concern. "By the eternal, the boy's right, *mi compañero!* It looks as if the *hacienda*'s on fire—we must get there with all speed, *Halcón!*"

"God Almighty!" John Cooper said, his face grim. Then, turning in his saddle, he cried, "*Hombres,* leave the *carretas* and the wagons. We're only a few miles from home now, and it looks as if someone set fire to the *hacienda!* Let's get there and help if we can!" And turning to Miguel, he muttered, "I pray to God that Catarina's safe and Don Diego and Doña Inez and Carlos—and all the children—let's go, Miguel! Come on, son!"

They galloped their horses toward the *hacienda,* and when they came upon the outskirts and saw the bunkhouse in ruins, the wing of the *hacienda* charred and crumbled, and the great new church itself charred all along one side, almost to the steeple, John Cooper burst into hoarse sobs. "What a fool I was to leave! I should have waited till spring! Oh, my God—"

"*Patrón, patrón,*" Miguel tried to console him, "how could you know? I'm sure everyone is safe; the Jicarilla guarded us, I know they did. And I'm thinking of my Bess just the way you are about your Catarina, *patrón.*"

They rode through the gateposts, and Carlos de Escobar and Esteban Morales, having worked through the night, were first to see them and shouted to them.

John Cooper dismounted and ran to his brother-in-law: "How's Catarina?"

Carlos gripped his arms and smiled at him. "She's well, John Cooper. She gave you a fine son last night. And you, Miguel, your Bess shot down some of the attackers. They had Comanche, and they had men in *americano* uniforms and others whom Esteban told me were Comancheros. And Teresa herself brought down a few of those murdering devils with her rifle! We lost five of the Jicarilla and about twelve *trabajadores* and *vaqueros.* Our guards were also killed when they came upon us late last night without warning. But they're beaten, and I don't think they'll ever be back."

"Take me to Catarina, Carlos! God bless all of you, for what you did in my absence," John Cooper exclaimed as he hurried into the *hacienda.*

Concepción and Bess were beside his wife, seated on

each side of the bed, and in her arms Catarina held her tiny son.

"I failed you, *mi corazón*," John Cooper groaned as he bent to kiss her and then to touch with his lips the forehead of his child. "And to think that you went through this agony in that terrible attack—" He turned to Bess and took her hand and kissed it, tears in his eyes: "God bless you, Bess. Carlos told me how you fought to save us, and how you protected my wife when she was in her time. God bless you."

"We have a son, Coop," Catarina faintly said, smiling up at him. "What shall we name him?"

"I know," he said gruffly, to hide the well of tears that surged within him. "We'll call him Coraje; it's the Spanish word for courage. And you have that, my darling. What a wife you are—what a lucky man I am to have won you."

"Coraje—yes," she murmured in reply. "And Andrew— is he safe and sound?"

"He is fine, and he is wonderful. He's a man now, Catarina." He took her hand in his and stroked her hair, and the tender smiles on their faces bespoke the fact that all would be well. After a time, John Cooper rose, kissed both Catarina and their son again, then said, "I must go talk to the others, dearest. There's work to be done rebuilding. And we will rebuild it—bigger than ever. You'll see!"

It was the day before Christmas in this year of 1825. The families of the Hacienda del Halcón were gathered before the church. Some of the *trabajadores* had already replaced the charred wood at the side with new beams, and the patchwork was so expert that it almost seemed there had been no fire at all. Later, after the holidays, there would be even sturdier reinforcements.

They watched now in awed silence as *trabajadores* began to install the great bell from Belgium into the steeple. It was made secure, and the bell rope dangled down. John Cooper turned to Jorge Pastronaz: "You shall be the first, Fra Pastronaz, to make the bell ring out to express our thanks to Him who gave us safety and the birthday of whose blessed Son we celebrate tomorrow," he said.

And the young priest made the sign of the cross over each of them, over John cooper and Catarina, who stood beside him holding their tiny son; over Don Diego and Doña

Inez; over Miguel and his Bess; over Carlos and Teresa, who stood side by side; and over all those others who had become the great, united family of the Hacienda del Halcón, a citadel and sanctuary of freedom in this new Southwest.

He walked into the church then, took hold of the long bell rope, and pulled it once, and then again, and then again. The bell sang with authority, sonority, and clarity, and it seemed to swell out over the river and through the forest and the tall grass and in all directions, borne on high by the winds of the earth.

It had a joyous sound, and it sang and tolled of peace and the love of God and the love of fellow man for all mankind that lived by God's will and fought the infamies of evil.

Coming in 1983 . . .

A SAGA OF THE SOUTHWEST: BOOK V

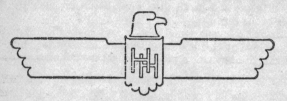

NIGHT
OF
THE HAWK
by Leigh Franklin James

In 1826, John Cooper Baines ventures to South America as the guest of a wealthy Argentine landowner, and there he pits his frontiersman's skills against the dangers of both man and nature in a land as wild as any in the young United States. Back home, there is the increasing threat of war in the great Southwest as the Mexican Army comes to blows with the intrepid settlers and traders in Texas and New Mexico. But on the Double H Ranch, Carlos de Escobar takes a lovely aristocratic widow for his bride and there is great joy—a joy that may be shattered by a maniacal killer bent on revenge.

Read NIGHT OF THE HAWK, coming in 1983 from Bantam Books.

★ WAGONS WEST ★

A series of unforgettable books that trace the lives of a dauntless band of pioneering men, women, and children as they brave the hazards of an untamed land in their trek across America. This legendary caravan of people forge a new link in the wilderness. They are Americans from the North and the South, alongside immigrants, Blacks, and Indians, who wage fierce daily battles for survival on this uncompromising journey—each to their private destinies as they fulfill their greatest dreams.

☐ **INDEPENDENCE! BOOK I** (22808)
The wagon train begins its journey on Long Island. Among the travellers are Whip Holt and Cathy von Ayl, whose lives are changed by the unseen forces of the vast frontier. $3.50

☐ **NEBRASKA! BOOK II** (20417)
Although some members remain behind, many people in the wagon train brave their way against incredible odds as they continue courageously toward their destination. $3.25

☐ **WYOMING! BOOK III** (23177)
Only the stalwart survive the hazardous trek through the Rockies—beset by Indian attacks and treachery by secret enemy agents on board the wagon train. $3.50

☐ **OREGON! BOOK IV** (22568)
The wagon train members are pawns in the clash between three great national powers, all gambling on the riches that lie in the great northwest. $3.50

☐ **TEXAS! BOOK V** (23168)
1843. The fledgling republic fights for its life against the onrush of Mexican soldiers. Some of the original wagon train members join the call to help this struggle. $3.50

☐ **CALIFORNIA! BOOK VI** (14260)
Gold is discovered in 1848 and its lure attracts friend and foe alike . . . in a mad scramble for new-found riches. But many lives become endangered as lawlessness overtakes the territory. $3.95

☐ **COLORADO- BOOK VII** (14717)
Now gold is found in Central City. and the frontier town of Denver becomes the magnet for hucksters, and many of the wagon train friends. Shocking events result from this highly volatile situation. $3.95

☐ **NEVADA- BOOK VIII** (20174)
In the midsa of a Civil War, Major General Lee Blake is summoned to spearhead a mission of utmost importance to the Union cause. Aided by his long time friend and wagon master. Whip Holt, Whip's courageous son, a beautiful, sharpshooting newswoman and a seductive courtesan, the vital journey begins. $3.50

☐ **WASHINGTON! BOOK IX** (20919)
Now it is the close of the Civil War. Wounded hero, Toby Hall, returns from battle and rides West to claim a homestead on the vast timberlands of WASHINGTON! Awaiting him are ruthless profiteers enticed by the promise of fabulous wealth and bent on robbing Toby of his land's riches. $3.50

THE EXCITING NEW FRONTIER SERIES BY THE CREATORS OF WAGONS WEST

STAGECOACH
by Hank Mitchum

"The STAGECOACH series is great frontier entertainment. Hank Mitchum really makes the West come alive in each story."

—Dana Fuller Ross,
author of *Wagons West*

Here's a powerful new series of adventures set in the West's most dramatic towns—filled with the danger, history, and romance of the bold men and women who conquered the frontier. There's a new STAGECOACH novel available every other month and the first three are on sale now.

STATION 1: DODGE CITY—A justice-seeking Federal marshal, a cunning gambler, and a beautiful young widow are swept up in the exploding action of the wickedest town in the West.

STATION 2: LAREDO—At high noon, the dusty border pueblo of Laredo will witness the hanging of a legendary outlaw—if the outlaw's band of longriders don't shoot him free first.

STATION 3: CHEYENNE—A beautiful, strong-willed woman and a proud, rugged rancher risk the dangers of the darkest corners of Cheyenne to save the lives of a wayward young man and a fiery Apache chieftan.

Read all of these STAGECOACH adventures, on sale wherever Bantam paperbacks are sold.

ST—11/82